PENGUIN BOOKS

THE PARADISE

ÉMILE ZOLA, born in Paris in 1840, was brought up at Aix-en-Provence in an atmosphere of struggling poverty after the death of his father in 1847. He was educated at the Collège Bourbon at Aix and then at the Lycée Saint-Louis in Paris. After failing the *baccalauréat* twice and taking menial clerical employment, he joined the newly founded publishing house Hachette in 1862 and quickly rose to become head of publicity. Having published his first novel in 1865, he left Hachette the following year to become a full-time journalist and writer. *Thérèse Raquin* appeared in 1867 and caused a scandal, to which he responded with his famous preface to the novel's second edition in 1868 in which he laid claim to being a "Naturalist." That same year he began work on a series of novels intended to trace scientifically the effects of heredity and environment in one family: *Les Rougon-Macquart*. This great cycle eventually contained twenty novels, which appeared between 1871 and 1893. In 1877 the seventh of these, *L'Assommoir* (*The Drinking Den*), a study of alcoholism in working-class Paris, brought him abiding wealth and fame. On completion of the Rougon-Macquart series he began a new cycle of novels, *Les Trois Villes: Lourdes, Rome, Paris* (1894–98), a violent attack on the Church of Rome, which led to another cycle, *Les Quatre Évangiles*. While his later writing was less successful, he remained a celebrated figure on account of the Dreyfus case, in which his powerful interventions played an important part of redressing a heinous miscarriage of justice. His marriage in 1870 had remained childless, but his happy, public relationship in later life with Jeanne Rozerot, initially one of his domestic servants, brought him a son and a daughter. He died in mysterious circumstances in 1902, the victim of an accident or murder.

The Paradise

A Novel

ÉMILE ZOLA

Translated by
ERNEST ALFRED VIZETELLY

PENGUIN BOOKS

PENGUIN BOOKS

Published by the Penguin Group
Penguin Group (USA) LLC
375 Hudson Street
New York, New York 10014

USA | Canada | UK | Ireland | Australia | New Zealand | India | South Africa | China
penguin.com
A Penguin Random House Company

This translation by Ernest Alfred Vizetelly first published in Great Britain
under the title *The Ladies' Paradise* by Vizetelly & Co 1886
Published in Penguin Books 2013

ISBN 978-0-14-312470-2

Printed in the United States of America
3 5 7 9 10 8 6 4 2

Set in Buccardi Std
Designed by Sabrina Bowers

The
Paradise

CHAPTER 1.

Denise had walked from the Saint-Lazare railway station, where a Cherbourg train had landed her and her two brothers, after a night passed on the hard seat of a third-class carriage. She was leading Pépé by the hand, and Jean was following her, all three fatigued after the journey, frightened and lost in this vast Paris, their eyes on every street name, asking at every corner the way to the Rue de la Michodière, where their uncle Baudu lived. But on arriving in the Place Gaillon, the young girl stopped short, astonished.

"Oh! look there, Jean," said she; and they stood still, nestling close to one another, all dressed in black, wearing the old mourning bought at their father's death. She, rather puny for her twenty years, was carrying a small parcel; on the other side, her little brother, five years old, was clinging to her arm; while behind her, the big brother, a strapping youth of sixteen, was standing empty-handed.

"Well," said she, after a pause, "that *is* a shop!"

They were at the corner of the Rue de la Michodière and the Rue Neuve-Saint-Augustin, in front of a draper's shop, which displayed a wealth of color in the soft October light. Eight o'clock was striking at the church of Saint-Roch; not many people were about, only a few clerks on their way to business, and housewives doing their morning shopping. Before the door, two shopmen, mounted on a step-ladder, were hanging up some woollen goods, whilst in a window in the Rue Neuve-Saint-Augustin another young man, kneeling with his back to the pavement, was delicately plaiting a piece of blue silk. In the shop, where there were as yet no customers, there was a buzz as of a swarm of bees at work.

"By Jove!" said Jean, "this beats Valognes. Yours wasn't such a fine shop."

Denise shook her head. She had spent two years there, at Cornaille's, the principal draper's in the town, and this shop, encountered so suddenly—this, to her, enormous place, made her heart swell, and kept her excited, interested, and oblivious of everything else. The high plate-glass door, facing the Place Gaillon, reached the first storey, amidst a complication of ornaments covered with gilding. Two allegorical figures, representing two laughing, bare-breasted women, unrolled the scroll bearing the sign, "The Ladies' Paradise." The establishment extended along the Rue de la Michodière and the Rue Neuve-Saint-Augustin, and comprised, beside the corner house, four others—two on the right and two on the left, bought and fitted up recently. It seemed to her an endless extension, with its display on the ground floor, and the plate-glass windows, through which could be seen the whole length of the counters. Upstairs a young lady, dressed all in silk, was sharpening a pencil, while two others, beside her, were unfolding some velvet mantles.

"The Ladies' Paradise," read Jean, with the tender laugh of a handsome youth who had already had an adventure with a woman. "That must draw the customers—eh?"

But Denise was absorbed by the display at the principal entrance. There she saw, in the open street, on the very pavement, a mountain of cheap goods—bargains, placed there to tempt the passers-by, and attract attention. Hanging from above were pieces of woollen and cloth goods, merinoes, cheviots, and tweeds, floating like flags; the neutral, slate, navy-blue, and olive-green tints being relieved by the large white price-tickets. Close by, round the doorway, were hanging strips of fur, narrow bands for dress trimmings, fine Siberian squirrel-skin, spotless snowy swansdown, rabbit-skin imitation ermine and imitation sable. Below, on shelves and on tables, amidst a pile of remnants, appeared an immense quantity of hosiery almost given away knitted woollen gloves, neckerchiefs, women's hoods, waist-coats, a winter show in all colors, striped, dyed, and variegated, with here and there a flaming patch of red. Denise saw some tartan at nine sous, some strips of American vison at a franc, and some mittens at five sous. There appeared to be an immense clearance sale going on; the establishment seemed bursting with goods, blocking up the pavement with the surplus.

Uncle Baudu was forgotten. Pépé himself, clinging tightly to his sister's hand, opened his big eyes in wonder. A vehicle coming up, forced them to quit the road-way, and they turned up the Rue Neuve-Saint-Augustin mechanically, following the shop windows and stopping at each fresh display. At first they were captivated by a complicated arrangement: above, a number of umbrellas, laid obliquely, seemed to form a rustic roof; beneath these a quantity of silk stockings, hung on rods, showed the roundness of the calves, some covered with rosebuds, others of all colors, black open-worked, red with embroidered corners, and flesh color, the silky grain of which made them look as soft as a fair woman's skin; and at the bottom of all, a symmetrical array of gloves, with their taper fingers and narrow palms, and that rigid virgin grace which characterizes such feminine articles before they are worn. But the last window especially attracted their attention. It was an exhibition of silks, satins, and velvets, arranged so as to produce, by a skilful artistic arrangement of colors, the most delicious shades imaginable. At the top were the velvets, from a deep black to a milky white: lower down, the satins—pink, blue, fading away into shades of a wondrous delicacy; still lower down were the silks, of all the colors of the rainbow, pieces set up in the form of shells, others folded as if round a pretty figure, arranged in a life-like natural manner by the clever fingers of the window dressers. Between each motive, between each colored phrase of the display ran a discreet accompaniment, a slight puffy ring of cream-colored silk. At each end were piled up enormous bales of the silk of which the house had made a specialty, the "Paris Paradise" and the "Golden Grain," two exceptional articles destined to work a revolution in that branch of commerce.

"Oh, that silk at five francs twelve sous!" murmured Denise, astonished at the "Paris Paradise."

Jean began to get tired. He stopped a passer-by. "Which is the Rue de la Michodière, please, sir?"

On hearing that it was the first on the right they all turned back, making the tour of the establishment. But just as she was entering the street, Denise was attracted by a window in which ladies' dresses were displayed. At Cornaille's that was her department, but she had never seen anything like this, and remained rooted to the spot with admiration. At the back a large sash of Bruges lace, of considerable value, was spread out like an altar-veil, with its two white wings extended; there were flounces of Alençon point, grouped in garlands; then from the top to the bottom fluttered, like a fall of snow, a cloud of lace of every description—Malines, Honiton, Valenciennes, Brussels, and Venetian-point. On each side the heavy columns were draped with cloth, making the background appear still more distant. And the dresses were in this sort of chapel raised to the worship of woman's beauty and grace. Occupying the centre was a magnificent article, a velvet mantle, trimmed with silver fox; on one side a silk cape lined with miniver, on the other a cloth cloak edged with cocks' plumes; and last of all, opera cloaks in white cashmere and white silk trimmed with swansdown or chenille. There was something for all tastes, from the opera cloaks at twenty-nine francs to the velvet mantle marked up at eighteen hundred. The well-rounded neck and graceful figures of the dummies exaggerated the slimness of the waist, the absent head being replaced by a large price-ticket pinned on the neck; whilst the mirrors, cleverly arranged on each side of the window, reflected and multiplied the forms without end, peopling the street with these beautiful women for sale, each bearing a price in big figures in the place of a head.

"How stunning they are!" murmured Jean, finding no other words to express his emotion.

This time he himself had become motionless, his mouth open. All this female luxury turned him rosy with pleasure. He had a girl's beauty—a beauty he seemed to have stolen from his sister—

a lovely skin, curly hair, lips and eyes overflowing with tenderness. By his side Denise, in her astonishment, appeared thinner still, with her rather long face and large mouth, fading complexion, and light hair. Pépé, also fair, in the way of most children, clung closer to her, as if wanting to be caressed, troubled and delighted at the sight of the beautiful ladies in the window. They looked so strange, so charming, on the pavement, those three fair ones, poorly dressed in black—the sad-looking young girl between the pretty child and the handsome youth—that the passers-by looked back smilingly.

For several minutes a stout man with grey hair and a large yellow face, standing at a shop-door on the other side of the street, had been looking at them. He was standing there with bloodshot eyes and contracted mouth, beside himself with rage at the display made by The Ladies' Paradise, when the sight of the young girl and her brothers completed his exasperation. What were those three simpletons doing there, gaping in front of the cheapjack's parade?

"What about uncle?" asked Denise, suddenly, as if just waking up.

"We are in the Rue de la Michodière," said Jean. "He must live somewhere about here."

They raised their heads and looked round. Just in front of them, above the stout man, they perceived a green sign-board bearing in yellow letters, discolored by the rain: "The Old Elbeuf. Cloths, Flannels. Baudu, late Hauchecorne." The house, coated with an ancient rusty white-wash, quite flat and unadorned, amidst the mansions in the Louis XIV. style which surrounded it, had only three front windows, and these windows, square, without shutters, were simply ornamented by a handrail and two iron bars in the form of a cross. But amidst all this nudity, what struck Denise the most, her eyes full of the light airy windows at The Ladies' Paradise, was the ground-floor shop, crushed by the ceiling, surmounted by a very low storey with half-moon windows, of a prison-like appearance. The wainscoting, of a bottle-green hue, which time had tinted with ochre and bitumen, encircled, right and left, two deep windows, black and dusty, in which the heaped up goods could hardly be seen. The open door seemed to lead into the darkness and dampness of a cellar.

"That's the house," said Jean.

"Well, we must go in," declared Denise. "Come on, Pépé."

They appeared, however, somewhat troubled, as if seized with fear. When their father died, carried off by the same fever which had, a month previous, killed their mother, their uncle Baudu, in the emotion which followed this double mourning, had written to Denise, assuring her there would always be a place for her in his house whenever she would like to come to Paris. But this was nearly a year ago, and the young girl was now sorry to have left Valognes in a moment of temper without informing her uncle. The latter did not know them, never having set foot in Valognes since the day he left, as a boy, to enter as junior in the drapery establishment kept by Hauchecorne, whose daughter he afterwards married.

"Monsieur Baudu?" asked Denise, deciding at last to speak to the stout man who was still eyeing them, surprised at their appearance.

"That's me," replied he.

Denise blushed and stammered out: "Oh, I'm so pleased! I am Denise. This is Jean, and this is Pépé. You see we have come, uncle."

Baudu seemed amazed. His big eyes rolled in his yellow face; he spoke slowly and with difficulty. He was evidently far from thinking of this family which suddenly dropped down on him.

"What—what, you here?" repeated he several times. "But you were at Valognes. Why aren't you at Valognes?"

With her sweet but rather faltering voice she then explained that since the death of her father, who had spent everything in his dye-works, she had acted as a mother to the two children, but the little she earned at Cornaille's did not suffice to keep the three of them. Jean worked at a cabinetmaker's, a repairer of old furniture, but didn't earn a sou. However, he had got to like the business, and had learned to carve in wood very well. One day, having found a piece of ivory, he amused himself by carving a head, which a gentleman staying in the town had seen and admired, and it was this gentleman who had persuaded them to leave Valognes, promising to find a place in Paris for Jean with an ivory-carver.

"So you see, uncle," continued Denise, "Jean will commence his apprenticeship at his new master's tomorrow. They ask no premium, and will board and lodge him. I felt sure Pépé and I could manage very well. We can't be worse off than we were at Valognes."

She said nothing about Jean's love affair, of certain letters written to the daughter of a nobleman living in the town, of kisses exchanged over a wall—in fact, quite a scandal which had determined her leaving. And she was especially anxious to be in Paris, to be able to look after her brother, feeling quite a mother's tender anxiety for this gay and handsome youth, whom all the women adored. Uncle Baudu couldn't get over it, and continued his questions. However, when he heard her speaking of her brothers in this way he became much kinder.

"So your father has left you nothing," said he. "I certainly thought there was still something left. Ah! how many times did I write advising him not to take that dye-work! A good-hearted fellow, but no head for business! And you've been obliged to keep and look after these two youngsters since?"

His bilious face had become clearer, his eyes were not so bloodshot as when he was glaring at The Ladies' Paradise. Suddenly he noticed that he was blocking up the doorway.

"Well," said he, "come in, now you're here. Come in, no use hanging about gaping at a parcel of rubbish."

And after having darted a last look of anger at The Ladies' Paradise, he made way for the children by entering the shop and calling his wife and daughter.

"Elizabeth, Geneviève, come down; here's company for you!"

But Denise and the two boys hesitated before the darkness of the shop. Blinded by the clear light of the street, they could hardly see. Feeling their way with their feet with an instinctive fear of encountering some treacherous step, and clinging still closer together from this vague fear, the child continuing to hold the young girl's skirts, and the big boy behind, they made their entry with a smiling, anxious grace. The clear morning light described the dark profile of their mourning clothes; an oblique ray of sunshine gilded their fair hair.

"Come in, come in," repeated Baudu.

In a few brief sentences he explained the matter to his wife and daughter. The first was a little woman, eaten up with anaemia, quite white—white hair, white eyes, white lips. Geneviève, in whom her mother's degenerateness appeared stronger still, had the debilitated, colorless appearance of a plant reared in the shade. However, her magnificent black hair, thick and heavy, marvellously vigorous for such a weak, poor soul, gave her a sad charm.

"Come in," said both the women in their turn; "you are welcome."

And they made Denise sit down behind a counter. Pépé immediately jumped up on his sister's lap, whilst Jean leant against some wood-work beside her. Looking round the shop the newcomers began to take courage, their eyes getting used to the obscurity. Now they could see it, with its low and smoky ceiling, oaken counters bright with use, and old-fashioned drawers with strong iron fittings. Bales of goods reached to the beams above; the smell of linen and dyed stuffs—a sharp chemical smell—seemed intensified by the humidity of the floor. At the further end two young men and a young woman were putting away pieces of white flannel.

"Perhaps this young gentleman would like to take something?" said Madame Baudu, smiling at Pépé.

"No, thanks," replied Denise, "we had a cup of milk in a café opposite the station." And as Geneviève looked at the small parcel she had laid down, she added: "I left our box there too."

She blushed, feeling that she ought not to have dropped down on her friends in this way. Even as she was leaving Valognes, she had been full of regrets and fears; that was why she had left the box, and given the children their breakfast.

"Come, come," said Baudu suddenly, "let's come to an understanding. 'Tis true I wrote to you, but that's a year ago, and since then business hasn't been flourishing, I can assure you, my girl."

He stopped, choked with an emotion he did not wish to show. Madame Baudu and Geneviève, with a resigned look, had cast their eyes down.

"Oh," continued he, "it's a crisis which will pass, no doubt, but I have reduced my staff; there are only three here now, and this is not the moment to engage a fourth. In short, my dear girl, I cannot take you as I promised."

Denise listened, and turned very pale. He dwelt upon the subject, adding: "It would do no good, either to you or to me."

"All right, uncle," replied she with a painful effort, "I'll try and manage all the same."

The Baudus were not a bad sort of people. But they complained of never having had any luck. When their business was flourishing, they had had to bring up five sons, of whom three had died before attaining the age of twenty; the fourth had gone wrong, and the fifth had just left for Mexico, as a captain. Geneviève was the only one left at home. But this large family had cost a great deal of money, and Baudu had made things worse by buying a great lumbering country house, at Rambouillet, near his wife's father's place. Thus, a sharp, sour feeling was springing up in the honest old tradesman's breast.

"You might have warned us," resumed he, gradually getting angry at his own harshness. "You could have written; I should have told you to stay at Valognes. When I heard of your father's death I said what is right on such occasions, but you drop down on us without a word of warning. It's very awkward."

He raised his voice, and that relieved him. His wife and daughter still kept their eyes on the ground, like submissive persons who would never think of interfering. However, whilst Jean had turned pale, Denise had hugged the terrified Pépé to her bosom. She dropped hot tears of disappointment.

"All right, uncle," she said, "we'll go away."

At that he stopped, an awkward silence ensued. Then he resumed in a harsh tone: "I don't mean to turn you out. As you are here you must stay the night; tomorrow we will see."

Then Madame Baudu and Geneviève understood they were free to arrange matters. There was no need to trouble about Jean, as he was to commence his apprenticeship the next day. As for Pépé, he would be well looked after by Madame Gras, an old lady living in the Rue des Orties, who boarded and lodged young children for forty francs a month. Denise said she had sufficient to pay for the first month, and as for herself they could soon find her a situation in the neighborhood, no doubt.

"Wasn't Vinçard wanting a saleswoman?" asked Geneviève.

"Of course!" cried Baudu; "we'll go and see him after lunch. Nothing like striking the iron while it's hot."

Not a customer had been in to interrupt this family discussion; the shop remained dark and empty. At the other end, the two young men and the young woman were still working, talking in a low hissing tone amongst themselves. However, three ladies arrived, and Denise was left alone for a moment. She kissed Pépé with a swelling heart, at the thought of their approaching separation. The child, affectionate as a kitten, hid his head without saying a word. When Madame Baudu and Geneviève returned, they remarked how quiet he was. Denise assured them he never made any more noise than that, remaining for days together without speaking, living on kisses and caresses. Until lunch-time the three women sat and talked about children, housekeeping, life in Paris and life in the country, in short, vague sentences, like relations feeling rather awkward through not knowing one another very well. Jean had gone to the shop-door, and stood there watching the passing crowd and smiling at the pretty girls. At ten o'clock a servant appeared. As a rule the cloth was laid for Baudu, Geneviève, and the first-hand. A second lunch was served at eleven o'clock for Madame Baudu, the other young man, and the young woman.

"Come to lunch!" called out the draper, turning towards his niece.

And as all sat ready in the narrow dining room behind the shop, he called the first-hand who had not come.

"Colomban!"

The young man apologized, having wished to finish arranging

the flannels. He was a big, stout fellow of twenty-five, heavy and freckled, with an honest face, large weak mouth, and cunning eyes.

"There's a time for everything," said Baudu, solidly seated before a piece of cold veal, which he was carving with a master's skill and prudence, weighing each piece at a glance to within an ounce.

He served everybody, and even cut up the bread. Denise had placed Pépé near her to see that he ate properly. But the dark close room made her feel uncomfortable. She thought it so small, after the large well-lighted rooms she had been accustomed to in the country. A single window opened on a small back-yard, which communicated with the street by a dark alley along the side of the house. And this yard, sodden and filthy, was like the bottom of a well into which a glimmer of light had fallen. In the winter they were obliged to keep the gas burning all day long. When the weather enabled them to do without gas it was duller still. Denise was several seconds before her eyes got sufficiently used to the light to distinguish the food on her plate.

"That young chap has a good appetite," remarked Baudu, observing that Jean had finished his veal. "If he works as well as he eats, he'll make a fine fellow. But you, my girl, you don't eat. And, I say, now we can talk a bit, tell us why you didn't get married at Valognes?"

Denise almost dropped the glass she had in her hand. "Oh! uncle—get married! How can you think of it? And the little ones!"

She was forced to laugh, it seemed to her such a strange idea. Besides, what man would care to have her—a girl without a sou, no fatter than a lath, and not at all pretty? No, no, she would never marry, she had quite enough children with her two brothers.

"You are wrong," said her uncle; "a woman always needs a man. If you had found an honest young fellow, you wouldn't have dropped on to the Paris pavement, you and your brothers, like a family of gypsies."

He stopped, to divide with a parsimony full of justice, a dish of bacon and potatoes which the servant brought in. Then, pointing to Geneviève and Colomban with his spoon, he added: "Those two will be married next spring, if we have a good winter season."

Such was the patriarchal custom of the house. The founder, Aristide Finet, had given his daughter, Desiree to his first-hand, Hauchecorne; he, Baudu, who had arrived in the Rue de la Michodière with seven francs in his pocket, had married old Hauchecorne's daughter, Elizabeth; and he intended, in his turn, to hand over Geneviève and the business to Colomban as soon as trade should improve. If he thus delayed a marriage, decided on for three years past, it was by a scruple, an obstinate probity. He had received the business, in a prosperous state, and did not wish to pass it on to his son-in-law less patronized or in a worse position than when he took it. Baudu continued, introducing Colomban, who came from Rambouillet, the same place as Madame Baudu's father; in fact they were distant cousins. A hardworking fellow, who for ten years had slaved in the shop, fairly earning his promotions! Besides, he was far from being a nobody; he had for father that noted toper, Colomban, a veterinary surgeon, known all over the department of Seine-et-Oise, an artist in his line, but so fond of the flowing bowl that he was ruining himself.

"Thank heaven!" said the draper in conclusion, "if the father drinks and runs after the women, the son has learnt the value of money here."

Whilst he was speaking Denise was examining Geneviève and Colomban. They sat close together at table, but remained very quiet, without a blush or a smile. From the day of his entry the young man had counted on this marriage. He had passed through the various stages: junior, counter-hand, etc., and had at last gained admittance into the confidence and pleasures of the family circle, all this patiently, and leading a clock-work style of life, looking upon this marriage with Geneviève as an excellent, convenient arrangement. The certainty of having her prevented him feeling any desire for her. And the young girl had also got to love him, but with the gravity of her reserved nature, and a real deep passion of which she herself was not aware, in her regular, monotonous daily life.

"Quite right, if they like each other, and can do it," said Denise, smiling, considering it her duty to make herself agreeable.

"Yes, it always finishes like that," declared Colomban, who had not spoken a word before, masticating slowly.

Geneviève, after giving him a long look, said in her turn: "When people understand each other, the rest comes naturally."

Their tenderness had sprung up in this gloomy house of old Paris like a flower in a cellar. For ten years she had known no one but him, living by his side, behind the same bales of cloth, amidst the darkness of the shop; morning and evening they found themselves elbow to elbow in the narrow dining room, so damp and dull. They could not have been more concealed, more utterly lost had they been in the country, in the woods. But a doubt, a jealous fear, began to suggest itself to the young girl, that she had given her hand, forever, amidst this abetting solitude through sheer emptiness of heart and mental weariness.

However, Denise, having remarked a growing anxiety in the look Geneviève cast at Colomban, good-naturedly replied: "Oh! when people are in love they always understand each other."

But Baudu kept a sharp eye on the table. He had distributed slices of Brie cheese, and, as a treat for the visitors, he called for a second dessert, a pot of red-currant jam, a liberality which seemed to surprise Colomban. Pépé, who up to then had been very good, behaved rather badly at the sight of the jam; whilst Jean, all attention during the conversation about Geneviève's marriage, was taking stock of the latter, whom he thought too weak, too pale, comparing her in his own mind to a little white rabbit with black ears and pink eyes.

"We've chatted enough, and must now make room for the others," said the draper, giving the signal to rise from table. "Just because we've had a treat is no reason why we should want too much of it."

Madame Baudu, the other shopman, and the young lady then came and took their places at the table. Denise, left alone again, sat near the door waiting for her uncle to take her to Vinçard's.

Pépé was playing at her feet, whilst Jean had resumed his post of observation at the door. She sat there for nearly an hour, taking an interest in what was going on around her. Now and again a few customers came in; a lady, then two others appeared, the shop retaining its musty odor, its half light, by which the old-fashioned business, good-natured and simple, seemed to be weeping at its desertion. But what most interested Denise was The Ladies' Paradise opposite, the windows of which she could see through the open door. The sky remained clouded, a sort of humid softness warmed the air, notwithstanding the season; and in this clear light, in which there was, as it were, a hazy diffusion of sunshine, the great shop seemed alive and in full activity.

Denise began to feel as if she were watching a machine working at full pressure, communicating its movement even as far as the windows. They were no longer the cold windows she had seen in the early morning; they seemed to be warm and vibrating from the activity within. There was a crowd before them, groups of women pushing and squeezing, devouring the finery with longing, covetous eyes. And the stuffs became animated in this passionate atmosphere: the laces fluttered, drooped, and concealed the depths of the shop with a troubling air of mystery; even the lengths of cloth, thick and heavy, exhaled a tempting odor, while the cloaks threw out their folds over the dummies, which assumed a soul, and the great velvet mantle particularly, expanded, supple and warm, as if on real fleshly shoulders, with a heaving of the bosom and a trembling of the hips. But the furnace-like glow which the house exhaled came above all from the sale, the crush at the counters, that could be felt behind the walls. There was the continual roaring of the machine at work, the marshalling of the customers, bewildered amidst the piles of goods, and finally pushed along to the pay-desk. And all that went on in an orderly manner, with mechanical regularity, quite a nation of women passing through the force and logic of this wonderful commercial machine.

Denise had felt herself being tempted all day. She was bewildered and attracted by this shop, to her so vast, in which she saw more people in an hour than she had seen at Cornaille's in six months; and there was mingled with her desire to enter it a vague sense of danger which rendered the seduction complete. At the same time her uncle's shop made her feel ill at ease; she felt an unreasonable disdain, an instinctive repugnance for this cold, icy place, the home of old-fashioned trading. All her sensations—her anxious entry, her friends' cold reception, the dull lunch eaten in a prison-like atmosphere, her waiting amidst the sleepy solitude of this old house doomed to a speedy decay—all these sensations reproduced themselves in her mind under the form of a dumb protestation, a passionate longing for life and light. And notwithstanding her really tender heart, her eyes turned to The Ladies' Paradise, as if the saleswoman within her felt the need to go and warm herself at the glow of this immense business.

"Plenty of customers over there!" was the remark that escaped her.

But she regretted her words on seeing the Baudus near her. Madame Baudu, who had finished her lunch, was standing up, quite white, with her pale eyes fixed on the monster; every time she caught sight of this place, a mute, blank despair swelled her heart, and filled her eyes with scalding tears. As for Geneviève, she was anxiously watching Colomban, who, not supposing he was being observed, stood in ecstasy, looking at the handsome young saleswomen in the dress department opposite, the counter being visible through the first-floor window. Baudu, his anger rising, merely said:

"All is not gold that glitters. Patience!"

The thought of his family evidently kept back the flood of rancor which was rising in his throat. A feeling of pride prevented him displaying his temper before these children, only that morning arrived. At last the draper made an effort, and tore himself away from the spectacle of the sale opposite.

"Well!" resumed he, "we'll go and see Vinçard. These situations are soon snatched up; it might be too late tomorrow."

But before going out he ordered the junior to go to the station and fetch Denise's box. Madame Baudu, to whom the young girl had confided Pépé, decided to run over and see Madame Gras, to arrange about the child. Jean promised his sister not to stir from the shop.

"It's two minutes' walk," explained Baudu as they went down the Rue Gaillon; "Vinçard has a silk business, and still does a fair trade. Of course he suffers, like everyone else, but he's an artful fellow, who makes both ends meet by his miserly ways. I fancy, though, he wants to retire, on account of his rheumatics."

The shop was in the Rue Neuve-des-Petits-Champs, near the Passage Choiseul. It was clean and light, well fitted up in the modern style, but rather small, and contained but a poor stock. They found Vinçard in consultation with two gentlemen.

"Never mind us," called out the draper; "we are in no hurry; we can wait." And returning to the door he whispered to Denise: "The thin fellow is at The Paradise, second in the silk department, and the stout man is a silk manufacturer from Lyons."

Denise gathered that Vinçard was trying to sell his business to Robineau of The Paradise. He was giving his word of honor in a frank open way, with the facility of a man who could take any number of oaths without the slightest trouble. According to his account, the business was a golden one; and in the splendor of his rude health he interrupted himself to whine and complain of those infernal pains which prevented him stopping and making his fortune. But Robineau, nervous and tormented, interrupted him impatiently. He knew what a crisis the trade was passing through, and named a silk warehouse already ruined by The Paradise. Vinçard, inflamed, raised his voice.

"No wonder! The fall of that great booby of a Vabre was certain. His wife spent everything he earned. Besides, we are more than five hundred yards away, whilst Vabre was almost next door to The Paradise."

Gaujean, the silk manufacturer, then chimed in, and their voices fell again. He accused the big establishments of ruining French manufacture; three or four laid down the law, reigning like masters over the market; and he gave it as his opinion that the only way of fighting them was to favor the small traders; above all, those who dealt in special classes of goods, to whom the future belonged. Therefore he offered Robineau plenty of credit.

"See how you have been treated at The Paradise," said he. "No notice taken of your long service. You had the promise of the first-hand's place long ago, when Bouthemont, an outsider without any claim, came in and got it at once."

Robineau was still smarting under this injustice. However, he hesitated to start on his own account, explaining that the money came from his wife, a legacy of sixty thousand francs she had just inherited, and he was full of scruples regarding this sum, saying that he would rather cut off his right hand than compromise her money in a doubtful affair.

"No," said he, "I haven't made up my mind; give me time to think over it. We'll have another talk about it."

"As you like," replied Vinçard, concealing his disappointment under a smiling countenance. "It's to my interest not to sell; and were it not for my rheumatics—"

And returning to the middle of the shop, he asked: "What can I do for you, Monsieur Baudu?"

The draper, who had been listening with one ear, introduced Denise, told him as much as he thought necessary of her story, adding that she had two years' country experience.

"And as I have heard you are wanting a good saleswoman."

Vinçard affected to be awfully sorry. "What an unfortunate thing!" said he. "I have, indeed, been looking for a saleswoman all the week; but I've just engaged one—not two hours ago."

A silence ensued. Denise seemed disheartened. Robineau, who was looking at her with interest, probably inspired with pity by her poor appearance, ventured to say:

"I know they're wanting a young person at our place, in the ready-made dress department."

Baudu could not help crying out fervently: "At your place? Never!"

Then he stopped, embarrassed. Denise had turned very red; she would never dare enter that great place, and yet the idea of being there filled her with pride.

"Why not?" asked Robineau, surprised. "It would be a good

opening for the young lady. I advise her to go and see Madame Aurélie, the first-hand, tomorrow. The worst that can happen to her is not to be accepted."

The draper, to conceal his inward revolt, began to talk vaguely. He knew Madame Aurélie, or, at least, her husband, Lhomme, the cashier, a stout man, who had had his right arm severed by an omnibus. Then turning suddenly to Denise, he added: "However, that's her business. She can do as she likes."

And he went out, after having said "good-day" to Gaujean and Robineau. Vinçard went with him as far as the door, reiterating his regrets. The young girl had remained in the middle of the shop, intimidated, desirous of asking Robineau for further particulars. But not daring to, she in her turn bowed, and simply said: "Thank you, sir."

On the way back Baudu said nothing to his niece, but walked very fast, forcing her to run to keep up with him, as if carried away by his reflections. Arrived in the Rue de la Michodière, he was going into his shop, when a neighboring shopkeeper, standing at his door, called him.

Denise stopped and waited.

"What is it, old Bourras?" asked the draper.

Bourras was a tall old man, with a prophet's head, bearded and hairy, and piercing eyes under thick and bushy eyebrows. He kept an umbrella and walking-stick shop, did repairs, and even carved handles, which had won for him an artistic celebrity in the neighborhood. Denise glanced at the shop-window, where the umbrellas and sticks were arranged in straight lines. But on raising her eyes she was astonished at the appearance of the house, a hovel squeezed between The Ladies' Paradise and a large building of the Louis XIV. style, sprung up one hardly knew how, in this narrow space, crushed by its two low storeys. Had it not been for the support on each side it must have fallen; the slates were old and rotten, and the two-windowed front was cracked and covered with stains, which ran down in long rusty lines over the worm-eaten sign-board.

"You know he's written to my landlord, offering to buy the

house?" said Bourras, looking steadily at the draper with his fiery eyes.

Baudu became paler still, and bent his shoulders. There was a silence, during which the two men remained face to face, looking very serious.

"Must be prepared for anything now," murmured Baudu at last.

Bourras then got angry, shaking his hair and flowing board. "Let him buy the house, he'll have to pay four times the value for it! But I swear that as long as I live he shall not touch a stone of it. My lease has twelve years to run yet. We shall see! we shall see!"

It was a declaration of war. Bourras looked towards The Ladies' Paradise, which neither had directly named. Baudu shook his head in silence, and then crossed the street to his shop, his legs almost failing under him. "Ah! good Lord! ah! good Lord!" he kept repeating.

Denise, who had heard all, followed her uncle. Madame Baudu had just come back with Pépé, whom Madame Gras had agreed to receive at anytime. But Jean had disappeared, and this made his sister anxious. When he returned with a flushed face, talking in an animated way of the boulevards, she looked at him with such a sad expression that he blushed with shame. The box had arrived, and it was arranged that they should sleep in the attic.

"How did you get on at Vinçard's?" asked Madame Baudu, suddenly.

The draper related his useless errand, adding that Denise had heard of a situation; and, pointing to The Ladies' Paradise with a scornful gesture, he cried out: "There—in there!"

The whole family felt wounded at the idea. The first dinner was at five o'clock. Denise and the two children took their places, with Baudu, Geneviève, and Colomban. A single jet of gas lighted and warmed the little dining room, reeking with the smell of hot food. The meal passed off in silence, but at dessert Madame Baudu, who could not rest anywhere, left the shop, and came and sat down near Denise. And then the storm, kept back all day, broke out, everyone feeling a certain relief in abusing the monster.

"It's your business, you can do as you like," repeated Baudu. "We don't want to influence you. But if you only knew what sort of place it is—" And he commenced to relate, in broken sentences, the history of this Octave Mouret. Wonderful luck! A fellow who had come up from the South of France with the amiable audacity of an adventurer; no sooner arrived than he commenced to distinguish himself by all sorts of disgraceful pranks with the ladies; had figured in an affair, which was still the talk of the neighborhood; and to crown all, had suddenly and mysteriously made the conquest of Madame Hédouin, who brought him The Ladies' Paradise as a marriage portion.

"Poor Caroline!" interrupted Madame Baudu. "We were distantly related. If she had lived things would be different. She wouldn't have let them ruin us like this. And he's the man who killed her. Yes, that very building! One morning, when visiting the works, she fell down a hole, and three days after she died. A fine, strong, healthy woman, who had never known what illness was! There's some of her blood in the foundation of that house."

She pointed to the establishment opposite with her pale and trembling hand. Denise, listening as to a fairy tale, slightly shuddered; the sense of fear which had mingled with the temptation she had felt since the morning, was caused perhaps by the presence of this woman's blood, which she fancied she could see in the red mortar of the basement.

"It seems as if it brought him good luck," added Madame Baudu, without mentioning Mouret by name.

But the draper shrugged his shoulders, disdaining these old women's tales, and resumed his story, explaining the situation commercially. The Ladies' Paradise was founded in 1822 by two brothers, named Deleuze. On the death of the elder, his daughter, Caroline, married the son of a linen manufacturer, Charles Hédouin; and, later on, becoming a widow, she married Mouret. She thus brought him a half share of the business. Three months after the marriage, the second brother Deleuze died childless; so that when Caroline met her death, Mouret became sole heir, sole proprietor of The Ladies' Paradise. Wonderful luck!

"A sharp fellow, a dangerous busybody, who will overthrow the whole neighborhood if allowed to!" continued Baudu. "I fancy that Caroline, a rather romantic woman, must have been carried away by the gentleman's extravagant ideas. In short, he persuaded her to buy the house on the left, then the one on the right; and he himself, on becoming his own master, bought two others; so that the establishment has continued to grow—extending in such a way that it now threatens to swallow us all up!"

He was addressing Denise, but was really speaking more to himself, feeling a feverish longing to go over this history which haunted him continually. At home he was always angry, always violent, clenching his fists as if longing to go for somebody. Madame Baudu ceased to interfere, sitting motionless on her chair; Geneviève and Colomban, their eyes cast down, were picking up and eating the crumbs off the table, just for the sake of something to do. It was so warm, so stuffy in the small room, that Pépé was sleeping with his head on the table, and even Jean's eyes were closing.

"Wait a bit!" resumed Baudu, seized with a sudden fit of anger, "such jokers always go to smash! Mouret is hard-pushed just now; I know that for a fact. He's been forced to spend all his savings on his mania for extensions and advertisements. Moreover, in order to raise money, he has induced most of his shop-people to invest all they possess with him. So that he hasn't a sou to help himself with now; and, unless a miracle be worked, and he treble his sales, as he hopes to do, you'll see what a crash there'll be! Ah! I'm not ill-natured, but that day I'll illuminate my shop-front, on my word of honor!"

And he went on in a revengeful voice; one would have thought that the fall of The Ladies' Paradise was to restore the dignity and prestige of compromised business. Had anyone ever seen such a thing? A draper's shop selling everything! Why not call it a bazaar at once? And the employees! a nice set they were too—a lot of puppies, who did their work like porters at a railway station, treating goods and customers like so many parcels; leaving the shop or getting the sack at a moment's notice. No affection, no manners, no taste! And all at once he quoted Colomban as an example of a good tradesman, brought up in the old school, knowing how long it took to learn all the cunning and tricks of the trade. The art was not to sell a large quantity, but to sell dear. Colomban could say how he had been treated, carefully looked after, his washing and mending done, nursed in illness, considered as one of the family—loved, in fact!

"Of course," repeated Colomban, after every statement the governor made.

"Ah, you're the last of the old stock," Baudu ended by declaring. "After you're gone there'll be none left. You are my sole consolation, for if they call all this sort of thing business I give up, I would rather clear out."

Geneviève, her head on one side, as if her thick hair were too heavy for her pale forehead, was watching the smiling shopman; and in her look there was a suspicion, a wish to see whether Colomban, stricken with remorse, would not blush at all this praise. But, like a fellow up to every trick of the old trade, he preserved his quiet manner, his good-natured and cunning look. However, Baudu still went on, louder than ever, condemning the people opposite, calling them a pack of savages, murdering each other in their struggle for existence, destroying all family ties. And he mentioned some country neighbors, the Lhommes—mother, father, and son—all employed in the infernal shop, people without any home life, always out, leading a comfortless, savage existence, never dining at home except on Sunday, feeding all the week at restaurants, hotels, anywhere. Certainly his dining room wasn't too large nor too well-lighted; but it was part of their home, and the family had grown up affectionately about the domestic hearth. Whilst speaking his eyes wandered about the room; and he shuddered at the unavowed idea that the savages might one day, if they succeeded in ruining his trade, turn him out of this house where he was so comfortable with his wife and child. Notwithstanding the assurance with which he predicted the utter downfall of his rivals, he was really terrified, feeling that the neighborhood was being gradually invaded and devoured.

"I don't want to disgust you," resumed he, trying to calm himself; "if you think it to your interest to go there, I shall be the first to say, 'go.'"

"I am sure of that, uncle," murmured Denise, bewildered, all this excitement rendering her more and more desirous of entering The Ladies' Paradise.

He had put his elbows on the table, and was staring at her so hard that she felt uneasy. "But look here," resumed he; "you who know the business, do you think it right that a simple draper's shop should sell everything? Formerly, when trade was trade, drapers sold nothing but drapery. Now they are doing their best to snap up every branch and ruin their neighbors. The whole neighborhood complains of it, for every small tradesman is beginning to suffer terribly. This Mouret is ruining them. Bédoré and his sister, who keep the hosiery shop in the Rue Gaillon, have already lost half their customers; Mademoiselle Tatin, at the under-linen warehouse in the Passage Choiseul, has been obliged to lower her prices, to be able to sell at all. And the effects of this scourge, this pest, are felt as far as the Rue Neuve-des-Petits-Champs, where I hear that Vanpouille Brothers, the furriers, cannot hold out much longer. Drapers selling fur goods—what a farce! another of Mouret's ideas!"

"And gloves," added Madame Baudu; "isn't it monstrous? He has even dared to add a glove department! Yesterday, as I was going along the Rue Neuve-Saint-Augustin, I saw Quinette, the glover, at his door, looking so downcast that I hadn't the heart to ask him how business was going."

"And umbrellas," resumed Baudu; "that's the climax! Bourras feels sure that Mouret simply wants to ruin him; for, in short, where's the rhyme between umbrellas and drapery? But Bourras is firm on his legs, and won't allow himself to be beggared. We shall see some fun one of these days."

He spoke of other tradesmen, passing the whole neigbourhood in review. Now and again he let slip a confession. If Vinçard wanted to sell it was time for the rest to pack up, for Vinçard was like the rats who leave a house when it threatens to fall in. Then, immediately after, he contradicted himself, alluded to an alliance, an understanding between the small tradesmen in order to fight the colossus. He hesitated an instant before speaking of himself, his hands shaking, and his mouth twitching in a nervous manner. At last he made up his mind.

"As for myself, I can't complain as yet. Of course he has done me harm, the scoundrel! But up to the present he only keeps ladies' cloths, light stuffs for dresses and heavier goods for mantles. People still come to me for men's goods, velvets for shooting suits, cloths for liveries, without speaking of flannels and serges, of which I defy him to show as good an assortment. But he thinks to annoy me by planting his cloth department right in front of my door. You've seen his display, haven't you? He always places his finest made-up goods there, surrounded by a framework of various cloths—a cheapjack parade to tempt the women. Upon my word, I should be ashamed to use such means! The Old Elbeuf has been known for nearly a hundred years, and has no need for such at its door. As long as I live, it shall remain as I took it, with a few samples on each side, and nothing more!"

The whole family was affected. Geneviève ventured to make a remark after a silence:

"You know, papa, our customers know and like us. We mustn't lose heart. Madame Desforges and Madame de Boves have been in today, and I am expecting Madame Marty for some flannel."

"I," declared Colomban, "I took an order from Madame Bourdelais yesterday. 'Tis true she spoke of an English cheviot marked up opposite ten sous cheaper than ours, and the same stuff, it appears."

"Fancy," murmured Madame Baudu in her weak voice, "we knew that house when it was scarcely larger than a handkerchief! Yes, my dear Denise, when the Deleuzes started it, it had only one window in the Rue Neuve-Saint-Augustin; and such a tiny one, in which there was barely room for a couple of pieces of print and two or three pieces of calico. There was no room to turn round in the shop, it was so small. At that time The Old Elbeuf, after sixty years' trading, was as you see it now. Ah! all that has greatly changed!"

She shook her head; the drama of her whole life was expressed in these few words. Born in the old house, she loved every part of it, living only for it and by it; and, formerly proud of this house, the finest, the best patronized in the neighborhood, she had had the daily grief of seeing the rival establishment gradually growing in importance, at first disdained, then equal to theirs, and finally towering above it, and threatening all the rest. This was for her a continual, open sore; she was slowly dying from sheer grief at seeing The Old Elbeuf humiliated, though still living, as if by the force of impulse, like a machine wound up. But she felt that the death of the shop would be hers as well, and that she would never survive the closing of it.

There was a painful silence. Baudu was softly beating a tattoo with his fingers on the American cloth on the table. He experienced a sort of lassitude, almost a regret at having relieved his feelings once more in this way. In fact, the whole family felt the effects of his despondency, and could not help ruminating on the bitter story. They never had had any luck. The children had been educated and started in the world, fortune was beginning to smile on them, when suddenly this competition sprang up and ruined their hopes. There was, also, the house at Rambouillet, that country house to which he had been dreaming of retiring for the last ten years—a bargain, he thought; but it had turned out to be an old building always wanting repairs, and which he had let to people who never paid any rent. His last profits were swallowed up by the place—the only folly he had committed in his honest, upright career as a tradesman, obstinately attached to the old ways.

"Come, come!" said he, suddenly, "we must make room for the others. Enough of this useless talk!"

It was like an awakening. The gas hissed, in the dead and stifling air of the small room. They all jumped up, breaking the melancholy silence. However, Pépé was sleeping so soundly that they laid him on some bales of cloth. Jean had already returned to the street door yawning.

"In short," repeated Baudu to his niece, "you can do as you like. We have explained the matter to you, that's all. You know your own business best."

He looked at her sharply, waiting for a decisive answer. Denise, whom these stories had inspired with a still greater longing to enter The Ladies' Paradise, instead of turning her from it, preserved her quiet gentle demeanor with a Norman obstinacy. She simply replied: "We shall see, uncle."

And she spoke of going to bed early with the children, for they were all three very tired. But it had only just struck six, so she decided to stay in the shop a little longer. Night had come on, and she found the street quite dark, enveloped in a fine close rain, which had been falling since sunset. She was surprised. A few minutes had sufficed to fill the street with small pools, a stream of dirty water was running along the gutters, the pavement was thick with a sticky black mud; and through the beating rain she saw nothing but a confused stream of umbrellas, pushing, swinging along in the gloom like great black wings. She started back at first, feeling very cold, oppressed at heart by the badly-lighted shop, very dismal at this hour of the day. A damp breeze, the breath of the old quarter, came in from the street; it seemed that the rain, streaming from the umbrellas, was running right into the shop, that the pavement with its mud and its puddles extended all over the place, putting the finishing touches to the moldiness of the old shop front, white with saltpetre. It was quite a vision of old Paris, damp and uncomfortable, which made her shiver, astonished and heart-broken to find the great city so cold and so ugly.

But opposite, the gas-lamps were being lighted all along the frontage of The Ladies' Paradise. She moved nearer, again attracted and, as it were, warmed by this wealth of illumination. The machine was still roaring, active as ever, hissing forth its last clouds of steam; whilst the salesmen were folding up the stuffs, and the cashiers counting up the receipts. It was, as seen through the hazy windows, a vague swarming of lights, a confused factory-like interior. Behind the curtain of falling rain, this apparition, distant and confused, assumed the appearance of a giant furnace-house, where the black shadows of the firemen could be seen passing by the red glare of the furnaces. The displays in the windows became indistinct also; one could only distinguish the snowy lace, heightened in its whiteness by the ground glass globes of a row of gas jets, and against this chapel-like background the ready-made goods stood out vigorously, the velvet mantle trimmed with silver fox threw into relief the curved profile of a headless woman running through the rain to some entertainment in the unknown of the shades of the Paris night.

Denise, yielding to the seduction, had gone to the door, heedless of the raindrops falling on her. At this hour, The Ladies' Paradise, with its furnace-like brilliancy, entirely conquered her. In the great metropolis, black and silent, beneath the rain—in this Paris, to which she was a stranger, it shone out like a lighthouse, and seemed to be of itself the life and light of the city. She dreamed of her future there, working hard to bring up the children, and of other things besides—she hardly knew what—far-off things, the desire and the fear of which made her tremble. The idea of this woman who had met her death amidst the foundations came back to her; she felt afraid, she thought she saw the lights bleeding; then, the whiteness of the lace quieting her, a vague hope sprang up in her heart, quite a certainty of happiness; whilst the fine rain, blowing on her, cooled her hands, and calmed her after the excitement of her journey.

"It's Bourras," said a voice behind her.

She leant forward, and perceived the umbrella-maker, motionless before the window containing the ingenious display of umbrellas and walking-sticks. The old man had slipped up there in the dark, to feast his eyes on the triumphant show; and so great was his grief that he was unconscious of the rain which was beating on his bare head, and trickling off his white hair.

"How stupid he is, he'll make himself ill," resumed the voice.

Turning round, Denise found the Baudus behind her again. Though they thought Bourras so stupid, they were obliged, against their will, to return to this spectacle which was breaking their hearts. Geneviève, very pale, had noticed that Colomban was watching the shadows of the saleswomen pass to and fro on the first floor opposite; and, whilst Baudu was choking with suppressed rancor, Madame Baudu was silently weeping.

"You'll go and see tomorrow, won't you, Denise?" asked the draper, tormented with uncertainty, but feeling that his niece was conquered like the rest.

She hesitated, then gently replied: "Yes, uncle, unless it pains you too much."

CHAPTER II.

The next morning, at half-past seven, Denise was outside The Ladies' Paradise, wishing to call there before taking Jean to his new place, which was a long way off, at the top of the Faubourg du Temple. But, accustomed to early hours, she had arrived too soon; the shop was hardly opened, and, afraid of looking ridiculous, full of timidity, she walked up and down the Place Gaillon for a moment.

The cold wind that blew had already dried the pavement. Shopmen were hurriedly turning out of every street in the neighborhood, their coat-collars turned up, and their hands in their pockets, taken unawares by this first chill of winter. Most of them hurried along alone, and disappeared in the depths of the warehouse, without addressing a word or look to their colleagues marching along by their side. Others were walking in twos and threes, talking fast, and taking up the whole of the pavement; while they all threw away with a similar gesture, their cigarette or cigar before crossing the threshold.

Denise noticed that several of these gentlemen took stock of her in passing. This increased her timidity; she felt quite unable to follow them, and resolved to wait till they had all entered before going in, blushing at the idea of being elbowed at the door by all these men. But the stream continued, so to escape their looks, she took a walk round. When she returned to the principal entrance, she found a tall young man, pale and awkward, who appeared to be waiting as she was.

"I beg your pardon, mademoiselle," he finished by stammering out, "but perhaps you belong to the establishment?"

She was so troubled at hearing a stranger address her in this way that she did not reply at first.

"The fact is," he continued, getting more confused than ever, "I thought of asking them to engage me, and you might have given me a little information."

He was as timid as she was, and had probably risked speaking to her because he felt she was trembling like himself.

"I would with pleasure, sir," replied she at last. "But I'm no better off than you are; I'm just going to apply myself."

"Ah, very good," said he, quite out of countenance.

And they blushed violently, their two timidities remaining face to face for a moment, affected by the similarity of their positions, not daring, however, to wish each other success openly. Then, as they said nothing further, and became more and more uncomfortable, they separated awkwardly, and recommenced their waiting, one on either side, a few steps apart.

The shopmen continued to arrive, and Denise could now hear them joking as they passed, casting side glances towards her. Her confusion increased at finding herself exposed to this unpleasant ordeal, and she had decided to take half an hour's walk in the neighborhood, when the sight of a young man coming rapidly through the Rue Port-Mahon, detained her for a moment. He was evidently the manager of a department, she thought, for the others raised their hats to him. He was tall, with a clear skin and carefully trimmed beard; and he had eyes the color of old gold, of a velvety softness, which he fixed on her for a moment as he crossed the street. He already entered the shop, indifferent that she remained motionless, quite upset by his look, filled with a singular emotion, in which there was more uneasiness than pleasure. She began to feel really afraid, and, to give herself time to collect her courage somewhat, she walked slowly down the Rue Gaillon, and then along the Rue Saint-Roch.

It was better than a manager of a department, it was Octave Mouret in person. He had not been to bed, for after having spent the evening at a stockbroker's, he had gone to supper with a friend and two women, picked up behind the scenes of a small theatre. His tightly buttoned overcoat concealed a dress suit and white tie. He quickly ran upstairs, performed his toilet, changed, and entered his office, quite ready for work, with beaming eyes, and complexion as fresh as if he had had ten hours' sleep. The spacious office, furnished in old oak and hung with green rep, had for sole ornament the portrait of that Madame Hédouin, who was still the talk of the neighborhood. Since her death Octave thought of her with a tender regret, showing himself grateful to the memory of her, who, by marrying him, had made his fortune. And before commencing to sign the drafts laid on his desk, he bestowed the contented smile of a happy man on the portrait. Was it not always before her that he returned to work, after his young widower's escapades, every time he issued from the alcoves where his craving for amusement attracted him?

There was a knock, and without waiting, a young man entered, a tall, thin fellow, with thin lips and a sharp nose, very gentlemanly and correct in his appearance, with his smooth hair already showing signs of turning grey. Mouret raised his eyes, then continuing to sign, said:

"I hope you slept well, Bourdoncle?"

"Very well, thanks," replied the young man, walking about as if quite at home.

Bourdoncle, the son of a poor farmer near Limoges, had started at The Ladies' Paradise at the same time as Mouret, when it only occupied the corner of the Place Gaillon. Very intelligent, very active, it seemed as if he ought to have easily supplanted his comrade, who was not so steady, and who had, besides various other faults, a careless manner and too many intrigues with women; but he lacked that touch of genius possessed by the impassioned Southerner, and had not his audacity, his winning grace. Besides, by a wise instinct, he had always, from the first, bowed before him, obedient and without a struggle; and when Mouret advised his people to put all their money into the business, Bourdoncle was one of the first to respond, even investing the proceeds of an unexpected legacy left him by an aunt; and little by little, after passing through the various grades, salesman, second, and then first-hand in the silk department, he had become one of the governor's most cherished and influential lieutenants, one of the six persons who assisted Mouret to govern The Ladies' Paradise—something like a privy council under an absolute king. Each one watched over a department. Bourdoncle exercised a general control.

"And you," resumed he, familiarly, "have you slept well?"

When Mouret replied that he had not been to bed, he shook his head, murmuring: "Bad habits."

"Why?" replied the other, gaily. "I'm not so tired as you are, my dear fellow. You are half asleep now, you lead too quiet a life. Take a little amusement, that'll wake you up a bit."

This was their constant friendly dispute. Bourdoncle had, at the commencement, beaten his mistresses, because, said he, they prevented him sleeping. Now he professed to hate women, having, no doubt, chance love affairs of which he said nothing, so small was the place they occupied in his life; he contented himself with encouraging the extravagance of his lady customers, feeling the greatest disdain for their frivolity, which led them to ruin themselves in stupid gewgaws. Mouret, on the contrary, affected to worship them, remained before them delighted and cajoling, continually carried away by fresh love-affairs; and this served as an advertisement for his business. One would have said that he enveloped all the women in the same caress, the better to bewilder them and keep them at his mercy.

"I saw Madame Desforges last night," said he; "she was looking delicious at the ball."

"But it wasn't with her that you went to supper, was it?" asked the other.

Mouret protested. "Oh! no, she's very virtuous, my dear fellow. I went to supper with little Heloise, of the Folly. Stupid as a donkey, but so comical!"

He took another bundle of drafts and went on signing. Bourdoncle continued to walk about. He went and took a look through the lofty plate-glass windows, into the Rue Neuve-Saint-Augustin, then returned, saying: "You know they'll have their revenge."

"Who?" asked Mouret, who had lost the thread of the conversation.

"Why, the women."

At this, Mouret became merrier still, displaying, beneath his sensual, adorative manner, his really brutal character. With a shrug of the shoulders he seemed to declare he would throw them all over, like so many empty sacks, when they had finished helping him to make his fortune. Bourdoncle obstinately repeated, in his cold way: "They will have their revenge; there will be one who will avenge all the others. It's bound to be."

"No fear," cried Mouret, exaggerating his Southern accent. "That one isn't born yet, my boy. And if she comes, you know—"

He had raised his penholder, brandishing it and pointing it in the air, as if he would have liked to stab some invisible heart with a knife. Bourdoncle resumed walking, bowing as usual before the superiority of the governor, whose genius, though faulty, had always got the better of him. He, so clear-headed, logical and passionless, incapable of falling, had yet to learn the feminine character of success, Paris yielding herself with a kiss to the boldest.

A silence reigned, broken only by Mouret's pen. Then, in reply to his brief questions, Bourdoncle gave him the particulars of the great sale of winter novelties, which was to commence the following Monday. This was an important affair, and the house was risking its fortune in it; for the rumor had some foundation, Mouret was throwing himself into speculation like a poet, with such ostentation, such a determination to attain the colossal, that everything seemed bound to give way under him. It was quite a new style of doing business, an apparent commercial recklessness which had formerly made Madame Hédouin anxious, and which even now, notwithstanding the first successes, quite dismayed those who had capital in the business. They blamed the governor in secret for going too quick; accused him of having enlarged the establishment to a dangerous extent, before making sure of a sufficient increase of custom; above all, they trembled on seeing him put all the capital into one venture, filling the place with a pile of goods without leaving a sou in the reserve fund. Thus, for this sale, after the heavy sums paid to the builders, the whole capital was out, and it was once more a question of victory or death. And he, in the midst of all this excitement, preserved a triumphant gaiety, a certainty of gaining millions, like a man worshipped by the women, and who cannot be betrayed. When Bourdoncle ventured to express certain fears with reference to the too great development given to several not very productive departments, he broke out into a laugh full of confidence, and exclaimed:

"No fear! my dear fellow, the place is too small!"

The other appeared dumbfounded, seized with a fear he no longer attempted to conceal. The house too small! a draper's shop having nineteen departments, and four hundred and three employees!

"Of course," resumed Mouret, "we shall be obliged to enlarge our premises before another eighteen months. I'm seriously thinking about the matter. Last night Madame Desforges promised to introduce me to someone. In short, we'll talk it over when the idea is ripe."

And having finished signing his drafts, he got up, and tapped his lieutenant on the shoulder in a friendly manner, but the latter could not get over his astonishment. The fright felt by the prudent people around him amused Mouret. In one of his fits of brusque frankness with which he sometimes overwhelmed his familiars, he declared he was at heart a bigger Jew than all the Jews in the world; he took after his father, whom he resembled physically and morally, a fellow who knew the value of money; and, if his mother had given him that particle of nervous fantasy, why it was, perhaps, the principal element of his luck, for he felt the invincible force of his daring reckless grace.

"You know very well that we'll stand by you to the last," Bourdoncle finished by saying.

Before going down into the various departments to give their usual look round, they settled certain other details. They examined the specimen of a little book of account forms, which Mouret had just invented for use at the counters. Having remarked that the old-fashioned goods, the dead stock, went off all the more rapidly when the commission given to the employees was high, he had based on this observation a new system. In future he intended to interest his people in the sale of all goods, giving them a commission on the smallest piece of stuff, the slightest article sold: a system which had caused a revolution in the drapery trade, creating between the salespeople a struggle for existence of which the proprietor reaped the benefit. This struggle formed his favorite method, the principle of organization he constantly applied. He excited his employees' passions, pitted one against the other, allowed the strongest to swallow up the weakest, fattening on this interested struggle. The specimen book was approved of; at the top of the two forms—the one retained, and the one torn off—were the particulars of the department and the salesman's number; then there were columns on both for the measurement, description of the articles sold, and the price; the salesman simply signed the bill before handing it to the cashier. In this way an easy account was kept, it sufficed to compare the bills delivered by the cashier's department to the clearing-house with the salesmen's counterfoils. Every week the latter would receive their commission, and that without the least possibility of any error.

"We sha'n't be robbed so much," remarked Bourdoncle, with satisfaction. "A very good idea of yours."

"And I thought of something else last night," explained Mouret. "Yes, my dear fellow, at the supper. I should like to give the clearing-house clerks a trifle for every error found in checking. You can understand that we shall then be certain they won't pass any, for they would rather invent some."

He began to laugh, whilst the other looked at him in admiration. This new application of the struggle for existence delighted Mouret; he had a real genius for administrative business, and dreamed of organizing the house, so as to play upon the selfish instincts of his employees, for the complete and quiet satisfaction of his own appetites. He often said that to make people do their best, and even to keep them fairly honest, it was necessary to excite their selfish desires first.

"Well, let's go downstairs," resumed Mouret. "We must look after this sale. The silk arrived yesterday, I believe, and Bouthemont must be getting it in now."

Bourdoncle followed him. The receiving office was on the basement floor, in the Rue Neuve-Saint-Augustin. There, on a level with the pavement, was a kind of glazed cage, where the vans discharged the goods. They were weighed, and then slipped down a rapid slide, its oak and iron work shining, brightened by the chafing of goods and cases. Everything entered by this yawning trap; it was a continual swallowing up, a fall of goods, causing a roaring like that of a cataract. At the approach of big sale times especially, the slide carried down a perpetual stream of Lyons silks, English woollens, Flemish linens, Alsatian calicoes, and Rouen printed goods; and the vans were sometimes obliged to wait their turn along the street; the bales running down produced the peculiar noise made by a stone thrown into deep water.

Mouret stopped a moment before the slide, which was in full activity. Rows of cases were going down of themselves, falling like rain from some upper stream. Then some huge bales appeared, toppling over in their descent like so many pebbles. Mouret looked on, without saying a word. But this wealth of goods rushing in at the rate of thousands of francs a minute, made his eyes glisten. He had never before had such a clear, definite idea of the struggle he was engaged in. Here was this mountain of goods that he had to launch to the four corners of Paris. He did not open his mouth, continuing his inspection.

By the grey light penetrating the air-holes, a squad of men were receiving the goods, whilst others were undoing and opening the cases and bales in presence of the managers of different departments. A dockyard agitation filled this cellar, this basement, where wrought-iron pillars supported the arches, and the bare walls of which were cemented.

"Have you got all there, Bouthemont?" asked Mouret, going up to a broad-shouldered young fellow who was checking the contents of a case.

"Yes, everything seems all right," replied he; "but the counting will take me all the morning."

The manager was glancing at the invoice every now and then, standing up before a large counter on which one of his salesmen was laying, one by one, the pieces of silk he was taking from the case. Behind them ran other counters, also encumbered with goods that a small army of shopmen were examining. It was a general unpacking, an apparent confusion of stuffs, examined, turned over, and marked, amidst a buzz of voices.

Bouthemont, a celebrity in the trade, had a round, jolly face, a coal-black beard, and fine hazel eyes. Born at Montpellier, noisy, too fond of company, he was not much good for the sales, but for buying he had not his equal. Sent to Paris by his father, who kept a draper's shop in his native town, he had absolutely refused to return when the old fellow thought he ought to know enough to succeed him in his business; and from that moment a rivalry sprung up between father and son, the former, all for his little country business, shocked to see a simple shopman earning three times as much as he did himself, the latter joking at the old man's routine, chinking his money, and throwing the whole house into confusion at every flying visit he paid. Like the other managers, Bouthemont drew, besides his three thousand francs regular pay, a commission on the sales. Montpellier, surprised and respectful, whispered that young Bouthemont had made fifteen thousand francs the year before, and that that was only a beginning—people prophesied to the exasperated father that this figure would certainly increase.

Bourdoncle had taken up one of the pieces of silk, and was examining the grain with the eye of a connoisseur. It was a faille with a blue and silver selvage, the famous Paris Paradise, with which Mouret hoped to strike a decisive blow.

"It is really very good," observed Bourdoncle.

"And the effect it produces is better than its real quality," said Bouthemont. "Dumonteil is the only one capable of manufacturing such stuff. Last journey when I fell out with Gaujean, the latter was willing to set a hundred looms to work on this pattern, but he asked five sous a yard more."

Nearly every month Bouthemont went to Lyons, staying there days together, living at the best hotels, with orders to treat the manufacturers with open purse. He enjoyed, moreover, a perfect liberty, and bought what he liked, provided that he increased the yearly business of his department in a certain proportion, settled beforehand; and it was on this proportion that his commission was based. In short, his position at The Ladies' Paradise, like that of all the managers, was that of a special tradesman, in a grouping of various businesses, a sort of vast trading city.

"So," resumed he, "it's decided we mark it five francs twelve sous? It's barely the cost price, you know."

"Yes, yes, five francs twelve sous," said Mouret, quickly; "and if I were alone, I'd sell it at a loss."

The manager laughed heartily. "Oh! I don't mind, that will just suit me; it will treble the sale, and as my only interest is to attain heavy receipts."

But Bourdoncle remained very grave, biting his lips. He drew his commission on the total profits, and it did not suit him to lower the prices. Part of his business was to exercise a control over the prices fixed upon, to prevent Bouthemont selling at too small a profit in order to increase the sales. Moreover, his former anxiety reappeared in the presence of these advertising combinations which he did not understand. He ventured to show his repugnance by saying:

"If we sell it at five francs twelve sous, it will be like selling it at a loss, as we must allow for our expenses, which are considerable. It would fetch seven francs anywhere."

At this Mouret got angry. He struck the silk with his open hand, crying out excitedly: "I know that, that's why I want to give it to our customers. Really, my dear fellow, you'll never understand women's ways. Don't you see they'll be crazy after this silk?"

"No doubt," interrupted the other, obstinately, "and the more they buy, the more we shall lose."

"We shall lose a few sous on the stuff, very likely. What matters, if in return we attract all the women here, and keep them at our mercy, excited by the sight of our goods, emptying their purses without thinking? The principal thing, my dear fellow, is to inflame them, and for that you must have one article which flatters them—which causes a sensation. Afterwards, you can sell the other articles as dear as anywhere else, they'll still think yours the cheapest. For instance, our Golden Grain, that taffeta at seven francs and a half, sold everywhere at that price, will go down as an extraordinary bargain, and suffice to make up for the loss on the Paris Paradise. You'll see, you'll see!"

He became quite eloquent.

"Don't you understand? In a week's time from today I want the Paris Paradise to make a revolution in the market. It's our master-stroke, which will save us, and get our name up. Nothing else will be talked of; the blue and silver selvage will be known from one end of France to the other. And you'll hear the furious complaints of our competitors. The small traders will lose another wing by it; they'll be done for, all those rheumatic old brokers shivering in their cellars!"

The shopmen checking the goods round about were listening and smiling. He liked to talk in this way without contradiction. Bourdoncle yielded once more. However, the case was empty, two men were opening another.

"It's the manufacturers who are not exactly pleased," said Bouthemont. "At Lyons they are all furious with you, they pretend that your cheap trading is ruining them. You are aware that Gaujean has positively declared war against me. Yes, he has sworn to give the little houses longer credit, rather than accept my prices."

Mouret shrugged his shoulders. "If Gaujean doesn't look sharp," replied he, "Gaujean will be floored. What do they complain of? We pay ready money and we take all they can make; it's strange if they can't work cheaper at that rate. Besides, the public gets the benefit, and that's everything."

The shopman was emptying the second case, whilst Bouthemont was checking the pieces by the invoice. Another shopman, at the end of the counter, was marking them in plain figures, and the checking finished, the invoice, signed by the manager, had to be sent to the chief cashier's office. Mouret continued looking at this work for a moment, at all this activity round this unpacking of goods which threatened to drown the basement; then, without adding a word, with the air of a captain satisfied with his troops, he went away, followed by Bourdoncle.

They slowly crossed the basement floor. The air-holes placed at intervals admitted a pale light; while in the dark corners, and along the narrow corridors, gas was constantly burning. In these corridors were situated the reserves, large vaults closed with iron railings, containing the surplus goods of each department. Mouret glanced in passing at the heating apparatus, to be lighted on Monday for the first time, and at the post of firemen guarding a giant gas-meter enclosed in an iron cage. The kitchen and dining rooms, old cellars turned into habitable apartments, were on the left at the corner of the Place Gaillon. At last he arrived at the delivery department, right at the other end of the basement floor. The parcels not taken away by the customers were sent down there, sorted on tables, placed in compartments each representing a district of Paris; then sent up by a large staircase opening just opposite The Old Elbeuf, to the vans standing alongside the pavement. In the mechanical working of The Ladies' Paradise, this staircase in the Rue de la Michodière disgorged without ceasing the goods swallowed up by the slide in the Rue Neuve-Saint-Augustin, after they had passed through the mechanism of the counters up above.

"Campion," said Mouret to the delivery manager, a retired sergeant with a thin face, "why weren't six pairs of sheets, bought by a lady yesterday about two o'clock, delivered in the evening?"

"Where does the lady live?" asked the employee.

"In the Rue de Rivoli, at the corner of the Rue d'Alger—Madame Desforges."

At this early hour the sorting tables were bare, the compartment only contained a few parcels left over night. Whilst Campion was searching amongst these packets, after having consulted a list, Bourdoncle was looking at Mouret, thinking that this wonderful fellow knew everything, thought of everything, even when at the supper-tables of restaurants or in the alcoves of his mistresses. At last Campion discovered the error; the cashier's department had given a wrong number, and the parcel had come back.

"What is the number of the pay-desk that debited that?" asked Mouret: "No. 10, you say?" And turning towards his lieutenant, he added: "No. 10; that's Albert, isn't it? We'll just say two words to him."

But before starting on their tour round the shops, he wanted to go up to the postal order department, which occupied several rooms on the second floor. It was there that all the provincial and foreign orders arrived; and he went up every morning to see the correspondence. For two years this correspondence had been increasing daily. At first occupying only about ten clerks, it now required more than thirty. Some opened the letters, others read them, seated at both sides of the same table; others again classed them, giving each one a running number, which was repeated on a pigeon-hole. Then when the letters had been distributed to the different departments and the latter had delivered the articles, these articles were put in the pigeon-holes as they arrived, according to the running numbers. There was then nothing to do but to check and tie them up, which was done in a neighboring room by a squad of workmen who were nailing and tying up from morning to night.

Mouret put his usual question: "How many letters this morning, Levasseur?"

"Five hundred and thirty-four, sir," replied the chief clerk. "After the commencement of Monday's sale, I'm afraid we sha'n't have enough hands. Yesterday we were driven very hard."

Bourdoncle expressed his satisfaction by a nod of the head. He had not reckoned on five hundred and thirty-four letters on a Tuesday. Round the table, the clerks continued opening and reading the letters amidst a noise of rustling paper, whilst the going and coming of the various articles commenced before the pigeon-holes. It was one of the most complicated and important departments of the establishment, one in which there was a continual rush, for, strictly speaking, all the orders received in the morning ought to be sent off the same evening.

"You shall have more hands if you want them," replied Mouret, who had seen at a glance that the work was well done. "You know that when there's work to be done we never refuse the men."

Up above, under the roof, were the small bedrooms for the saleswomen. But he went downstairs again and entered the chief cashier's office, which was near his own. It was a room with a glazed wicket, and contained an enormous safe, fixed in the wall. Two cashiers there centralized the receipts which Lhomme, the chief cashier at the counters, brought in every evening; they also settled the current expenses, paid the manufacturers, the staff, all the crowd of people who lived by the house. The cashiers' office communicated with another, full of green cardboard boxes, where ten clerks checked the invoices. Then came another office, the clearing-house: six young men bending over black desks, having behind them quite a collection of registers, were getting up the discount accounts of the salesmen, by checking the debit-notes. This work, which was new to them, did not get on very well.

Mouret and Bourdoncle had crossed the cashiers' office and the invoice room. When they passed through the other office the young men, who were laughing and joking, started up in surprise. Mouret, without reprimanding them, explained the system of the little bonus he thought of giving them for each error discovered in the debit-notes; and when he went out the clerks left off laughing, as if they had been whipped, and commenced working in earnest, looking up the errors.

On the ground floor, occupied by the shops, Mouret went straight to the pay-desk No. 10, where Albert Lhomme was cleaning his nails, waiting for customers. People regularly spoke of "the Lhomme dynasty," since Madame Aurélie, first-hand at the dress department, after having helped her husband on to the post of chief cashier, had managed to get a pay desk for her son, a tall fellow, pale and vicious, who couldn't stop anywhere, and who caused her an immense deal of anxiety. But on reaching the young man, Mouret kept in the background, not wishing to render himself unpopular by performing a policeman's duty, and retaining from policy and taste his part of amiable god. He nudged Bourdoncle gently with his elbow—Bourdoncle, the infallible man, that model of exactitude, whom he generally charged with the work of reprimanding.

"Monsieur Albert," said the latter, severely, "you have taken another address wrong; the parcel has come back. It's unbear-able!"

The cashier, thinking it his duty to defend himself, called as a witness the messenger who had tied up the packet. This messen-ger, named Joseph, also belonged to the Lhomme dynasty, for he was Albert's foster brother, and owed his place to Madame Aurélie's influence, As the young man wanted to make him say it was the customer's mistake, Joseph stuttered, twisted the shaggy beard that ornamented his scarred face, struggling between his old soldier's conscience and gratitude towards his protectors.

"Let Joseph alone," Bourdoncle exclaimed at last, "and don't say any more. Ah! it's a lucky thing for you that we are mindful of your mother's good services!"

But at this moment Lhomme came running up. From his office near the door he could see his son's pay-desk, which was in the glove department. Quite white-haired already, deadened by his sedentary life, he had a flabby, colorless face, as if worn out by the reflection of the money he was continually handling. His am-putated arm did not at all incommode him in this work, and it was quite a curiosity to see him verify the receipts, so rapidly did the notes and coins slip through his left one, the only one he had. Son of a tax-collector at Chablis, he had come to Paris as a clerk in the office of a merchant of the Port-aux-Vins. Then, whilst lodging in the Rue Cuvier, he married the daughter of his doorkeeper, a small tailor, an Alsatian; and from that day he had bowed submissively before his wife, whose commercial ability filled him with respect. She earned more than twelve thousand francs a year in the dress department, whilst he only drew a fixed salary of five thousand francs. And the deference he felt for a woman bringing such sums into the home was extended to the son, who also belonged to her.

"What's the matter?" murmured he; "is Albert in fault?"

Then, according to his custom, Mouret appeared on the scene, to play the part of good-natured prince. When Bourdoncle had made himself feared, he looked after his own popularity.

"Nothing of consequence!" murmured he. "My dear Lhomme,

your son Albert is a careless fellow, who should take an example from you." Then, changing the subject, showing himself more amiable than ever, he continued; "And that concert the other day—did you get a good seat?"

A blush overspread the white cheeks of the old cashier. Music was his only vice, a vice which he indulged in solitarily, frequenting the theatres, the concerts, the rehearsals. Notwithstanding the loss of his arm, he played on the French horn, thanks to an ingenious system of keys; and as Madame Lhomme detested noise, he wrapped up his instrument in cloth in the evening, delighted all the same, in the highest degree, with the strangely dull sounds he drew from it. In the forced irregularity of their domestic life he had made himself an oasis of this music—that and the cash-box, he knew of nothing else, beyond the admiration he felt for his wife.

"A very good seat," replied he, with sparkling eyes. "You are really too kind, sir."

Mouret, who enjoyed a personal pleasure in satisfying other people's passions, sometimes gave Lhomme the tickets forced on him by the lady patronesses of such entertainments, and he completed the old man's delight by saying:

"Ah, Beethoven! ah, Mozart! What music!" And without waiting for a reply, he went off, rejoining Bourdoncle, already on his tour of inspection through the departments.

In the central hall, an inner courtyard with a glass roof formed the silk department. Both went along the Rue Neuve-Saint-Augustin, occupied by the linen department, from one end to the other. Nothing unusual striking them, they passed on through the crowd of respectful assistants. They then turned into the cotton and hosiery departments, where the same order reigned. But in the department devoted to woollens, occupying the gallery which ran through to the Rue de la Michodière, Bourdoncle resumed the character of executioner, on observing a young man, seated on the counter, looking knocked up after a night passed without sleep. And this young man, named Liénard, son of a rich Angers draper, bowed his head beneath the reprimand, fearing nothing in his idle, careless life of pleasure except to be recalled by his father. The reprimands now began to shower down, and the gallery of the Rue de la Michodière received the full force of the storm. In the drapery department a salesman, a fresh hand, who slept in the house, had come in after eleven o'clock; in the haberdashery department, the second counterman had just allowed himself to be caught downstairs smoking a cigarette. But the tempest burst with especial violence in the glove department, on the head of one of the rare Parisians in the house, handsome Mignot, as they called him, the illegitimate son of a music-mistress: his crime was having caused a scandal in the dining room by complaining of the food. As there were three tables, one at half-past nine, one at half-past ten, and another at half-past eleven, he wished to explain that belonging to the third table, he always had the leavings, the worst of everything.

"What! the food not good?" asked Mouret, naïvely, opening his mouth at last.

He only gave the head cook, a terrible Auvergnat, a franc and a half a head per day, out of which this man still managed to make a good profit; and the food was really execrable. But Bourdoncle shrugged his shoulders: a cook who had four hundred luncheons and four hundred dinners to serve, even in three series, had no time to waste on the refinements of his art.

"Never mind," said the governor, good-naturedly, "I wish all our employees to have good, abundant food. I'll speak to the cook." And Mignot's complaint was shelved.

Then returning to their point of departure, standing up near the door, amidst the umbrellas and neckties, Mouret and Bourdoncle received the report of one of the four inspectors, charged with the superintendence of the establishment. Old Jouve, a retired captain, decorated at Constantine, a fine-looking man still, with his big sensual nose and majestic baldness, having drawn their attention to a salesman, who, in reply to a simple remonstrance on his part, had called him "an old humbug," the salesman was immediately discharged.

However, the shop was still without customers, except a few housewives of the neighborhood who were going through the

almost deserted galleries. At the door the time-keeper had just
closed his book, and was making out a separate list of the late
comers. The salesmen were taking possession of their departments, which had been swept and brushed by the messengers
before their arrival. Each young man hung up his hat and great-
coat as he arrived, stifling a yawn, still half asleep. Some exchanged a few words, gazed about the shop and seemed to be
pulling themselves together ready for another day's work; others
were leisurely removing the green baize with which they had
covered the goods over night, after having folded them up; and
the piles of stuffs appeared symmetrically arranged, the whole
shop was in a clean and orderly state, brilliant in the morning
gaiety, waiting for the rush of business to come and obstruct it,
and, as it were, narrow it by the unpacking and display of linen,
cloth, silk, and lace.

In the bright light of the central hall, two young men were
talking in a low voice at the silk counter. One, short and charming, well set, and with a pink skin, was endeavoring to blend the
colors of some silks for indoor show. His name was Hutin, his father kept a café at Yvetot, and he had managed after eighteen
months' service to become one of the principal salesmen, thanks
to a natural flexibility of character, a continual flow of caressing
flattery, under which was concealed a furious rage for business,
grasping everything, devouring everybody, even without hunger,
just for the pleasure of the thing.

"Look here, Favier, I should have struck him if I had been in
your place, honor bright!" said he to the other, a tall bilious fellow with a dry and yellow skin, who was born at Besançon of a
family of weavers, and who, without the least grace, concealed
under a cold exterior a disquieting will.

"It does no good to strike people," murmured he, phlegmati-
cally; "better wait."

They were both speaking of Robineau, who was looking after
the shopmen during the manager's absence downstairs. Hutin
was secretly undermining Robineau, whose place he coveted. He
had already, to wound him and make him leave, introduced
Bouthemont to fill the vacancy of manager which had been

promised to Robineau. However, the latter stood firm, and it was now an hourly battle. Hutin dreamed of setting the whole department against him, to hound him out by means of ill-will and vexations. At the same time he went to work craftily, exciting Favier especially, who stood next to him as salesman, and who appeared to allow himself to be led on, but with certain brusque reserves, in which could be felt quite a private campaign carried on in silence.

"Hush! seventeen!" said he, quickly, to his colleague, to warm him by this peculiar cry of the approach of Mouret and Bourdoncle.

These latter were continuing their inspection by traversing the hall. They stopped to ask Robineau for an explanation with regard to a stock of velvets of which the boxes were encumbering a table. And as the latter replied that there wasn't enough room:

"I told you so, Bourdoncle," cried out Mouret, smiling; "the place is already too small. We shall soon have to knock down the walls as far as the Rue de Choiseul. You'll see what a crush there'll be next Monday."

And respecting the coming sale, for which they were preparing at every counter, he asked Robineau further questions and gave him various orders. But for several minutes, and without having stopped talking, he had been watching Hutin, who was contrasting the silks—blue, grey, and yellow—drawing back to judge of the harmony of the tones. Suddenly he interfered:

"But why are you endeavoring to please the eyes? Don't be afraid; blind them. Look! red, green, yellow."

He had taken the pieces, throwing them together, crushing them, producing an excessively fast effect. Everyone allowed the governor to be the best displayer in Paris, of a regular revolutionary stamp, who had founded the brutal and colossal school in the science of displaying. He delighted in a tumbling of stuffs, as if they had fallen from the crowded shelves by chance, making them glow with the most ardent colors, lighting each other up by the contrast, declaring that the customers ought to have sore eyes on going out of the shop. Hutin, who belonged, on the contrary, to the classic school, in which symmetry and harmony of color were cherished, looked at him lighting up this fire of stuff on a table, not venturing on the least criticism, but biting his lip with the pout of an artist whose convictions are wounded by such a debauch.

"There!" exclaimed Mouret when he had finished. "Leave it; you'll see if it doesn't fetch the women on Monday."

Just as he rejoined Bourdoncle and Robineau, there arrived a woman, who remained stock-still, suffocated before this show. It was Denise, who, having waited for nearly an hour in the street, the prey to a violent attack of timidity, had at last decided to go in. But she was so beside herself with bashfulness that she mistook the clearest directions; and the shopmen, of whom she had stutteringly asked for Madame Aurélie, directed her in vain to the lower staircase; she thanked them, and turned to the left if they told her to turn to the right; so that for the last ten minutes she had been wandering about the ground floor, going from department to department, amidst the ill-natured curiosity and ill-tempered indifference of the salesmen. She longed to run away, and was at the same time retained by a wish to stop and admire. She felt herself lost, she, so little, in this monster place, in this machine at rest, trembling for fear she should be caught in the movement with which the walls already began to shake. And the thought of The Old Elbeuf, black and narrow, increased the immensity of this vast establishment, presenting it to her as bathed in light, like a city with its monuments, squares, and streets, in which it seemed impossible that she should ever find her way.

However, she had not dared to risk herself in the silk hall, the high glass roof, luxurious counters, and cathedral-like air of which frightened her. Then when she did venture in, to escape the shopmen in the linen department, who were grinning, she had stumbled right on to Mouret's display; and, notwithstanding her fright, the woman was aroused within her, her cheeks suddenly became red, and she forgot everything in looking at the glow of these silks.

"Hullo!" said Hutin in Favier's ear; "there's the girl we saw in the Place Gaillon."

Mouret, whilst affecting to listen to Bourdoncle and Rob-ineau, was at heart flattered by the startled look of this poor girl, as a marchioness might be by the brutal desire of a passing dray-man. But Denise had raised her eyes, and her confusion increased at the sight of this young man, whom she took for a manager. She thought he was looking at her severely. Then not knowing how to get away, quite lost, she applied to the nearest shopman, who happened to be Favier.

"Madame Aurélie, please?"

But Favier, who was disagreeable, contented himself with re-plying sharply: "First floor."

And Denise, longing to escape the looks of all these men, thanked him, and had again turned her back to the stairs she ought to have mounted, when Hutin, yielding naturally to his in-stinct of gallantry, stopped her with his most amiable salesman's smile.

"No—this way, mademoiselle; if you don't mind."

And he even went with her a little way to the foot of the stair-case on the left-hand side of the hall under the gallery. There he bowed, smiling tenderly, as he smiled at all women.

"When you get upstairs turn to the left. The dress department is straight in front."

This caressing politeness affected Denise deeply. It was like a brotherly hand extended to her; she raised her eyes and looked at Hutin, and everything in him touched her—his handsome face, his looks which dissolved her fears, and his voice which seemed to her of a consoling softness. Her heart swelled with gratitude, and she bestowed her friendship in the few disjointed words her emotion allowed her to utter.

"Really, sir, you are too kind. Pray don't trouble to come any further. Thank you very much."

Hutin had already rejoined Favier, to whom he coarsely whis-pered: "What a bag of bones—eh?"

Upstairs the young girl suddenly found herself in the midst of the dress department. It was a vast room, with high carved oak cupboards all round, and clear glass windows looking on to the Rue de la Michodière. Five or six women in silk dresses, looking very coquettish with their frizzed chignons and crinolines drawn back, were moving about, talking. One, tall and thin, with a long head, having a runaway-horse appearance, was leaning against a cupboard, as if already knocked up with fatigue.

"Madame Aurélie?" inquired Denise.

The saleswoman looked at her without replying, with an air of disdain for her shabby dress, then turning to one of her friends, a short girl with a sickly white skin and an innocent and disgusted appearance, she asked: "Mademoiselle Vadon, do you know where Madame Aurélie is?"

The young girl, who was arranging some mantles according to their sizes, did not even take the trouble to raise her head. "No, Mademoiselle Prunaire, I don't know at all," replied she in a mincing tone.

A silence ensued. Denise stood still, and no one took any further notice of her. However, after waiting a moment, she ventured to put another question: "Do you think Madame Aurélie will be back soon?"

The second-hand, a thin, ugly woman, whom she had not noticed before, a widow with a projecting jaw-bone and coarse hair, cried out from a cupboard, where she was checking some tickets: "You'd better wait if you want to speak to Madame Aurélie herself." And, addressing another saleswoman, she added: "Isn't she downstairs?"

"No, Madame Frédéric, I don't think so," replied the young lady. "She said nothing before going, so she can't be far off."

Denise, thus instructed, remained standing. There were several chairs for the customers; but as they had not told her to sit down, she did not dare to take one, although she felt ready to drop with fatigue. All these ladies had evidently put her down as an applicant for the vacancy, and they were taking stock of her, pulling her to pieces ill-naturedly, with the secret hostility of people at table who do not like to close up to make room for hungry outsiders. Her confusion increased; she crossed the room quietly and looked out of the window into the street, just for something to do. Opposite, The Old Elbeuf, with its rusty front and lifeless windows, appeared to her so ugly, so miserable, seen thus from amidst the luxury and life of her present standpoint, that a sort of remorse filled her already swollen heart with grief.

"I say," whispered tall Prunaire to little Vadon, "have you seen her boots?"

"And her dress!" murmured the other.

With her eyes still towards the street, Denise felt herself being devoured. But she was not angry; she did not think them handsome, neither the tall one with her carroty chignon falling over her horse-like neck, nor the little one with her sour milk complexion, which gave her flat and, as it were, boneless face a flabby appearance. Clara Prunaire, daughter of a clog maker in the forest of Vilet, debauched by the footmen at the Chateau de Mareuil, where the countess engaged her as needlewoman, had come later on from a shop at Langres, and was avenging herself in Paris on the men for the kicks with which her father had regaled her when at home. Marguerite Vadon, born at Grenoble, where her parents kept a linen shop, had been obliged to come to The Ladies' Paradise to conceal an accident she had met with—a brat which had made its appearance one day. She was a well-conducted girl, and intended to return to Grenoble to take charge of her parents' shop, and marry a cousin who was waiting for her.

"Well," resumed Clara, in a low voice, "there's a girl who won't do much good here!"

But they stopped talking. A woman of about forty-five came in. It was Madame Aurélie, very stout, tightly laced in her black silk dress, the body of which, strained over her massive shoulders and full bust, shone like a piece of armor. She had, under very dark folds of hair, great fixed eyes, a severe mouth, and large and rather drooping cheeks; and in the majesty of her position as first-hand, her face assumed the bombast of a puffy mask of Caesar.

"Mademoiselle Vadon," said she, in an irritated voice, "you didn't return the pattern of that mantle to the workroom yesterday, it seems?"

"There was an alteration to make, madame," replied the saleswoman, "so Madame Frédéric kept it."

The second-hand then took the pattern out of a cupboard, and the explanation continued. Everyone gave way to Madame Aurélie, when she thought it necessary to assert her authority. Very vain, even going so far as not to wish to be called by her real name, Lhomme, which annoyed her, and to deny her father's humble position, always referring to him as a regularly established tailor, she was only gracious towards those young ladies who showed themselves flexible and caressing, bowing down in admiration before her. Some time previously, whilst she was trying to establish herself in a shop of her own, her temper had become sour, continually thwarted by the worst of luck, exasperated to feel herself born to fortune and to encounter nothing but a series of catastrophes; and now, even after her success at The Ladies' Paradise, where she earned twelve thousand francs a year, it seemed that she still nourished a secret spite against everyone, and she was very hard with beginners, as life had shown itself hard for her at first.

"That will do!" said she, sharply; "you are no more reasonable than the others, Madame Frédéric. Let the alteration be made immediately."

During this explanation, Denise had ceased to look into the street. She had no doubt this was Madame Aurélie; but, frightened at her sharp voice, she remained standing, still waiting. The two saleswomen, delighted to have set their two superiors at variance, had returned to their work with an air of profound indifference. A few minutes elapsed, nobody being charitable enough to draw the young girl from her uncomfortable position. At last, Madame Aurélie herself perceived her, and astonished to see her standing there without moving, asked her what she wanted.

"Madame Aurélie, please."

"I am Madame Aurélie."

Denise's mouth became dry and parched, and her hands cold; she felt some such fear as when she was a child and trembled at the thought of being whipped. She stammered out her request, but was obliged to repeat it to make herself understood. Madame Aurélie looked at her with her great fixed eyes, not a line of her imperial mask deigning to relax.

"How old are you?"

"Twenty, madame."

"What, twenty years old? You don't look sixteen!"

The saleswomen again raised their heads. Denise hastened to add: "Oh, I'm very strong!"

Madame Aurélie shrugged her broad shoulders, then coldly declared: "Well! I don't mind entering your name. We enter the names of all those who apply. Mademoiselle Prunaire, give me the book."

But the book could not be found; Jouve, the inspector had probably got it. As tall Clara was going to fetch it, Mouret arrived, still followed by Bourdoncle. They had made the tour of the other departments—the lace, the shawls, the furs, the furniture, the under-linen, and were winding up with the dresses. Madame Aurélie left Denise a moment to speak to them about an order for some cloaks she thought of giving to one of the large Paris houses; as a rule, she bought direct, and on her own responsibility; but, for important purchases, she preferred consulting the chiefs of the house. Bourdoncle then related her son Albert's latest act of carelessness, which seemed to fill her with despair. That boy would kill her; his father, although not a man of talent, was at least well-conducted, careful, and honest. All this dynasty of Lhommes, of which she was the acknowledged head, very often caused her a great deal of trouble. However, Mouret, surprised to see Denise again, bent down to ask Madame Aurélie what the young lady was doing there; and, when the first-hand replied that she was applying for a saleswoman's situation, Bourdoncle, with his disdain for women, seemed suffocated at this pretension.

"You don't mean it," murmured he; "it must be a joke, she's too ugly!"

"The fact is, there's nothing handsome about her," said Mouret, not daring to defend her, although still moved by the rapture she had displayed downstairs before his arrangement of silks.

But the book having been brought in, Madame Aurélie returned to Denise, who had certainly not made a favorable impression. She looked very clean in her thin black woollen dress; the question of shabbiness was of no importance, as the house furnished a uniform, the regulation silk dress; but she appeared rather weak and puny, and had a melancholy face. Without insisting on handsome girls, one liked them to be of agreeable appearance for the sale rooms. And beneath the gaze of all these ladies and gentlemen who were studying her, weighing her like farmers would a horse at a fair, Denise completely lost countenance.

"Your name?" asked Madame Aurélie, at the end of a counter, pen in hand, ready to write.

"Denise Baudu, madame."

"Your age?"

"Twenty years and four months." And she repeated, risking a glance at Mouret, at this supposed manager, whom she met everywhere and whose presence troubled her so: "I don't look like it, but I am really very strong."

They smiled. Bourdoncle showed evident signs of impatience; her remark fell, moreover, amidst a most discouraging silence.

"What house have you been in, in Paris?" resumed Madame Aurélie.

"I've just arrived from Valognes."

This was a fresh disaster. As a rule, The Ladies' Paradise only took saleswomen with a year's experience in one of the small houses in Paris. Denise thought all was lost; and, had it not been for the children, had she not been obliged to work for them, she would have closed this useless interview and left the place.

"Where were you at Valognes?"

"At Cornaille's."

"I know him—good house," remarked Mouret.

It was very rarely that he interfered in the engagement of the employees, the manager of each department being responsible for his staff. But with his delicate appreciation of women, he divined in this young girl a hidden charm, a wealth of grace and tenderness of which she herself was ignorant. The good name enjoyed by the house in which the candidate had started was of great importance, often deciding the question in his or her favor. Madame Aurélie continued, in a kinder tone: "And why did you leave Cornaille's?"

"For family reasons," replied Denise, turning scarlet. "We have lost our parents, I have been obliged to follow my brothers. Here is a certificate."

It was excellent. Her hopes were reviving, when another question troubled her.

"Have you any other references in Paris? Where do you live?"

"At my uncle's," murmured she, hesitating about naming him, fearing they would never take the niece of a competitor. "At my uncle Baudu's, opposite."

At this, Mouret interfered a second time. "What! are you Baudu's niece? Is it Baudu who sent you here?"

"Oh! no, sir!"

And she could not help laughing, the idea appeared to her so singular. It was a transfiguration; she became quite rosy, and the smile round her rather large mouth lighted up her whole face. Her grey eyes sparkled with a tender flame, her cheeks filled with delicious dimples, and even her light hair seemed to partake of the frank and courageous gaiety that pervaded her whole being.

"Why, she's really pretty," whispered Mouret to Bourdoncle.

The partner refused to admit it, with a gesture of annoyance. Clara bit her lips, and Marguerite turned away; but Madame Aurélie seemed won over, and encouraged Mouret with a nod when he resumed: "Your uncle was wrong not to bring you; his recommendation sufficed. They say he has a grudge against us. We are people of more liberal minds, and if he can't find employment for his niece in his house, why we will show him that she has only to knock at our door to be received. Just tell him I still like him very much, and that he must blame, not me, but the new style of business. Tell him, too, that he will ruin himself if he insists on keeping to his ridiculous old-fashioned ways."

Denise turned quite white again. It was Mouret; no one had mentioned his name, but he had revealed himself, and now she guessed who it was, she understood why this young man had caused her such emotion in the street, in the silk department, and again now. This emotion, which she could not analyse, pressed on her heart more and more, like a too-heavy weight. All the stories related by her uncle came back to her, increasing Mouret's importance, surrounding him with a sort of halo, making of him the master of the terrible machine by whose wheels she had felt herself being seized all the morning. And, behind his handsome face, well-trimmed beard, and eyes of the color of old gold, she beheld the dead woman, that Madame Hédouin, whose blood had helped to cement the stones of the house. The shiver she had felt the previous night again seized her; and she thought she was merely afraid of him.

Meanwhile, Madame Aurélie had closed the book. She only wanted one saleswoman, and she already had ten applications. But she was too anxious to please the governor to hesitate for a moment. However, the application would follow its course, Jouve, the inspector, would go and make enquiries, send in his report, and then she would come to a decision.

"Very good, mademoiselle," said she majestically, to preserve her authority; "we will write to you."

Denise stood there, unable to move for a moment, hardly knowing how to take her leave in the midst of all these people. At last she thanked Madame Aurélie, and on passing by Mouret and Bourdoncle, she bowed. These gentlemen, occupied in examining the pattern of a mantle with Madame Frédéric, did not take the slightest notice. Clara looked in a vexed way towards Marguerite, as if to predict that the new-comer would not have a very pleasant time of it in the place. Denise doubtless felt this indifference and rancor behind her, for she went downstairs with the same troubled feeling she had on going up, asking herself whether she ought to be sorry or glad to have come. Could she count on having the situation? She did not even know that, her uncomfortable state having prevented her understanding clearly. Of all her sensations, two remained and gradually effaced all the others—the emotion, almost the fear, inspired in her by Mouret, and Hutin's amiability, the only pleasure she had enjoyed the whole morning, a souvenir of charming sweetness which filled her with gratitude. When she crossed the shop to go out she looked for the young man, happy at the idea of thanking him again with her eyes; and she was very sorry not to see him.

"Well, mademoiselle, have you succeeded?" asked a timid voice, as she at last stood on the pavement outside. She turned round and recognized the tall, awkward young fellow who had spoken to her in the morning. He also had just come out of The Ladies' Paradise, appearing more frightened than she did, still bewildered with the examination he had just passed through.

"I really don't know yet, sir," replied she.

"You're like me, then. What a way of looking at and talking to you they have in there—eh? I'm applying for a place in the lace department. I was at Crèveccœur's in the Rue du Mail."

They were once more standing facing each other; and, not knowing how to take leave, they commenced to blush. Then the young man, just for something to say in the excess of his timidity, ventured to ask in his good-natured, awkward way: "What is your name, mademoiselle?"

"Denise Baudu."

"My name is Henri Deloche."

Now they smiled, and, yielding to the fraternity of their positions, shook each other by the hand.

"Good luck!"

"Yes, good luck!"

CHAPTER III.

Every Saturday, between four and six, Madame Desforges offered a cup of tea and a few cakes to those friends who were kind enough to visit her. She occupied the third floor of a house at the corner of the Rue de Rivoli and the Rue d'Alger; and the windows of both drawing-rooms overlooked the Tuileries Gardens. This Saturday, just as a footman was about to introduce him into the principal drawing-room, Mouret perceived from the anteroom, through an open door, Madame Desforges, who was crossing the little drawing-room. She stopped on seeing him, and he went in that way, bowing to her with a ceremonious air. But when the footman had closed the door, he quickly seized the young woman's hand, and tenderly kissed it.

"Take care, I have company!" she said, in a low voice, glancing towards the door of the larger room. "I've just been to fetch this fan to show them," and she playfully tapped him on the face with the tip of the fan. She was dark, rather stout, with big jealous eyes.

But he still held her hand and asked: "Will he come?" "Certainly," replied she. "I have his promise." Both of them referred to Baron Hartmann, director of the Crédit Immobilier. Madame Desforges, daughter of a Councillor of State, was the widow of a stock-broker, who had left her a fortune, denied by some, exaggerated by others. Even during her husband's lifetime people said she had shown herself grateful towards Baron Hartmann, whose financial tips had proved very useful to them; and later on, after her husband's death, the acquaintance had probably continued, but always discreetly, without imprudence or dis-

play; for she never courted notoriety in any way, and was received everywhere in the upper-middle classes amongst whom
she was born. Even at this time, when the passion of the banker,
a sceptical, crafty man, had subsided into a simple paternal affection, if she permitted herself certain lovers whom he tolerated, she displayed in these treasons of the heart such a delicate
reserve and tact, a knowledge of the world so adroitly applied,
that appearances were saved, and no one would have ventured
to openly express any doubt as to her conduct. Having met Mouret at a mutual friend's, she had at first detested him; but she had
yielded to him later on, as if carried away by the violent love
with which he attacked her, and since he had commenced to approach Baron Hartmann through her, she had gradually got to
love him with a real profound tenderness, adoring him with the
violence of a woman already thirty-five, although only acknowledging twenty-nine, and in despair at feeling him younger than
herself, trembling lest she should lose him.

"Does he know about it?"

"No, you'll explain the affair to him yourself," she replied.

She looked at him, thinking that he couldn't know anything
or he would not employ her in this way with the baron, affecting
to consider him simply as an old friend of hers. But he still held
her hand, he called her his good Henriette, and she felt her heart
melting. Silently she presented her lips, pressed them to his, then
whispered: "Oh, they're waiting for me. Come in behind me."

They could hear voices issuing from the principal drawing-
room, deadened by the heavy curtains. She pushed the door,
leaving its two folds open, and handed the fan to one of the four
ladies who were seated in the middle of the room.

"There it is," said she; "I didn't know exactly where it was.
My maid would never have found it." And she added in her
cheerful way: "Come in, Monsieur Mouret, come through the
little drawing-room; it will be less solemn."

Mouret bowed to the ladies whom he knew. The drawing-
room, with its flowered brocatel Louis XVI. furniture, gilded
bronzes and large green plants, had a tender feminine air,
notwithstanding the height of the ceiling; and through the two

windows could be seen the chestnut trees in the Tuileries Gardens, their leaves blowing about in the October wind.

"But it isn't at all bad, this Chantilly!" exclaimed Madame Bourdelais, who had taken the fan.

She was a short fair woman of thirty, with a delicate nose and sparkling eyes, an old school-fellow of Henriette's, and who had married a chief clerk in the Treasury. Of an old middle-class family, she managed her household and three children with a rare activity and good grace, and an exquisite knowledge of practical life.

"And you paid twenty-five francs for it?" resumed she, examining each mesh of the lace. "At Luc, I think you said, to a country woman? No, it isn't dear; but you had to get it mounted, hadn't you?"

"Of course," replied Madame Desforges. "The mounting cost me two hundred francs."

Madame Bourdelais began to laugh. And that was what Henriette called a bargain! Two hundred francs for a plain ivory mount, with a monogram! And that for a simple piece of Chantilly, over which she had saved five francs, perhaps. Similar fans could be had ready mounted for a hundred and twenty francs, and she named a shop in the Rue Poissonniere.

However, the fan was handed round to all the ladies. Madame Guibal barely glanced at it. She was a tall, thin woman, with red hair, and a face full of indifference, in which her grey eyes, occasionally penetrating her unconcerned air, cast the terrible gleams of selfishness. She was never seen out with her husband, a barrister well-known at the Palais de Justice, who led, it was said, a pretty free life, dividing himself between his law business and his pleasures.

"Oh," murmured she, passing the fan to Madame de Boves, "I've scarcely bought one in my life. One always receives too many of such things."

The countess replied with delicate malice: "You are fortunate, my dear, in having a gallant husband." And bending over to her daughter, a tall girl of twenty, she added: "Just look at the monogram, Blanche. What pretty work! It's the monogram that must have increased the price like that."

Madame de Boves had just turned forty. She was a superb woman, with the neck of a goddess, a large regular face, and big sleepy eyes, whom her husband, Inspector-General of the Stud, had married for her beauty. She appeared quite moved by the delicacy of the monogram, as if seized with a desire the emotion of which made her turn pale, and turning round suddenly, she continued: "Give us your opinion, Monsieur Mouret. Is it too dear—two hundred francs for this mount?"

Mouret had remained standing in the midst of the five women, smiling, taking an interest in what interested them. He picked up the fan, examined it, and was about to give his opinion, when the footman opened the door and announced:

"Madame Marty."

And there entered a thin, ugly woman, ravaged with the small-pox, dressed with a complicated elegance. She was of uncertain age, her thirty-five years appearing sometimes equal to thirty, and sometimes to forty, according to the intensity of the nervous fever which agitated her. A red leather bag, which she had not let go, hung from her right hand.

"Dear madame," said she to Henriette, "excuse me bringing my bag. Just fancy, as I was coming along I went into The Paradise, and as I have again been very extravagant, I did not like to leave it in my cab for fear of being robbed." But having perceived Mouret, she resumed laughingly: "Ah! sir, I didn't mean to give you an advertisement, for I didn't know you were here. But you really have some extraordinary fine lace just now."

This turned the attention from the fan, which the young man laid on the table. The ladies were all anxious to see what Madame Marty had bought. She was known to be very extravagant, totally unable to resist temptation, strict in her conduct and incapable of yielding to a lover, but weak and cowardly, easily conquered before the least bit of finery. Daughter of a city clerk, she was ruining her husband, a master at the Lycée Bonaparte, who was obliged to double his salary of six thousand francs a year by giving private lessons, in order to meet the constantly increasing household expenses. She did not open her bag, but held it tight on her lap, and commenced to talk about her daughter Valentine, fourteen years old, one of her dearest coquetries, for she dressed her like herself, with all the fashionable novelties of which she submitted to the irresistible seduction.

"You know," she said, "they are making dresses trimmed with a narrow lace for young girls this winter. So when I saw, a very pretty Valenciennes—"

And she at last decided to open her bag. The ladies were stretching out their necks, when, in the midst of the silence, the door-bell was heard.

"It's my husband," stammered Madame Marty, very confused. "He promised to fetch me on leaving the Lycée Bonaparte."

She quickly shut the bag again, and put it under her chair with an instinctive movement. All the ladies set up a laugh. This made her blush for her precipitation, and she put the bag on her knees again, explaining that men never understood, and that they need not know.

"Monsieur de Boves, Monsieur de Vallagnosc," announced the footman.

It was quite a surprise. Madame de Boves herself did not expect her husband. The latter, a fine man, wearing a moustache and an imperial with the military correctness so much liked at the Tuileries, kissed the hand of Madame Desforges, whom he had known as a young girl at her father's. And he made way to allow his companion, a tall, pale fellow, of an aristocratic poverty of blood, to make his bow to the lady of the house. But the conversation had hardly recommenced when two exclamations were heard:

"What! Is that you, Paul?"

"Why, Octave!"

Mouret and Vallagnosc then shook hands, much to Madame Desforges's surprise. They knew each other, then? Of course, they had grown up side by side at the college at Plassans, and it was quite by chance they had not met at her house before. However, with their hands still united, they went into the little drawing-room, just as the servant brought in the tea, a china service on a silver waiter, which he placed near Madame Desforges, on a small round marble table with a light copper mounting. The ladies drew up and began talking louder, all speaking at once, producing a cross-fire of short disjointed sentences; whilst Monsieur de Boves, standing up behind them, put in an occasional word with the gallantry of a handsome functionary. The vast room, so prettily and cheerfully furnished, became merrier still with these gossiping voices, and the frequent laughter.

"Ah! Paul, old boy," repeated Mouret.

He was seated near Vallagnosc, on a sofa. And alone in the little drawing-room, very coquettish with its pretty silk hangings, out of hearing of the ladies, and not even seeing them, except through the open door, the two old friends commenced grinning, examining each other's looks, exchanging slaps on the knees. Their whole youthful career was recalled, the old college at Plassans, with its two courtyards, its damp classrooms, and the dining room in which they had consumed so much cod-fish, and the dormitories where the pillows used to fly from bed to bed as soon as the monitor began to snore. Paul, belonging to an old parliamentary family, noble, poor, and proud, was a good scholar, always at the top of his class, continually held up as an example by the master, who prophesied for him a brilliant future; whilst Octave remained at the bottom, stuck amongst the dunces, fat and jolly, indulging in all sorts of pleasures outside. Notwithstanding the difference in their characters, a fast friendship had rendered them inseparable, until their final examinations, which they passed, the one with honors, the other in a passable manner after two vexatious trials. Then they went out into the world, and had now met again, after ten years, already changed and looking older.

"Well," said Mouret, "what's become of you?"

"Nothing at all," replied the other.

Vallagnosc, in the joy of their meeting, retained his tired and disenchanted air; and as his friend, astonished, insisted, saying: "But you must do something. What do you do?"

"Nothing," replied he.

Octave commenced to laugh. Nothing! That wasn't enough. Little by little he succeeded in drawing Paul out to tell his story. It was the usual story of penniless younger sons, who think themselves obliged by their birth to choose a liberal profession, burying themselves in a sort of vain mediocrity, happy to escape starvation, notwithstanding their numerous degrees. He had studied law by a sort of family tradition; and had since remained a burden on his widowed mother, who even then hardly knew how to dispose of her two daughters. Having at last got quite ashamed, he left the three women to vegetate on the remnants of their fortune, and accepted an appointment in the Ministry of the Interior, where he buried himself like a mole in its hole.

"What do you get there?" resumed Mouret.

"Three thousand francs."

"But that's pitiful pay! Ah! old man, I'm really sorry for you. What! a clever fellow like you, who floored all of us! And they only give you three thousand francs a year, after having already ground you down for five years! No, it isn't right!" He interrupted himself, and returned to his own doings. "As for me, I made them a humble bow. You know what I'm doing?"

"Yes," said Vallagnosc, "I heard you were in business. You've got that big place in the Place Gaillon, haven't you?"

"That's it. Counter-jumper, my boy!"

Mouret raised his head, again slapped him on the knee, and repeated, with the solid gaiety of a fellow who did not blush for the trade by which he was making his fortune:

"Counter-jumper, and no mistake! You remember, no doubt, I didn't bite much at their machines, although at heart I never thought myself duller than the others. When I took my degree, just to please the family, I could have become a barrister or a doctor quite as easily as any of my school-fellows, but those trades frightened me. I saw so many who were starving at them that I just threw them over without the least regret, and pitched head-first into business."

Vallagnosc smiled with an awkward air, and ultimately said: "It's very certain your degree can't be much good to you for selling calico."

"Well!" replied Mouret, joyously, "all I ask is, that it shall not stand in my way, and you know, when one has been stupid enough to burden one's self with it, it is difficult to get rid of it. One goes at a tortoise's pace through life, whilst those who are bare-footed run like madmen." Then, noticing that his friend seemed troubled, he took his hand in his, and continued: "Come, come, I don't want to hurt your feelings, but confess that your degrees have not satisfied any of your wants. Do you know that my manager in the silk department will draw more than twelve thousand francs this year. Just so! a fellow of very clear intelligence, whose knowledge is confined to spelling, and the first four rules. The ordinary salesmen in my place make from three to four thousand francs a year, more than you can earn yourself; and their education was not so expensive as yours, nor were they launched into the world with a written promise to conquer it. Of course, it is not everything to make money; but between the poor devils possessed of a smattering of science who now block up the liberal professions, without earning enough to keep themselves from starving, and the practical fellows armed for life's struggle, knowing every branch of their trade, by Jove! I don't hesitate a moment, I'm for the latter against the former, I think they thoroughly understand the age they live in!"

His voice had become impassioned. Henriette, who was pouring out the tea, turned her head. When he caught her smile, at the further end of the large drawing-room, and saw the other ladies were listening, he was the first to make merry over his own big phrases.

"In short, old man, every counter-jumper who commences, has, at the present day, a chance of becoming a millionaire."

Vallagnosc threw himself back on the sofa indolently, half-closing his eyes in a fatigued and disdainful attitude, in which a suspicion of affectation was added to his real hereditary exhaustion.

"Bah!" murmured he, "life isn't worth all that trouble. There is nothing worth living for." And as Mouret, shocked, looked at him with an air of surprise, he added: "Everything happens and nothing happens; one may as well stay with one's arms folded."

He then explained his pessimism—the mediocrities and the abortions of existence. For a time he had thought of literature, but his intercourse with certain poets had filled him with universal despair. He always arrived at the conclusion that all effort was useless, every hour equally weary and empty, and the world incurably stupid and dull. All enjoyment was a failure, and there was no pleasure in wrong-doing even.

"Just tell me, do you enjoy life yourself?" asked he at last.

Mouret was now in a state of astonished indignation, and exclaimed: "What? Do I enjoy myself? What are you talking about? Why, of course I do, my boy, and even when things give way, for then I am furious at hearing them cracking. I am a passionate fellow myself, and don't take life quietly; that's what interests me in it perhaps." He glanced towards the drawing-room, and lowered his voice. "Oh! there are some women who've bothered me awfully, I must confess. But when I've got hold of one, I keep her. She doesn't always escape me, and then I take my share, I assure you. But it is not so much the women, for to speak truly, I don't care a hang for them; it's the wish to act—to create, in short. You have an idea; you fight for it, you hammer it into people's heads, and you see it grow and triumph. Ah! yes, my boy, I enjoy life!"

All the joy of action, all the gaiety of existence, resounded in these words. He repeated that he went with the times. Really, a man must be badly constituted, have his brain and limbs out of order, to refuse to work in an age of such vast undertakings, when the entire century was pressing forward with giant strides. And he laughed at the despairing ones, the disgusted ones, the pessimists, all those weak, sickly members of our budding sciences, who assumed the weeping airs of poets, or the minting ways of skeptics, amidst the immense activity of the present day. A fine part to play, proper and intelligent, that of yawning before other people's labor!

"That's my only pleasure, yawning in other's faces," said Vallagnosc, smiling with his cold look.

At this Mouret's passion subsided, and he became affectionate again. "Ah, Paul, you're not changed. Just as paradoxical as ever! However, we've not met to quarrel. Each one has his own ideas, fortunately. But you must come and see my machine at work; you'll see it isn't a bad idea. Come, what news? Your mother and sisters are quite well, I hope? And weren't you supposed to get married at Plassans, about six months ago?"

A sudden movement made by Vallagnosc stopped him; and as the former was looking round the drawing-room with an anxious expression, Mouret also turned round, and noticed that Mademoiselle de Boves was closely watching them. Blanche, tall and stout, resembled her mother; but her face was already puffed out, her large, coarse features swollen with unhealthy fat. Paul, in reply to a discreet question, intimated that nothing was yet settled; perhaps nothing would be settled. He had made the young person's acquaintance at Madame Desforges's, where he had visited a good deal last winter, but where he very rarely came now, which explained why he had not met Octave there sooner. In their turn, the De Boves invited him, and he was especially fond of the father, a very amiable man, formerly well known about town, who had retired into his present position. On the other hand, no money. Madame de Boves having brought her husband nothing but her Juno-like beauty as a marriage portion, the family were living poorly on the last mortgaged farm, to which modest revenue was added, fortunately, the nine thousand francs a year drawn by the count as Inspector-General of the Stud. And the ladies, mother and daughter, kept very short of money by him, impoverished by tender escapades outside, were sometimes reduced to turning their dresses themselves.

"In that case, why marry?" was Mouret's simple question.

"Well! I can't go on like this forever," said Vallagnosc, with a weary movement of the eyelids. "Besides, there are certain expectations; we are waiting the death of an aunt."

However, Mouret still kept his eye on Monsieur de Boves, who, seated next to Madame Guibal, was most attentive, and laughing tenderly like a man on an amorous campaign; he turned to his friend with such a significant twinkle of the eye that the latter added:

"Not that one. At least not yet. The misfortune is, that his duty calls him to the four corners of France, to the breeding depots, so that he has continual pretexts for absenting himself. Last month, whilst his wife supposed him to be at Perpignan, he was living at a hotel, in an out-of-the-way neighborhood, with a music-mistress."

There ensued a pause. Then the young man, who was also watching the count's gallantries towards Madame Guibal, resumed in a low tone: "Really, I think you are right. The more so as the dear lady is not exactly a saint, if all they say is true. There's a very amusing story about her and an officer. But just look at him! Isn't he comical, magnetizing her with his eyes? The old-fashioned gallantry, my dear fellow! I adore that man, and if I marry his daughter, he can safely say it's for his sake!"

Mouret laughed, greatly amused. He questioned Vallagnosc again, and when he found that the first idea of a marriage between him and Blanche came from Madame Desforges, he thought the story better still. That good Henriette took a widow's delight in marrying people, so much so, that when she had provided for the girls, she sometimes allowed their fathers to choose friends from her company; but all so naturally, with such a good grace, that no one ever found any food for scandal. And Mouret, who loved her with the love of an active, busy man, accustomed to reducing his tenderness to figures, forgot all his calculations of captivation, and felt for her a comrade's friendship.

At that moment she appeared at the door of the little drawing-room, followed by a gentleman, about sixty years old, whose entry had not been observed by the two friends. Occasionally the ladies' voices became sharper, accompanied by the tinkling of the small spoons in the china cups; and there was heard, from time to time, in the interval of a short silence, the noise of a saucer laid down too roughly on the marble table. A sudden gleam of the setting sun, which had just emerged from behind a thick cloud, gilded the top of the chestnut-trees in the gardens, and streamed through the windows in a red, golden flame, the fire of which lighted up the brocatel and brass-work of the furniture.

"This way, my dear baron," said Madame Desforges. "Allow me to introduce Monsieur Octave Mouret, who is longing to ex-

press the admiration he feels for you." And turning round towards Octave, she added: "Baron Hartmann."

A smile played on the old man's lips. He was a short, vigorous
man, with a large Alsatian head, and a heavy face, which lighted
up with a gleam of intelligence at the slightest curl of his mouth,
the slightest movement of his eyelids. For the last fortnight he
had resisted Henriette's wish that he should consent to this
interview; not that he felt any immoderate jealousy, accepting,
like a man of the world, his position of father; but because it was
the third friend Henriette had introduced to him, and he was
afraid of becoming ridiculous at last. So that on approaching
Octave he put on the discreet smile of a rich protector, who, if
good enough to show himself charming, does not consent to be
a dupe.

"Oh! sir," said Mouret, with his Southern enthusiasm, "the
Crédit Immobilier's last operation was really astonishing! You
cannot think how happy and proud I am to know you."

"Too kind, sir, too kind," repeated the baron, still smiling.

Henriette looked at them with her clear eyes without any awkwardness, standing between the two, lifting her head, going
from one to the other; and, in her lace dress, which revealed her
delicate neck and wrists, she appeared delighted to see them so
friendly together.

"Gentlemen," said she at last, "I leave you to your conversation." Then, turning towards Paul, who had got up, she resumed:
"Will you accept of a cup of tea, Monsieur de Vallagnosc?"

"With pleasure, madame," and they both returned to the
drawing-room.

Mouret resumed his place on the sofa, when Baron Hartmann
had sat down; the young man then broke out in praise of the
Crédit Immobilier's operations. From that he went on to the
subject so near his heart, speaking of the new thoroughfare, of
the lengthening of the Rue Reaumur, of which they were going
to open a section under the name of the Rue du Dix-Décembre,
between the Place de la Bourse and the Place de l'Opera. It had
been declared a work of public utility eighteen months previously; the expropriation jury had just been appointed. The

whole neighborhood was excited about this new opening, anxiously awaiting the commencement of the work, taking an interest in the condemned houses. Mouret had been waiting three years for this work—first, in the expectation of an increase of business; secondly, with certain schemes of enlargement which he dared not openly avow, so extensive were his ideas. As the Rue du Dix-Décembre was to cut through the Rue de Choiseul and the Rue de la Michodière, he saw The Ladies' Paradise invading the whole block, surrounded by these streets and the Rue Neuve-Saint-Augustin; he already imagined it with a princely frontage in the new thoroughfare, lord and master of the conquered city. Hence his strong desire to make Baron Hartmann's acquaintance, when he learnt that the Crédit Immobilier had made a contract with the authorities to open and build the Rue du Dix-Décembre, on condition that they received the frontage ground on each side of the street.

"Really," repeated he, trying to assume a naïve look, "you'll hand over the street ready-made, with sewers, pavements, and gas lamps. And the frontage ground will suffice to compensate you. Oh! it's curious, very curious!"

At last he came to the delicate point. He was aware that the Crédit Immobilier was buying up the houses which surrounded The Ladies' Paradise, not only those which were to fall under the demolisher's hands, but the others as well, those which were to remain standing; and he suspected the projectment of some future establishment. He was very anxious about the enlargements of which he continued to extend the dream, seized with fear at the idea of one day clashing with a powerful company, owning property which they certainly would not part with. It was precisely this fear which had decided him to establish a connection immediately between himself and the baron—the amiable connection of a woman, so powerful between men of a gallant nature. No doubt he could have seen the financier in his office, and talked over the affair in question at his ease; but he felt himself stronger in Henriette's house; he knew how much the mutual possession of a mistress serves to render men pliable and tender. To be both near her, within the beloved perfume of her presence, to have her ready to convince them with a smile, seemed to him a certainty of success.

"Haven't you bought the old Hôtel Duvillard, that old building next to mine?" he asked suddenly.

The baron hesitated a moment, and then denied it. But Mouret looked in his face and smiled, playing, from that moment, the part of a good young man, open-hearted, simple, and straightforward in business.

"Look here, baron," said he, "as I have the unexpected honor of meeting you, I must make a confession. Oh, I don't ask you any of your secrets, but I am going to entrust you with mine, certain that I couldn't place them in wiser hands. Besides, I want your advice. I have long wished to call and see you, but dared not do so."

He did make his confession, he related his start, not even concealing the financial crisis through which he was passing in the midst of his triumph. Everything was brought up, the successive enlargements, the profits continually put back into the business, the sums brought by his employees, the house risking its existence at every fresh sale, in which the entire capital was staked, as it were, on a single throw of the dice. However, it was not money he wanted, for he had a fanatic's faith in his customers; his ambition ran higher; he proposed to the baron a partnership, into which the Crédit Immobilier should bring the colossal palace he saw in his dreams, whilst he, for his part, would give his genius and the business already created. The estate could be valued, nothing appeared to him easier to realize.

"What are you going to do with your land and buildings?" asked he, persistently. "You have a plan, no doubt. But I'm quite certain your idea is not so good as mine. Think of that.

"We build a gallery on the ground, we pull down or re-arrange the houses, and we open the most extensive establishment in Paris—a bazaar which will bring in millions." And he let slip the fervent heartfelt exclamation: "Ah! if I could only do without you! But you get hold of everything now. Besides, I shall never have the necessary capital. Come, we must come to an understanding. It would be a crime not to do so."

"How you go ahead, my dear sir!" Baron Hartmann contented himself with replying. "What an imagination!"

He shook his head, and continued to smile, determined not to return confidence for confidence. The intention of the Crédit Immobilier was to create in the Rue du Dix-Décembre a rival to the Grand Hôtel, a luxurious establishment, the central position of which would attract foreigners. At the same time, as the hotel was only to occupy a certain frontage, the baron could also have entertained Mouret's idea, and treated for the rest of the block of houses, occupying a vast surface. But he had already advanced funds to two of Henriette's friends, and he was getting tired of his position as complacent protector. Besides, notwithstanding his passion for activity, which prompted him to open his purse to every fellow of intelligence and courage, Mouret's commercial genius astonished more than captivated him. Was it not a fanciful, imprudent operation, this gigantic shop? Would he not risk a certain failure in thus enlarging out of all bounds the drapery trade? In short, he didn't believe in it; he refused.

"No doubt the idea is attractive, but it's a poet's idea. Where would you find the customers to fill such a cathedral?"

Mouret looked at him for a moment silently, as if stupefied at his refusal. Was it possible?—a man of such foresight, who smelt money at no matter what depth! And suddenly, with an extremely eloquent gesture, he pointed to the ladies in the drawing-room and exclaimed: "There are my customers!"

The sun was going down, the golden-red flame was now but a pale light, dying away in a farewell gleam on the silk of the hangings and the panels of the furniture. At this approach of twilight, an intimacy bathed the large room in a sweet softness. While Monsieur de Boves and Paul de Vallagnosc were talking near one of the windows, their eyes wandering far away into the gardens, the ladies had closed up, forming in the middle of the room a narrow circle of petticoats, from which issued sounds of laughter, whispered words, ardent questions and replies, all the passion felt by woman for expenditure and finery. They were talking about dress, and Madame de Boves was describing a costume she had seen at a ball.

"First of all, a mauve silk skirt, then over that flounces of old Alençon lace, twelve inches deep."

"Oh! is it possible!" exclaimed Madame Marty. "Some women are fortunate!"

Baron Hartmann, who had followed Mouret's gesture, was looking at the ladies through the door, which was wide open. He was listening to them with one ear, whilst the young man, inflamed by the desire to convince him, went deeper into the question, explaining the mechanism of the new style of drapery business. This branch of commerce was now based on a rapid and continual turning over of the capital, which it was necessary to turn into goods as often as possible in the same year. Thus, that year his capital, which only amounted to five hundred thousand francs, had been turned over four times, and had thus produced business to the amount of two millions. But this was a mere trifle, which could be increased tenfold, for later on he certainly hoped to turn over the capital fifteen or twenty times in certain departments.

"You will understand, baron, that the whole system lies in this. It is very simple, but it had to be found out. We don't want a very large working capital; our sole effort is to get rid as quickly as possible of our stock to replace it by another, which will give our capital as many times its interest. In this way we can content ourselves with a very small profit; as our general expenses amount to the enormous figure of sixteen per cent, and as we seldom make more than twenty per cent, on our goods, it is only a net profit of four per cent at most; but this will finish by bringing in millions when we can operate on considerable quantities of goods incessantly renewed. You follow me, don't you? Nothing can be clearer."

The baron shook his head again. He who had entertained the boldest combinations, of whom people still quoted the daring flights at the time of the introduction of gas, still remained uneasy and obstinate.

"I quite understand," said he; "you sell cheap to sell a quantity, and you sell a quantity to sell cheap. But you must sell, and I repeat my former question: Whom will you sell to? How do you hope to keep up such a colossal sale?"

The sudden burst of a voice, coming from the drawing-room, cut short Mouret's explanation. It was Madame Guibal, who was saying she would have preferred the flounces of old Alençon down the front only.

"But, my dear," said Madame de Boves, "the front was covered with it as well. I never saw anything richer."

"Ah, that's a good idea," resumed Madame Desforges, "I've got several yards of Alençon somewhere; I must look them up for a trimming."

And the voices fell again, becoming nothing but a murmur. Prices were quoted, quite a traffic stirred up their desires, the ladies were buying lace by the mile.

"Why!" said Mouret, when he could speak, "we can see what we like when we know how to sell! There lies our triumph."

And with his southern spirit, he showed the new business at work in warm, glowing phrases which evoked whole pictures. First came the wonderful power of the piling up of the goods, all accumulated at one point, sustaining and pushing each other, never any stand-still, the article of the season always on hand; and from counter to counter the customer found herself seized, buying here the material, further on the cotton, elsewhere the mantle, everything necessary to complete her dress in fact, then falling into unforeseen purchases, yielding to her longing for the useless and the pretty. He then went on to sing the praises of the plain figure system. The great revolution in the business sprung from this fortunate inspiration. If the old-fashioned small shops were dying out it was because they could not struggle against the low prices guaranteed by the tickets. The competition was now going on under the very eyes of the public; a look into the windows enabled them to contrast the prices; every shop was lowering its rates, contenting itself with the smallest possible profit; no cheating, no stroke of fortune prepared long beforehand on an article sold at double its value, but current operations, a regular percentage on all goods, success depending solely on the orderly working of a sale all the larger from the fact of its being carried on in broad daylight. Was it not an astonish-

ing creation? It was causing a revolution in the market, transforming Paris, for it was made of woman's flesh and blood.

"I have the women, I don't care a hang for the rest!" said Mouret, in a brutal confession which passion snatched from him.

At this cry Baron Hartmann appeared moved. His smile lost
its touch of irony; he looked at the young man, won over gradually by his confidence, feeling a growing tenderness for him.

"Hush!" murmured he, paternally, "they will hear you."

But the ladies were now all speaking at once, so excited that
they weren't even listening to each other. Madame de Boves was
finishing the description of a dinner-dress; a mauve silk tunic,
draped and caught up by bows of lace; the bodice cut very low,
with more bows of lace on the shoulders.

"You'll see," said she. "I am having a bodice made like it, with
some satin—"

"I," interrupted Madame Bourdelais, "I wanted some velvet.
Oh! such a bargain!"

Madame Marty asked: "How much for the silk?"

And off they started again, all together. Madame Guibal, Henriette, and Blanche were measuring, cutting out, and making up.
It was a pillage of material, a ransacking of all the shops, an appetite for luxury which expended itself in toilettes longed for
and dreamed of—such a happiness to find themselves in an atmosphere of finery, that they lived buried in it, as in the warm
air necessary to their existence.

Mouret, however, had glanced towards the other drawing-
room, and in a few phrases whispered into the baron's ear, as if
he were confiding to him one of those amorous secrets that men
sometimes risk among themselves, he finished explaining the
mechanism of modern commerce. And, above the facts already
given, right at the summit, appeared the exploitation of woman.
Everything depended on that, the capital incessantly renewed,
the system of piling up goods, the cheapness which attracts, the
marking in plain figures which tranquilizes. It was for woman
that all the establishments were struggling in wild competition;
it was woman that they were continually catching in the snare of

their bargains, after bewildering her with their displays. They had awakened new desires in her flesh; they were an immense temptation, before which she succumbed fatally, yielding at first to reasonable purchases of useful articles for the household, then tempted by their coquetry, then devoured. In increasing their business tenfold, in popularizing luxury, they became a terrible spending agency, ravaging the households, working up the fashionable folly of the hour, always dearer. And if woman reigned in their shops like a queen, cajoled, flattered, overwhelmed with attentions, she was an amorous one, on whom her subjects traffic, and who pays with a drop of her blood each fresh caprice. Through the very gracefulness of his gallantry, Mouret thus allowed to appear the brutality of a Jew, selling woman by the pound. He raised a temple to her, had her covered with incense by a legion of shopmen, created the rite of a new religion, thinking of nothing but her, continually seeking to imagine more powerful seductions; and, behind her back, when he had emptied her purse and shattered her nerves, he was full of the secret scorn of a man to whom a woman had just been stupid enough to yield herself.

"Once have the women on your side," whispered he to the baron, and laughing boldly, "you could sell the very world."

Now the baron understood. A few sentences had sufficed, he guessed the rest, and such a gallant exploitation inflamed him, stirring up in him the memory of his past life of pleasure. His eyes twinkled in a knowing way, and he ended by looking with an air of admiration at the inventor of this machine for devouring the women. It was really clever. He made the same remark as Bourdoncle, suggested to him by his long experience: "You know they'll make you suffer for it."

But Mouret shrugged his shoulders in a movement of overwhelming disdain. They all belonged to him, were his property, and he belonged to none of them. After having drawn from them his fortune and his pleasure, he intended to throw them all over for those who might still find their account in them. It was the rational, cold disdain of a Southerner and a speculator.

"Well! my dear baron," asked he in conclusion, "will you join me? Does this affair appear possible to you?"

The baron, half conquered, did not wish, however, to engage himself yet. A doubt remained beneath the charm which was gradually operating on him. He was going to reply in an evasive manner, when a pressing call from the ladies spared him the trouble. Voices were repeating, amidst silvery laughter: "Monsieur Mouret! Monsieur Mouret!"

And as the latter, annoyed at being interrupted, pretended not to hear, Madame de Boves, who had just got up, came as far as the door of the little drawing-room.

"You are wanted, Monsieur Mouret. It isn't very gallant of you to bury yourself in a corner to talk over business."

He then decided to go, with an apparent good grace, an air of rapture which astonished the baron. Both rose up and passed into the other drawing-room.

"But I am quite at your service, ladies," said he on entering, a smile on his lips.

He was greeted with a burst of triumph. He was obliged to go further forward; the ladies made room for him in their midst. The sun had just gone down behind the trees in the gardens, the day was departing, a fine shadow was gradually invading the vast apartment. It was the tender hour of twilight, that minute of discreet voluptuousness in the Parisian houses, between the dying brightness of the street and the lighting of the lamps downstairs. Monsieur de Boves and Vallagnosc, still standing up before a window, threw a shadow on the carpet: whilst, motionless in the last gleam of light which came in by the other window, Monsieur Marty, who had quietly entered, and whom the conversation of these ladies about dress had completely confused, placed his poor profile, a frock-coat, scanty but clean, his face pale and wan from teaching.

"Is your sale still fixed for next Monday?" Madame Marty was just asking.

"Certainly, madame," replied Mouret, in a soft, sweet voice, an actor's voice, which he assumed when speaking to women.

Henriette then intervened. "We are all going, you know. They say you are preparing wonders."

"Oh! wonders!" murmured he, with an air of modest fatuity. "I simply try to deserve your patronage."

But they pressed him with questions: Madame Bourdelais, Madame Guibal, Blanche even wanted to know.

"Come, give us some details," repeated Madame de Boves, persistently. "You are making us die of curiosity."

And they were surrounding him, when Henriette observed that he had not even taken a cup of tea. It was distressing. Four of them set about serving him, but on condition that he would answer them afterwards. Henriette poured it out, Madame Marty held the cup, whilst Madame de Boves and Madame Bourdelais contended for the honor of sweetening it. Then, when he had declined to sit down, and commenced to drink his tea slowly, standing up in the midst of them, they all approached, imprisoning him in the narrow circle of their skirts; and with their heads raised, their eyes sparkling, they sat there smiling at him.

"Your silk, your Paris Paradise, that all the papers are taking about?" resumed Madame Marty, impatiently.

"Oh!" replied he, "an extraordinary article, coarse-grained, supple and strong. You'll see it, ladies, and you'll see it nowhere else, for we have bought the exclusive right of it."

"Really! a fine silk at five francs twelve sous!" said Madame Bourdelais, enthusiastic. "One cannot credit it."

Ever since the advertisement had appeared, this silk had occupied a considerable place in their daily life. They talked of it, promising themselves some of it, worked up with desire and doubt. And, beneath the gossiping curiosity with which they overwhelmed the young man, there appeared their various temperaments as buyers.

Madame Marty, carried away by her rage for spending, took everything at The Ladies' Paradise, without choosing, just as the articles appeared; Madame Guibal walked about the shop for hours without ever buying anything, happy and satisfied to simply feast her eyes; Madame de Boves, short of money, always tortured by some immoderate wish, nourished a feeling of rancor against the goods she could not carry away; Madame Bourdelais, with the sharp eye of a careful practical housewife, made straight for the bargains, using the big establishments with such a clever housewife's skill that she saved a heap of money; and lastly, Henriette, who, very elegant, only procured certain articles there, such as gloves, hosiery, and her coarser linen.

"We have other stuffs of astonishing cheapness and richness," continued Mouret, with his musical voice. "For instance, I recommend you our Golden Grain, a taffeta of incomparable brilliancy. In the fancy silks there are some charming lines, designs chosen from among thousands by our buyer: and in velvets you will find an exceedingly rich collection of shades. I warn you that cloth will be greatly worn this year; you'll see our checks and our cheviots."

They had ceased to interrupt him, and narrowed the circle, their mouths half open with a vague smile, their eager faces close to his, as in a sudden rush of their whole being towards the tempter. Their eyes grew dim, a slight shudder ran through them. All this time he retained his calm, conquering air, amidst the intoxicating perfumes which their hair exhaled; and between each sentence he continued to sip a little of his tea, the aroma of which cooled those sharper odors, in which there was a particle of the savage. Before a captivating grace so thoroughly master of itself, strong enough to play with woman in this way without being overcome by the intoxication which she exhales, Baron Hartmann, who had not ceased to look at him, felt his admiration increasing.

"So cloth will be worn?" resumed Madame Marty, whose ravished face sparkled with coquettish passion.

Madame Bourdelais, who kept a cool look-out, said, in her turn: "Your sale of remnants takes place on Thursday, doesn't it? I shall wait. I have all my little ones to clothe." And turning her delicate blonde head towards the mistress of the house: "Sauveur is still your dressmaker, I suppose?"

"Yes," replied Henriette, "Sauveur is very dear, but she is the only one in Paris who knows how to make a bodice. Besides, Monsieur Mouret may say what he likes, she has the prettiest designs, designs that are not seen anywhere else. I can't bear to see my dresses on every woman's back."

Mouret smiled discreetly at first. Then he intimated that Madame Sauveur bought her material at his shop; no doubt she went to the manufacturers direct for certain designs of which she acquired the sole right of sale: but for all black silks, for instance, she watched for The Paradise bargains, laying in a considerable stock, which she disposed of at double and treble the price she gave.

"Thus I am quite sure her buyers will snap up all our Paris Paradise. Why should she go to the manufacturers and pay dearer for this silk than she would at my place? On my word of honor, we shall sell it at a loss."

This was a decisive blow for the ladies. The idea of getting goods below cost price awoke in them all the greed felt by women, whose enjoyment as buyers is doubled when they think they are robbing the tradesman. He knew them to be incapable of resisting anything cheap.

"But we sell everything for nothing!" exclaimed he gaily, taking up Madame Desforges's fan, which was behind him on the table. "For instance, here's this fan. I don't know what it cost."

"The Chantilly lace was twenty-five francs, and the mounting cost two hundred," said Henriette.

"Well, the Chantilly isn't dear. However, we have the same at eighteen francs; as for the mount, my dear madame, it's a shameful robbery. I should not dare to sell one like it for more than ninety francs."

"Just what I said!" exclaimed Madame Bourdelais.

"Ninety francs!" murmured Madame de Boves; "one must be very poor indeed to go without one at that price."

She had taken up the fan, and was again examining it with her daughter Blanche; and, on her large regular face, in her big sleepy eyes, there arose an expression of the suppressed and despairing longing of a caprice in which she could not indulge. The fan once more went the round of the ladies, amidst various remarks and exclamations. Monsieur de Boves and Vallagnosc, however, had left the window. Whilst the former had returned to his place behind Madame Guibal, the charms of whose bust he was admiring, with his correct and superior air, the young man was leaning over Blanche, endeavoring to find something agreeable to say.

"Don't you think it rather gloomy, mademoiselle, this white mount and black lace?"

"Oh," replied she, gravely, not a blush coloring her inflated cheeks, "I once saw one made of mother-of-pearl and white lace. Something truly virginal!"

Monsieur de Boves, who had doubtless observed the heartbroken, longing looks with which his wife was following the fan, at last added his word to the conversation. "These flimsy things don't last long, they soon break," said he.

"Of course they do!" declared Madame Guibal, with an air of indifference. "I'm tired of having mine mended."

For several minutes, Madame Marty, excited by the conversation, was feverishly turning her red leather bag about on her lap, for she had not yet been able to show her purchases. She was burning to display them, with a sort of sensual desire; and, suddenly forgetting her husband's presence, she took out a few yards of narrow lace wound on a piece of cardboard.

"It's the Valenciennes for my daughter," said she. "It's an inch and a half wide. Isn't it delicious? One franc eighteen sous."

The lace was passed from hand to hand. The ladies were astonished. Mouret assured them he sold these little trimmings at cost price. However, Madame Marty had closed the bag, as if to conceal certain things she could not show. But after the success obtained by the Valenciennes she was unable to resist the temptation of taking out a handkerchief.

"There was this handkerchief as well. Real Brussels, my dear. Oh! a bargain! Twenty francs!"

And after that the bag became inexhaustible, she blushed with pleasure, a modesty like that of a woman undressing herself made her appear more charming and embarrassed at each fresh article she took out. There was a Spanish blonde-lace cravat, thirty francs: she didn't want it, but the shopman had sworn it was the last, and that in future the price would be raised. Next came a Chantilly veil: rather dear, fifty francs; if she didn't wear it she could make it do for her daughter.

"Really, lace is so pretty!" repeated she with her nervous laugh. "Once I'm inside I could buy everything."

"And this?" asked Madame de Boves, taking up and examining a remnant of Maltese lace.

"That," replied she, "is for an insertion. There are twenty-six yards—a franc a yard. Just fancy!"

"But," said Madame Bourdelais, surprised, "what are you going to do with it?"

"I'm sure I don't know. But it was such a funny pattern!"

At this moment she raised her eyes and perceived her terrified husband in front of her. He had turned paler than usual, his whole person expressed the patient, resigned anguish of a man assisting, powerless, at the reckless expenditure of his salary, so dearly earned. Every fresh bit of lace was for him a disaster; bitter days of teaching swallowed up, long journeys to pupils through the mud devoured, the continued effort of his life resulting in a secret misery, the hell of a necessitous household. Before the increasing wildness of his look, she wanted to catch up the veil, the cravat, and the handkerchief, moving her feverish hands about, repeating with forced laughter: "You'll get me a scolding from my husband. I assure you, my dear, I've been very reasonable; for there was a fine piece of point at five hundred francs, oh! a marvel!"

"Why didn't you buy it?" asked Madame Guibal, calmly. "Monsieur Marty is the most gallant of men."

The poor professor was obliged to bow and say his wife was perfectly welcome. But the idea of this point at five hundred francs was like a lump of ice dripping down his back; and as Mouret was just at that moment affirming that the new shops increased the comfort of the middle-class households, he glared at him with a terrible expression, the flash of hatred of a timid man who would have throttled him had he dared.

But the ladies had still kept hold of the bits of lace, fascinated, intoxicated. The pieces were unrolled, passed from one to the other, drawing the admirers closer still, holding them in the delicate meshes. On their laps there was a continual caress of this tissue, so miraculously fine, and amidst which their culpable fingers fondly lingered. They still kept Mouret a close prisoner, overwhelming him with fresh questions. As the day continued to decline, he was now and again obliged to bend his head, grazing their hair with his beard, to examine a stitch, or indicate a design. But in this soft voluptuousness of twilight, in the midst of this warm feminine atmosphere, Mouret still remained their master beneath the rapture he affected. He seemed to be a woman himself, they felt themselves penetrated and overcome by this delicate sense of their secret that he possessed, and they abandoned themselves, captivated; whilst he, certain from that moment to have them at his mercy, appeared, brutally triumphing over them, the despotic monarch of dress.

"Oh, Monsieur Mouret!" stammered they, in low, hysterical voices, in the gloom of the drawing-room.

The last rays of the setting sun were dying away on the brass-work of the furniture. The laces alone retained a snowy reflex on the dark dresses of the ladies, of which the confused group seemed to surround the young man with a vague appearance of kneeling, worshipping women. A light still shone on the side of the silver teapot, a short flame like that of a night-light, burning in an alcove warmed by the perfume of the tea. But suddenly the servant entered with two lamps, and the charm was destroyed. The drawing-room became light and cheerful. Madame Marty was putting her lace in her little bag, Madame de Boves was eating a sponge cake, whilst Henriette who had got up, was talking in a half-whisper to the baron, near one of the windows.

"He's a charming fellow," said the baron.

"Isn't he?" exclaimed she, with the involuntary cry of a woman in love.

He smiled, and looked at her with a paternal indulgence. This was the first time he had seen her so completely conquered; and, too proud to suffer from it, he experienced nothing but a feeling of compassion on seeing her in the hands of this handsome fellow, so tender and yet so cold-hearted. He thought he ought to warn her, and murmured in a joking tone: "Take care, my dear, or he'll eat you all up."

A flash of jealousy lighted up Henriette's eyes. Perhaps she understood Mouret had simply made use of her to get at the baron; and she determined to render him mad with passion, he whose hurried style of making love had the easy charm of a song thrown to the four winds of heaven. "Oh," said she, affecting to joke in her turn, "the lamb always finishes up by eating the wolf."

The baron, greatly amused, encouraged her with a nod. Could she be the woman who was to avenge all the others?

When Mouret, after having reminded Vallagnosc that he wanted to show him his machine at work, came up to take his leave, the baron retained him near the window opposite the gardens, now buried in darkness. He yielded at last to the seduction; his confidence had come on seeing him in the midst of these ladies. Both conversed for a moment in a low tone, then the banker said: "Well, I'll look into the affair. It's settled if your Monday's sale proves as important as you expect."

They shook hands, and Mouret, delighted, took his leave, for he did not enjoy his dinner unless he went and gave a look at the day's receipts at The Ladies' Paradise.

CHAPTER IV.

The following Monday, the 10th of October, a clear, victorious sun pierced the grey clouds which had darkened Paris during the previous week. It had drizzled all the previous night, a sort of watery mist, the humidity of which dirtied the streets; but in the early morning, thanks to the sharp wind which was driving the clouds away, the pavement had become drier, and the blue sky had a limpid, spring-like gaiety.

Thus The Ladies' Paradise, after eight o'clock, blazed forth beneath the clear rays of the sun, in all the glory of its great sale of winter novelties. Flags were flying at the door, and pieces of woollens were flapping about in the fresh morning air, animating the Place Gaillon with the bustle of a country fair; whilst in both streets the windows developed symphonies of displays, the clearness of the glass showing up still further the brilliant tones. It was like a debauch of color, a street pleasure which burst forth there, a wealth of goods publicly displayed, where everybody could go and feast their eyes.

But at this hour very few people entered, only a few rare customers, housewives of the neighborhood, women desirous of avoiding the afternoon crush. Behind the stuffs which decorated it, one could feel the shop to be empty, under arms and waiting for customers, with its waxed floors and counters overflowing with goods.

The busy morning crowd barely glanced at the windows, without lingering a moment. In the Rue Neuve-Saint-Augustin and in the Place Gaillon, where the carriages were to take their stand, there were only two cabs at nine o'clock. The inhabitants of the district, especially the small traders, stirred up by such a show of streamers and decorations, formed little groups in the doorways, at the corners of the streets, gazing at the shop, making bitter remarks. What most filled them with indignation was the sight of one of the four delivery vans just introduced by Mouret, which was standing in the Rue de la Michodière, in front of the delivery office. They were green, picked out with yellow and red, their brilliantly varnished panels sparkling in the sun with the brightness of purple and gold. This van, with its brand-new medley of colors, the name of the house painted on each side, and surmounted with an advertisement of the day's sale, finished by going off at a trot, drawn by a splendid horse, after being filled up with the previous night's parcels; and Baudu, who was standing on the threshold of The Old Elbeuf, watched it as far as the boulevard, where it disappeared, to spread all over Paris in a starry radiance the hated name of The Ladies' Paradise.

However, a few cabs were arriving and forming a line. Every time a customer entered, there was a movement amongst the shop messengers, who were drawn up under the lofty doorway, dressed in livery consisting of a light green coat and trousers, and striped red and yellow waistcoat. Jouve, the inspector and retired captain, was also there, in a frockcoat and white tie, wearing his decoration like a sign of respectability and probity, receiving the ladies with a gravely polite air, bending over them to point out the departments. Then they disappeared in the vestibule, which was transformed into an oriental saloon.

From the very threshold it was a marvel, a surprise, which enchanted all of them. It was Mouret who had been struck with this idea. He was the first to buy, in the Levant, at very advantageous rates, a collection of old and new carpets, articles which up to the present had only been sold at curiosity shops, at high prices; and he intended to flood the market with these goods, selling them at a little over cost price, simply drawing from them a splendid decoration destined to attract the best class of art customers to his establishment. From the centre of the Place Gaillon could be seen this oriental saloon, composed solely of carpets and door curtains which had been hung under his orders.

The ceiling was covered with a quantity of Smyrna carpets, the complicated designs of which stood out boldly on a red ground. Then from each side there hung Syrian and Karamanian door-curtains, speckled with green, yellow, and vermilion; Diarbekir door-curtains of a commoner type, rough to the touch, like shepherds' cloaks; besides these there were carpets which could be used as door-curtains and hangings—long Ispahan, Teheran, and Kermancha rugs, the larger Schoumaka and Madras carpets, a strange florescence of peonies and palms, the fancy let loose in a garden of dreams. On the floor were more carpets, a heap of greasy fleeces: in the centre was an Agra carpet, an extraordinary article with a white ground and a broad delicate blue border, through which ran violet-colored ornaments of exquisite design. Everywhere there was an immense display of marvellous fabrics; Mecca carpets with a velvety reflection, prayer carpets from Daghestan with a symbolic point, Kurdistan carpets covered with blossoming flowers; and finally, piled up in a corner, a heap of Gherdes, Koula, and Kirchur rugs from fifteen francs a piece.

This sumptuous pacha's tent was furnished with divans and arm-chairs, made with camel sacks, some ornamented with many-colored lozenges, others with primitive roses. Turkey, Arabia, and the Indies were all there. They had emptied the palaces, plundered the mosques and bazaars. A barbarous gold tone prevailed in the weft of the old carpets, the faded tints of which still preserved a somber warmth, as of an extinguished furnace, a beautiful burnt hue suggestive of the old masters. Visions of the East floated beneath the luxury of this barbarous art, amid the strong odor which the old wools had retained of the country of vermin and of the rising sun.

In the morning at eight o'clock, when Denise, who was to commence on that very Monday, had crossed the oriental saloon, she stood there, lost in astonishment, unable to recognize the shop entrance, entirely overcome by this harem-like decoration planted at the door. A messenger having shown her to the top of the house, and handed her over to Madame Cabin, who cleaned and looked after the rooms, this person installed her in

No. 7, where her box had already been put. It was a narrow cell, opening on the roof by a skylight, furnished with a small bed, a walnut-wood wardrobe, a toilet-table, and two chairs. Twenty similar rooms ran along the convent-like corridor, painted yellow; and, out of the thirty-five young ladies in the house, the twenty who had no friends in Paris slept there, whilst the remaining fifteen lodged outside, a few with borrowed aunts and cousins. Denise at once took off her shabby woollen dress, worn thin by brushing and mended at the sleeves, the only one she had brought from Valognes; she then put on the uniform of her department, a black silk dress which had been altered for her and which she found ready on the bed. This dress was still too large, too wide across the shoulders; but she was so hurried in her emotion that she paid no heed to these details of coquetry. She had never worn silk before. When she went downstairs again, dressed up, uncomfortable, she looked at the shining skirt, feeling ashamed of the noisy rustling of the silk.

Down below, as she was entering her department, a quarrel burst out. She heard Clara say, in a shrill voice:

"Madame, I came in before her."

"It isn't true," replied Marguerite. "She pushed past me at the door, but I had already one foot in the room."

It was for the inscription on the list of turns, which regulated the sales. The saleswomen wrote their names on a slate in the order of their arrival, and whenever one of them had served a customer, she re-wrote her name beneath the others. Madame Aurélie finished by deciding in Marguerite's favor.

"Always some injustice here!" muttered Clara, furiously.

But Denise's entry reconciled these young ladies. They looked at her, then smiled to each other. How could a person truss herself up in that way! The young girl went and awkwardly wrote her name on the list, where she found herself last. Meanwhile, Madame Aurélie was examining her with an anxious face. She could not help saying:

"My dear, two like you could get into your dress; you must have it taken in. Besides, you don't know how to dress yourself. Come here and let me arrange you a bit."

And she placed herself before one of the tall glasses alternating with the doors of the cupboards containing the dresses. The vast apartment, surrounded by these glasses and the woodwork in carved oak, the floor covered with red Wilton carpet of a large pattern, resembled the commonplace drawing-room of a hotel, traversed by a continual stream of travelers. The young ladies completed the resemblance, dressed in the regulation silk, promenading their commercial charms about, without ever sitting down on the dozen chairs reserved for the customers. All wore between two buttonholes of the body of their dresses, as if stuck in their bosoms, a long pencil, with its point in the air; and half out of their pockets, could be seen the white cover of the book of debit-notes. Several risked wearing jewelry—rings, brooches, chains; but their great coquetry, the luxury they all struggled for in the forced uniformity of their dress, was their bare hair, quantities of it, augmented by plaits and chignons when their own did not suffice, combed, curled, and decked out in every way.

"Pull the waist down in front," said Madame Aurélie. "There, you have now no hump on your back. And your hair, how can you massacre it like that? It would be superb, if you only took a little trouble."

This was, in fact, Denise's only beauty. Of a beautiful flaxen hue, it fell down to her ankles; and when she did it up, it was so troublesome that she simply rolled it in a knot, keeping it together under the strong teeth of a bone comb. Clara, greatly annoyed by this head of hair, affected to laugh at it, so strange did it look, twisted up anyhow in its savage grace. She made a sign to a saleswoman in the under-linen department, a girl with a large face and agreeable manner. The two departments, which were close together, were in continual hostility; but the young ladies sometimes joined together in laughing at other people.

"Mademoiselle Cugnot, just look at that mane," said Clara, whom Marguerite was nudging, feigning also to be on the point of bursting out laughing.

But Mademoiselle Cugnot was not in the humor for joking. She had been looking at Denise for a moment, and she remembered what she had suffered herself during the first few months of her arrival in the establishment.

"Well, what?" said she. "Everybody hasn't got a mane like that!"

And she returned to her place, leaving the two others very crestfallen. Denise, who had heard all, followed her with a look of thanks, while Madame Aurélie gave our heroine a book of debit-notes with her name on it, saying: "Tomorrow you'll get yourself up better; and, now, try and pick up the ways of the house, wait your turn for selling. Today's work will be very hard; we shall be able to judge of your capabilities."

However, the department still remained deserted; very few customers came up at this early hour. The young ladies reserved themselves, prudently preparing for the fatigues of the afternoon. Denise, intimidated by the thought that they were watching her, sharpened her pencil, for the sake of something to do; then, imitating the others, she stuck it into her bosom, between two buttonholes, and summoned up all her courage, determined to conquer a position. The previous evening they had told her she entered as a probationer, that is to say without any fixed salary; she would simply have the commission and a certain allowance on everything she sold. But she fully hoped to earn twelve hundred francs a year in this way, knowing that the good saleswomen earned as much as two thousand, when they liked to take the trouble. Her expenses were regulated; a hundred francs a month would enable her to pay Pépé's board and lodging, assist Jean, who did not earn a sou, and procure some clothes and linen for herself. But, in order to attain this large sum, she would have to show herself industrious and pushing, taking no notice of the ill-will displayed by those around her, fighting for her share, even snatching it from her comrades if necessary. As she was thus working herself up for the struggle, a tall young man, passing the department, smiled at her; and when she saw it was Deloche, who had been engaged in the lace department the previous day, she returned his smile, happy at the friendship which thus presented itself, accepting this smile as a good omen.

At half-past nine a bell rang for the first luncheon. Then a fresh peal announced the second; and still no customers appeared. The second-hand, Madame Frédéric, who, in her disagreeable widow's harshness, delighted in prophesying disasters, declared in short sentences that the day was lost, that they would not see a soul, that they might close the cupboards and go away; predictions which darkened Marguerite's flat face, she being a girl who looked sharp after her profits, whilst Clara, with her runaway-horse appearance, was already dreaming of an excursion to the Verrières woods, if the house failed. As for Madame Aurélie, she was there, silent and serious, promenading her Caesar-like mask about the empty department, like a general who has a certain responsibility in victory and in defeat. About eleven o'clock a few ladies appeared. Denise's turn for serving had arrived. Just at that moment a customer came up.

"The fat old girl from the country," murmured Marguerite.

It was a woman of forty-five, who occasionally journeyed to Paris from the depths of some out-of-the-way place. There she saved up for months; then, hardly out of the train, she made straight for The Ladies' Paradise, and spent all her savings. She very rarely ordered anything by letter, she liked to see and handle the goods, and laid in a stock of everything, even down to needles, which she said were excessively dear in her small town. The whole staff knew her, that her name was Boutarel, and that she lived at Albi, but troubled no further about her, neither about her position nor her mode of life.

"How do you do, madame?" graciously asked Madame Aurélie, who had come forward. "And what can we show you? You shall be attended to at once." Then, turning round: "Now, young ladies!"

Denise approached; but Clara had sprung forward. As a rule, she was very careless and idle, not caring about the money she earned in the shop, as she could get plenty outside, without trouble. But the idea of doing the new-comer out of a good customer spurred her on.

"I beg your pardon, it's my turn," said Denise, indignantly.

Madame Aurélie set her aside with a severe look, saying:

"There are no turns. I alone am mistress here. Wait till you know, before serving our regular customers."

The young girl retired, and as the tears were coming in her eyes, and she wished to conceal this excess of sensibility, she turned her back, standing up before the window, pretending to be looking into the street. Were they going to prevent her selling? Would they all arrange together to deprive her of the important sales, like that? A fear for the future seized her, she felt herself crushed between so many interests let loose. Yielding to the bitterness of her abandonment, her forehead against the cold glass, she gazed at The Old Elbeuf opposite, thinking she ought to have implored her uncle to keep her. Perhaps he himself regretted his decision, for he seemed to her greatly affected the previous evening. Now she was quite alone in this vast house, where no one liked her, where she found herself hurt, lost. Pépé and Jean, who had never left her side, were living with strangers; it was a cruel separation, and the big tears which she kept back made the street dance in a sort of fog. All this time, the hum of voices continued behind her.

"This one makes me look a fright," Madame Boutarel was saying.

"You really make a mistake, madame," said Clara; "the shoulders fit perfectly—but perhaps you would prefer a pelisse to a mantle?"

But Denise started. A hand was laid on her arm. Madame Aurélie addressed her severely:

"Well, you're doing nothing now—eh? Only looking at the people passing. Things can't go on this way, you know!"

"But they prevent me selling, madame."

"Oh, there's other work for you, mademoiselle! Begin at the beginning. Do the folding-up."

In order to please the few customers who had called, they had been obliged to ransack all the cupboards, and on the two long oaken tables, to the right and the left, were heaps of mantles, pelisses, and capes, garments of all sizes and all materials. Without replying, Denise set about sorting them, folding them carefully and arranging them again in the cupboards. This was the lowest work, generally performed by beginners. She ceased to protest, knowing that they required the strictest obedience, waiting till the first-hand should be good enough to let her sell, as she seemed at first to have the intention of doing. She was still folding, when Mouret appeared on the scene. This was a violent shock for her; she blushed without knowing why, she felt herself invaded by a strange fear, thinking he was going to speak to her. But he did not even see her; he no longer remembered this little girl whom the charming impression of an instant had induced him to support.

"Madame Aurélie," called he in a brief voice.

He was rather pale, but his eyes were clear and resolute. In making the tour of the departments he had found them empty, and the possibility of a defeat had suddenly presented itself in the midst of his obstinate faith in fortune. True, it was only eleven o'clock; he knew by experience that the crowd never arrived much before the afternoon. But certain symptoms troubled him. At the previous sales, a general movement had taken place from the morning even; besides he did not see any of those bareheaded women, customers living in the neighborhood, who usually dropped into his shop as into a neighbor's. Like all great captains, he felt at the moment of giving battle a superstitious weakness, notwithstanding his habitually resolute attitude. Things would not go on well, he was lost, and he could not have explained why; he thought he could read his defeat on the faces of the passing ladies even.

Just at that moment, Madame Boutarel, she who always bought something, was going away, saying: "No, you have nothing that pleases me. I'll see, I'll decide later on."

Mouret watched her depart. Then, as Madame Aurélie ran up at his call, he took her aside, and they exchanged a few rapid words. She wore a despairing air, and was evidently admitting that things were looking bad. For a moment they remained face to face, seized with one of those doubts which generals conceal from their soldiers. Ultimately he said out loud in his brave way: "If you want assistance, understand, take a girl from the workroom. She'll be a little help to you."

He continued his inspection in despair. He had avoided Bour-doncle all the morning, for his anxious doubts irritated him. On leaving the under-linen department, where business was still worse, he dropped right on to him, and was obliged to submit to the expression of his fears. He did not hesitate to send him to the devil, with a brutality that even his principal employees came in for when things were looking bad.

"Get out of my way!" said he. "Everything is going on all right. I shall end by pitching out the tremblers."

Mouret planted himself alone on the landing of the hallstair-case. From there he commanded the whole shop; around him the departments on the first floor; beneath, those of the ground floor. Above, the emptiness seemed heart-breaking; in the lace department, an old woman was having everything turned over and buying nothing; whilst three good-for-nothing minxes in the under-linen department were slowly choosing some collars at eighteen sous. Down below, under the covered galleries, in the ray of light which came in from the street, he noticed that the customers were commencing to get more numerous. It was a slow, broken procession, a promenade before the counters; in the mercery and the haberdashery departments some women of the commoner class were pushing about, but there was hardly a customer in the linen or in the woollen departments. The shop messengers, in their green coats, the buttons of which shone brilliantly, were waiting for customers, their hands dangling about. Now and again there passed an inspector with a ceremo-nious air, very stiff in his white necktie. Mouret was especially grieved by the mortal silence which reigned in the hall, where the light fell from above from a ground glass window, showing a white dust, diffuse and suspended, as it were, under which the silk department seemed to be sleeping, amid a shivering reli-gious silence. A shopman's footstep, a few whispered words, the rustling of a passing skirt, were the only noises heard, and they were almost stifled by the hot air of the heating apparatus. How-ever, carriages began to arrive, the sudden pulling up of the horses was heard, and immediately after the banging of the car-riage doors. Outside, a distant tumult was commencing to make itself heard, groups of idlers were pushing in front of the windows, cabs were taking up their positions in the Place Gaillon, there were all the appearances of an approaching crowd. But on seeing the idle cashiers leaning back on their chairs behind their wickets, and observing that the parceltables with their boxes of string and reams of blue packing-paper remained unoccupied, Mouret, though indignant with himself for being afraid, thought he felt his immense machine stop and turn cold beneath him.

"I say, Favier," murmured Hutin, "look at the governor up there. He doesn't seem to be enjoying himself."

"This is a rotten shop!" replied Favier. "Just fancy, I've not sold a thing yet."

Both of them, waiting for customers, whispered such short remarks from time to time without looking at each other. The other salesmen of the department were occupied in arranging large bales of the Paris Paradise under Robineau's orders; whilst Bouthemont, in full consultation with a thin young woman, seemed to be taking an important order. Around them, on frail and elegant shelves, the silks, folded in long pieces of creamy paper, were heaped up like pamphlets of an unusual size; and, encumbering the counters, were fancy silks, moirés, satins, velvets, presenting the appearance of mown flowers, quite a harvest of delicate precious tissues. This was the most elegant of all the departments, a veritable drawing-room, where the goods, so light and airy, were nothing but a luxurious furnishing.

"I must have a hundred francs by Sunday," said Hutin. "If I don't make an average of twelve francs a day, I'm lost. I'd reckoned on this sale."

"By Jove! a hundred francs; that's rather stiff," said Favier. "I only want fifty or sixty. You must go in for swell women, then?"

"Oh, no, my dear fellow. It's a stupid affair; I made a bet and lost. So I have to stand a dinner for five persons, two fellows and three girls. Hang me! the first one that passes I'll let her in for twenty yards of Paris Paradise!"

They continued talking for several minutes, relating what they had done the previous day, and what they intended to do the next week. Favier did a little betting, Hutin did a little boating, and kept music-hall singers. But they were both possessed by the same desire for money, struggling for it all the week, and spending it all on Sunday. It was their sole preoccupation in the shop, an hourly and pitiless struggle. And that cunning Bouthemont had just managed to get hold of Madame Sauveur's messenger, the skinny woman with whom he was talking! good business, three or four dozen pieces, at least, for the celebrated dressmaker always gave good orders. At that moment Robineau took it into his head to do Favier out of a customer.

"Oh! as for that fellow, we must settle up with him," said Hutin, who took advantage of the slightest thing in order to stir up the salesmen against the man whose place he coveted. "Ought the first- and second-hands to sell? My word of honor! my dear fellow, if ever I become second you'll see how well I shall act with the others."

And all his little Norman person, so fat and jolly, played the good-natured man energetically. Favier could not help casting a side glance towards him, but he preserved his phlegmatical air, contenting himself with replying: "Yes, I know. I should be only too pleased." Then, as a lady came up, he added in a lower tone: "Look out! Here's one for you."

It was a lady with a blotchy face, a yellow bonnet, and a red dress. Hutin immediately recognized in her a woman who would buy nothing. He quickly stooped behind the counter, pretending to be doing up his boot-lace; and, thus concealed, he murmured: "No fear, let someone else take her. I don't want to lose my turn!"

However, Robineau called out: "Whose turn, gentlemen? Monsieur Hutin's? Where's Monsieur Hutin?"

And as this gentleman still gave no reply, it was the next salesman who served the lady with the blotches. Hutin was right, she simply wanted some samples with the prices; and she kept the salesman more than ten minutes, overwhelming him with questions. However, Robineau had seen Hutin get up from behind the counter; so that when another customer arrived, he interfered with a stern air, stopping the young man, who was rushing forward.

"Your turn is passed. I called you, and as you were there behind."

"But I didn't hear you, sir."

"That'll do! Write your name at the bottom. Now, Monsieur
Favier, it's your turn."

Favier, greatly amused at heart at this adventure, threw a
glance at his friend, as if to excuse himself. Hutin, with pale lips,
had turned his head away. What enraged him was that he knew
the customer very well, an adorable blonde who often came to
their department, and whom the salesmen called amongst themselves "the pretty lady," knowing nothing of her, not even her
name. She bought a great deal, had her purchases taken to her
carriage, and immediately disappeared. Tall, elegant, dressed
with exquisite taste, she appeared to be very rich, and to belong
to the best society.

"Well! and your courtesan?" asked Hutin of Favier, when the
latter returned from the pay-desk, where he had accompanied
the lady.

"Oh! a courtesan!" replied the other. "I fancy she looks too
lady-like for that. She must be the wife of a stockbroker or a doctor, or something of that sort."

"Don't tell me! it's a courtesan. With their grand lady airs it's
impossible to tell now-a-days!"

Favier looked at his book of debit-notes. "I don't care!" said he,
"I've stuck her for two hundred and ninety-three francs. That
makes nearly three francs for me."

Hutin bit his lips, and vented his spleen on the debit note-
books. Another invention for cramming their pockets. There
was a secret rivalry between these two. Favier, as a rule, pretended to sing small, to recognize Hutin's superiority, but in re-
ality devouring him all the while behind his back. Thus Hutin
was wild at the thought of the three francs pocketed so easily by
a salesman whom he considered to be his inferior in business. A
fine day's work! If it went on like this, he would not earn enough
to pay for the seltzer water for his guests. And in the midst of the
battle, which was now becoming fiercer, he walked along the

counters with hungry eyes, eager for his share, jealous even of his superior, who was just showing the thin young woman out, and saying to her:

"Very well! it's understood. Tell her I'll do my best to obtain this favor from Monsieur Mouret."

Mouret had quitted his post on the stairs some time before. Suddenly he reappeared on the landing of the principal staircase which communicated with the ground floor; and from there he commanded a view of the whole establishment. His face had regained its color, his faith was restored and increasing before the crowd which was gradually filling the place. It was the expected rush at last, the afternoon crush, which he had for a moment despaired of. All the shopmen were at their posts, a last ring of the bell had announced the end of the third lunch; the disastrous morning, due no doubt to a shower which fell about nine o'clock, could still be repaired, for the blue sky of early morn had resumed its victorious gaiety. Now that the first-floor departments were becoming animated, he was obliged to stand back to make way for the women who were going up to the under-clothing and dress departments; whilst, behind him, in the lace and the shawl departments, he heard large sums bandied about. But the sight of the galleries on the ground floor especially reassured him. There was a crowd at the haberdashery department, and even the linen and woollen departments were invaded. The procession of buyers closed up, nearly all of a higher class at present, with a few lingering housewives. Under the pale light of the silk hall, ladies had taken off their gloves to feel the Paris Paradise, talking in half-whispers. And there was no longer any mistaking the noises arriving from outside, rolling of cabs, banging of carriage-doors, an increasing tumult in the crowd. He felt the machine commencing to work under him, getting up steam and reviving, from the pay-desks where the money was jingling, and the tables where the messengers were hurriedly packing up the goods, down to the basement, in the delivery-room, which was quickly filling up with the parcels sent down, and the underground rumbling of which seemed to shake the whole house. In the midst of the crowd was the inspector, Jouve, walking about gravely, watching for thieves.

"Hullo! is that you?" said Mouret, all at once, recognizing Paul de Vallagnosc whom a messenger had conducted to him. "No, no, you are not in my way. Besides, you've only to follow me if you want to see everything, for today I stay at the breach."

He still felt anxious. No doubt there were plenty of people, but would the sale prove to be the triumph he hoped for? However, he laughed with Paul, carrying him off gaily.

"It seems to be picking up a bit," said Hutin to Favier. "But somehow I've no luck; there are some days that are precious bad, my word! I've just made another miss, that old frump hasn't bought anything."

And he glanced towards a lady who was walking off, casting looks of disgust at all the goods. He was not likely to get fat on his thousand francs a year, unless he sold something; as a rule he made seven or eight francs a day commission, which gave him with his regular pay an average of ten francs a day. Favier never made much more than eight, and there was this animal taking the bread out of his mouth, for he had just sold another dress—a cold-natured fellow who had never known how to amuse a customer! It was exasperating.

"Those chaps over there seem to be doing very well," remarked Favier, speaking of the salesmen in the hosiery and haberdashery departments.

But Hutin, who was looking all round the place, suddenly asked: "Do you know Madame Desforges, the governor's sweetheart? Look! that dark woman in the glove department, who is having some gloves tried on by Mignot." He stopped, then resumed in a low tone, as if speaking to Mignot, on whom he continued to keep his eyes: "Oh, go on, old man, you may pull her fingers about as much as you like, that won't do you any good! We know your conquests!"

There was a rivalry between himself and the glove-man, the rivalry of two handsome fellows, who both affected to flirt with the lady-customers. As a matter of fact they had neither had any real conquests to boast about. Mignot lived on the legend of a police superintendent's wife who had fallen in love with him, whilst Hutin had really conquered a lace-maker who had got tired of wandering about in the doubtful hotels in the neighborhood; but they invented a lot of mysterious adventures, leading people to believe in all sorts of appointments made by titled ladies, between two purchases.

"You should get hold of her," said Favier, in his sly, artful way.

"That's a good idea!" exclaimed Hutin. "If she comes here I'll let her in for something extensive; I want a five-franc piece!"

In the glove department quite a row of ladies were seated before the narrow counter covered with green velvet and edged with nickel silver; and the smiling shopmen were heaping up before them the flat boxes of a bright red, taken out of the counter itself, and resembling the ticketed drawers of a secrétaire. Mignot especially was bending his pretty doll-like face over his customer, his thick Parisian voice full of tender inflections. He had already sold Madame Desforges a dozen pairs of kid gloves, the Paradise gloves, one of the specialities of the house. She then took three pairs of Swedish, and was now trying on some Saxon gloves, for fear the size should not be exact.

"Oh! quite perfect, madame!" repeated Mignot. "Six and a quarter would be too large for a hand like yours."

Half lying on the counter, he was holding her hand, taking the fingers one by one, slipping the glove on with a long, renewed, and persistently caressing air, looking at her as if he expected to see in her face the signs of a voluptuous joy. But she, with her elbow on the velvet counter, her wrist raised, gave him her fingers with the unconcerned air with which she gave her foot to her maid to allow her to button her boot. For her he was not a man; she employed him for such private work with the familiar disdain she showed for the people in her service, without looking at him even.

"I don't hurt you, madame?"

She replied "No," with a shake of the head. The smell of the Saxon gloves—that savage smell as of sugared musk—troubled her as a rule; and she sometimes laughed about it, confessing her taste for this equivocal perfume, in which there is a suspicion of the wild beast fallen into some girl's powder-box. But seated at this commonplace counter she did not notice the smell of the gloves, it raised no sensual feeling between her and this salesman doing his work.

"And what next, madame?"

"Nothing, thanks. Be good enough to carry the parcel to the pay-desk No. 10, for Madame Desforges."

Being a constant customer, she gave her name at a pay-desk, and had each purchase sent there without wanting a shopman to follow her. When she had gone away, Mignot turned towards his neighbor and winked, and would have liked him to believe that wonderful things had just taken place.

"By Jove! I'd like to dress her all over!" said he, coarsely.

Meanwhile, Madame Desforges continued her purchases. She turned to the left, stopping in the linen department to procure some dusters; then she walked round the shop, going as far as the woollen department at the further end of the gallery. As she was satisfied with her cook, she wanted to make her a present of a dress. The woollen department overflowed with a compact crowd, all the lower middle-class women were there, feeling the stuff, absorbed in mute calculations; and she was obliged to sit down for a moment. The shelves were piled up with great rolls of stuff which the salesmen were taking down one by one, with a sudden pull. They were beginning to get confused with these encumbered counters, on which the stuffs were mixing up and tumbling over each other. It was a rising tide of neutral tints, heavy woollen tones, iron-greys, and blue-greys, with here and there a Scotch tartan, and a blood-red ground of flannel breaking out. And the white tickets on the pieces were like a shower of rare white flakes falling on a black December soil.

Behind a pile of poplin, Liénard was joking with a tall girl without hat or bonnet, a work-girl, sent by her mistress to match some merino. He detested these big-sale days, which tired him to death, and he endeavored to shirk his work, getting plenty of money from his father, not caring a fig about the business, doing just enough to avoid being dismissed.

"Listen to me, Mademoiselle Fanny," he was saying; "you are

always in a hurry. Did the striped vicugna do the other day? I shall come and see you, and ask for my commission."

But the girl escaped, laughing, and Liénard found himself before Madame Desforges, whom he could not help asking: "What can I serve you with, madame?"

She wanted a dress, not too dear but yet strong. Liénard, with the view of sparing his arms, which was his principal care, maneuvered to make her take one of the stuffs already unfolded on the counter. There were cashmeres, serges, vicugnas, and he declared that there was nothing better to be had, they never wore out. But none of these seemed to satisfy her. On one of the shelves she had observed a blue serge, which she wished to see. He made up his mind at last, and took down the roll, but she thought it too rough. Then he showed her a cheviot, some diagonal, some greys, every sort of woollens, which she felt out of curiosity, for the pleasure of doing so, decided at heart to take no matter what. The young man was thus obliged to empty the highest shelves; his shoulders cracked, the counter had disappeared under the silky grain of the cashmeres and poplins, the rough nap of the cheviot, and the tufty down of the vicugna; there were samples of every material and every tint. Though she had not the least wish to buy any, she asked to see some grenadine and some Chambéry gauze. Then, when she had seen enough, she said:

"Oh! after all, the first is the best; it's for my cook. Yes, the serge, the one at two francs." And when Liénard had measured it, pale with suppressed anger, she added: "Have the goodness to carry that to pay-desk No. 10, for Madame Desforges."

Just as she was going away, she recognized Madame Marty close to her, accompanied by her daughter Valentine, a tall girl of fourteen, thin and bold, who was already casting a woman's covetous looks on the goods.

"Ah! it's you, dear madame?"

"Yes, dear madame; what a crowd—eh?"

"Oh! don't speak of it, it's stifling. And such a success! Have you seen the oriental saloon?"

"Superb—wonderful!"

And amidst the pushing and crushing of the growing crowd of modest purses eagerly seeking the cheap lines in the woollen goods, they went into ecstasies over the exhibition of carpets. Then Madame Marty explained she was looking for some material for a mantle; but she was not quite decided; she wanted to see some check patterns.

"Look, mamma," murmured Valentine, "it's too common."

"Come to the silk department," said Madame Desforges, "you must see their famous Paris Paradise."

Madame Marty hesitated for a moment. It would be very dear, and she had faithfully promised her husband to be careful! She had been buying for an hour, quite a pile of articles were following her already: a muff and some cuffs and collars for herself, some stockings for her daughter. She finished by saying to the shopman who was showing her the checks:

"Well—no; I'm going to the silk department; you've nothing to suit me."

The shopman took the articles and walked before the ladies.

In the silk department there was also a crowd, the principal crush being opposite the inside display, arranged by Hutin, and to which Mouret had given the finishing touches. It was at the further end of the hall, around one of the small wrought-iron columns which supported the glass roof, a veritable torrent of stuffs, a puffy sheet falling from above and spreading out down to the floor. At first stood out the light satins and tender silks, the satins *à la Reine* and Renaissance, with the pearly tones of spring water; light silks, transparent as crystals—Nile-green, Indian-azure, May-rose, and Danube-blue. Then came the stronger fabrics: marvellous satins, duchess silks, warm tints, rolling in great waves; and right at the bottom, as in a fountain-basin, reposed the heavy stuffs, the figured silks, the damasks, brocades, and lovely silvered silks in the midst of a deep bed of velvet of every sort—black, white, and colored—skillfully disposed on silk and satin grounds, hollowing out with their medley of colors a still lake in which the reflex of the sky seemed to be dancing. The women, pale with desire, bent over as if to look at themselves. And before this falling cataract they all remained standing, with the secret fear of being carried away by the irruption of such luxury, and with the irresistible desire to jump in amidst it and be lost.

"Here you are, then!" said Madame Desforges, on finding Madame Bourdelais installed before a counter.

"Ah! good-morning!" replied the latter, shaking hands with the ladies. "Yes, I've come to have a look."

"What a prodigious exhibition! It's like a dream. And the oriental saloon! Have you seen the oriental saloon?"

"Yes, yes; extraordinary!"

But beneath this enthusiasm, which was to be decidedly the fashionable note of the day, Madame Bourdelais retained her practical housekeeper's coolness. She was carefully examining a piece of Paris Paradise, for she had come on purpose to take advantage of the exceptional cheapness of this silk, if she found it really advantageous. She was doubtless satisfied with it, for she took twenty-five yards, hoping it would be sufficient to make a dress for herself and a cloak for her little girl.

"What! you are going already?" resumed Madame Desforges. "Take a walk round with us."

"No, thanks; they are waiting for me at home. I didn't like to risk bringing the children into this crowd."

And she went away, preceded by the salesman carrying the twenty-five yards of silk, and who led her to pay-desk No. 10, where young Albert was getting confused with all the demands for bills with which he was besieged. When the salesman was able to approach, after having inscribed his sale on the debit-note, he called out the item, which the cashier entered in a register; then it was checked over, and the leaf torn off the salesman's book of debit-notes was stuck on a file near the receipting stamp.

"One hundred and forty francs," said Albert.

Madame Bourdelais paid and gave her address, for having come on foot she did not wish to be troubled with a parcel. Joseph had already got the silk behind the pay-desk, and was tying it up; and the parcel, thrown into a basket on wheels, was sent down to the delivery department, where all the goods in the shop seemed to be swallowed up with a sluice-like noise.

Meanwhile, the block was becoming so great in the silk department that Madame Desforges and Madame Marty could not at first find a salesman disengaged. They remained standing, mingling with the crowd of ladies who were looking at the silks and feeling them, staying there hours without making up their minds. But the Paris Paradise was a great success; around it pressed one of those crowds which decides the fortune of a fashion in a day. A host of shopmen were engaged in measuring off this silk; one could see, above the customers' heads, the pale glimmer of the unfolded pieces, in the continual coming and going of the fingers along the oak yard measures hanging from brass rods; one could hear the noise of the scissors cutting the silk, without ceasing, as the sale went on, as if there were not enough shopmen to suffice for all the greedy outstretched hands of the customers.

"It really isn't bad for five francs twelve sous," said Madame Desforges, who had succeeded in getting hold of a piece at the edge of the table.

Madame Marty and her daughter experienced a disappointment. The newspapers had said so much about it, that they had expected something stronger and more brilliant. But Bouthemont had just recognized Madame Desforges, and in order to get in the good graces of such a handsome lady, who was supposed to be all-powerful with the governor, he came up, with his rather coarse amiability. What! no one was serving her! it was unpardonable! He begged her to be indulgent, for really they did not know which way to turn. And he went to look for some chairs amongst the neighboring skirts, laughing with his good-natured laugh, full of a brutal love for the sex, which did not seem to displease Henriette.

"I say," murmured Favier, on going to take some velvet from a shelf behind Hutin, "there's Bouthemont making up to your mash."

Hutin had forgotten Madame Desforges, beside himself with rage with an old lady, who, after having kept him a quarter of an hour, had finished by buying a yard of black satin for a pair of stays. In the busy moments they took no notice of the turns, each salesman served the customers as they arrived. And he was answering Madame Boutarel, who was finishing her afternoon at The Ladies' Paradise, where she had already spent three hours in the morning, when Favier's warning made him start. Was he going to miss the governor's friend, from whom he had sworn to draw a five-franc piece? That would be the height of ill-luck, for he hadn't made three francs as yet with all those other chignons who were mooning about the place! Bouthemont was just then calling out loudly:

"Come, gentlemen, someone this way!"

Hutin passed Madame Boutarel over to Robineau, who was doing nothing.

"Here's the second-hand, madame. He will answer you better than I can."

And he rushed off to take Madame Marty's purchases from the woollen salesman who had accompanied the ladies. That day a nervous excitement must have troubled his delicate scent. As a rule, the first glance told him if a customer would buy, and how much. Then he domineered over the customer, he hastened to serve her to pass on to another, imposing his choice on her, persuading her that he knew best what material she wanted.

"What sort of silk, madame?" asked he in his most gallant manner. Madame Desforges had no sooner opened her mouth than he added: "I know, I've got just what you want."

When the piece of Paris Paradise was unfolded on a narrow corner of the counter, between heaps of other silks, Madame Marty and her daughter approached. Hutin, rather anxious, understood that it was at first a question of serving these two. Whispered words were exchanged, Madame Desforges was advising her friend.

"Oh! certainly," murmured she. "A silk at five francs twelve sous will never be equal to one at fifteen, or even ten."

"It is very light," repeated Madame Marty. "I'm afraid that it has not sufficient body for a mantle."

This remark induced the salesman to intervene. He smiled with the exaggerated politeness of a man who cannot make a mistake.

"But, madame, flexibility is the chief quality of this silk. It will not crumple. It's exactly what you want."

Impressed by such an assurance, the ladies said no more. They had taken the silk up, and were examining it again, when they felt a touch on their shoulders. It was Madame Guibal, who had been slowly walking about the shop for an hour past, feasting her eyes on the heaped-up riches, without buying even a yard of calico. And there was another explosion of gossip.

"What! Is that you?"

"Yes, it's me, rather knocked about though."

"What a crowd—eh? One can't get about. And the oriental saloon?"

"Ravishing!"

"Good heavens! what a success! Stay a moment, we will go upstairs together."

"No, thanks, I've just come down."

Hutin was waiting, concealing his impatience with a smile that did not quit his lips. Were they going to keep him there long? Really the women took things very coolly, it was like taking his money out of his pocket. At last Madame Guibal went away and continued her stroll, turning round the splendid display of silks with an enraptured air.

"If I were you I should buy the mantle ready-made," said Madame Desforges, suddenly returning to the Paris Paradise. "It won't cost you so much."

"It's true that the trimmings and making-up," murmured Madame Marty. "Besides, one has more choice."

All three had risen. Madame Desforges turned to Hutin, saying: "Have the goodness to show us to the ready-made department."

He remained dumbfounded, not being used to such defeats. What! the dark lady bought nothing! Had he then made a mistake? He abandoned Madame Marty and attacked Madame Desforges, trying his powerful abilities as salesman on her.

"And you, madame, would you not like to see our satins, our velvets? We have some extraordinary bargains."

"Thanks, another time," replied she coolly, not looking at him any more than she had at Mignot.

Hutin had to take up Madame Marty's purchases and walk before the ladies to show them to the ready-made department. But he had also the grief of seeing that Robineau was selling Madame Boutarel a good quantity of silk. Decidedly his scent was playing him false, he wouldn't make four sous. Beneath the amiable correctness of his manners there was the rage of a man being robbed and swallowed up by the others.

"On the first floor, ladies," said he, without ceasing to smile.

It was no easy matter to get to the staircase. A compact crowd of heads was surging under the galleries, expanding like an overflowing river into the middle of the hall. Quite a battle of business was going on, the salesmen had this population of women at their mercy, passing them from one to the other with feverish haste. The moment of the formidable afternoon rush had arrived, when the over-heated machine led the dance of customers, drawing the money from their very flesh. In the silk department especially a breath of folly seemed to pervade all, the Paris Paradise collected such a crowd that for several minutes Hutin could not advance a step; and Henriette, half-suffocated, having raised her eyes, beheld Mouret at the top of the stairs, his favorite position, from which he could see the victory. She smiled, hoping that he would come down and extricate her. But he did not even recognize her in the crowd; he was still with Vallagnosc, showing him the house, his face beaming with triumph.

The trepidation within was now stifling all outside noise; one no longer heard the rumbling of the vehicles, nor the banging of the carriage-doors; nothing remained above the vast murmur of business but the sentiment of this enormous Paris, of such immensity that it would always furnish buyers. In the heavy still air, in which the fumes of the heating apparatus warmed the odor of the stuffs, the hubbub increased, made up of all sorts of noises, of the continual walking about, of the same phrases, a hundred times repeated around the counters, of the gold jingling on the brass of the pay-desks, besieged by a legion of purses, and of the baskets on wheels loaded with parcels which were constantly disappearing into the gaping cellars. And, amidst the fine dust, everything finished by getting mixed up, it became impossible to recognize the divisions of the different departments; the haberdashery department over there seemed drowned; further on, in the linen department, a ray of sunshine, entering by the window in the Rue Neuve-Saint-Augustin, was like a golden dart in a heap of snow; close by, in the glove and woollen departments, a dense mass of bonnets and chignons hid the background of the shop from view. The toilettes were no longer visible, the head-dresses alone appeared, decked with feathers and ribbons. A few men's hats introduced here and there a black spot, whilst the women's pale complexions assumed in the fatigue and heat the transparencies of the camellia. At last, Hutin— thanks to his vigorous elbows—was able to open a way for the ladies, by keeping in front of them. But on ascending the stairs, Henriette could not find Mouret, who had just plunged Vallagnosc right into the crowd to complete his bewilderment, himself feeling the physical want of a dip into this bath of success. He lost his breath deliciously, he felt against his limbs a sort of caress from all his customers.

"To the left, ladies," said Hutin, still attentive, notwithstanding his increasing exasperation.

Up above there was the same block. It invaded even the furnishing department, usually the quietest. The shawl, the fur, and the under-clothing departments swarmed with people. As the ladies were crossing the lace department another meeting took place. Madame de Boves was there with her daughter Blanche, both buried in the articles Deloche was showing them. And Hutin had to make another halt, bundle in hand.

"Good afternoon! I was just thinking of you."

"I've been looking for you myself. But how can you expect to find anyone in this crowd?"

"It's magnificent, isn't it?"

"Dazzling, my dear. We can hardly stand."

"And you're buying?"

"Oh! no, we're only looking round. It rests us a little to be seated."

As a fact, Madame de Boves, scarcely possessing more than her cab-fare in her purse, was having all sorts of laces handed down, simply for the pleasure of seeing and handling them. She had guessed Deloche to be a new salesman, slow and awkward, who dared not resist the customers' whims; and she took advantage of his bewildered good-nature, and kept him there half an hour, still asking for fresh articles. The counter was covered, she dived her hands into this increasing mountain of lace, Malines, Valenciennes, and Chantilly, her fingers trembling with desire, her face gradually warming with a sensual joy; whilst Blanche, close to her, agitated by the same passion, was very pale, her flesh inflated and soft. The conversation continued; Hutin, standing there waiting their good pleasure, could have slapped their faces.

"Ah!" said Madame Marty, "you're looking at some cravats and handkerchiefs like those I showed you the other day."

It was true, Madame de Boves, tormented by Madame Marty's lace since the previous Saturday, had been unable to resist the desire to at least handle some like it, as the allowance her husband made her did not permit her to carry any away. She blushed slightly, explaining that Blanche wanted to see the Spanish-blonde cravats. Then she added: "You're going to the ready-made department—Well! we'll see you again. Shall we say in the oriental saloon?"

"That's it, in the oriental saloon—Superb, isn't it?"

And they separated enraptured, amidst the obstruction produced by the sale of the insertions and small trimmings at low prices. Deloche, glad to be occupied, recommenced emptying the boxes before the mother and daughter. And amidst the groups pressed along the counters, Jouve, the inspector, was slowly walking about with his military air, displaying his decoration, watching over these fine and precious goods, so easy to conceal up a sleeve. When he passed behind Madame de Boves, surprised to see her with her arms plunged in such a heap of lace he cast a quick glance at her feverish hands.

"To the right, ladies," said Hutin, resuming his march.

He was beside himself with rage. Was it not enough that he had missed a sale down below? Now they kept him waiting at each turning of the shop! And in his annoyance there was a strong feeling of the rancor existing between the textile departments and the ready-made departments, which were in continual hostility, fighting over the customers, stealing each other's percentage and commission. Those of the silk department were more enraged than those of the woollen, whenever they were obliged to show a lady to where the ready-made articles were kept, when she decided to take a mantle after looking at various sorts of silk.

"Mademoiselle Vadon!" said Hutin, in an angry voice, when he at last arrived in the department.

But she passed by without listening, absorbed in a sale which she was conducting. The room was full, a stream of people were crossing it, coming in by the door of the lace department and going out by the door of the under-clothing department, whilst to the right customers were trying on garments, and posing before the glasses. The red carpet stifled the noise of the footsteps, the distant roar from the ground floor died away, giving place to a discreet murmur, a drawing-room warmth deadened by the crowd of women.

"Mademoiselle Prunaire!" cried out Hutin. And as she took no notice either, he added between his teeth, so as not to be heard: "A set of frights!"

He certainly was not fond of them, tired to death as he was by climbing the stairs to bring them customers, furious at the profits which he accused them of taking out of his pocket. It was a secret war, in which the young ladies themselves entered with equal fierceness; and in their mutual fatigue, always on foot, worked to death, all difference of sex disappeared, nothing remained but these contrary interests, irritated by the fever of business.

"So there's no one here to serve?" asked Hutin.

But he suddenly caught sight of Denise. They had kept her folding all the morning, only giving her a few doubtful customers to whom she had not sold anything. When he recognized her, occupied in clearing off the counter an enormous heap of garments, he ran up to her.

"Look here, mademoiselle! serve these ladies who are waiting." And he quickly slipped Madame Marty's purchases into her arms, tired of carrying them about the place. His smile returned, and in this smile there was the ill-natured expression of the experienced salesman, who shrewdly guessed into what an awkward position he had just thrown both the ladies and the young girl. The latter, however, remained quite troubled before this unhoped-for sale which suddenly presented itself. For the second time Hutin appeared to her like an unknown friend, fraternal and tender, always ready to spring out of darkness and save her. Her eyes glistened with gratitude; she followed him with a lingering look, whilst he was elbowing his way towards his department.

"I want a mantle," said Madame Marty.

Then Denise questioned her. What style of mantle? But the lady had no idea, she wished to see what the house had got. And the young girl, already very tired, bewildered by the crowd, lost her head; she had never served any but the rare customers who came to Cornaille's, at Valognes; she didn't even know the number of the models, nor their places in the cupboards. She hardly knew how to reply to the ladies, who were beginning to lose patience, when Madame Aurélie perceived Madame Desforges, of whose connection with Mouret she was no doubt aware, for she hastened over and asked with a smile:

"Are these ladies being served?"

"Yes, that young person over there is attending to us," replied Henriette. "But she does not appear to be very well up to her work; she can't find anything."

At this, the first-hand completely paralyzed Denise by saying to her in a whisper: "You see very well you know nothing. Don't interfere any more, please." And turning round she called out: "Mademoiselle Vadon, these ladies require a mantle!"

She remained there whilst Marguerite showed the models. The girl assumed with the customers a dry polite voice, the disagreeable attitude of a young person dressed up in silk, with a sort of varnish of elegance, of which she retained, unknown to herself, the jealousy and rancor. When she heard Madame Marty say she did not wish to exceed two hundred francs, she made a grimace of pity. Oh! madame would give more, it would be impossible to find anything respectable for two hundred francs. And she threw some of the common mantles on a counter with a gesture which signified: "Just see, aren't they pitiful?" Madame Marty dared not think of them after that; she bent over to murmur in Madame Desforges's ear:

"Don't you prefer to be served by men? One feels more comfortable?"

At last Marguerite brought a silk mantle trimmed with jet, which she treated with more respect. And Madame Aurélie abruptly called Denise.

"Come, do something for your living. Just put that on your shoulders."

Denise, wounded to the heart, despairing of ever succeeding in the house, had remained motionless, her hands hanging by her side. No doubt she would be sent away, and the children would be without food. The tumult of the crowd buzzed in her head, she felt herself tottering, her arms bruised by the handling of so many armfuls of garments, hard work which she had never done before. However, she was obliged to obey and allow Marguerite to put the mantle on her, as on a dummy.

"Stand upright," said Madame Aurélie.

But a moment after they forgot Denise. Mouret had just come in with Vallagnosc and Bourdoncle; and he bowed to the ladies, who complimented him on his magnificent exhibition of winter novelties. Of course they went into raptures over the oriental saloon. Vallagnosc, who was finishing his walk round the counters, displayed more surprise than admiration; for, after all, thought he, in his pessimist supineness, it was nothing more than an immense collection of calico. Bourdoncle, forgetting that he belonged to the establishment, also congratulated the governor, to make him forget his anxious doubts and persecutions of the early part of the day.

"Yes, yes; things are going on very well, I'm quite satisfied," repeated Mouret, radiant, replying with a smile to Madame Desforges's tender looks. "But I must not interrupt you, ladies."

Then all eyes were again fixed on Denise. She placed herself entirely in the hands of Marguerite, who was making her turn round slowly.

"What do you think of it—eh?" asked Madame Marty of Madame Desforges.

The latter gave her advice, like a supreme umpire of fashion. "It isn't bad, the cut is original, but it doesn't seem to me very graceful about the figure."

"Oh!" interrupted Madame Aurélie, "it must be seen on the lady herself. You can understand it does not look much on this young person, who is not very stout. Hold up your head, mademoiselle, give it all its importance."

They smiled. Denise had turned very pale. She felt ashamed at being thus turned into a machine, which they were examining and joking about so freely.

Madame Desforges, yielding to the antipathy of a contrary nature, and annoyed by the young girl's sweet face, maliciously added: "No doubt it would set better if the young person's dress were not so loose-fitting."

And she cast at Mouret the mocking look of a Parisian beauty, greatly amused by the absurd ridiculous dress of a country girl. He felt the amorous caress of this glance, the triumph of a woman proud of her beauty and of her art. Therefore, out of pure gratitude, the gratitude of a man who felt himself adored, he thought himself obliged to joke in his turn, notwithstanding his good-will towards Denise, whose secret charm had conquered his gallant nature.

"Besides, her hair should be combed," murmured he.

This was the last straw. The director deigned to laugh, all the young ladies were bursting. Marguerite risked a slight chuckle, like a well-behaved girl who restrains herself; Clara had left a customer to enjoy the fun at her ease; even the saleswomen from another department had come, attracted by the talking. As for the ladies they took it more quietly, with an air of well-bred enjoyment. Madame Aurélie was the only one who did not laugh, as if Denise's splendid wild-looking head of hair and elegant virginal shoulders had dishonored her, in the orderly well-kept department. The young girl had turned paler still, in the midst of all these people who were laughing at her. She felt herself violated, exposed to all their looks, without defense. What had she done that they should thus attack her thin figure, and her too luxuriant hair? But she was especially wounded by Madame Desforges's and Mouret's laughter, instinctively divining their connection, her heart sinking with an unknown grief. This lady was very ill-natured to attack a poor girl who had said nothing; and as for Mouret, he most decidedly froze her up with a sort of fear, before which all her other sentiments disappeared, without her being able to analyze them. And, totally abandoned, attacked in her most cherished womanly feelings of modesty, and shocked at their injustice, she was obliged to stifle the sobs which were rising in her throat.

"I should think so; let her comb her hair tomorrow," said the terrible Bourdoncle to Madame Aurélie. He had condemned Denise the first day she came, full of scorn for her small limbs.

At last the first-hand came and took the mantle off Denise's shoulders, saying to her in a low tone: "Well! mademoiselle, here's a fine start. Really, if this is the way you show off your capabilities. Impossible to be more stupid!"

Denise, fearing the tears might gush from her, hastened back to the heap of garments, which she began to sort out on the counter. There at least she was lost in the crowd. Fatigue prevented her thinking. But she suddenly felt Pauline near her, a saleswoman in the under-clothing department, who had already defended her that morning. The latter had followed the scene, and murmured in Denise's ear:

"My poor child, don't be so sensitive. Keep that to yourself, or they'll go on worse and worse. I come from Chartres. Yes, exactly, Pauline Cugnot is my name; and my parents are millers. Well! they would have devoured me the first few days if I had not stood up firm. Come, be brave! give me your hand, we'll have a talk together whenever you like."

This hand held out redoubled Denise's confusion; she shook it furtively, hastening to take up a load of cloaks, fearing to be doing wrong and to get a scolding if they knew she had a friend.

However, Madame Aurélie herself, had just put the mantle on

Madame Marty, and they all exclaimed: "Oh! how nice! delight-ful!" It at once looked quite different. Madame Desforges de-cided it would be impossible to improve on it. There was a good deal of bowing. Mouret took his leave, whilst Vallagnosc, who had perceived Madame de Boves and her daughter in the lace de-partment, hastened to offer his arm to the mother. Marguerite, standing before one of the pay-desks, was already calling out the different purchases made by Madame Marty, who settled for them and ordered the parcel to be taken to her cab. Madame Desforges had found her articles at pay-desk No. 10. Then the la-dies met once more in the oriental saloon. They were leaving, but it was amidst a loquacious feeling of admiration. Even Ma-dame Guibal became enthusiastic.

"Oh! delicious! makes you think you are in the East; doesn't it?"

"A real harem, and not at all dear!"

"And the Smyrnas! oh, the Smyrnas! what tones, what deli-cacy!"

"And this Kurdestan! Just look, a Delacroix!"

The crowd was slowly diminishing. The bell, at an hour's inter-val, had already announced the two first dinners; the third was about to be served, and in the departments there were now only a few lingering customers, whose fever for spending had made them forget the time. Outside nothing was heard but the rolling of the last carriages amidst the husky voice of Paris, the snort of a satiated ogre digesting the linens and cloths, silks and lace, with which he had been gorged since the morning. Inside, be-neath the flaming gas-jets, which, burning in the twilight, had lighted up the supreme efforts of the sale, everything appeared like a field of battle still warm with the massacre of the various goods. The salesmen, harassed and fatigued, camped amidst the contents of their shelves and counters, which appeared to have been thrown into the greatest confusion by the furious blast of a hurricane. It was with difficulty that one traversed the galleries on the ground floor, blocked up with a crowd of chairs, and in the glove department it was necessary to step over a pile of cases heaped up around Mignot; in the woollen department there was no means of passing at all, Liénard was dozing on a sea of bales, in which certain piles, still standing, though half destroyed, seemed to be houses that an overflowing river was carrying away; and, further on, the linen department was like a heavy fall of snow, one ran up against icebergs of napkins, and walked on light flakes of handkerchiefs.

The same disorder prevailed upstairs, in the departments of the floor: the furs were scattered over the flooring, the ready-made clothes were heaped up like the great-coats of wounded soldiers, the lace and the under-linen, unfolded, crumpled, thrown about everywhere, made one think of an army of women who had disrobed there in the disorder of some sudden desire; whilst downstairs, at the other end of the house, the delivery department in full activity was still disgorging the parcels with which it was bursting, and which were carried off by the vans—last vibration of the overheated machine. But it was in the silk department especially that the customers had flung themselves with the greatest ardour. There they had cleared off everything, there was plenty of room to pass, the hall was bare; the whole of the colossal stock of Paris Paradise had been cut up and carried away, as if by a swarm of devouring locusts. And in the midst of this emptiness, Hutin and Favier were running through the counterfoils of their debit-notes, calculating their commission, still out of breath after the struggle. Favier had made fifteen francs, Hutin had only managed to make thirteen, thoroughly beaten that day, enraged at his bad luck. Their eyes sparkled with the passion for money. The whole shop around them was also adding up figures, glowing with the same fever, in the brutal gaiety of the evening of the battle.

"Well, Bourdoncle!" cried out Mouret, "are you trembling still?"

He had returned to his favorite position at the top of the stairs of the first floor, against the balustrade; and, in the presence of the massacre of stuffs which was spread out under him, he indulged in a victorious laugh. His fears of the morning, that moment of unpardonable weakness which nobody would ever know of, inspired him with a greater desire to triumph. The battle was definitely won, the small trades-people of the neighborhood were done for, and Baron Hartmann was conquered, with his millions and his land. Whilst he was looking at the cashiers bending over their ledgers, adding up long columns of figures, whilst he was listening to the sound of the gold, falling from their fingers into the metal bowls, he already saw The Ladies' Paradise growing beyond all bounds, enlarging its hall and prolonging its galleries as far as the Rue du Dix-Décembre.

"And now are you convinced, Bourdoncle," he resumed, "that the house is really too small? We could have sold twice as much."

Bourdoncle humbled himself, enraptured, moreover, to find himself in the wrong. But a new spectacle rendered them grave. As was the custom every evening, Lhomme, the chief cashier, had just collected the receipts from each pay-desk; after having added them up, he usually posted up the total amount after placing the paper on which it was written on his file. He then took the receipts up to the chief cashier's office, in a leather case and in bags, according to the nature of the cash. On this occasion the gold and silver predominated, and he was slowly walking upstairs, carrying three enormous bags. Deprived of his right arm, cut off at the elbow, he clasped them in his left arm against his breast, holding one up with his chin to prevent it slipping. His heavy breathing could be heard at a distance, he passed along, staggering and superb, amidst the respectful shopmen.

"How much, Lhomme?" asked Mouret.

"Eighty thousand seven hundred and forty-two francs two sous," replied the cashier.

A joyous laugh stirred up The Ladies' Paradise. The amount ran through the establishment. It was the highest figure ever attained in one day by a draper's shop.

That evening, when Denise went up to bed, she was obliged to lean against the partition in the corridor under the zine roof. When in her room, and with the door closed, she fell down on the bed; her feet pained her so much. For a long time she continued to look with a stupid air at the dressing-table, the wardrobe, all the hotel-like nudity. This, then, was where she was going to live; and her first day tormented her—an abominable, endless day. She would never have the courage to go through another. Then she perceived she was dressed in silk; and this uniform depressed her. She was childish enough, before unpacking her box, to put on her old woollen dress, which hung on the back of a chair. But when she was once more dressed in this poor garment of hers, a painful emotion choked her; the sobs which she had kept back all day burst forth suddenly in a flood of hot tears. She fell back on the bed, weeping at the thought of the two children, and she wept on, without feeling to have the strength to take off her boots, completely overcome with fatigue and grief.

CHAPTER V.

The next day Denise had scarcely been downstairs half an hour, when Madame Aurélie said to her in her sharp voice: "You are wanted at the directorate, mademoiselle."

The young girl found Mouret alone, in the large office hung with green repp. He had suddenly remembered the "unkempt girl," as Bourdoncle called her; and he, who usually detested the part of fault-finder, had had the idea of sending for her and waking her up a bit, if she were still dressed in the style of a country wench. The previous day, notwithstanding his pleasantry, he had experienced, in Madame Desforges's presence, a feeling of wounded vanity, on seeing the elegance of one of his saleswomen discussed. He felt a confused sentiment, a mixture of sympathy and anger.

"We have engaged you, mademoiselle," commenced he, "out of regard for your uncle, and you must not put us under the sad necessity—"

But he stopped. Opposite him, on the other side of the desk, stood Denise, upright, serious, and pale. Her silk dress was no longer too big for her, but fitted tight round her pretty figure, displaying the pure lines of her virgin shoulders; and if her hair, knotted in thick tresses, still appeared untidy, she tried at least to keep it in order. After having gone to sleep with her clothes on, her eyes red with weeping, the young girl had felt ashamed of this attack of nervous sensibility on waking up about four o'clock, and she had immediately set about taking in her dress. She had spent an hour before the small looking-glass, combing her hair, without being able to reduce it as she would have liked to.

"Ah! thank heavens!" said Mouret, "you look better this morning. But there's still that dreadful hair!" He rose from his seat and went up to her to try and smooth it down in the same familiar way Madame Aurélie had attempted to do it the previous day. "There! just tuck that in behind your ear. The chignon is too high."

She did not speak, but let him continue to arrange her hair; notwithstanding her vow to be strong, she had arrived at the office full of misgivings, certain that she had been sent for to be informed of her dismissal. And Mouret's evident kindliness did not reassure her; she still felt afraid of him, feeling when near him that uneasiness which she attributed to a natural anxiety in the presence of a powerful man on whom her fate depended. When he saw her so trembling under his hands, which were grazing her neck, he was sorry for his movement of good-nature, for he feared above all to lose his authority.

"In short, mademoiselle," resumed he, once more placing the desk between himself and her, "try and look to your appearance. You are no longer at Valognes; study our Parisian young ladies. If your uncle's name has sufficed to gain your admittance to our house, I feel sure you will carry out what your person seemed to promise to me. Unfortunately, everybody here is not of my opinion. Let this be a warning to you. Don't make me tell a falsehood."

He treated her like a child, with more pity than kindness, his curiosity in matters feminine simply awakened by the troubling, womanly charm which he felt springing up in this poor and awkward child. And she, whilst he was lecturing her, having suddenly perceived Madame Hédouin's portrait—the handsome regular face smiling gravely in the gold frame—felt herself shivering again, notwithstanding the encouraging words he addressed to her. This was the dead lady, she whom people accused him of having killed, in order to found the house with the blood of her body.

Mouret was still speaking. "Now you may go," said he at last, sitting down and taking up his pen. She went away, heaving a deep sigh of relief.

From that day forward, Denise displayed her great courage. Beneath these rare attacks of sensitiveness, a strong sense of reason was constantly working, quite a feeling of bravery at finding herself weak and alone, a cheerful determination to carry out her self-imposed task. She made very little noise, but went straight ahead to her goal, with an invincible sweetness, overcoming all obstacles, and that simply and naturally, for such was her real character.

At first she had to surmount the terrible fatigues of the department. The parcels of garments tired her arms, so much so that during the first six weeks she cried with pain when she turned over at night, bent almost double, her shoulders bruised. But she suffered still more from her shoes, thick shoes brought from Valognes, want of money preventing her replacing them with light boots. Always on her feet, trotting about from morning to night, scolded if seen leaning for a moment against any support, her feet became swollen, little feet, like those of a child, which seemed ground up in these torturing bluchers; her heels throbbed with fever, the soles were covered with blisters, the skin of which chafed off and stuck to the stocking. She felt her entire frame shattered, her limbs and organs contracted by the lassitude of her legs, the certain sudden weaknesses incident to her sex betraying themselves by the paleness of her flesh. And she, so thin, so frail, resisted courageously, whilst a great many saleswomen around her were obliged to quit the business, attacked with special maladies. Her good grace in suffering, her valiant obstinacy maintained her, smiling and upright, when she felt ready to give way, thoroughly worn out and exhausted by work to which men would have succumbed.

Another torment was to have the whole department against her. To the physical martyrdom there was added the secret persecution of her comrades. Two months of patience and gentleness had not disarmed them. She was constantly exposed to wounding remarks, cruel inventions, a series of slights which cut her to the heart, in her longing for affection. They had joked for a long time over her unfortunate first appearance; the words "clogs" and "numbskull" circulated. Those who missed a sale were sent to Valognes; she passed, in short, for the fool of the place. Then, when she revealed herself later on as a remarkable saleswoman, well up in the mechanism of the house, the young ladies arranged together so as never to leave her a good customer. Marguerite and Clara pursued her with an instinctive hatred, closing up the ranks in order not to be swallowed up by this new-comer, whom they really feared in spite of their affectation of disdain. As for Madame Aurélie, she was hurt by the proud reserve displayed by the young girl, who did not hover round her skirts with an air of caressing admiration; she therefore abandoned Denise to the rancor of her favorites, to the favored ones of her court, who were always on their knees, engaged in feeding her with a continual flattery, which her large authoritative person needed to make it blossom forth. For a while, the second-hand, Madame Frédéric, appeared not to enter into the conspiracy, but this must have been by inadvertence, for she showed herself equally harsh the moment she saw to what annoyances her good-nature was likely to expose her. Then the abandonment became complete, they all made a butt of the "unkempt girl," who lived in an hourly struggle, only managing by the greatest courage to hold her own in the department.

Such was her life now. She had to smile, look brave and gracious in a silk dress which did not belong to her, although dying with fatigue, badly fed, badly treated, under the continual menace of a brutal dismissal. Her room was her only refuge, the only place where she could abandon herself to the luxury of a cry, when she had suffered too much during the day. But a terrible coldness fell from the zinc roof, covered with the December snow; she was obliged to nestle in her iron bedstead, throw all her clothes over her, and weep under the counterpane to prevent the frost chapping her face. Mouret never spoke to her now. When she caught Bourdoncle's severe looks during business hours she trembled, for she felt in him a born enemy who would not forgive her the slightest fault. And amidst this general hostility, Jouve the inspector's strange friendliness astonished her. If he met her in any out-of-the-way corner he smiled at her, made some amiable remark; twice he had saved her from being reprimanded without any show of gratitude on her part, for she was more troubled than touched by his protection.

One evening, after dinner, as the young ladies were setting the cupboards in order, Joseph came and informed Denise that a young man wanted her below. She went down, feeling very anxious.

"Hullo!" said Clara, "the 'unkempt girl' has got a young man."

"He must be hard up for a sweetheart," declared Marguerite.

Downstairs, at the door, Denise found her brother Jean. She had formally prohibited him from coming to the shop in this way, as it looked very bad. But she did not dare to scold him, so excited did he appear, bareheaded, out of breath through running from the Faubourg du Temple.

"Have you got ten francs?" stammered he. "Give me ten francs, or I'm a lost man."

The young rascal looked so comical, with his flowing locks and handsome girlish face, launching out with this melodramatic phrase, that she could have smiled had it not been for the anguish which this demand for money caused her.

"What! ten francs?" she murmured. "Whatever's the matter?"

He blushed, and explained that he had met a friend's sister. Denise stopped him, feeling embarrassed, not wishing to know any more about it. Twice already had he rushed in to obtain similar loans, but the first time it was only twenty-five sous, and the next thirty. He was always getting mixed up with women.

"I can't give you ten francs," resumed she. "Pépé's board isn't paid yet, and I've only just the money. I shall have hardly enough to buy a pair of boots, which I want badly. You really are not reasonable, Jean. It's too bad of you."

"Well, I'm lost," repeated he, with a tragical gesture. "Just listen, little sister; she's a tall, dark girl; we went to the café with her brother. I never thought the drinks—"

She had to interrupt him again, and as tears were coming into his eyes, she took out her purse and slipped a ten-franc piece into his hand. He at once set up a laugh.

"I was sure—But my word of honor! never again! A fellow would have to be a regular scamp."

And he ran off, after having kissed his sister, like a madman. The fellows in the shop seemed astonished.

That night Denise did not sleep much. Since her entry in The Ladies' Paradise, money had been her cruel anxiety. She was still a probationer, without salary; the young ladies in the department frequently prevented her from selling, and she just managed to pay Pépé's board and lodging, thanks to the unimportant customers they were good enough to leave her. It was a time of black misery—misery in a silk dress. She was often obliged to spend the night repairing her small stack of clothes, darning her linen, mending her chemises as if they had been lace; without mentioning the patches she put on her boots, as cleverly as any bootmaker could have done. She even risked washing things in her hand basin. But her old woollen dress was an especial cause of anxiety to her; she had no other, and was forced to put it on every evening when she quitted the uniform silk, and this wore it terribly; a spot on it gave her the fever, the least tear was a catastrophe. And she had nothing, not a sou, not even enough to buy the trifling articles which a woman always wants; she had been obliged to wait a fortnight to renew her stock of needles and cotton. Thus it was a real disaster when Jean, with his love affairs, dropped down all at once and pillaged her purse. A franc piece taken away caused a gulf which she did not know how to fill up. As for finding ten francs on the morrow it was not to be thought of for a moment. The whole night she slept an uncomfortable sleep, haunted by the nightmare, in which she saw Pépé thrown into the street, whilst she was turning over the flagstones with her bruised fingers to see if there were not some money underneath.

It happened that the next day she had to play the part of the well-dressed girl. Some well-known customers came in, and Madame Aurélie called her several times in order that she should show off the new styles. And whilst she was posing there, with the stiff graces of a fashion-plate, she was thinking of Pépé's board and lodging, which she had promised to pay that evening. She could very well do without boots for another month; but even on adding the thirty francs she had left to the four francs which she had saved sou by sou, that would never make more than thirty-four francs, and where was she to find six francs to complete the sum? It was an anguish in which her heart failed her.

"You will notice the shoulders are free," Madame Aurélie was saying. "It's very fashionable and very convenient. The young person can fold her arms."

"Oh! easily," replied Denise, who continued to smile amiably. "One can't feel it. I am sure you will like it, madame."

She now blamed herself for having gone to fetch Pépé from Madame Gras's, the previous Sunday, to take him for a walk in the Champs-Elysées. The poor child so seldom went out with her! But she had had to buy some gingerbread and a little spade, and then take him to see Punch and Judy, and that had mounted at once to twenty-nine sous. Really Jean could not think much about the little one, or he would not be so foolish. Afterwards, everything fell upon her shoulders.

"Of course, if it does not suit you, madame—" resumed the first-hand. "Just put this cloak on, mademoiselle, so that the lady may judge."

And Denise walked slowly round, with the cloak on, saying: "This is warmer. It's this year's fashion."

And she continued to torture herself, behind her professional good graces, until the evening, to know where she was to find this money. The young ladies, who were very busy, had left her an important sale; but it was only Tuesday, and she had four days to wait before drawing any money. After dinner she decided to postpone her visit to Madame Gras till the next day. She would excuse herself, say she had been detained, and before then she would have the six francs, perhaps.

As Denise avoided the slightest expense, she went to bed early. What could she do in the streets, with her unsociableness, still frightened by the big city in which she only knew the streets near the shop? After having ventured as far as the Palais-Royal, to get a little fresh air, she would quickly return, lock herself in her room and set about sewing or washing.

It was, along the corridor of the bedrooms, a barrack-like

promiscuity—girls, who were often not very tidy, a gossiping over dirty water and dirty linen, quite a disagreeable feeling, which manifested itself in frequent quarrels and continual rec- onciliations. They were, moreover, prohibited from going up to their rooms in the day-time; they did not live there, but merely slept there at night, not going up till the last minute, leaving again in the morning still half asleep, hardly awakened by a rapid wash; and this gust of wind which was continually sweep- ing through the corridor, the fatigue of the thirteen hours' work which threw them on their beds thoroughly worn out, changed this upper part of the house into an inn traversed by the tired ill-temper of a host of travellers. Denise had no friend. Of all the young ladies, one alone, Pauline Cugnot, showed her a certain tenderness; and the ready-made and under-clothing departments being close to one another, and in open war, the sympathy between the two saleswomen had hitherto been con- fined to a few rare words hastily exchanged. Pauline occupied a neighboring room, to the right of Denise's; but as she disap- peared immediately after dinner and only returned at eleven o'clock, the latter only heard her get into bed, without ever meeting her after business hours.

This evening, Denise had made up her mind to play the part of bootmaker once more. She was holding her shoes, turning them about, wondering how she could make them last another month. At last she decided to take a strong needle and sew on the soles, which were threatening to leave the uppers. During this time a collar and a pair of cuffs were soaking in the basin full of soapsuds.

Every evening she heard the same noises, the young ladies coming in one by one, short whispered conversations, laughing, and sometimes a dispute, which they stifled as much as possible. Then the beds creaked, the tired occupants yawned, and fell into a heavy slumber. Denise's left hand neighbor often talked in her sleep, which frightened her very much at first. Perhaps others, like herself, stopped up to mend their things, in spite of the rules; but if so they probably took the same precautions as she did herself, keeping very quiet, avoiding the least shock, for a shivering silence reigned in all the rooms.

It had struck eleven about ten minutes before when a sound of footsteps made her raise her head. Another young lady late! And she recognized it to be Pauline, by hearing the latter open the door next to hers.

But she was astonished when Pauline returned quietly and knocked at her door.

"Make haste, it's me!"

The saleswomen not being allowed to visit each other in their rooms, Denise quickly unlocked the door, so that her neighbor should not be caught by Madame Cabin, who was supposed to see this rule strictly carried out.

"Was she there?" asked Denise, closing the door.

"Who? Madame Cabin?" replied Pauline. "Oh, I'm not afraid of her, she's easily settled with a five-franc piece!" Then she added: "I've wanted to have a talk with you for a long time past. But it's impossible to do so downstairs. Besides, you looked so downhearted tonight at table."

Denise thanked her, and invited her to sit down, touched by her good-natured air. But in the trouble caused by the sudden visit she had not laid down the shoe she was mending, and Pauline's eyes fell on it at once. She shook her head, looked round and perceived the collar and cuffs in the basin.

"My poor child, I thought as much," resumed she. "Ah, I know what it is! When I first came up from Chartres, and old Cugnot didn't send me a sou, I many a time washed my own chemises! Yes, yes, even my chemises! I had two, and there was always one in soak."

She sat down, still out of breath from running. Her large face, with small bright eyes, and big tender mouth, had a certain grace, notwithstanding the rather coarse features. And, without transition, all of a sudden, she related her history; her childhood at the mill; old Cugnot ruined by a lawsuit; her being sent to Paris to make her fortune with twenty francs in her pocket; then her start as a shop-girl in a shop at Batignolles, then at The Ladies' Paradise—a terrible start, all the sufferings and all the privations imaginable; she then spoke of her present life, of the two hundred francs she earned a month, the pleasures she indulged in, the carelessness in which she allowed her days to glide away. Some jewelry, a brooch, a watch-chain, glistened on her dark-blue cloth dress, coquettishly made to the figure; and she wore a velvet hat, ornamented with a large grey feather.

Denise had turned very red, with her shoe. She began to stammer out an explanation.

"But the same thing happened to me," repeated Pauline. "Come, come, I'm older than you, I'm over twenty-six, though I don't look it. Just tell me your little troubles."

Denise yielded, conquered by this friendship so frankly offered. She sat down in her petticoat, with an old shawl over her shoulders, near Pauline in full dress; and an interesting gossip ensued.

It was freezing in the room, the cold seemed to run down the bare prison-like walls; but they did not notice that their fingers were almost frost-bitten, they were so fully taken up by their conversation. Little by little, Denise opened her heart entirely, spoke of Jean and Pépé, and how much the money question tortured her; which led them both to abuse the young ladies in the dress department. Pauline relieved her mind.

"Oh, the hussies! If they treated you properly and in a friendly manner, you could make more than a hundred francs a month."

"Everybody is down on me, and I'm sure I don't know why," said Denise, beginning to cry. "Look at Monsieur Bourdoncle, he's always watching me for a chance of finding me in fault, as if I were in his way. Old Jouve is about the only one—"

The other interrupted her. "What, that old monkey of an inspector! Ah! my dear, don't you trust him. You know, men with big noses like his! He may display his decoration as much as he likes, there's a story about something that happened to him in our department. But what a child you are to grieve like this! What a misfortune it is to be so sensitive! Of course, what is happening to you happens to everyone; they are making you pay your footing."

She seized her hands and kissed her carried away by her good heart. The money-question was a graver one. Certainly a poor girl could not support her two brothers, pay the little one's board and lodging, and regale the big one's mistresses with the few paltry sous picked up from the others' cast-off customers; for it was to be feared that she would not get any salary until business improved in March.

"Listen to me, it's impossible for you to live in this way any longer. If I were you" said Pauline.

But a noise in the corridor stopped her. It was probably Marguerite, who was accused of prowling about at night to watch the others. Pauline, who was still pressing her friend's hand, looked at her for a moment in silence, listening. Then she resumed in a very low tone, with an air of tender conviction: "If I were you I should take someone."

"How someone?" murmured Denise, not understanding at first.

When she understood, she withdrew her hands, looking very confused. This advice made her feel awkward, like an idea which had never occurred to her, and of which she could not see the advantage.

"Oh! no," replied she simply.

"Then," continued Pauline, "you'll never manage, I tell you so, plainly. Here are the figures: forty francs for the little one, a five-franc piece now and again for the big one; and then there's yourself, you can't always go about dressed like a pauper, with boots that make the other girls laugh at you; yes, really, your boots do you a deal of harm. Take someone, it would be much better."

"No," repeated Denise.

"Well! you are very foolish. It's inevitable, my dear, and so natural. We all do it sooner or later. Look at me, I was a probationer, like you, without a sou. We are boarded and lodged, it's true; but there's our dress; besides, it's impossible to go without a copper in one's pocket, shut up in one's room, watching the flies. So you see girls forcibly drift into it."

She then spoke of her first lover, a lawyer's clerk whom she had met at a party at Meudon. After him, came a post-office clerk. And, finally, ever since the autumn, she had been keeping company with a salesman at the Bon Marché, a very nice tall fellow, with whom she spent all her leisure time. Never more than one sweetheart at a time, however. She was very respectable in her way, and became indignant when she heard talk of those girls who yielded to the first-comer.

"I don't tell you to misconduct yourself, you know!" said she quickly. "For instance, I should not like to be seen with your Clara, for fear people should say I was as bad as she. But when a girl stays quietly with one lover, and has nothing to blame herself for—do you think that wrong?"

"No," replied Denise. "But I don't care for it, that's all." There was a fresh silence. In the small icy-cold room they were smiling to each other, greatly affected by this whispered conversation. "Besides, one must have some affection for someone before doing so," resumed she, her cheeks scarlet.

Pauline was astonished. She set up a laugh, and embraced her a second time, saying: "But, my darling, when you meet and like each other! You are funny! People won't force you. Look here, would you like Baugé to take us somewhere in the country on Sunday? He'll bring one of his friends."

"No," said Denise, in her gently obstinate way.

Pauline insisted no longer. Each one was free to act as she liked. What she had said was out of pure kindness of heart, for she felt really grieved to see a comrade so miserable. And as it was nearly midnight, she got up to leave. But before doing so she forced Denise to accept the six francs she wanted, begging her not to trouble about the matter, but to repay the amount when she earned more.

"Now," added she, "blow your candle out, so that they can't see which door opens; you can light it again immediately."

The candle blown out, they shook hands; and Pauline ran off to her room, without leaving any trace in the darkness but the vague rustling of her petticoats amidst the deep slumber of the occupants of the other little rooms.

Before going to bed Denise wanted to finish her boot and do her washing. The cold became sharper still as the night advanced; but she did not feel it, this conversation had stirred up her heart's blood. She was not shocked, it seemed to her that everyone had a right to arrange her life as she liked, when alone and free in the world. She had never given way to such ideas; her sense of right and her healthy nature maintained her naturally in the respectability in which she had always lived. About one o'clock she at last went to bed. No, she did not love anyone. So what was the use of disarranging her life, of spoiling the maternal devotion she had vowed for her two brothers? However, she did not sleep; a crowd of indistinct forms passed before her closed eyes, vanishing in the darkness.

From this moment Denise took an interest in the love-stories of the department. During the slack moments they were constantly occupied by their affairs with the men. Gossiping tales flew about, stories of adventures amused the girls for a week. Clara was a scandal; she had three lovers, without counting a string of chance admirers whom she had in tow; and, if she did not leave the shop, where she did the least work possible, disdaining the money which she could easily and more agreeably earn elsewhere, it was to shield herself from her family; for she was mortally afraid of old Prunaire, who threatened to come to Paris and break her arms and legs with his clogs. Marguerite, on the contrary, behaved very well, and was not known to have any lover; this caused some surprise, for all knew of her adventure— her coming to Paris to be confined in secret; how had she come to have the child, if she were so virtuous? And there were some who hinted at an accident, adding that she was now reserving herself for her cousin at Grenoble. The young ladies also joked about Madame Frédéric, declaring that she was discreetly connected with certain great personages; the truth was that they knew nothing of her love-affairs; for she disappeared every evening, stiff as starch in her widow's ill-temper, evidently in a great hurry, though nobody knew where she was running off to so eagerly. As to Madame Aurélie's passions, her pretended larks with obedient young men, they were certainly false; mere inventions, spread abroad by discontented saleswomen just for fun. Perhaps she had formerly displayed rather too much motherly feeling for one of her son's friends, but she now occupied too high a place in the drapery business to allow her to amuse herself with such childish matters. Then there was the crowd leaving in the evening, nine girls out of every ten having young men waiting for them at the door; in the Place Gaillon, along the Rue de la Michodière, and the Rue Neuve-Saint-Augustin, there was always quite a troop of men standing motionless, watching for the girls coming out; and, when they came, each one gave his arm to his lady and disappeared, talking with a marital tranquility.

But what troubled Denise most was to have discovered Colomban's secret. He was continually to be seen on the other side of the street, at the door of The Old Elbeuf, his eyes raised, and never quitting the young ladies in the ready-made department. When he felt Denise was watching him he blushed and turned away his head, as if afraid she might betray him to Geneviève, although there had been no further connection between the Baudus and their niece since her engagement at The Ladies' Paradise. At first she had thought he was in love with Marguerite, on seeing his despairing looks, for Marguerite, being very quiet, and sleeping in the building, was not very easy to get at. But what was her astonishment to find that Colomban's ardent glances were intended for Clara. He had been like that for months, devoured by passion on the opposite side of the way, without finding the courage to declare himself; and that for a girl who was perfectly free, who lived in the Rue Louis-le-Grand, and whom he could have spoken to any evening before she walked off on the arm of a fresh fellow! Clara herself appeared to have no idea of her conquest. Denise's discovery filled her with a painful emotion. Was love, then, such a stupid thing as that? What! this fellow, who had real happiness within his reach, was ruining his life, enraptured with this good-for-nothing girl as if she were a saint! From that day she was seized with a feeling of grief every time she saw Geneviève's pale and suffering face behind the green panes of The Old Elbeuf.

In the evening, Denise could not help thinking a great deal, on seeing the young ladies march off with their sweethearts. Those who did not sleep at The Ladies' Paradise, disappeared until the next day, bringing back into their departments an outside odor, a sort of troubling, unknown impression. The young girl was sometimes obliged to reply with a smile to a friendly nod from Pauline, whom Baugé waited for every evening regularly at half-past eight, at the corner of the fountain in the Place Gaillon. Then, after having gone out the last and taken a furtive walk, always alone, she was invariably the first in, going upstairs to work, or to bed, her head filled with dreams, full of curiosity about this outdoor life, of which she knew nothing. She certainly did not envy the young ladies, she was happy in her solitude, in that unsociableness to which her timidity condemned her, as to a refuge; but her imagination carried her away, she tried to guess things, evoking the pleasures constantly described before her, the cafés, the restaurants, the theatres, the Sundays spent on the water and in the country taverns. This filled her with a mental weakness, a desire mingled with lassitude; and she seemed to be already tired of those amusements which she had never tasted.

However, there was but little room for these dangerous dreams in her daily working life. During the thirteen hours' hard work in the shop, there was no time for any display of tenderness between the salesmen and the saleswomen. If the continual fight for money had not abolished the sexes, the unceasing press of business which occupied their minds and fatigued their bodies would have sufficed to kill all desire. But very few love-affairs had been known in the establishment amidst the hostilities and friendships between the men and the women, the constant elbowings from department to department. They were all nothing but the wheels, turned round by the immense machine, abdicating their personalities, simply contributing their strength to this commonplace, powerful total. It was only outside that they resumed their individual lives, with the abrupt flame of awakening passions.

Denise, however, one day saw Albert Lhomme slipping a note into the hand of a young lady in the under-clothing department, after having several times passed through with an air of indifference. The dead season, which lasts from December to February was commencing; and she had periods of rest, hours spent on her feet, her eyes wandering all over the shop, waiting for customers. The young ladies of her department were especially

friendly with the salesmen who served the lace, but their intimacy never went any further than some rather risky jokes, exchanged in whispers. In the lace department there was a
second-hand, a gay youth who pursued Clara with all sorts of
abominable stories, simply for a joke—so careless at heart that he
made no effort to meet her outside; and thus it was from counter
to counter, between the gentlemen and the young ladies, a series
of winks, nods, and remarks, which they alone understood. At
times they indulged in some sly gossip with their backs half
turned and with a dreamy air, in order to put the terrible Bourdoncle off the scent. As for Deloche, for a long time he contented
himself with smiling at Denise when he met her; but, getting
bolder, he occasionally murmured a friendly word. The day she
had noticed Madame Aurélie's son giving a note to the young
lady in the under-linen department, Deloche was asking her if
she had enjoyed her lunch, feeling to want to say something, and
unable to find anything more amiable. He also saw the white
paper; and looking at the young girl, they both blushed at this
intrigue carried on before them.

But under these rumors which gradually awoke the woman in
her, Denise still retained her infantine peace of mind. The one
thing that stirred her heart was meeting with Hutin. But even
that was only gratitude in her eyes; she simply thought herself
touched by the young man's politeness. He could not bring a customer to the department without her feeling quite confused.
Several times, on returning from a pay-desk, she found herself
making a *détour*, uselessly passing the silk counter, her bosom
heaving with emotion. One afternoon she met Mouret there,
who seemed to follow her with a smile. He paid no more attention to her now, only addressing a few words to her from time to
time, to give her a few hints about her toilet, and to joke with
her, as an impossible girl, a little savage almost like a boy, of
whom he would never make a coquette, notwithstanding all his
knowledge of women; sometimes he even ventured to laugh at
and tease her, without wishing to acknowledge to himself the
charm which this little saleswoman inspired in him, with her
comical head of hair. Before this mute smile, Denise trembled, as

if she were in fault. Did he know why she was going through the silk department, when she could not herself have explained what made her make such a *détour*?

Hutin, moreover, did not seem to be aware in any way of the young girl's grateful looks. The shop-girls were not his style, he affected to despise them, boasting more than ever of extraordinary adventures with the lady customers; a baroness had been struck with him at his counter, and the wife of an architect had fallen into his arms one day when he went to her house about an error in measuring he had made. Beneath this Norman boasting he simply concealed girls picked up in cafés and music-halls. Like all young gentlemen in the drapery line, he had a mania for spending, fighting in his department the whole week with a miser's greediness, with the sole wish to squander his money on Sunday on the racecourses, in the restaurants, and dancing-saloons; never thinking of saving a penny, spending his salary as soon as he drew it, absolutely indifferent about the future. Favier did not join him in these parties. Hutin and he, so friendly in the shop, bowed to each other at the door, where all further intercourse ceased. A great many of the shopmen, in continual contact indoors, became strangers, ignorant of each other's lives, as soon as they set foot in the streets. But Liénard was Hutin's intimate friend. Both lived in the same lodging-house, the Hôtel de Smyrne, in the Rue Sainte-Anne, a murky building entirely inhabited by shop assistants. In the morning they arrived together; then, in the evening, the first one free, after the folding was done, waited for the other at the Café Saint-Roch, in the Rue Saint-Roch, a little café where the employees of The Ladies' Paradise usually met, brawling, drinking, and playing cards amidst the smoke of their pipes. They often stopped there till one in the morning, until the tired landlord turned them out. For the last month they had been spending three evenings a week at a free-and-easy at Montmartre; and they took their friends with them, creating a success for Mademoiselle Laure, a music-hall singer, Hutin's latest conquest, whose talent they applauded with such violent blows and such a clamor that the police had been obliged to interfere on two occasions.

The winter passed in this way, and Denise at last obtained three hundred francs a year fixed salary. It was quite time, for her shoes were completely worn out. For the last month she had avoided going out, for fear of bursting them entirely.

"What a noise you make with your shoes, mademoiselle!" Madame Aurélie very often remarked, with an irritated look. "It's intolerable. What's the matter with your feet?"

The day Denise appeared with a pair of cloth boots, for which she had given five francs, Marguerite and Clara expressed their astonishment in a kind of half whisper, so as to be heard.

"Hullo! the 'unkempt girl' has given up her galoshes," said the one.

"Ah," retorted the other, "she must have cried over them. They were her mother's."

In point of fact, there was a general uprising against Denise. The girls of her department had found out her friendship with Pauline, and thought they saw a certain bravado in this affection displayed for a saleswoman of a rival counter. They spoke of treason, accused her of going and repeating their slightest words. The war between the two departments became more violent than ever, it had never waxed so warm; hard words were exchanged like cannon-balls, and there was even a slap given one evening behind some boxes of chemises. Perhaps this remote quarrel arose from the fact that the young ladies in the underlinen department wore woollen dresses, whilst those in the ready-made one wore silk. In any case, the former spoke of their neighbors with the shocked air of respectable girls; and facts proved that they were right, for it had been remarked that the silk dresses appeared to have a certain influence on the dissolute habits of the young ladies who wore them. Clara was taunted with her troop of lovers, even Marguerite had, so to say, had her child thrown in her face, whilst Madame Frédéric was accused of all sorts of concealed passions. And this was solely on account of that Denise!

"Now, young ladies, no ugly words; behave yourselves!" Madame Aurélie would say with her imperial air, amidst the rising passions of her little kingdom. "Show who you are."

At heart she preferred to remain neutral. As she confessed one day, when talking to Mouret, these girls were all about the same, one was as good as the other. But she suddenly became impassioned when she learnt from Bourdoncle that he had just caught her son downstairs kissing a young girl belonging to the under-linen department, the saleswoman to whom he had passed several letters. It was abominable, and she roundly accused the under-linen department of having laid a trap for Albert. Yes, it was a got-up affair against herself, they were trying to dishonor her by ruining a child without experience, after seeing that it was impossible to attack her department. Her only object in making such a noise was to complicate the business, for she knew what her son was, fully aware that he was capable of doing all sorts of stupid things. For a time the matter assumed a grave aspect, Mignot, the glove salesman, was mixed up in it. He was a great friend of Albert's, and the rumor got circulated that he favored the mistresses Albert sent him, girls with big chignons, who rummaged in the boxes for hours together; and there was also a story about some Swedish kid gloves given to the girl of the under-linen department which was never properly cleared up. At last the scandal was hushed up out of regard for Madame Aurélie, whom Mouret himself treated with deference. Bourdoncle contented himself a week after with dismissing, for some slight offence, the girl who allowed herself to be kissed. If they shut their eyes to the terrible doings of their employees outdoors, the managers did not tolerate the least nonsense in the house.

And it was Denise who suffered for all this. Madame Aurélie, although perfectly well aware of what was going on, nourished a secret rancor against her; she saw her laughing one evening with Pauline, and took it for bravado, concluding that they were gossiping over her son's love-affairs. And she caused the young girl to be isolated more than ever in the department. For some time she had been thinking of inviting the young ladies to spend a Sunday near Rambouillet, at Rigolles, where she had bought a country house with the first hundred thousand francs she had saved; and she suddenly decided to do so; it would be a means of punishing Denise, of putting her openly on one side. She was the only one not invited. For a fortnight in advance, nothing was talked of but this party; the girls kept their eyes on the sky, and had already mapped out the whole day, looking forward to all sorts of pleasures: donkey-riding, milk and brown bread. And they were to be all women, which was more amusing still! As a rule, Madame Aurélie killed her holidays in this way, going out with her lady friends; for she was so little accustomed to being at home, she always felt so uncomfortable, so strange, during the rare occasions she could dine with her husband and son, that she preferred to throw up even those occasions, and go and dine at a restaurant. Lhomme went his own way, enraptured to resume his bachelor existence, and Albert, greatly relieved, went off with his beauties; so that, unaccustomed to being at home, feeling in each other's way, and wearying each other when together on a Sunday, they paid nothing more than a flying visit to the house, as to some common hotel where people take a bed for the night. Regarding the excursion to Rambouillet, Madame Aurélie simply declared that propriety prevented Albert joining them, and that the father himself would display great tact by refusing to come; a declaration which enchanted the two men. However, the happy day was drawing near, and the young girls chattered more than ever, relating their preparations in the way of dress, as if they were going on a six months' tour, whilst Denise had to listen to them, pale and silent in her abandonment.

"Ah, they make you wild, don't they?" said Pauline to her one morning. "If I were you I would just catch them nicely! They are going to enjoy themselves. I would enjoy myself too. Come with us on Sunday, Baugé is going to take me to Joinville."

"No, thanks," said the young girl with her quiet obstinacy.

"But why not? Are you still afraid of being taken by force?"

And Pauline laughed heartily. Denise also smiled. She knew how such things came about; it was always during some similar excursions that the young ladies had made the acquaintance of their first lovers, brought by chance by a friend; and she did not want to.

"Come," resumed Pauline, "I assure you that Baugé won't bring anyone. We shall be all by ourselves. As you don't want to, I won't go and marry you off, of course."

Denise hesitated, tormented by such a strong desire to go that the blood flew to her cheeks. Since the girls had been talking about their country pleasures she had felt stifled, overcome by a longing for fresh air, dreaming of the tall grass into which she could sink down up to the neck, of the giant trees the shadows of which should flow over her like so much cooling water. Her childhood, spent in the rich verdure of the Cotentin, was awakening with a regret for sun and air.

"Well! yes," said she at last.

Everything was soon arranged. Baugé was to come and fetch them at eight o'clock, in the Place Gaillon; from there they would take a cab to the Vincennes Station. Denise, whose twenty-five francs a month was quickly swallowed up by the children, had only been able to do up her old black woollen dress, by trimming it with strips of check poplin; and she had also made herself a bonnet, a shape covered with silk and ornamented with a simple blue ribbon. In this simple attire she looked very young, like an overgrown girl, exceedingly clean, rather shamefaced and embarrassed by her luxuriant hair, which appeared through the nakedness of her bonnet. Pauline, on the contrary, displayed a pretty violet and white striped silk dress, a hat richly trimmed and laden with feathers, jewels round her neck and rings on her fingers, which gave her the appearance of a well-to-do tradesman's wife. It was like a Sunday revenge on the woollen dress she was obliged to wear all the week in the shop; whilst Denise, who wore her uniform silk from Monday to Saturday, resumed, on Sunday, her thin woollen dress of misery.

"There's Baugé," said Pauline, pointing to a tall fellow standing near the fountain.

She introduced her lover, and Denise felt at her ease at once, he seemed such a nice fellow. Baugé, big, strong as an ox, had a long Flemish face, in which his expressionless eyes twinkled with an infantine puerility. Born at Dunkerque, the younger son of a grocer, he had come to Paris, almost turned out by his father and brother, who thought him a fearful dunce. However, he made three thousand five hundred francs a year at the Bon Marché. He was rather stupid, but a very good hand in the linen department. The women thought him nice.

"And the cab?" asked Pauline.

They had to go as far as the Boulevard. It was already rather warm in the sun, the glorious May morning seemed to laugh on the street pavement. There was not a cloud in the sky; quite a gaiety floated in the blue air, transparent as crystal. An involuntary smile played on Denise's lips; she breathed freely; it seemed to her that her bosom was throwing off the stifling sensation of six months. At last she no longer felt the stuffy air and the heavy stones of The Ladies' Paradise weighing her down! She had then the prospect of a long day in the country before her! and it was like a new lease of life, an endless joy, into which she entered with all the glee of a little child. However, when in the cab, she turned her eyes away, feeling very awkward as Pauline bent over to kiss her lover.

"Oh, look!" said she, her head still at the window, "there's Monsieur Lhomme. How he does walk!"

"He's got his French horn," added Pauline, leaning out. "What an old stupid! One would think he was running to meet his girl!"

Lhomme, with his instrument under his arm, was spinning along past the Gymnase Theatre, his nose in the air, laughing with delight at the thought of the treat in store for him. He was going to spend the day at a friend's, a flautist at a small theatre, where a few amateurs indulged in a little chamber music on Sundays as soon as breakfast was over.

"At eight o'clock! what a madman!" resumed Pauline. "And you know that Madame Aurélie and all her clique must have taken the Rambouillet train that left at half-past six. It's very certain the husband and wife won't come across each other."

Both then commenced talking of the Rambouillet excursion. They did not wish it to be rainy for the others, because they themselves would be obliged to suffer as well; but if a cloud could burst over there without extending to Joinville, it would be funny all the same. Then they attacked Clara, a dirty slut, who hardly knew how to spend the money her men gave her: hadn't she bought three pairs of boots all at the same time, which she threw away the next day, after having cut them with her scissors, on account of her feet, which were covered with bunions. In fact, the young ladies were just as bad as the fellows, they squandered everything, never saving a sou, wasting two or three hundred francs a month on dress and dainties.

"But he's only got one arm," said Baugé all of a sudden. "How does he manage to play the French horn?"

He had kept his eyes on Lhomme. Pauline, who sometimes amused herself by playing on his stupidity, told him the cashier kept the instrument up by placing it against a wall. He thoroughly believed her, and thought it very ingenious. Then, when stricken with remorse, she explained to him in what way Lhomme had adapted to his stump a system of keys which he made use of as a hand, he shook his head, full of suspicion, declaring that they wouldn't make him swallow that.

"You are really too stupid!" she retorted, laughingly. "Never mind, I love you all the same."

They reached the Vincennes Station just in time for a train. Baugé paid; but Denise had previously declared that she wished to pay her share of the expenses; they would settle up in the evening. They took second-class tickets, and found the train full of a gay, noisy throng. At Nogent, a wedding party got out, amidst a storm of laughter. At last they arrived at Joinville, and went straight to the island to order lunch; and they stopped there, lingering on the banks of the Marne, under the tall poplars. It was rather cold in the shade, a sharp breeze was blowing in the sunshine, extending far into the distance, on the other side of the river, the limpid purity of a plain dotted with cultivated fields. Denise lingered behind Pauline and her lover, who were walking with their arms round each other's waists. She had picked a handful of buttercups, and was watching the flow of the river, happy, her heart beating, her head drooping, each time Baugé leant over to kiss his mistress. Her eyes filled with tears. And yet she was not suffering. What was the matter with her that she had this feeling of suffocation? And why did this vast landscape, where she had looked forward to having so much enjoyment, fill

her with a vague regret she could not explain? Then, at lunch,
Pauline's noisy laugh bewildered her. That young lady, who loved
the suburbs with the passion of an actress living in the gas-light,
in the thick air of a crowd, wanted to lunch in an arbor, notwithstanding the sharp wind. She was delighted with the sudden
gusts which blew up the table-cloth, she thought the arbor very
funny in its nudity, with the freshly-painted trelliswork, the lozenges of which cast a reflection on the cloth. She ate ravenously,
devouring everything with the voracity of a girl badly fed at the
shop, making up for it outside by giving herself an indigestion
with the things she liked; this was her vice, she spent most of her
money in cakes and indigestible dainties of all kinds, favorite
dishes stowed away in her leisure moments. As Denise seemed to
have had enough of the eggs, fried fish, and stewed chicken, she
restrained herself, not daring to order any strawberries, a luxury
still very dear, for fear of running the bill up too high.

"Now, what are we going to do?" asked Baugé when the coffee
was served.

As a rule Pauline and he returned to Paris to dine, and finish
their day in some theatre. But at Denise's request, they decided
to stay at Joinville all day; they would be able to have their fill of
the country. So they stopped and wandered about the fields all
the afternoon. They spoke for a moment of going for a row, but
abandoned the idea; Baugé was not a good waterman. But they
found themselves walking along the banks of the Marne, all the
same, and were greatly interested by the life on the river, the
squadrons of yawls and other boats, and the young men who
formed the crews. The sun was going down, they were returning
to Joinville, when they saw two boats coming down stream at a
racing speed, exchanging volleys of insults, in which the repeated cries of "Sawbones!" and "Counter-jumpers!" dominated.

"Hallo!" said Pauline, "it's Monsieur Hutin."

"Yes," said Baugé, shading his face with his hand, "I recognize
his mahogany boat. The other one is manned by students, no
doubt."

And he explained the deadly hatred existing between the
young students and the shopmen. Denise, on hearing Hutin's

name mentioned, suddenly stopped, and followed, with fixed eyes, the frail skiff spinning along like an arrow. She tried to distinguish the young man among the rowers, but could only manage to make out the white dresses of two women, one of whom, who was steering, wore a red hat. Their voices were drowned by the rapid flow of the river.

"Pitch 'em in, the sawbones!"

"Duck 'em, the counter-jumpers!"

In the evening they returned to the restaurant on the island. But it had turned too chilly, they were obliged to dine in one of the closed rooms, where the table-cloths were still damp from the humidity of the winter. After six o'clock the tables were all occupied, yet the excursionists still hurried in, looking for a corner; and the waiters continued to bring in more chairs and forms, putting the plates closer together, and crowding the people up. It was stifling, they had to open the windows. Outdoors, the day was waning, a greenish twilight fell from the poplars so quickly that the proprietor, unprepared for these meals under cover, and having no lamps, was obliged to put a wax candle on each table. The uproar became deafening with laughing, calling out, and the clacking of the table utensils; the candles flared and melted in the draught from the windows, whilst moths fluttered about in the air, warmed by the odor of the food, and traversed by sudden gusts of cold wind.

"What fun they're having, eh?" said Pauline, very busy with a plate of matelote, which she declared extraordinary. She leant over to add: "Didn't you see Monsieur Albert over there?"

It was really young Lhomme, in the middle of three questionable women, a vulgar-looking old lady in a yellow bonnet, suspiciously like a procuress, and two young girls of thirteen or fourteen, forward and painfully impudent creatures. He, already intoxicated, was knocking his glass on the table, and talking of drubbing the waiter if he did not bring some "liqueurs" immediately.

"Well!" resumed Pauline, "there's a family, if you like! the mother at Rambouillet, the father in Paris; and the son at Joinville; they won't tread on one another's toes!"

Denise, who detested noise, smiled, however, and tasted the joy of ceasing to think, amid such uproar. But all at once they heard a noise in the other room, a burst of voices which drowned the others. They were yelling, and must have come to blows, for one could hear a scuffle, chairs falling down, quite a struggle, amid which the river-cries again resounded:

"Duck 'em, the counter-jumpers!"

"Pitch 'em in, the sawbones!"

And when the hotel-keeper's loud voice had calmed this tempest, Hutin suddenly made his appearance, wearing a red jersey, and a little cap at the back of his head; he had on his arm the tall, fair girl, who had been steering, and who, in order to wear the boat's colors, had planted a bunch of poppies behind her ear. They were greeted on entering by a storm of applause; and his face beamed with pride, he swelled out his chest, assuming a nautical rolling gait, showing off a blow which had blackened his cheek, puffed up with joy at being noticed. Behind them followed the crew. They took a table by storm, and the uproar became something fearful.

"It appears," explained Baugé, after having listened to the conversation behind him, "it appears that the students have recognized the woman with Hutin as an old friend from their neighborhood, who now sings in a music-hall at Montmartre. So they were kicking up a row for her. These students never pay their women."

"In any case," said Pauline, stiffly, "she's jolly ugly, with her carroty hair. Really, I don't know where Monsieur Hutin picks them up, but they're an ugly, dirty lot."

Denise had turned pale, and felt an icy coldness, as if her heart's blood were flowing away, drop by drop. She had already, on seeing the boats from the bank, felt a shiver; but now she no longer had any doubt, this girl was certainly with Hutin. With trembling hands, and a choking sensation in her throat, she ceased eating.

"What's the matter?" asked her friend.

"Nothing," stammered she; "it's rather warm here."

But Hutin's table was close to theirs, and when he perceived

Baugé, whom he knew, he commenced a conversation in a shrill voice, in order to attract further attention.

"I say," cried he, "are you as virtuous as ever at the Bon Marché?"

"Not so much as all that," replied Baugé, turning very red.

"That won't do! You know they only take virgins there, and there's a confessional box permanently fixed for the salesmen who venture to look at them. A house where they marry you—no, thanks!"

The other fellows began to laugh. Liénard, who belonged to the crew, added: "It isn't like the Louvre. There they have a midwife attached to the ready-made department. My word of honor!"

The gaiety increased; Pauline herself burst out, the idea of the midwife seemed so funny. But Baugé was annoyed by the jokes about the innocence of his house. He launched out all at once: "Oh, you're not too well off at The Ladies' Paradise. Sacked for the slightest thing! And a governor who seems to tout for his lady customers."

Hutin no longer listened to him, but commenced to praise the house in the Place Clichy. He knew a young girl there so excessively aristocratic that the customers dared not speak to her for fear of humiliating her. Then, drawing up closer, he related that he had made a hundred and fifteen francs that week; oh! a capital week. Favier left behind with fifty-two francs, the whole lot floored. And it was visible he was bursting with money, he would not go to bed till he had liquidated the hundred and fifteen francs. Then, as he gradually became intoxicated, he attacked Robineau, that fool of a second-hand who affected to keep himself apart, going so far as to refuse to walk in the street with one of his salesmen.

"Shut up," said Liénard; "you talk too much, old man."

The heat had increased, the candles were guttering down on to the table-cloths stained with wine; and through the open windows, when the noise within ceased for an instant, there entered a distant prolonged voice, the voice of the river, and of the tall poplars sleeping in the calm night. Baugé had just called for the bill, seeing that Denise was now quite white, her throat choked by the tears she withheld; but the waiter did not appear, and she had to submit to Hutin's loud talk. He was now boasting of being more superior to Liénard, because Liénard cared for nothing, simply squandering his father's money, whilst he, Hutin, was spending his own earnings, the fruit of his intelligence. At last Baugé paid, and the two girls went out.

"There's one from the Louvre," murmured Pauline in the outer room, looking at a tall thin girl putting on her mantle.

"You don't know her. You can't tell," said the young man.

"Oh, can't I? They've got a way of draping themselves. She belongs to the midwife's department! If she heard, she must be pleased."

They got outside at last, and Denise heaved a sigh of relief. For a moment she had thought she was going to die in that suffocating heat, amidst all those cries; and she still attributed her faintness to the want of air. Now she breathed freely in the freshness of the starry night. As the two young girls were leaving the garden of the restaurant, a timid voice murmured in the shade: "Good evening, ladies."

It was Deloche. They had not seen him at the further end of the front room, where he was dining alone, after having come from Paris on foot, for the pleasure of the walk. On recognizing this friendly voice, Denise, suffering, yielded mechanically to the want of some support.

"Monsieur Deloche, come back with us," said she. "Give me your arm."

Pauline and Baugé had already gone on in front. They were astonished, never thinking it would turn out like this, and with this fellow above all. However, as there was still an hour before the train started, they went to the end of the island, following the bank, under the tall poplars; and, from time to time, they turned round, murmuring: "But where are they? Ah, there they are. It's rather funny, all the same."

At first Denise and Deloche remained silent. The noise from the restaurant was slowly dying away, changing into a musical sweetness in the calmness of the night; and they went further in amongst the cool of the trees, still feverish from that furnace, the lights of which were disappearing one by one behind the foliage. Opposite them there was a sort of shadowy wall, a mass of shade in which the trunks and branches buried themselves so compact that they could not even distinguish any trace of the path. However, they went forward quietly, without fear. Then, their eyes getting more accustomed to the darkness, they saw on the right the trunks of the poplars, resembling somber columns upholding the domes of their branches, pierced with stars; whilst on the right the water assumed occasionally in the darkness the brightness of a mirror. The wind was subsiding, they no longer heard anything but the flowing of the river.

"I am very pleased to have met you," stammered Deloche at last, making up his mind to speak first. "You can't think how happy you render me in consenting to walk with me."

And, aided by the darkness, after many awkward attempts, he ventured to tell her he loved her. He had long wanted to write to her and tell her so; and perhaps she would never have known it had it not been for this lovely night coming to his assistance, this water that murmured so softly, and these trees which screened them with their shade. But she did not reply; she continued to walk by his side with the same suffering air. And he was trying to look into her face, when he heard a sob.

"Oh! good heavens!" he exclaimed, "you are crying, mademoiselle, you are crying! Have I offended you?"

"No, no," she murmured.

She tried to keep back her tears, but she could not. Even when at table, she had thought her heart was about to burst. She abandoned herself in the darkness entirely, stifled by her sobs, thinking that if Hutin had been in Deloche's place and said such tender things to her, she would have been unable to resist. This confession made to herself filled her with confusion. A feeling of shame burnt her face, as if she had already fallen into the arms of that Hutin, who was disporting himself with those girls.

"I didn't mean to offend you," continued Deloche, almost crying also.

"No, but listen," said she, her voice still trembling; "I am not at all angry with you. But never speak to me again as you have just done. What you ask is impossible. Oh! you're a good fellow, and I'm quite willing to be your friend, but nothing more. You understand—your friend."

He shuddered. After a few steps taken in silence, he stammered: "In fact, you don't love me?"

And as she spared him the pain of a brutal "no," he resumed in a soft, heart-broken voice: "Oh, I was prepared for it. I have never had any luck, I know I can never be happy. At home, they used to beat me. In Paris, I've always been a drudge. You see, when one does not know how to rob other fellows of their mistresses, and when one is too awkward to earn as much as the others, why the best thing is to go into some corner and die. Never fear, I sha'n't torment you any more. As for loving you, you can't prevent me, can you? I shall love you for nothing, like a dog. There, everything escapes me, that's my luck in life."

And he, too, burst into tears. She tried to console him, and in their friendly effusion they found they belonged to the same department—she to Valognes, he to Briquebec, eight miles from each other, and this was a fresh tie. His father, a poor, needy bailiff, and sickly jealous, used to drub him, calling him a bastard, exasperated with his long pale face and tow-like hair, which, said he, did not belong to the family. And they got talking about the vast pastures, surrounded with quick-set hedges, of the shady paths winding beneath the elm trees, and of the grass grown roads, like the alleys in a park. Around them night was getting darker, but they could still distinguish the rushes on the banks, and the interlaced foliage, black beneath the twinkling stars; and a peacefulness came over them, they forgot their troubles, brought nearer by their ill-luck, in a closer feeling of friendship.

"Well?" asked Pauline of Denise, taking her aside when they arrived at the station.

The young girl understood by the smile and the stare of tender curiosity; she turned very red and replied: "But—never, my dear! I told you I did not wish to! He belongs to my part of the country. We were talking about Valognes." Pauline and Baugé were perplexed, put out in their ideas, not knowing what to think. Deloche left them in the Place de la Bastille; like all young probationers, he slept at the house, where he had to be in by eleven o'clock. Not wishing to go in with him, Denise, who had got permission to go to the theatre, accepted Baugé's invitation to accompany Pauline to his home—he, in order to be nearer his mistress, had moved into the Rue Saint-Roch. They took a cab, and Denise was stupefied on learning on the way that her friend was going to stay all night with the young man—nothing was easier, they only had to give Madame Cabin five francs, all the young ladies did it. Baugé did the honors of his room, which was furnished with old Empire furniture, given him by his father. He got angry when Denise spoke of settling up, but at last accepted the fifteen francs twelve sous which she had laid on the chest of drawers; but he insisted on making her a cup of tea, and he struggled with a spirit-lamp and saucepan, and then was obliged to go and fetch some sugar. Midnight struck as he was pouring out the tea.

"I must be off," said Denise.

"Presently," replied Pauline. "The theatres don't close so early."

Denise felt uncomfortable in this bachelor's room. She had seen her friend take off her things, turn down the bed, open it, and pat the pillows with her naked arms; and these preparations for a night of love-making carried on before her, troubled her, and made her feel ashamed, awakening once in her wounded heart the recollection of Hutin. Such ideas were not very salutary. At last she left them, at a quarter past twelve. But she went away confused, when in reply to her innocent "good night," Pauline cried out, thoughtlessly:

"Thanks, we are sure to have a good one!"

The private door leading to Mouret's apartments and to the employees' bedrooms was in the Rue Neuve-Saint-Augustin. Madame Cabin opened the door and gave a glance in order to mark the return. A night-light was burning dimly in the hall, and Denise, finding herself in this uncertain light, hesitated, and was seized with fear, for on turning the corner of the street, she had seen the door close on the vague shadow of a man. It must have been the governor coming home from a party; and the idea that he was there in the dark waiting for her, perhaps, caused her one of those strange fears with which he still inspired her, without any reasonable cause. Someone moved on the first floor, a boot creaked, and losing her head entirely, she pushed open a door which led into the shop, and which was always left open for the night-watch. She was in the printed cotton department.

"Good heavens! what shall I do?" she stammered, in her emotion.

The idea occurred to her that there was another door upstairs leading to the bedrooms; but she would have to go right across the shop. She preferred this, notwithstanding the darkness reigning in the galleries. Not a gas-jet was burning, there were only a few oil-lamps hung here and there on the branches of the lustres; and these scattered lights, like yellow patches, their rays lost in the gloom, resembled the lanterns hung up in a mine. Big shadows loomed in the air; one could hardly distinguish the piles of goods, which assumed alarming profiles: fallen columns, squatting beasts, and lurking thieves. The heavy silence, broken by distant respirations, increased still more the darkness. However, she saw where she was. The linen department on her left formed a dead color, like the blueness of houses in the street under a summer sky; then she wished to cross the hall immediately, but running up against some piles of printed calico, she thought it safer to follow the hosiery department, and then the woollen one. There she was frightened by a loud noise of snoring. It was Joseph, the messenger, sleeping behind some articles of mourning. She quickly ran into the hall, now illuminated by the skylight, with a sort of crepuscular light which made it appear larger, full of a nocturnal church-like terror, with the immobility of its shelves, and the shadows of its yard-measures which described reversed crosses. She now fairly ran away. In the mercery and glove departments she nearly walked over some more messengers, and only felt safe when she at last found herself on the staircase. But upstairs, before the ready-made department, she was seized with fear on perceiving a lantern moving forward, twinkling in the darkness. It was the watch, two firemen marking their passage on the faces of the indicators. She stood a moment unable to understand it, watched them passing from the shawl to the furniture department, then to the under-linen one, terrified by their strange maneuvers, by the grinding of the key, and by the closing of the iron doors which made a murderous noise. When they approached, she took refuge in the lace department, but a sound of talking made her hastily depart, and run off to the outer door. She had recognized Deloche's voice. He slept in his department, on a little iron bedstead which he set up himself every evening; and he was not asleep yet, recalling the pleasant hours he had just spent.

"What! it's you, mademoiselle?" said Mouret, whom Denise found before her on the staircase, a small pocket-candlestick in his hand.

She stammered, and tried to explain that she had come to look for something. But he was not angry. He looked at her with his paternal, and at the same time curious, air.

"You had permission to go to the theatre, then?"

"Yes, sir."

"And have you enjoyed yourself? What theatre did you go to?"

"I have been in the country, sir."

That made him laugh. Then he asked, laying a certain stress on his question: "All alone?"

"No, sir; with a lady friend," replied she, her cheeks burning, shocked at the idea which he no doubt entertained.

He said no more; but he was still looking at her in her simple black dress and hat trimmed with a single blue ribbon. Was this little savage going to turn out a pretty girl? She looked all the better for her day in the open air, charming with her splendid hair falling over her forehead. And he, who during the last six months had treated her like a child, sometimes giving her advice, yielding to a desire to gain experience, to a wicked wish to know how a woman sprung up and lost herself in Paris, no longer laughed, experiencing a feeling of surprise and fear mingled with tenderness. No doubt it was a lover who embellished her like this. At this thought he felt as if stung to the quick by a favorite bird, with which he was playing.

"Good night, sir," murmured Denise, continuing her way without waiting.

He did not answer, but stood watching her till she disappeared. Then he entered his own apartments.

CHAPTER VI.

When the dead summer season arrived, there was quite a panic at The Ladies' Paradise. The reign of terror commenced, a great many employees were sent away on leave, and others were dismissed in dozens by the principals, who wished to clear the shop, no customers appearing during the July and August heat. Mouret, on making his daily inspection with Bourdoncle, called aside the managers, whom he had prompted during the winter to engage more men than were necessary, so that the business should not suffer, leaving them to weed out their staff later on. It was now a question of reducing expenses by getting rid of quite a third of the shop people, the weak ones who allowed themselves to be swallowed up by the strong ones.

"Come," he would say, "you must have some who don't suit you. We can't keep them all this time doing nothing."

And if the manager hesitated, hardly knowing whom to sacrifice, he would continue; "Make your arrangements, six salesmen must suffice; you can take on others in October, there are plenty to be had!"

As a rule Bourdoncle undertook the executions. He had a terrible way of saying: "Go and be paid!" which fell like a blow from an axe. Anything served him as a pretext for clearing off the superfluous staff. He invented misdeeds, speculating on the slightest negligence. "You were sitting down, sir; go and be paid!" "You dare to answer me; go and be paid!" "Your shoes are not clean; go and be paid!" And even the bravest trembled in presence of the massacre which he left behind him. Then, this system not working quick enough, he invented a trap by which he got rid in a few days, without fatigue, of the number of salesmen condemned beforehand. At eight o'clock, he took his stand at the door, watch in hand; and at three minutes past the hour, the breathless young people were greeted with the implacable "Go and be paid!" This was a quick and cleanly method of doing the work.

"You've an ugly mug," he ended by saying one day to a poor wretch whose nose, all on one side, annoyed him, "go and be paid!"

The favored ones obtained a fortnight's holiday without pay, which was a more humane way of lessening the expenses. The salesmen accepted their precarious situation, obliged to do so by necessity and habit. Since their arrival in Paris, they had roamed about, commencing their apprenticeship here, finishing it there, getting dismissed or themselves resigning all at once, as interest dictated. When business stood still, the workmen were deprived of their daily bread; and this was well understood in the indifferent march of the machine, the useless workmen were quietly thrown aside, like so much old plant, there was no gratitude shown for services rendered. So much the worse for those who did not know how to look after themselves!

Nothing else was now talked of in the various departments. Fresh stories circulated every day. The dismissed salesmen were named, as one counts the dead in time of cholera. The shawl and the woollen departments suffered especially; seven employees disappeared from them in one week. Then the under-linen department was thrown into confusion, a customer had nearly fainted away, accusing the young person who had served her of eating garlic; and the latter was dismissed at once, although, badly fed and dying of hunger, she was simply finishing a collection of bread crusts at the counter. The authorities were pitiless at the least complaint from the customers; no excuse was admitted, the employee was always wrong, and had to disappear like a defective instrument, hurtful to the proper working of the business; and the others bowed their heads, not even attempting any defense. In the panic which was raging each one trembled for himself. Mignot, going out one day with a parcel under his coat, notwithstanding the rules, was nearly caught, and really thought himself lost. Liénard, who was celebrated for his idleness, owed to his father's position in the drapery trade that he was not turned away one afternoon that Bourdoncle found him dozing between two piles of English velvets. But the Lhommes were especially anxious, expecting every day to see their son Albert sent away, the governor being very dissatisfied with his conduct at the pay-desk. He frequently had women there who distracted his attention from his work; and twice Madame Aurélie had been obliged to plead for him with the principals.

Denise was so menaced amid this general clearance, that she lived in the continual expectation of a catastrophe. It was in vain that she summoned up her courage struggling with all her gaiety and all her reason not to yield to the misgivings of her tender nature; she burst out into blinding tears as soon as she had closed the door of her bedroom, desolated at the thought of seeing herself in the street, on bad terms with her uncle, not knowing where to go, without a sou saved, and having the two children to look after. The sensations she had felt the first few weeks sprang up again, she fancied herself a grain of seed under a powerful millstone; and, utterly discouraged, she abandoned herself entirely to the thought of what a small atom she was in this great machine, which would certainly crush her with its quiet indifference. There was no illusion possible; if they sent away anyone from her department she knew it would be her. No doubt, during the Rambouillet excursion, the other young ladies had incensed Madame Aurélie against her, for since then that lady had treated her with an air of severity in which there was a certain rancor. Besides, they could not forgive her going to Join-ville, regarding it as a sign of revolt, a means of setting the whole department at defiance, by parading about with a young lady from a rival counter. Never had Denise suffered so much in the department, and she now gave up all hope of conquering it.

"Let them alone!" repeated Pauline, "a lot of stuck-up things, as stupid as donkeys!"

But it was just these fine lady airs which intimidated Denise. Nearly all the saleswomen, by their daily contact with the rich customers, assumed certain graces, and finished by forming a vague nameless class, something between a work-girl and a middle-class lady. But beneath their art in dress, and the manners and phrases learnt by heart, there was often only a false superficial education, the fruits of attending cheap theatres and music-halls, and picking up all the current stupidities of the Paris pavement.

"You know the 'unkempt girl' has got a child?" said Clara one morning, on arriving in the department. And, as they seemed astonished, she continued: "I saw her yesterday myself taking the child out for a walk! She's got it stowed away in the neighborhood, somewhere."

Two days after, Marguerite came up after dinner with another piece of news. "A nice thing, I've just seen the 'unkempt girl's' lover—a workman, just fancy! Yes, a dirty little workman, with yellow hair, who was watching her through the windows."

From that moment it was an accepted truth: Denise had a workman for a lover, and an infant concealed somewhere in the neighborhood. They overwhelmed her with spiteful allusions. The first time she understood she turned quite pale before the monstrosity of their suppositions. It was abominable; she tried to explain, and stammered out: "But they are my brothers!"

"Oh! oh! her brothers!" said Clara in a bantering tone.

Madame Aurélie was obliged to interfere. "Be quiet! young ladies. You had better go on changing those tickets. Mademoiselle Baudu is quite free to misbehave herself out of doors, if only she worked a bit when here."

This curt defense was a condemnation. The young girl, feeling choked as if they had accused her of a crime, vainly endeavored to explain the facts. They laughed and shrugged their shoulders, and she felt wounded to the heart. On hearing the rumor, Deloche was so indignant that he wanted to slap the faces of the young ladies in Denise's department; and was only restrained by the fear of compromising her. Since the evening at Joinville, he entertained a submissive love, an almost religious friendship for her, which he proved by his faithful dog-like looks. He was careful not to show his affection before the others, for they would have laughed at them; but that did not prevent his dreaming of the avenging blow, if ever anyone should attack her before him.

Denise finished by not answering the insults. It was too odious, nobody would believe it. When any girl ventured a fresh allusion, she contented herself with looking at her with a sad, calm air. Besides, she had other troubles, material anxieties which took up her attention. Jean went on as bad as ever, always worrying her for money. Hardly a week passed that she did not receive some fresh story from him, four pages long; and when the house postman brought her these letters, in a big, passionate handwriting, she hastened to hide them in her pocket, for the saleswomen affected to laugh, and sung snatches of some doubtful ditties. Then after having invented a pretext to go to the other end of the establishment and read the letters, she was seized with fear; poor Jean seemed to be lost. All his fibs went down with her, she believed all his extraordinary love adventures, her complete ignorance of such things making her exaggerate the danger. Sometimes it was a two-franc piece to enable him to escape the jealousy of some woman; at other times five francs, six francs, to get some poor girl out of a scrape, whose father would otherwise kill her. So that as her salary and commission did not suffice, she had conceived the idea of looking for a little work after business hours. She spoke about it to Robineau, who had shown a certain sympathy for her since their meeting at Vinçard's, and he had procured her the making of some neckties at five sous a dozen. At night, between nine and one o'clock, she could do six dozen, which made thirty sous, out of which she had to deduct four sous for a candle. But as this sum kept Jean going she did not complain of the want of sleep, and would have thought herself very happy had not another catastrophe once more overthrown her budget calculations. At the end of the second fortnight, when she went to the necktie-dealer, she found the door closed; the woman had failed, become bankrupt, thus carrying off her eighteen francs six sous, a considerable sum on which she had been counting for the last week. All the annoyances in the department disappeared before this disaster.

"You look dull," said Pauline, meeting her in the furniture gallery, looking very pale. "Are you in want of anything?"

But as Denise already owed her friend twelve francs, she tried to smile and replied: "No, thanks. I've not slept well, that's all."

It was the twentieth of July, when the panic caused by the dismissals was at its worst. Out of the four hundred employees, Bourdoncle had already sacked fifty, and there were rumors of fresh executions. She thought but little of the menaces which were flying about, entirely taken up by the anguish of one of Jean's adventures, still more terrifying than the others. This very day he wanted fifteen francs, which sum alone could save him from the vengeance of an outraged husband. The previous evening she had received the first letter opening the drama; then, one after the other, came two more; in the last, which she was finishing when Pauline met her, Jean announced his death for that evening, if she did not send the money. She was in agony. Impossible to take it out of Pépé's board, paid two days before. Every sort of bad luck was pursuing her, for she had hoped to get her eighteen francs six sous through Robineau, who could perhaps find the necktie-dealer; but Robineau having got a fortnight's holiday, had not returned the previous night as he was expected to do.

However, Pauline still questioned her in a friendly way; when they met, in an out-of-the-way department, they conversed for a few minutes, keeping a sharp look-out the while. Suddenly, Pauline made a move as if to run off, having observed the white tie of an inspector who was coming out of the shawl department.

"Ah! it's only old Jouve!" murmured she in a relieved tone. "I can't think what makes the old man grin as he does when he sees us together. In your place I should beware, for he's too kind to you. He's an old humbug, as spiteful as a cat, and thinks he's still got his troopers to talk to."

It was quite true; Jouve was detested by all the salespeople for the severity of his treatment. More than half the dismissals were the result of his reports; and with his big red nose of a rakish ex-captain, he only exercised his leniency in the departments served by women.

"Why should I be afraid?" asked Denise.

"Well!" replied Pauline, laughing, "perhaps he may exact some return. Several of the young ladies try to keep well with him."

Jouve had gone away, pretending not to see them; and they heard him dropping on to a salesman in the lace department, guilty of watching a fallen horse in the Rue Neuve-Saint-Augustin.

"By the way," resumed Pauline, "weren't you looking for Monsieur Robineau yesterday? He's come back."

Denise thought she was saved. "Thanks, I'll go round the other way then, and pass through the silk department. So much the worse! They sent me upstairs to the work-room to fetch a bodkin."

And they separated. The young girl, with a busy look, as if she were running from pay-desk to pay-desk in search of something, arrived on the stairs and went down into the hall. It was a quarter to ten, the first lunch-bell had rung. A warm sun was playing on the windows, and notwithstanding the grey linen blinds, the heat penetrated into the stagnant air. Now and then a refreshing breath arose from the floor, which the messengers were gently watering. It was a somnolence, a summer siesta, in the midst of the empty space around the counters, like the interior of a church wrapt in sleeping shadow after the last mass. Some listless salesmen were standing about, a few rare customers were crossing the galleries and the hall, with the fatigued step of women annoyed by the sun.

Just as Denise went down, Favier was measuring a dress length of light silk, with pink spots, for Madame Boutarel, arrived in Paris the previous day from the South. Since the commencement of the month, the provinces had been sending up their detachments; one saw nothing but queerly-dressed ladies with yellow shawls, green skirts, and flaring bonnets. The shopmen, indifferent, were too indolent to laugh at them even. Favier accompanied Madame Boutarel to the mercery department, and on returning, said to Hutin:

"Yesterday they were all Auvergnat women, today they're all Provençales. I'm sick of them."

But Hutin rushed forward, it was his turn, and he had recognized "the pretty lady," the lovely blonde whom the department thus designated, knowing nothing about her, not even her name. They all smiled at her, not a week passed without her coming to The Ladies' Paradise, always alone. This time she had a little boy of four or five with her, and this gave rise to some comment.

"She's married, then?" asked Favier, when Hutin returned from the pay-desk, where he had debited her with thirty yards of Duchess satin.

"Possibly," replied he, "although the youngster proves nothing. Perhaps he belongs to a lady friend. What's certain is, that she must have been weeping. She's so melancholy, and her eyes are so red!"

A silence ensued. The two salesmen gazed vaguely into the depths of the shop. Then Favier resumed in a low voice; "If she's married, perhaps her husband's given her a drubbing."

"Possibly," repeated Hutin, "unless it be a lover who has left her." And after a fresh silence, he added: "Any way, I don't care a hang!"

At this moment Denise crossed the silk department, slackening her pace and looking around her, trying to find Robineau. She could not see him, so she went into the linen department, then passed through again. The two salesmen had noticed her movements.

"There's that bag of bones again," murmured Hutin.

"She's looking for Robineau," said Favier. "I can't think what they're up to together. Oh! nothing smutty; Robineau's too big a fool. They say he has procured her a little work, some neckties. What a spec, eh?"

Hutin was meditating something spiteful. When Denise passed near him, he stopped her, saying: "Is it me you're looking for?"

She turned very red. Since the Joinville excursion, she dared not read her heart, full of confused sensations. She was constantly recalling his appearance with that red-haired girl, and if she still trembled before him, it was doubtless from uneasiness.

Had she ever loved him? Did she love him still? She hardly liked to stir up these things, which were painful to her.

"No, sir," she replied, embarrassed.

Hutin then began to laugh at her uneasy manner. "Would you like us to serve him to you? Favier, just serve this young lady with Robineau."

She looked at him fixedly, with the sad calm look with which she had received the wounding remarks the young ladies had made about her. Ah! he was spiteful, he attacked her as well as the others! And she felt a sort of supreme anguish, the breaking of a last tie. Her face expressed such real suffering, that Favier, though not of a very tender nature, came to her assistance.

"Monsieur Robineau is in the stock-room," said he. "No doubt he will be back for lunch. You'll find him here this afternoon, if you want to speak to him."

Denise thanked him, and went up to her department, where Madame Aurélie was waiting for her in a terrible rage. What! she had been gone half an hour! Where had she just sprung from? Not from the work-room, that was quite certain! The poor girl hung down her head, thinking of this avalanche of misfortunes. All would be over if Robineau did not come in. However, she resolved to go down again.

In the silk department, Robineau's return had provoked quite a revolution. The salesmen had hoped that, disgusted with the annoyances they were incessantly causing him, he would not return; and, in fact, there was a moment, when pressed by Vinçard to take over his business, he had almost decided to do so. Hutin's secret working, the mine he had been laying under the second-hand's feet for months past, was about to be sprung. During Robineau's holidays, Hutin, who had taken his place as second-hand, had done his best to injure him in the minds of the principals, and get possession of his situation by an excess of zeal; he discovered and reported all sorts of trifling irregularities, suggested improvements, and invented new designs. In fact, everyone in the department, from the unpaid probationer, longing to become a salesman, up to the first salesman who coveted the situation of manager, they all had one fixed idea, and that was to dislodge the comrade above them, to ascend another rung of the ladder, swallowing him up if necessary; and this struggle of appetites, this pushing the one against the other, even contributed to the better working of the machine, provoking business and increasing tenfold the success which was astonishing Paris. Behind Hutin, there was Favier; then behind Favier came the others, in a long line. One heard a loud noise as of jaw-bones working. Robineau was condemned, each one was grabbing after his bone. So that when the second-hand reappeared there was a general grumbling. The matter had to be settled, the salesmen's attitude appeared so menacing, that the head of the department had sent Robineau to the stock-room, in order to give the authorities time to come to a decision.

"We would sooner all leave, if they keep him," declared Hutin,

This affair bothered Bouthemont, whose gaiety ill-accorded with such an internal vexation. He was pained to see nothing but scowling faces around him. However, he wished to be just.

"Come, leave him alone, he doesn't hurt you."

But they protested energetically. "What! doesn't hurt us! An insupportable object, always irritable, capable of walking over your body, he's so proud!"

This was the great bitterness of the department. Robineau, nervous as a woman, was intolerably stiff and susceptible. They related scores of stories, a poor little fellow who had fallen ill through it, and lady customers even who had been humiliated by his nasty remarks.

"Well, gentlemen, I won't take anything on myself," said Bouthemont. "I've notified the directors, and am going to speak about it shortly."

The second lunch-bell rang, the clang of which came up from the basement, distant and deadened in the close air of the shop. Hutin and Favier went down. From all the counters, the salesmen were arriving one by one, helter-skelter, hastening below to the narrow entrance to the kitchen, a damp passage always lighted with gas. The throng pushed forward, without a laugh or a word, amidst an increasing noise of crockery and a strong odor of food. At the extremity of the passage there was a sudden halt, before a wicket. Flanked with piles of plates, armed with forks and spoons, which he was plunging in the copper-pans, a cook was distributing the portions. And when he stood aside, the flaring kitchen could be seen behind his white-covered belly.

"Of course!" muttered Hutin, consulting the bill of fare, written on a black-board above the wicket. "Beef and pungent sauce, or skate. Never any roast meat in this rotten shop! Their boiled beef and fish don't do a bit of good to a fellow!"

Moreover, the fish was universally neglected, for the pan was quite full. Favier, however, took some skate. Behind him, Hutin stooped down, saying: "Beef and pungent sauce."

With a mechanical movement, the cook picked up a piece of meat, and poured a spoonful of sauce over it; and Hutin, suffocated by the ardent breath from the kitchen, had hardly got his portion, before the words, "Beef, pungent sauce; beef, pungent sauce," followed each other like a litany; whilst the cook continued to pick up the meat and pour over the sauce, with the rapid and rhythmical movement of a well-regulated clock.

"But the skate's cold," declared Favier, whose hand felt no warmth from the plate.

They were all hurrying along now, with their plates held out straight, for fear of running up against one another. Ten steps further was the bar, another wicket with a shiny zinc counter, on which were ranged the shares of wine, small bottles, without corks, still damp from rinsing. And each took one of these bottles in his empty hand as he passed, and then, completely laden, made for his table with a serious air, careful not to spill anything.

Hutin grumbled, "This is a fine dance, with all this crockery!"

Their table, Favier's and his, was at the end of the corridor in the last dining room. The rooms were all alike, old cellars twelve feet by fifteen, which had been cemented over and fitted up as refectories; but the damp came through the paint-work, the yellow walls were covered with greenish spots; and, from the narrow air-holes, opening on the street, on a level with the pavement, there fell a livid light, incessantly traversed by the vague shadows of the passers-by. In July as in December, one was stifled in the warm air, laden with nauseous smells, coming from the neighborhood of the kitchen.

Hutin went in first. On the table, which was fixed at one end to the wall, and covered with American cloth, there were only the glasses, knives, and forks, marking off the places. A pile of clean plates stood at each end; whilst in the middle was a big loaf, a knife sticking in it, with the handle in the air. Hutin got rid of his bottle and laid down his plate; then, after having taken his napkin from the bottom of a set of pigeonholes, the sole ornament on the walls, he heaved a sigh and sat down.

"And I'm fearfully hungry, too!" he murmured.

"It's always like that," replied Favier, who took his place on the left. "Nothing to eat when one is starving."

The table was rapidly filling. It contained twenty-two places. At first nothing was heard but a loud clattering of knives and forks, the gormandizing of big fellows with stomachs emptied by thirteen hours' daily work. Formerly the employees had an hour for meals, which enabled them to go outside to a café and take their coffee; and they would dispatch their dinner in twenty minutes, anxious to get into the street. But this stirred them up too much, they came back careless, indisposed for business; and the managers had decided that they should not go out, but pay an extra three sous for a cup of coffee, if they wanted it. So that now they were in no hurry, but prolonged the meal, not at all anxious to go back to work before time. A great many read some newspaper, between mouthfuls, the journal folded and placed against their bottle. Others, their first hunger satisfied, talked noisily, always returning to the eternal grievance of the bad food, the money they had earned, what they had done the previous Sunday, and what they were going to do on the next one.

"I say, what about your Robineau?" asked a salesman of Hutin.

The struggle between the salesmen of the silk department and their second-hand occupied all the counters. The question was discussed every evening at the Café Saint-Roch until midnight. Hutin, who was busy with his piece of beef, contented himself with replying:

"Well! he's come back, Robineau has." Then, suddenly getting angry, he resumed: "But confound it! they've given me a bit of a donkey, I believe! It's becoming disgusting, my word of honor!"

"You needn't grumble!" said Favier. "I was flat enough to ask for skate. It's putrid."

They were all speaking at once, some complaining, some joking. At a corner of the table, against the wall, Deloche was silently eating. He was afflicted with an enormous appetite, which he had never been able to satisfy, and not earning enough to afford any extras, he cut himself enormous chunks of bread, and swallowed up the least savory platefuls, with an air of greediness. They all laughed at him, crying: "Favier, pass your skate to Deloche. He likes it like that. And your meat, Hutin; Deloche wants it for his dessert."

The poor fellow shrugged his shoulders, and did not even reply. It wasn't his fault if he was dying of hunger. Besides, the others might abuse the food as much as they liked, they swallowed it up all the same.

But a low whistling stopped their talk; Mouret and Bourdoncle were in the corridor. For some time the complaints had become so frequent that the principals pretended to come and judge for themselves the quality of the food. They gave thirty sous a head per day to the chief cook, who had to pay everything, provisions, coal, gas, and staff, and they displayed a naïve astonishment when the food was not good. This very morning even, each department had deputed a spokesman. Mignot and Liénard had undertaken to speak for their comrades. And in the sudden silence, all ears were stretched out to catch the conversation going on in the next room, where Mouret and Bourdoncle had just entered. The latter declared the beef excellent; and Mignot, astounded by this quiet affirmation, was repeating, "But chew it, and see;" whilst Liénard, attacking the skate, was gently saying, "But it stinks, sir!" Mouret then launched into a cordial speech: he would do everything for his employees' welfare, he was their father, and would rather eat dry bread than see them badly fed.

"I promise you to look into the matter," said he in conclusion, raising his voice so that they should hear it from one end of the passage to the other.

The inquiry being finished, the noise of the knives and forks commenced once more. Hutin muttered, "Yes, reckon on that, and drink water! Ah, they're not stingy of soft words. Want some promises, there you are! And they continue to feed you on old boot-leather, and to chuck you out like dogs!"

The salesman who had already questioned him repeated: "You say that Robineau—"

But a noise of heavy crockery-ware drowned his voice. The men changed their plates themselves, and the piles at both ends were diminishing. When a kitchen-help brought in some large tin dishes, Hutin cried out: "Baked rice! this is a finisher!"

"Good for a penn'orth of gum!" said Favier, serving himself.

Some liked it, others thought it too sticky. There were some who remained quite silent, plunged in the fiction of their newspaper, not even knowing what they were eating. They were all mopping their foreheads, the narrow cellar-like apartment was full of a ruddy steam, whilst the shadows of the passers-by were continually passing in black bands over the untidy cloth.

"Pass Deloche the bread," cried out one of the wags.

Each one cut a piece, and then dug the knife into the loaf up to the handle; and the bread still went round.

"Who'll take my rice for a dessert?" asked Hutin.

When he had concluded his bargain with a short, thin young fellow, he attempted to sell his wine also; but no one would take it, it was known to be detestable.

"As I was telling you, Robineau is back," he continued, amid the cross-fire of laughter and conversation that was going on. "Oh! his affair is a grave one. Just fancy, he has been debauching the saleswomen! Yes, and he gets them cravats to make!"

"Silence!" exclaimed Favier. "They're just judging him."

And he pointed to Bouthemont, who was walking in the passage between Mouret and Bourdoncle, all three absorbed in an animated conversation, carried on in a low tone. The dining room of the managers and second-hands happened to be just opposite.

Therefore, when Bouthemont saw Mouret pass he got up, having finished, and related the affair, explaining the awkward position he was in. The other two listened, still refusing to sacrifice Robineau, a first-class salesman, who dated from Madame Hédouin's time. But when he came to the story of the neckties, Bourdoncle got angry. Was this fellow mad to interfere with the saleswomen and procure them extra work? The house paid dear enough for the women's time; if they worked on their own account at night they worked less during the day in the shop, that was certain; therefore it was a robbery, they were risking their health which did not belong to them. No, the night was made for sleep; they must all sleep, or they would be sent to the right-about!

"Getting rather warm!" remarked Hutin.

Every time the three men passed the dining room, the shop-men watched them, commenting on the slightest gestures. They had forgotten the baked rice, in which a cashier had just found a brace-button.

"I heard the word 'cravat,'" said Favier. "And you saw how Bourdoncle's face turned pale at once."

Mouret shared his partner's indignation. That a saleswoman should be reduced to work at night, seemed to him an attack on the organization of The Ladies' Paradise. Who was the stupid that couldn't earn enough in the business? But when Bouthemont named Denise he softened down, and invented excuses. Ah! yes, that poor little girl; she wasn't very sharp, and was greatly burdened, it was said. Bourdoncle interrupted him to declare they ought to send her off immediately. They would never do anything with such an ugly creature, he had always said so; and he seemed to be indulging a spiteful feeling. Mouret, perplexed, affected to laugh. Dear me! what a severe man! couldn't they forgive her for once? They could call in the culprit and give her a scolding. In short, Robineau was the most to blame, for he ought to have dissuaded her, he, an old hand, knowing the ways of the house.

"Well! there's the governor laughing now!" resumed Favier, astonished, as the group again passed the door.

"Ah, by Jove!" exclaimed Hutin, "if they persist in shoving Robineau on our shoulders, we'll make it lively for them!"

Bourdoncle looked straight at Mouret. Then he simply assumed a disdainful expression, to intimate that he saw how it was, and thought it idiotic. Bouthemont resumed his complaints; the salesmen threatened to leave, and there were some very good men amongst them. But what appeared to touch these gentlemen especially, was the rumor of Robineau's friendly relations with Gaujean; the latter, it was said, was urging the former to set up for himself in the neighborhood, offering him any amount of credit, to run in opposition to The Ladies' Paradise. There was a pause. Ah! Robineau was thinking of showing fight, was he! Mouret had become serious; he affected a certain scorn, avoided coming to a decision, treating it as a matter of no importance. They would see, they would speak to him. And he immediately commenced to joke with Bouthemont, whose father, arrived two days before from his little shop at Montpellier, had been nearly choked with rage and indignation on seeing the immense hall in which his son reigned. They were still laughing about the old man, who, recovering his Southern assurance, had immediately commenced to run everything down, pretending that the drapery business would soon go to the dogs.

"Here's Robineau," said Bouthemont. "I sent him to the stockroom to avoid any unpleasant occurrence. Excuse me if I insist, but things are in such an unpleasant state that something must be done."

Robineau, who had just come in, passed by the group with a bow, on his way to the table. Mouret simply repeated: "All right, we'll see about it."

And they separated. Hutin and Favier were still waiting for them, but on seeing they did not return, relieved their feelings. Was the governor coming down like this to every meal, to count the mouthfuls? A nice thing, if they could not even eat in peace! The truth was, they had just seen Robineau come in, and the governor's good-humor made them anxious for the result of the struggle they were engaged in. They lowered their voices, trying to find fresh subjects for grumbling.

"But I'm dying of hunger!" continued Hutin, aloud. "One is hungrier than ever on getting up from table!" And yet he had eaten two portions of dessert, his own and the one he had exchanged for his plate of rice. All at once he cried out: "Hang it, I'm going in for an extra! Victor, give me another dessert!"

The waiter was finishing serving the dessert. He then brought in the coffee, and those who took it gave him their three sous there and then. A few fellows had gone away, dawdling along the corridor, looking for a dark corner in which they could smoke a cigarette. The others remained at table before the heaps of greasy plates and dishes, rolling up the bread-crumbs into little bullets, going over the same old stories, in the odor of broken food, and the sweltering heat that was reddening their ears. The walls reeked with moisture, a slow asphyxia fell from the moldy ceiling. Standing against the wall was Deloche, stuffed with bread, digesting in silence, his eyes on the air-hole; his daily recreation, after lunch, was to watch the feet of the passers-by spinning along the street, a continual procession of living feet, big boots, elegant boots, and ladies' tiny boots, without head or body. On rainy days it was very dirty.

"What! Already?" exclaimed Hutin.

A bell rang at the end of the passage, they had to make way for the third lunch. The waiters came in with pails of warm water and big sponges to clean the American cloth. Gradually the rooms became empty, the salesmen returned to their departments, lingering on the stairs. In the kitchen, the head cook had resumed his place at the wicket, between the pans of skate, beef, and sauce, armed with his forks and spoons, ready to fill the plates anew with the rhythmical movement of a well-regulated clock. As Hutin and Favier slowly withdrew, they saw Denise coming down.

"Monsieur Robineau is back, mademoiselle," said the former with sneering politeness.

"He is still at table," added the other. "But if it's anything important you can go in."

Denise continued on her way without replying or turning

round; but when she passed the dining room of the managers and second-hands, she could not help just looking in, and saw that Robineau was really there. She resolved to try and speak to him in the afternoon, and continued her journey along the corridor to her dining room, which was at the other end.

The women took their meals apart, in two special rooms. Denise entered the first one. It was also an old cellar, transformed into a refectory; but it had been fitted up with more comfort. On the oval table, in the middle of the apartment, the fifteen places were further apart and the wine was in decanters, a dish of skate and a dish of beef with pungent sauce occupied the two ends of the table. Waiters in white aprons attended to the young ladies, and spared them the trouble of fetching their portions from the wicket. The management had thought that more decent.

"You went round, then?" asked Pauline, already seated and cutting herself some bread.

"Yes," replied Denise, blushing, "I was accompanying a customer."

But this was a falsehood. Clara nudged her neighbor. What was the matter with the "unkempt girl"? She was quite strange in her ways. One after the other she had received letters from her lover; then, she went running all over the shop like a madwoman, pretending to be going to the work-room, where she did not even make an appearance. There was something up, that was certain. Then Clara, eating her skate without disgust, with the indifference of a girl who had been used to nothing better than rancid bacon, spoke of a frightful drama, the account of which filled the newspapers.

"You've heard about that man cutting his mistress's throat with a razor, haven't you?"

"Well!" said a little quiet delicate-looking girl belonging to the under-linen department, "he found her with another fellow. Serve her right!"

But Pauline protested. What! just because one had ceased to love a man, he should be allowed to cut your throat? Ah! no, never! And stopping all at once, she turned round to the waiter, saying: "Pierre, I can't get through this beef. Just tell them to do me an extra, an omelet, nice and soft, if possible."

To pass away the time, she took out some chocolate which she began eating with her bread, for she always had her pockets full of sweetmeats.

"Certainly it isn't very amusing with such a fellow," resumed Clara. "And some people are fearfully jealous, you know! Only the other day there was a workman who pitched his wife into a well."

She kept her eyes on Denise, thinking she had guessed her trouble on seeing her turn pale. Evidently this little prude was afraid of being beaten by her lover, whom she no doubt deceived. It would be a lark if he came right into the shop after her, as she seemed to fear he would. But the conversation took another turn, one of the girls was giving a recipe for cleaning velvet. They then went on to speak of a piece at the Gaiety, in which some darling little children danced better than any grown-up persons. Pauline, saddened for a moment at the sight of her omelet, which was overdone, resumed her gaiety on finding it went down fairly well.

"Pass the wine," said she to Denise. "You should go in for an omelet."

"Oh! the beef is enough for me," replied the young girl, who, to avoid expense, confined herself to the food provided by the house, no matter how repugnant it might be.

When the waiter brought in the baked rice, the young ladies protested. They had refused it the previous week, and hoped it would not appear again. Denise, inattentive, worrying about Jean after Clara's stories, was the only one to eat it; all the others looked at her with an air of disgust. There was a great demand for extras, they gorged themselves with jam. This was a sort of elegance, they felt obliged to feed themselves with their own money.

"You know the gentlemen have complained," said the little delicate girl from the under-linen department, "and the management has promised—"

They interrupted her with a burst of laughter, and commenced to talk about the management. All the girls took coffee but Denise, who couldn't bear it, she said. And they lingered there before their cups, the young ladies from the under-linen department in woollen dresses, with a middle-class simplicity, the young ladies from the dress department in silk, their napkins tucked under their chins, in order not to stain their dresses, like ladies who might have come down to the servants' hall to dine with their chamber-maids. They had opened the glazed sash of the air-hole to change the stifling poisoned air; but they were obliged to close it at once, the cab-wheels seemed to be passing over the table.

"Hush!" exclaimed Pauline; "here's that old beast!"

It was Jouve, the inspector, who was rather fond of prowling about at meal times, when the young ladies were there. He was supposed, in fact, to look after their dining rooms. With a smiling face he would come in and walk round the tables; sometimes he would even indulge in a little gossip, and inquire if they had made a good lunch. But as he annoyed them and made them feel uncomfortable, they all hastened to get away. Although the bell had not rung, Clara was the first to disappear; the others followed her, so that soon only Denise and Pauline remained. The latter, after having drunk her coffee, was finishing her chocolate drops. All at once she got up, saying: "I'm going to send the messenger for some oranges. Are you coming?"

"Presently," replied Denise, who was nibbling at a crust, determined to wait till the last, so as to be able to see Robineau on going upstairs.

However, when she found herself alone with Jouve she felt uneasy, so she quitted the table; but as she was going towards the door he stopped her saying: "Mademoiselle Baudu—"

Standing before her, he smiled with a paternal air. His thick grey moustache and short cropped hair gave him a respectable military appearance; and he threw out his chest, on which was displayed the red ribbon of his decoration.

"What is it, Monsieur Jouve?" asked she, feeling reassured.

"I caught you again this morning talking upstairs behind the carpet department. You know it is not allowed, and if I reported you—she must be very fond of you, your friend Pauline." His moustache quivered, a flame lighted up his enormous nose. "What makes you so fond of each other, eh?"

Denise, without understanding, was again becoming seized with an uneasy feeling. He was getting too close, and was speaking right in her face.

"It's true we were talking, Monsieur Jouve," she stammered, "but there's no harm in talking a bit. You are very good to me, and I'm very much obliged to you."

"I ought not to be good," said he. "Justice, and nothing more, is my motto. But when it's a pretty girl—"

And he came closer still, and she felt really afraid. Pauline's words came back to her memory; she now remembered the stories going about, stories of girls terrified by old Jouve into buying his good-will. In the shop, as a rule, he confined himself to little familiarities, such as pinching the cheeks of the complaisant young ladies with his fat fingers, taking their hands in his and keeping them there as if he had forgotten them. This was very paternal, and he only gave way to his real nature outdoors, when they consented to accept a little refreshment at his place in the Rue des Moineaux.

"Leave me alone," murmured the young girl, drawing back.

"Come," said he, "you are not going to play the savage with me, who always treats you well. Be amiable, come and take a cup of tea and a slice of bread-and-butter with me this evening. You are very welcome."

She was struggling now. "No! no!"

The dining room was empty, the waiter had not come back. Jouve, listening for the sound of any footsteps, cast a rapid glance around him; and, very excited, losing control over himself, going beyond his fatherly familiarities, he tried to kiss her on the neck.

"What a spiteful, stupid little girl. When one has a head of hair like yours one should not be so stupid. Come round this evening, just for fun."

But she was very excited, shocked, and terrified at the approach of this burning face, of which she could feel the breath.

Suddenly she pushed him, so roughly that he staggered and nearly fell on to the table. Fortunately, a chair saved him; but in the shock, some wine left in a glass spurted on to his white neck-tie, and soaked his decoration. And he stood there, without wiping himself, choked with anger at such brutality. What! when he was expecting nothing, when he was not exerting his strength, and was yielding simply to his kindness of heart!

"Ah, you will be sorry for this, on my word of honor!"

Denise ran away. Just at that moment the bell rang; but troubled, still shuddering, she forgot Robineau, and went straight to her counter, not daring to go down again. As the sun fell on the frontage of the Place Gaillon of an afternoon, they were all stifling in the first-floor rooms, notwithstanding the grey linen blinds. A few customers came, put the young ladies into a very uncomfortable, warm state, and went away without buying anything. Everyone was yawning even under Madame Aurélie's big sleepy eyes. Towards three o'clock, Denise, seeing the first-hand falling off to sleep, quietly slipped off, and resumed her journey across the shop, with a busy air. To put the curious ones, who might be watching her, off the scent, she did not go straight to the silk department; pretending to want something in the lace department, she went up to Deloche, and asked him a question; then, on the ground floor, she passed through the printed cottons department, and was just going into the cravat one, when she stopped short, startled and surprised. Jean was before her,

"What! it's you?" she murmured, quite pale.

He had on his working blouse, and was bare-headed, with his hair in disorder, the curls falling over his girlish face. Standing before a show-case of narrow black neckties, he appeared to be thinking deeply.

"What are you doing here?" resumed Denise.

"What do you think?" replied he. "I was waiting for you. You won't let me come. So I came in, but haven't said anything to anybody. You may feel quite safe. Pretend not to know me, if you like."

Some salesmen were already looking at them with astonishment. Jean lowered his voice. "She wanted to come with me you know. Yes, she is close by, opposite the fountain. Give me the fifteen francs quick, or we are done for as sure as the sun is shining on us!"

Denise lost her head. The lookers-on were grinning, listening to this adventure. And as there was a staircase behind the cravat department leading to the lower floor, she pushed her brother along, and quickly led him below. Downstairs he continued his story, embarrassed, inventing his facts, fearing not to be believed.

"The money is not for her. She is too respectable for that. And as for her husband, he does not care a straw for fifteen francs. Not for a million would he allow his wife. A glue manufacturer, I tell you. People very well off indeed. No, it's for a low fellow, one of her friends, who has seen us together; and if I don't give him this money this evening—"

"Be quiet," murmured Denise. "Presently, do get along."

They were now in the parcels office. The dead season had thrown the vast floor into a sort of torpor, in the pale light from the air-holes. It was cold as well, a silence fell from the ceiling. However, a porter was collecting from one of the compartments the few packets for the neighborhood of the Madeleine; and, on the large sorting-table, was seated Campion, the chief clerk, his legs dangling, and his eyes wandering about.

Jean began again: "The husband, who has a big knife—"

"Get along!" repeated Denise, still pushing him forward.

They followed one of the narrow corridors, where the gas was kept continually burning. To the right and the left in the dark vaults the reserve goods threw out their shadows behind the gratings. At last she stopped opposite one of these. Nobody was likely to pass that way; but it was not allowed, and she shuddered.

"If this rascal says anything," resumed Jean, "the husband, who has a big knife—"

"Where do you expect I can find fifteen francs?" exclaimed Denise in despair. "Can't you be more careful? You're always getting into some stupid scrape!"

He struck his chest. Amidst all his romantic inventions, he had almost forgotten the exact truth. He dramatized his money wants, but there was always some immediate necessity behind this display. "By all that's sacred, it's really true this time. I was holding her like this, and she was kissing me."

She stopped him again, and lost her temper, feeling on thorns, completely at a loss. "I don't want to know. Keep your wicked conduct to yourself. It's too bad, you ought to know better! You're always tormenting me. I'm killing myself to keep you in money. Yes, I have to stay up all night at work. Not only that, you are taking the bread out of your little brother's mouth."

Jean stood there with his mouth wide open, and all the color left his face. What! it was not right? And he could not understand, he had always treated his sister like a comrade, he thought it quite a natural thing to open his heart to her. But what choked him above all, was to learn she stopped up all night. The idea that he was killing her, and taking Pépé's share as well, affected him so much that he began to cry.

"You're right; I'm a scamp," exclaimed he. "But it isn't wicked, really, far from it, and that's why one always does it! This woman, Denise, is twenty, and thought it such fun, because I'm only seventeen. Really now! I am quite furious with myself! I could slap my face!" He had taken her hands, and was kissing them and inundating them with tears. "Give me the fifteen francs, and this shall be the last time. I swear to you. Or rather—no!—don't give me anything. I prefer to die. If the husband murders me it will be a good riddance for you." And as she was crying as well, he was stricken with remorse. "I say that, but of course I'm not sure. Perhaps he doesn't want to kill anyone. We'll manage. I promise you that, darling. Good-bye, I'm off."

But a sound of footsteps at the end of the corridor frightened them. She quickly drew him close to the grating, in a dark corner. For an instant they heard nothing but the hissing of a gas-burner near them. Then the footsteps drew nearer; and, on stretching out her neck, she recognized Jouve, the inspector, who had just entered the corridor, with his stiff military walk.

Was he there by chance, or had someone at the door warned him of Jean's presence? She was seized with such a fright that she knew not what to do; and she pushed Jean out of the dark spot where they were concealed, and drove him before her, stammering out: "Be off! Be off!"

Both galloped along, hearing Jouve behind them, for he also had began to run. They crossed the parcels office again, and arrived at the foot of the stairs leading out into the Rue de la Michodière.

"Be off!" repeated Denise, "be off! If I can, I'll send you the fifteen francs all the same."

Jean, bewildered, scampered away. The inspector, who came up panting, out of breath, could only distinguish a corner of his white blouse, and his locks of fair hair flying in the wind. He stood a moment to get his breath, and resume his correct appearance. He had on a brand-new white necktie, the large bow of which shone like a snow-flake.

"Well! this is nice behavior, mademoiselle!" said he, his lips trembling. "Yes, it's nice, very nice! If you think I'm going to stand this sort of thing in the basement, you're mistaken."

And he pursued her with this whilst she was returning to the shop, overcome with emotion, unable to find a word of defense. She was sorry now she had run away. Why hadn't she explained the matter, and brought her brother forward? They would now go and imagine all sorts of villainies, and say what she might, they would not believe her. Once more she forgot Robineau, and went straight to her counter. Jouve immediately went to the manager's office to report the matter. But the messenger told him Monsieur Mouret was with Monsieur Bourdoncle and Monsieur Robineau; they had been talking together for the last quarter of an hour. In fact, the door was half-open, and he could hear Mouret gaily asking Robineau if he had had a pleasant holiday; there was not the least question of a dismissal—on the contrary, the conversation fell on certain things to be done in the department.

"Do you want anything, Monsieur Jouve?" exclaimed Mouret. "Come in."

But a sudden instinct warned the inspector. As Bourdoncle had come out, he preferred to relate the affair to him. They slowly passed through the shawl department, walking side by side, the one leaning over and talking in a low tone, the other listening, not a sign on his severe face betraying his impressions.

"All right," said the latter at last.

And as they had arrived close to the dress department, he went in. Just at that moment Madame Aurélie was scolding Denise. Where had she come from, again? This time she couldn't say she had been to the work-room. Really, these continual absences could not be tolerated any longer.

"Madame Aurélie!" cried Bourdoncle.

He had decided on a bold stroke, not wishing to consult Mouret, for fear of some weakness. The first-hand came up, and the story was once more related in a low voice. They were all waiting in the expectation of some catastrophe. At last, Madame Aurélie turned round with a solemn air.

"Mademoiselle Baudu!" And her puffy emperor's mask assumed the immobility of the all-powerful: "Go and be paid!"

The terrible phrase sounded very loud in the empty department. Denise stood there pale as a ghost, without saying a word. At last she was able to ask in broken sentences:

"Me! me! What for? What have I done?"

Bourdoncle replied, harshly, that she knew very well, that she had better not provoke any explanation; and he spoke of the cravats, and said that it would be a fine thing if all the young ladies received men down in the basement.

"But it was my brother!" cried she with the grievous anger of an outraged virgin.

Marguerite and Clara commenced to laugh. Madame Frédéric, usually so discreet, shook her head with an incredulous air. Always her brother! Really it was very stupid! Denise looked round at all of them: Bourdoncle, who had taken a dislike to her the first day; Jouve, who had stopped to serve as a witness, and from whom she expected no justice; then these girls whom she had not been able to soften by nine months of smiling courage, who were happy, in fact, to turn her out of doors. What was the good of struggling? What was the use of trying to impose herself on them when no one liked her? And she went away without a word, not even casting a last look towards this room where she had so long struggled. But as soon as she was alone, before the hall staircase, a deeper sense of suffering filled her grieved heart. No one liked her, and the sudden thought of Mouret had just deprived her of all idea of resignation. No! no! she could not accept such a dismissal. Perhaps he would believe this villainous story, this rendezvous with a man down in the cellars. At the thought, a feeling of shame tortured her, an anguish with which she had never before been afflicted. She wanted to go and see him, to explain the matter to him, simply to let him know the truth; for she was quite ready to go away as soon as he knew this. And her old fear, the shiver which chilled her when in his presence, suddenly developed into an ardent desire to see him, not to leave the house without telling him she had never belonged to another.

It was nearly five o'clock, and the shop was waking up into life again in the cool evening air. She quickly started off for Mouret's office. But when she arrived at the door, a hopeless melancholy feeling again took possession of her. Her tongue refused its office, the intolerable burden of existence again fell on her shoulders. He would not believe her, he would laugh like the others, she thought; and this idea made her almost faint away. All was over, she would be better alone, out of the way, dead! And, without informing Pauline or Deloche, she went at once and took her money.

"You have, mademoiselle," said the clerk, "twenty-two days; that makes eighteen francs and fourteen sous; to which must be added seven francs for commission. That's right, isn't it?"

"Yes, sir. Thanks."

And Denise was going away with her money, when she at last met Robineau. He had already heard of her dismissal, and promised to find the necktie-dealer. In a lower tone he tried to console her, but lost his temper: what an existence, to be at the continual mercy of a whim! to be thrown out at an hour's notice, without even being able to claim a full month's salary. Denise went up to inform Madame Cabin, saying that she would try and send for her box during the evening. It was just striking five when she found herself on the pavement of the Place Gaillon, bewildered, in the midst of the crowd of people and cabs.

The same evening when Robineau got home he received a letter from the management informing him, in a few lines, that for certain reasons relating to the internal arrangements they were obliged to deprive themselves of his services. He had been in the house seven years, and it was only that afternoon that he was talking to the principals; this was a heavy blow for him. Hutin and Favier were crowing in the silk department, as loudly as Clara and Marguerite in the dress one. A jolly good riddance! Such clean sweeps make room for the others! Deloche and Pauline were the only ones to regret Denise's departure, exchanging, in the rush of business, bitter words of regret at losing her, so kind, so well behaved.

"Ah," said the young man, "if ever she succeeds anywhere else, I should like to see her come back here, and trample on the others; a lot of good-for-nothing creatures!"

It was Bourdoncle who in this affair had to bear the brunt of Mouret's anger. When the latter heard of Denise's dismissal, he was exceedingly annoyed. As a rule he never interfered with the staff; but this time he affected to see an encroachment on his power, an attempt to over-ride his authority. Was he no longer master in the place, that they dared to give orders? Everything must pass through his hands, absolutely everything; and he would immediately crush anyone who should resist. Then, after making personal inquiries, all the while in a nervous torment which he could not conceal, he lost his temper again. This poor girl was not lying; it was really her brother. Campion had fully recognized him. Why was she sent away, then? He even spoke of taking her back.

However, Bourdoncle, strong in his passive resistance, bent before the storm. He watched Mouret, and one day when he saw him a little calmer, ventured to say in a meaning voice: "It's better for everybody that she's gone."

Mouret stood there looking very awkward, the blood rushing to his face. "Well!" replied he, laughing, "perhaps you're right. Let's go and take a turn down stairs. Things are looking better, we took nearly a hundred thousand francs yesterday"

CHAPTER VII.

For a moment Denise stood bewildered on the pavement, in the sun which still shone fiercely at five o'clock. The July heat warmed the gutters, Paris was blazing with the chalky whiteness peculiar to it in summer-time, and which produced quite a blinding glare. The catastrophe had happened so suddenly, they had turned her out so roughly, that she stood there, turning her money over in her pocket in a mechanical way, asking herself where she was to go, and what she was to do.

A long line of cabs prevented her quitting the pavement near The Ladies' Paradise. When she at last risked herself amongst the wheels she crossed over the Place Gaillon, as if she intended to go into the Rue Louis-le-Grand; then she altered her mind, and walked towards the Rue Saint-Roch. But still she had no plan, for she stopped at the corner of the Rue Neuve-des-Petits-Champs, and finally followed it, after looking around her with an undecided air. Arrived at the Passage Choiseul, she passed through, and found herself in the Rue Monsigny, without knowing how, and ultimately came into the Rue Neuve-Saint-Augustin again. Her head was filled with a fearful buzzing sensation, she thought of her box on seeing a commissionaire; but where was she to have it taken to, and why all this trouble, when an hour ago she had a bed to go to?

Then her eyes fixed on the houses, she began to examine the windows. There were any number of bills, "Apartments to Let." She saw them confusedly, repeatedly seized by the inward emotion which was agitating her whole being. Was it possible? Left alone so suddenly, lost in this immense city in which she was a stranger, without support, without resources. She must eat and sleep, however. The streets succeeded one another, the Rue des Moulins, the Rue Sainte-Anne. She wandered about the neighborhood, frequently retracing her steps, always brought back to the only spot she knew really well. Suddenly she was astonished, she was again standing before The Ladies' Paradise; and to escape this obsession she plunged into the Rue de la Michodière. Fortunately Baudu was not at his door. The Old Elbeuf appeared to be dead, behind its murky windows. She would never have dared to show herself at her uncle's, for he affected not to recognize her any more, and she did not wish to become a burden to him, in the misfortune he had predicted for her. But, on the other side of the street, a yellow bill attracted her attention. "Furnished room to let." It was the first that did not frighten her, so poor did the house appear. She soon recognized it, with its two low storeys, and rusty-colored front, crushed between The Ladies' Paradise and the old Hôtel Duvillard. On the threshold of the umbrella shop, old Bourras, hairy and bearded like a prophet, and with his glasses on his nose, stood studying the ivory handle of a walking-stick. Hiring the whole house, he under-let the two upper floors furnished, to lighten the rent.

"You have a room, sir?" asked Denise, obeying an instinctive impulse.

He raised his great bushy eyes, surprised to see her, for he knew all the young persons at The Ladies' Paradise. And, after observing her clean dress and respectable appearance, he replied: "It won't suit you."

"How much is it, then?" replied Denise.

"Fifteen francs a month."

She asked to see it. On arriving in the narrow shop, and seeing that he was still eyeing her with an astonished air, she told him of her departure from the shop and of her wish not to trouble her uncle. The old man then went and fetched a key hanging on a board in the back-shop, a small dark room, where he did his cooking and had his bed; beyond that, behind a dirty window, could be seen a back-yard about six feet square.

"I'll walk in front to prevent you falling," said Bourras, entering the damp corridor which ran along the shop.

He stumbled against the lower stair, and commenced the ascent, reiterating his warnings to be careful. Look out! the rail was close against the wall, there was a hole at the corner, sometimes the lodgers left their dust-boxes there. Denise, in complete obscurity, could distinguish nothing, only feeling the chilliness of the old damp plaster. On the first floor, however, a small window looking into the yard enabled her to see vaguely, as at the bottom of a piece of sleeping water, the rotten staircase, the walls black with dirt, the cracked and discolored doors.

"If only one of these rooms were vacant," resumed Bourras. "You would be very comfortable there. But they are always occupied by ladies."

On the second floor the light increased, showing up with a raw paleness the distress of the house. A journeyman-baker occupied the first room, and it was the other, the further one, that was vacant. When Bourras had opened the door he was obliged to stay on the landing in order that Denise might enter with ease. The bed placed in the corner nearest the door, left just room enough for one person to pass. At the other end there was a small walnut-wood chest of drawers, a deal table stained black, and two chairs. The lodgers who did any cooking were obliged to kneel before the fire-place, where there was an earthenware stove.

"You know," said the old man, "it is not luxurious, but the view from the window is gay. You can see the people passing in the street." And, as Denise was looking with surprise at the ceiling just above the bed, where a chance lady-lodger had written her name—Ernestine—by drawing the flame of the candle over it, he added with a good-natured smile; "If I did a lot of repairs, I should never make both ends meet. There you are; it's all I have to offer."

"I shall be very well here," declared the young girl.

She paid a month in advance, asked for the linen—a pair of sheets and two towels, and made her bed without delay, happy, relieved to know where she was going to sleep that night. An hour after she had sent a commissionaire to fetch her box, and was quite at home.

During the first two months she had a terribly hard time of it. Being unable to pay for Pépé's board, she had taken him away, and slept him on an old sofa lent by Bourras. She could not do with less than thirty sous a day, including the rent, even by consenting to live on dry bread herself, in order to procure a bit of meat for the little one. During the first fortnight she got on pretty well, having begun her housekeeping with about ten francs; besides she had been fortunate enough to find the cravat-dealer, who paid her her eighteen francs six sous. But after that she became completely destitute. It was in vain she applied to the various shops, at La Place Clichy, the Bon Marché, the Louvre: the dead season had stopped business everywhere, they told her to apply again in the autumn, more than five thousand employees, dismissed like her, were wandering about Paris in want of places. She then tried to obtain a little work elsewhere; but in her ignorance of Paris she did not know where to apply, often accepting most ungrateful tasks, and sometimes even not getting her money. Certain evenings she gave Pépé his dinner alone, a plate of soup, telling him she had dined out; and she would go to bed, her head in a whirl, nourished by the fever which was burning her hands. When Jean dropped suddenly into the midst of this poverty, he called himself a scoundrel with such a despairing violence that she was obliged to tell some falsehood to reassure him; and often found means of slipping a two-franc piece into his hand, to prove that she still had money. She never wept before the children. On Sundays, when she would cook a piece of veal in the stove, on her knees before the fire, the narrow room re-echoed with the gaiety of children, careless about existence. Then, when Jean had returned to his master's and Pépé was sleeping, she spent a frightful night, in anguish about the coming day.

Other fears kept her awake. The two ladies on the first floor received visitors up to a late hour; and sometimes a visitor mistook the floor and came banging at Denise's door. Bourras having quietly told her not to answer, she buried her face under her pillow to escape hearing their oaths. Then, her neighbor, the baker, had shown a disposition to annoy her: he never came home till the morning, and would lay in wait for her, as she went to fetch her water; he even made holes in the wall, to watch her washing herself, so that she was obliged to hang her clothes against the wall. But she suffered still more from the annoyances of the street, the continual persecution of the passers-by. She could not go downstairs to buy a candle, in these streets swarming with the debauchees of the old quarters, without feeling a warm breath behind her, and hearing crude, insulting remarks; and the men pursued her to the very end of the dark passage, encouraged by the sordid appearance of the house. Why had she no lover? It astonished people, and seemed ridiculous. She would certainly have to yield one day. She herself could not have explained why she resisted, menaced as she was by hunger, and perturbed by the desires with which the air around her was warm.

One evening Denise had not even any bread for Pépé's soup, when a gentleman, wearing a decoration, commenced to follow her. On arriving opposite the passage he became brutal, and it was with a disgusted, shocked feeling that she banged the door in his face. Then, upstairs, she sat down, her hands trembling. The little one was sleeping. What should she say if he woke up and asked for bread? And yet she had only to consent and her misery would be over, she could have money, dresses, and a fine room. It was very simple, everyone came to that, it was said; for a woman alone in Paris could not live by her labor. But her whole being rose up in protestation, without indignation against the others, simply averse to the disgrace of the thing. She considered life a matter of logic, good conduct, and courage.

Denise frequently questioned herself in this way. An old love story floated in her memory, the sailor's betrothed whom her love guarded from all perils. At Valognes she had often hummed over this sentimental ballad, gazing on the deserted street. Had she also a tender affection in her heart that she was so brave? She still thought of Hutin, full of uneasiness. Morning and evening she saw him pass under her window. Now that he was second-hand he walked by himself, amid the respect of the simple salesmen. He never raised his head, she thought she suffered from his vanity, and watched him pass without any fear of being discovered. And as soon as she saw Mouret, who also passed every day, she began to tremble, and, quickly concealed herself, her bosom heaving. He had no need to know where she was lodging. Then she felt ashamed of the house, and suffered at the idea of what he thought of her, although perhaps they would never meet again.

Denise still lived amidst the agitation caused by The Ladies' Paradise. A simple wall separated her room from her old department; and, from early morning, she went over her day's work, feeling the arrival of the crowd, the increased bustle of business. The slightest noise shook the old house hanging on the flank of the colossus; she felt the gigantic pulse beating. Besides, she could not avoid certain meetings. Twice she had found herself face to face with Pauline, who had offered her services, grieved to see her so unfortunate; and she had even been obliged to tell a falsehood to avoid receiving her friend or paying her a visit, one Sunday, at Baugé's. But it was more difficult still to defend herself against Deloche's desperate affection; he watched her, aware of all her troubles, waited for her in the doorways. One day he wanted to lend her thirty francs, a brother's savings, he said, with a blush. And these meetings made her regret the shop, continually occupying her with the life they led inside, as if she had not quitted it.

No one ever called upon Denise. One afternoon she was surprised by a knock. It was Colomban. She received him standing. He, looking very awkward, stammered at first, asked how she was getting on, and spoke of The Old Elbeuf. Perhaps it was Uncle Baudu who had sent him, regretting his rigor; for he continued to pass his niece without taking any notice of her, although quite aware of her miserable position. But when she plainly questioned her visitor, he appeared more embarrassed than ever. No, no, it was not the governor who had sent him; and he finished by naming Clara—he simply wanted to talk about Clara. Little by little he became bolder, and asked Denise's advice, supposing that she could be useful to him with her old friend. It was in vain that she tried to dishearten him, by reproaching him with the pain he was causing Geneviève, all for this heartless girl. He came up another day, and got into the habit of coming to see her. This sufficed for his timid passion; he continually commenced the same conversation, unable to resist, trembling with joy to be with a girl who had approached Clara. And this caused Denise to live more than ever at The Ladies' Paradise.

It was towards the end of September that the young girl experienced the blackest misery. Pépé had fallen ill, having caught a severe cold. He ought to have been nourished with good broth, and she had not even a piece of bread. One evening, completely conquered, she was sobbing, in one of those somber straits which drive women on to the streets, or into the Seine, when old Bourras gently knocked at the door. He brought a loaf, and a milk-can full of broth.

"There! there's something for the youngster," said he in his abrupt way. "Don't cry like that; it annoys my lodgers." And as she thanked him in a fresh outburst of tears, he resumed: "Do keep quiet! Tomorrow come and see me. I've some work for you."

Bourras, since the terrible blow dealt him by The Ladies' Paradise by their opening an umbrella department, had ceased to employ any workwomen. He did everything himself to save expenses—the cleaning, mending, and sewing. His trade was also diminishing, so that he was sometimes without work. And he was obliged to invent something to do the next day, when he installed Denise in a corner of his shop. He felt that he could not let anyone die of hunger in his house.

"You'll have two francs a day," said he. "When you find something better, you can leave me."

She was afraid of him, and did the work so quickly that he hardly knew what else to give her to do. He had given her some silk to stitch, some lace to repair. During the first few days she did not dare raise her head, uncomfortable to know he was close to her, with his lion-like mane, hooked nose, and piercing eyes, under his thick bushy eyebrows. His voice was harsh, his gestures extravagant, and the mothers of the neighborhood often frightened their youngsters by threatening to send for him, as they would for a policeman. However, the boys never passed his door without calling out some insulting words, which he did not even seem to hear. All his maniacal anger was directed against the scoundrels who dishonored his trade by selling cheap trashy articles, which dogs would not consent to use.

Denise trembled whenever he burst out thus: "Art is done for, I tell you! There's not a single respectable handle made now. They make sticks, but as for handles, it's all up! Bring me a proper handle, and I'll give you twenty francs!"

He had a real artist's pride; not a workman in Paris was capable of turning out a handle like his, light and strong. He carved the knobs especially with charming ingenuity, continually inventing fresh designs, flowers, fruit, animals, and heads, subjects conceived and executed in a free and life-like style. A little pocket-knife sufficed, and he spent whole days, spectacles on nose, chipping bits of boxwood and ebony.

"A pack of ignorant beggars," said he, "who are satisfied with sticking a certain quantity of silk on so much whalebone! They buy their handles by the gross, handles ready-made. And they sell just what they like! I tell you, art is done for!"

Denise began to take courage. He had insisted on having Pépé down in the shop to play, for he was wonderfully fond of children. When the little one was crawling about on all fours, neither of them had room to move, she in her corner doing the mending, he near the window, carving with his little pocket-knife. Every day now brought on the same work and the same conversation. Whilst working, he continually pitched into The Ladies' Paradise; never tired of explaining how affairs stood. He had occupied his house since 1845, and had a thirty years' lease, at a rent of eighteen hundred francs a year; and, as he made a thousand francs out of his four furnished rooms, he only paid eight hundred for the shop. It was a mere trifle, he had no expenses, and could thus hold out for a long time still. To hear him, there was no doubt about his triumph; he would certainly swallow up the monster. Suddenly he would interrupt himself.

"Have they got any dog's heads like that?"

And he would blink his eyes behind his glasses, to judge the dog's head he was carving, with its lip turned up and fangs out, in a life-like growl. Pépé, delighted with the dog, would get up, placing his two little arms on the old man's knee.

"As long as I make both ends meet I don't care a hang about the rest," the latter would resume, delicately shaping the dog's tongue with the point of his knife. "The scoundrels have taken away my profits; but if I'm making nothing I'm not losing anything yet, or at least but very little. And, you see, I'm ready to sacrifice everything rather than yield."

He would brandish his knife, and his white hair would blow about in a storm of anger.

"But," Denise would mildly observe, without raising her eyes from her needle, "if they made you a reasonable offer, it would be wiser to accept."

Then his ferocious obstinacy would burst forth. "Never! If my head were under the knife I would say no, by heavens! I've another ten years' lease, and they shall not have the house before then, even if I should have to die of hunger within the four bare walls. Twice already have they tried to get over me. They offered me twelve thousand francs for my good-will, and eighteen thousand francs for the last ten years of my lease; in all thirty thousand. Not for fifty thousand even! I have them in my power, and intend to see them licking the dust before me!"

"Thirty thousand francs! it's a good sum," Denise would resume. "You could go and establish yourself elsewhere. And suppose they were to buy the house?"

Bourras, putting the finishing touches to his dog's tongue, would appear absorbed for a moment, an infantine laugh pervading his venerable prophet's face. Then he would continue: "The house, no fear! They spoke of buying it last year, and offered eighty thousand francs, twice as much as it's worth. But the landlord, a retired fruiterer, as big a scoundrel as they, wanted to make them shell out more. But not only that, they are suspicious about me; they know I'm not so likely to give way. No! no! here I am, and here I intend to stay. The emperor with all his cannon could not turn me out."

Denise never dared say any more, she would go on with her work, whilst the old man continued to break out in short sentences, between two cuts with his knife, muttering something to the effect that the game had hardly commenced, later on they would see wonderful things, he had certain plans which would sweep away their umbrella counter; and, in his obstinacy, there appeared a personal revolt of the small manufacturer against the threatening invasion of the great shops. Pépé, however, would at last climb on his knees, and impatiently stretch out his hand towards the dog's head.

"Give it me, sir."

"Presently, my child," the old man would reply in a voice that suddenly became tender. "He hasn't any eyes; we must make his eyes now." And whilst carving the eye he would continue talking to Denise. "Do you hear them? Isn't there a roar next door? That's what exasperates me more than anything, my word of honor! to have them always on my back with their infernal locomotive-like noise."

It made his little table tremble, he asserted. The whole shop was shaken, and he would spend the entire afternoon without a customer, in the trepidation of the crowd which overflowed The Ladies' Paradise. It was from morning to night a subject for eternal grumbling. Another good day's work, they were knocking against the wall, the silk department must have cleared ten thousand francs; or else he made merry over a showery day which had killed the receipts. And the slightest rumors, the most unimportant noises, furnished him with subjects of endless comment.

"Ah! someone has slipped down! Ah, if they could only all fall and break their backs! That, my dear, is a dispute between some ladies. So much the better! So much the better! Do you hear the parcels falling on to the lower floor? It's disgusting!"

It did not do for Denise to discuss his explanations, for he retorted bitterly by reminding her of the shameful way they had dismissed her. She was obliged to relate for the hundredth time her life in the dress department, the hardships she had endured at first, the small unhealthy bedrooms, the bad food, and the continual struggle between the salesmen; and they were thus talking about the shop from morning to night, absorbing it hourly in the very air they breathed.

"Give it me, sir," Pépé would repeat, with eager outstretched hands.

The dog's head finished, Bourras would hold it at a distance, then examine it closely with childish glee. "Take care, it will bite you! There, go and play, and don't break it, if you can help it." Then resuming his fixed idea, he would shake his fist at the wall. "You may do all you can to knock the house down. You sha'n't have it, even if you invade the whole neighborhood."

Denise had now her daily bread assured her, and she was extremely grateful to the old umbrella-dealer, whose good heart she felt beneath his strange violent ways. She had a strong desire, however, to find some work elsewhere, for she often saw him inventing some trifle for her to do; she fully understood that he did not require a workwoman in the present slack state of his business, and that he was employing her out of pure charity. Six months had passed thus, and the dull winter season had again returned. She was despairing of finding a situation before March, when, one evening in January, Deloche, who was watching for her in a doorway, gave her a bit of advice. Why did she not go and see Robineau; perhaps he might want someone?

In September, Robineau had decided to buy Vinçard's silk business, trembling all the time lest he should compromise his wife's sixty thousand francs. He had paid forty thousand for the good-will and stock, and was starting with the remaining twenty thousand. It was not much, but he had Gaujean behind him to back him up with any amount of credit. Since his disagreement with The Ladies' Paradise, the latter had been longing to stir up a system of competition against the colossus; and he thought victory certain, by creating special shops in the neighborhood, where the public could find a large and varied choice of articles. The rich Lyons manufacturers, such as Dumonteil, were the only ones who could accept the big shops' terms, satisfied to keep their looms going with them, looking for their profits by selling to less important houses. But Gaujean was far from having the solidity and staying power possessed by Dumonteil. For a long time a simple commission agent, it was only during the last five or six years that he had had looms of his own, and he still had a lot of work done by other makers, furnishing them with the raw material and paying them by the yard. It was precisely this system which, increasing his manufacturing expenses, had prevented him competing with Dumonteil for the supply of the Paris Paradise. This had filled him with rancor; he saw in Robineau the instrument of a decisive battle to be declared against these drapery bazaars which he accused of ruining the French manufacturers.

When Denise called she found Madame Robineau alone. Daughter of an overseer in the Department of Highways, entirely ignorant of business matters, she still retained the charming awkwardness of a girl educated in a Blois convent. She was dark, very pretty, with a gentle, cheerful manner, which gave her a great charm. She adored her husband, living solely by his love. As Denise was about to leave her name Robineau came in, and engaged her at once, one of his two saleswomen having left the previous day to go to The Ladies' Paradise.

"They don't leave us a single good hand," said he. "However, with you I shall feel quite easy, for you are like me, you can't be very fond of them. Come tomorrow."

In the evening Denise hardly knew how to announce her departure to Bourras. In fact, he called her an ungrateful girl, and lost his temper. Then when, with tears in her eyes, she tried to defend herself by intimating that she could see through his charitable conduct, he softened down, said that he had plenty of work, that she was leaving him just as he was about to bring out an umbrella of his invention.

"And Pépé?" asked he.

This was Denise's great trouble; she dared not take him back to Madame Gras, and could not leave him alone in the bedroom, shut up from morning to night.

"Very good, I'll keep him," said the old man; "he'll be all right in my shop. We'll do the cooking together." Then, as she refused, fearing it might inconvenience him, he thundered out: "Great heavens! have you no confidence in me? I sha'n't eat your child!"

Denise was much happier at Robineau's. He only paid her sixty francs a month, with her food, without giving her any commission on the sales, just the same as in the old-fashioned houses. But she was treated with great kindness, especially by Madame Robineau, always smiling at her counter. He, nervous, worried, was sometimes rather abrupt. At the expiration of the first month, Denise was quite one of the family, like the other saleswoman, a silent, consumptive, little body. The Robineaus were not at all particular before them, talking of the business at table in the back shop, which looked on to a large yard. And it was there they decided one evening on starting the campaign against The Ladies' Paradise. Gaujean had come to dinner. After the usual roast leg of mutton, he had broached the subject in his Lyons voice, thickened by the Rhône fogs.

"It's getting unbearable," said he. "They go to Dumonteil, purchase the sole right in a design, and take three hundred pieces straight off, insisting on a reduction of ten sous a yard; and, as they pay ready money, they enjoy moreover the profit of eighteen per cent, discount. Very often Dumonteil barely makes four sous a yard out of it. He works to keep his looms going, for a loom that stands still is a dead loss. Under these circumstances how can you expect that we, with our limited plant, and especially with our makers, can keep up the struggle?"

Robineau, pensive, forgot his dinner. "Three hundred pieces!" he murmured. "I tremble when I take a dozen, and at ninety days. They can mark up a franc or two francs cheaper than us. I have calculated there is a reduction of at least fifteen per cent, on their catalogued articles, when compared with our prices. That's what kills the small houses."

He was in a period of discouragement. His wife, full of anxiety, was looking at him with a tender air. She understood very little about the business, all these figures confused her; she could not understand why people took such trouble, when it was so easy to be gay and love one another. However, it sufficed that her husband wished to conquer, and she became as impassioned as he himself, and would have stood to her counter till death.

"But why don't all the manufacturers come to an understanding together?" resumed Robineau, violently. "They could then lay down the law, instead of submitting to it."

Gaujean, who had asked for another slice of mutton, was slowly masticating. "Ah! why, why? The looms must be kept going, I tell you. When one has weavers everywhere, in the neighborhood of Lyons, in the Gard, in the Isere, they can't stand still a day without an enormous loss. Then we who sometimes employ makers having ten or fifteen looms are better able to control the output, as far as regards the stock, whilst the big manufacturers are obliged to have continual outlets, the quickest and largest possible, so that they are on their knees before the big shops. I know three or four who out-bid each other, and who would sooner work at a loss than not obtain the orders. But they make up for it with the small houses like yours. Yes, if they exist through them, they make their profit out of you. Heaven knows how the crisis will end!"

"It's odious!" exclaimed Robineau, relieved by this cry of anger.

Denise was quietly listening. She was secretly for the big shops, with her instinctive love of logic and life.

They had relapsed into silence, and were eating some potted French beans; at last she ventured to say in a cheerful tone: "The public does not complain."

Madame Robineau could not suppress a little laugh, which annoyed her husband and Gaujean. No doubt the customer was satisfied, for, in the end, it was the customer who profited by the fall in prices. But everybody must live; where would they be if, under the pretext of the general welfare, the consumer was fattened at the expense of the producer? And then commenced a long discussion. Denise affected to be joking, all the while producing solid arguments. All the middle-men disappeared, the manufacturing agents, representatives, commission agents, and this greatly contributed to cheapen the articles; besides, the manufacturers could no longer live without the big shops, for as soon as one of them lost their custom, failure became a certainty; in short, it was a natural commercial evolution. It would be impossible to prevent things going on as they ought to, when everybody was working for that, whether they liked it or not.

"So you are for those who turned you out into the street?" asked Gaujean.

Denise became very red. She herself was surprised at the vivacity of her defense. What had she at heart, that such a flame should have invaded her bosom?

"Dear me, no!" replied she. "Perhaps I'm wrong, for you are more competent to judge than I. I simply express my opinion. The prices, instead of being settled as formerly by fifty houses, are now fixed by four or five, which have lowered them, thanks to the power of their capital, and the strength of their immense business. So much the better for the public, that's all!"

Robineau was not angry, but had become grave, keeping his eyes fixed on the tablecloth. He had often felt this breath of the new style of business, this evolution of which the young girl spoke; and he would ask himself in his clear, quiet moments, why he should wish to resist such a powerful current, which must carry everything before it. Madame Robineau herself, on seeing her husband deep in thought, glanced with approval at Denise, who had modestly resumed her silent attitude.

"Come," resumed Gaujean, to cut short the argument, "all that is simply theory. Let's talk of our matter."

After the cheese, the servant brought in some jam and some pears. He took some jam, eating it with a spoon, with the unconscious greediness of a big man very fond of sugar.

"To begin with, you must attack their Paris Paradise, which has been their success of the year. I have come to an understanding with several of my brother manufacturers at Lyons, and have brought you an exceptional offer—a black silk, that you can sell at five and a half. They sell theirs at five francs twelve sous, don't they? Well! this will be two sous less, and that will suffice to upset them."

At this Robineau's eyes lighted up again. In his continual nervous torment, he often skipped like this from despair to hope.

"Have you got a sample?" asked he. And when Gaujean drew from his pocket-book a little square of silk, he went into raptures, exclaiming: "Why, this is a handsomer silk than the Paris Paradise! In any case it produces a better effect, the grain is coarser. You are right, we must make the attempt. If I don't bring them to my feet, I'll give up this time!"

Madame Robineau, sharing this enthusiasm, declared the silk superb, and Denise herself thought they would succeed. The latter part of the dinner was thus very gay. They talked in a loud tone; it seemed that The Ladies' Paradise was at its last gasp. Gaujean, who was finishing the pot of jam, explained what enormous sacrifices he and his colleagues would be obliged to make to deliver such an article at this low price; but they would ruin themselves rather than yield; they had sworn to kill the big shops. As the coffee came in the gaiety was greatly increased by the arrival of Vinçard, who had just called, in passing, to see how his successor was getting on.

"Famous!" cried he, feeling the silk. "You'll floor them, I stake my life! Ah! you owe me a rare good thing; I told you this was a golden affair!"

He had just taken a restaurant at Vincennes. It was an old, cherished idea, slyly nourished while he was struggling in the silk business, trembling for fear he should not sell it before the crash came, and swearing to himself that he would put his money into an undertaking where he could rob at his ease. The idea of a restaurant had struck him at the wedding of a cousin, who had been made to pay ten francs for a bowl of dish water, in which floated some Italian paste. And, in presence of the Robineaus, the joy he felt in having saddled them with a badly-paying business of which he despaired of ever getting rid, enlarged still further his face with its round eyes and large loyal-looking mouth, a face beaming with health.

"And your pains?" asked Madame Robineau, good-naturedly.

"My pains?" murmured he, astonished.

"Yes, those rheumatic pains which tormented you so much when you were here."

He then recollected, and blushed slightly. "Oh I suffer from

them still! However, the country air, you know, has done wonders for me. Never mind, you've done a good stroke of business.
Had it not been for my rheumatics, I could soon have retired
with ten thousand francs a year. My word of honor!"

A fortnight later, the struggle commenced between Robineau
and The Ladies' Paradise. It became celebrated, and occupied for
a time the whole Parisian market. Robineau, using his adversary's weapons, had advertised extensively in the newspapers.
Besides that, he made a fine display, piling up enormous bales of
the famous silk in his windows, with immense white tickets, displaying in giant figures the price, five francs and a half. It was
this figure that caused a revolution among the women; two sous
cheaper than at The Ladies' Paradise, and the silk appeared
stronger. From the first day a crowd of customers flocked in. Madame Marty bought a dress she did not want, pretending it to be
a bargain; Madame Bourdelais thought the silk very fine, but
preferred waiting, guessing no doubt what would happen. And,
indeed the following week, Mouret boldly reduced The Paris
Paradise by four sous, after a lively discussion with Bourdoncle
and the other managers, in which he had succeeded in inducing
them to accept the challenge, even at a sacrifice; for these four
sous represented a dead loss, the silk being sold already at strict
cost price. It was a heavy blow to Robineau, who did not think
his rival would reduce; for this suicidal competition, these losing
sales, were then unknown; and the tide of customers, attracted
by the cheapness, had immediately flown back towards the Rue
Neuve-Saint-Augustin, whilst the shop in the Rue Neuve-des-
Petits-Champs gradually emptied.

Gaujean came up from Lyons; there were hasty confabula-
tions, and they finished by coming to a most heroic resolution;
the silk should be lowered in price, they would sell it at five
francs six sous, beneath which no one could go, without folly.
The next day Mouret marked his at five francs four sous. After
that it became a mania: Robineau replied by five francs three
sous, when Mouret at once ticketed his at five francs and two
sous. Neither lowered more than a sou at a time now, losing considerable sums as often as they made this present to the public.

The customers laughed, delighted with this duel, moved by the terrible blows dealt each other by the two houses to please them. At last Mouret ventured as low as five francs; his staff paled before such a challenge thrown down to fortune. Robineau, utterly beaten, out of breath, stopped also at five francs, not having the courage to go any lower. And they rested at their positions, face to face, with the massacre of their goods around them.

But if honor was saved on both sides, the situation was becoming fatal for Robineau. The Ladies' Paradise had money at its disposal and a patronage which enabled it to balance its profits; whilst he, sustained by Gaujean alone, unable to recoup his losses on other articles, was exhausted, and slipped daily a little further on the verge of bankruptcy. He was dying from his hardihood, notwithstanding the numerous customers that the hazards of the struggle had brought him. One of his secret torments was to see these customers slowly quitting him, returning to The Ladies' Paradise, after the money he had lost and the efforts he had made to conquer them.

One day he quite lost patience. A customer, Madame de Boves, had come to his shop for some mantles, for he had added a ready-made department to his business. She could not make up her mind, complaining of the quality of the goods. At last she said: "Their Paris Paradise is a great deal stronger."

Robineau restrained himself, assuring her that she was mistaken, with a tradesman's politeness, all the more respectful, because he was afraid to allow his anger to burst forth.

"But just look at the silk of this mantle!" resumed she, "one would really take it for so much cobweb. You may say what you like, sir, their silk at five francs is like leather compared with this."

He did not reply, the blood rushing to his face, and his lips tightly closed. In point of fact he had ingeniously thought of buying some of his rival's silk for these mantles. So that it was Mouret, not he, who lost on the material. He simply cut off the selvage.

"Really you think the Paris Paradise thicker?" murmured he.

"Oh! a hundred times!" said Madame de Boves. "There's no comparison."

This injustice on her part, her running down the goods in this way, filled him with indignation. And, as she was still turning the mantle over with a disgusted air, a little piece of the blue and silver selvage, not cut off, appeared under the lining. He could not contain himself any longer; he confessed he would even have given his head.

"Well, madame, this *is* Paris Paradise. I bought it myself! Look at the border."

Madame de Boves went away greatly annoyed, and a number of ladies quitted him when the affair became known. And he, amid this ruin, when the fear for the future seized him, only trembled for his wife, who had been brought up in a happy, peaceful home, and would never be able to endure a life of poverty. What would become of her if a catastrophe threw them into the street, with a load of debts? It was his fault, he ought never to have touched her money. She was obliged to comfort him. Wasn't the money as much his as hers? He loved her dearly, and she wanted nothing more; she gave him everything, her heart and her life. They could be heard in the back shop embracing one another. Little by little, the affairs and ways of the house became more regular; every month their losses increased, in a slow proportion which postponed the fatal issue. A tenacious hope sustained them, they still announced the near discomfiture of The Ladies' Paradise.

"Pooh!" he would say, "we are young yet. The future is ours."

"And besides, what matters, if you have done what you wanted to do?" resumed she. "As long as you are satisfied, I am as well, darling."

Denise's affection increased for them on seeing their tenderness. She trembled, feeling their inevitable fall; but she dared not interfere. It was then she fully understood the power of the new system of business, and became impassioned for this force which was transforming Paris. Her ideas were ripening, a woman's grace was developing out of the savage child newly arrived from

Valognes. In fact, her life was a pretty pleasant one, notwith-standing the fatigue and the little money she earned. When she had spent all the day on her feet, she had to go straight home, and look after Pépé, whom old Bourras insisted on feeding, for-tunately; but there was still a lot to do: a shirt to wash, stockings to mend; without mentioning the noise made by the youngster, which made her head ache fit to split. She never went to bed be-fore midnight. Sunday was her hardest day: she cleaned her room, and mended her own things, so busy that it was often five o'clock before she could dress. However, she sometimes went out for health's sake, taking (the little one for a long walk, out to-wards Neuilly; and their treat was to drink a cup of milk there at a dairyman's, who allowed them to sit down in his yard. Jean dis-dained these excursions; he put in an appearance now and again on week-day evenings, then disappeared, pretending to have other visits to pay; he asked for no more money, but he arrived with such a melancholy face, that his sister, anxious, always man-aged to keep a five-franc piece for him. That was her sole luxury.

"Five francs!" he would exclaim each time. "My stars! you're too good! It just happens, there's the stationer's wife—"

"Not another word," Denise would say; "I don't want to know."

But he thought she was accusing him of boasting. "I tell you she's the wife of a stationer! Oh! something magnificent!"

Three months passed away, spring was returning. Denise re-fused to return to Joinville with Pauline and Baugé. She some-times met them in the Rue Saint-Roch, when she left the shop in the evening. Pauline, one evening when she was alone, confided to her that she was very likely going to marry her lover; it was she who was hesitating, for they did not care for married sales-women at The Ladies' Paradise. This idea of marriage surprised Denise, she did not dare to advise her friend. One day, just as Co-lomban had stopped her near the fountain to talk about Clara, the latter was crossing the road; and Denise was obliged to run away, for he implored her to ask her old comrade if she would marry him. What was the matter with them all? Why were they tormenting themselves like this? She thought herself very fortu-nate not to be in love with anyone.

"You've heard the news?" cried out the umbrella dealer to her one evening on her return home from business.

"No, Monsieur Bourras."

"Well! the scoundrels have bought the Hôtel Duvillard. I'm hemmed in on all sides!" He was waving his long arms about, in a burst of fury which made his white mane stand up on end. "A regular mixed-up affair," resumed the old man. "It appears that the hotel belonged to the Crédit Immobilier, the president of which, Baron Hartmann, has just sold it to our famous Mouret. Now they've got me on the right, on the left, and at the back, just in the way I'm holding the knob of this stick in my hand!"

It was true, the sale was to have been concluded the previous day. Bourras's small house, hemmed in between The Ladies' Paradise and the Hôtel Duvillard, hanging on like a swallow's nest in a crack of a wall, seemed sure to be crushed, as soon as the shop invaded the hotel, and the time had now arrived. The colossus had turned the feeble obstacle, and was surrounding it with a pile of goods, threatening to swallow it up, to absorb it by the sole force of its giant aspiration. Bourras could feel the embrace which was making his shop creak. He thought he could see the place getting smaller; he was afraid of being absorbed himself, of being carried to the other side with his umbrellas and sticks, so loudly was the terrible machine roaring just then.

"Do you hear them?" asked he. "One would think they were eating up the walls even! And in my cellar, in the attic, everywhere, there's the same noise as of a saw going through the plaster. Never mind! I don't fancy they'll flatten me out like a sheet of paper. I'll stick here, even if they blow up my roof, and the rain should fall in bucketfuls on my bed!"

It was just at this moment that Mouret caused fresh proposals to be made to Bourras; they would increase the figure, they would give him fifty thousand francs for his good-will and the remainder of the lease. This offer redoubled the old man's anger; he refused in an insulting manner. How these scoundrels must rob people to be able to pay fifty thousand francs for a thing not worth ten thousand. And he defended his shop as a young girl defends her virtue, for honor's sake.

Denise noticed Bourras was pre-occupied during the next fortnight. He wandered about in a feverish manner, measuring the walls of his house, surveying it from the middle of the street with the air of an architect. Then one morning some workmen arrived. This was the decisive blow. He had conceived the bold idea of beating The Ladies' Paradise on its own ground by making certain concessions to modern luxury. The customers, who often reproached him about his dark shop, would certainly come back again, when they saw it bright and new. In the first place, the workmen stopped up the crevices and whitewashed the frontage, then they painted the woodwork a light green, and even carried the splendor so far as to gild the sign-board. A sum of three thousand francs, held in reserve by Bourras as a last resource, was swallowed up in this way. The whole neighborhood was in a state of revolution; people came to look at him amid all these riches, losing his head, no longer able to find the things he was accustomed to. He did not seem to be at home in this shining frame, in this tender setting; he seemed frightened, with his long beard and white hair. The people passing on the opposite side of the street were astonished on seeing him waving his arms about and carving his handles. And he was in a state of fever, afraid of dirtying his shop, plunging further into this luxurious business, which he did not at all understand.

The same as with Robineau, the campaign against The Ladies' Paradise was opened by Bourras. The latter had just brought out his invention, the automatic umbrella, which later on was to become popular. But The Paradise people immediately improved on the invention, and a struggle of prices commenced. Bourras had an article at one franc and nineteen sous, in zanella, with steel mounting, everlasting, said the ticket. But he was especially anxious to vanquish his competitors with his handles—bamboo, dogwood, olive, myrtle, rattan, every imaginable sort of handle. The Paradise people, less artistic, paid more attention to the material, extolling their alpacas and mohairs, their twills and sarcenets. And they came out victorious. Bourras, in despair, repeated that art was done for, that he was reduced to carving his handles for pleasure, without any hope of selling them.

"It's my fault!" cried he to Denise. "I never ought to have kept a lot of rotten articles, at one franc nineteen sous! That's where these new notions lead one to. I wanted to follow the example of these brigands; so much the better if I'm ruined by it!"

The month of July was very warm, and Denise suffered greatly in her narrow room, under the roof. So after leaving the shop, she sometimes went and fetched Pépé, and instead of going upstairs at once, went for a stroll in the Tuileries Gardens until the gates were closed. One evening as she was walking under the chestnut-trees she suddenly stopped with surprise; a few yards off, walking straight towards her, she thought she recognized Hutin. But her heart commenced to beat violently. It was Mouret, who had dined over the water, and was hurrying along on foot to call on Madame Desforges. At the abrupt movement she made to escape him, he caught sight of her. The night was coming on, but still he recognized her.

"Ah, it's you, mademoiselle!"

She did not reply, astonished that he should deign to stop, lie, smiling, concealed his constraint beneath an air of amiable protection.

"You are still in Paris?"

"Yes, sir," said she at last.

She was slowly drawing back, desirous of making a bow and continuing her walk. But he turned and followed her under the black shadows of the chestnut-trees. The air was getting cooler, some children were laughing in the distance, trundling their hoops.

"This is your brother, is it not?" resumed he, looking at Pépé.

The little boy, frightened by the unusual presence of a gentleman, was gravely walking by his sister's side, holding her tightly by the hand.

"Yes, sir," replied she once more.

She blushed, thinking of the abominable inventions circulated by Marguerite and Clara. No doubt Mouret understood why she was blushing, for he quickly added: "Listen, mademoiselle, I have to apologize to you. Yes, I should have been happy to have told you sooner how much I regret the error that has been made. You were accused too lightly of a fault. But the evil is done. I simply wanted to assure you that everyone in our establishment now knows of your affection for your brothers," he continued, with a respectful politeness to which the saleswomen in The Ladies' Paradise were little accustomed. Denise's confusion had increased; but her heart was filled with joy. He knew, then, that she had given herself to no one! Both remained silent; he continued beside her, regulating his walk to the child's short steps; and the distant murmurs of the city were dying away under the black shadows of the spreading chestnut-trees. "I have only one reparation to offer you," resumed he. "Naturally, if you would like to come back to us—"

She interrupted him, and refused with a feverish haste. "No, sir, I cannot. Thank you all the same, but I have found another situation."

He knew it, they had informed him she was with Robineau; and leisurely, on a footing of amiable equality, he spoke of the latter, rendering him full justice. A very intelligent fellow, but too nervous. He would certainly come to grief: Gaujean had burdened him with a very heavy business, in which they would both suffer. Denise, conquered by this familiarity, opened her mind further, and allowed it to be seen that she was for the big shops in the war between them and the small traders: she became animated, citing examples, showing herself well up in the question, even expressing new and enlightened ideas. He, charmed, listened to her in surprise; and turned round, trying to distinguish her features in the growing darkness. She seemed still the same with her simple dress and sweet face; but from this modest bashfulness, there seemed to exhale a penetrating perfume, of which he felt the powerful influence. Decidedly this little girl had got used to the air of Paris, she was becoming quite a woman, and was really perturbing, so sensible, with her beautiful hair, overflowing with tenderness.

"As you are on our side," said he, laughing, "why do you stay with our adversaries? I fancy, too, they told me you lodged with Bourras."

"A very worthy man," murmured she.

"No, not a bit of it! he's an old idiot, a madman who will force me to ruin him, though I should be glad to get rid of him with a fortune! Besides, your place is not in his house, which has a bad reputation. He lets to certain women."

But feeling that the young girl was confused, he hastened to add: "One can be respectable anywhere, and there's even more merit in remaining so when one is so poor."

They went on a few steps in silence. Pépé seemed to be listening with the attentive air of a sharp child. Now and again he raised his eyes to his sister, whose burning hand, quivering with sudden starts, astonished him.

"Look here!" resumed Mouret, gaily, "will you be my ambassador? I intended increasing my offer tomorrow—of proposing eighty thousand francs to Bourras. Do you speak to him first about it. Tell him he's cutting his own throat. Perhaps he'll listen to you, as he has a liking for you, and you'll be doing him a real service."

"Very well!" said Denise, smiling also, "I will deliver your message, but I am afraid I shall not succeed."

And a fresh silence ensued, neither of them having anything more to say. He attempted to talk of her uncle Baudu; but had to give it up on seeing the young girl's uneasiness. However, they continued to walk side by side, and at last found themselves near the Rue de Rivoli, in a path where it was still light. On coming out of the darkness of the trees it was like a sudden awakening. He understood that he could not detain her any longer.

"Good night, mademoiselle."

"Good night, sir."

But he did not go away. On raising his eyes he perceived in front of him, at the corner of the Rue d'Alger, the lighted windows at Madame Desforges's, whither he was bound. And looking at Denise, whom he could now see, in the pale twilight, she appeared to him very puny beside Henriette. Why was it she touched his heart in this way? It was a stupid caprice.

"This little man is getting tired," resumed he, just for something to say. "Remember, mind, that our house is always open to you; you've only to knock, and I'll give you every compensation possible. Good night, mademoiselle."

"Good night, sir."

When Mouret quitted her, Denise went back under the chestnut-trees, in the black shadow. For a long time she walked on without any object, between the enormous trunks, her face burning, her head in a whirl of confused ideas. Pépé still had hold of her hand, stretching out his short legs to keep pace with her. She had forgotten him. At last he said:

"You go too quick, little mother."

At this she sat down on a bench; and as he was tired, the child went to sleep on her lap. She held him there, nestling to her virgin bosom, her eyes lost far away in the darkness. When, an hour later on, they returned slowly to the Rue de la Michodière, she had regained her usual quiet, sensible expression.

"Hell and thunder!" shouted Bourras, when he saw her coming, "the blow is struck. That rascal of a Mouret has just bought my house." He was half mad, and was striking himself in the middle of the shop with such outrageous gestures that he almost threatened to break the windows. "Ah! the scoundrel! It's the fruiterer who's written to tell me this. And how much do you think he has got for the house? One hundred and fifty thousand francs, four times its value! There's another thief, if you like! Just fancy, he has taken advantage of my embellishments, making capital out of the fact that the house has been done up. How much longer are they going to make a fool of me?"

The thought that his money spent on paint and white-wash had brought the fruiterer a profit exasperated him. And now Mouret would be his landlord; he would have to pay him! It was beneath this detested competitor's roof that he must live in future! Such a thought raised his fury to the highest possible pitch.

"Ah! I could hear them digging a hole through the wall. At this moment, they are here eating out of my very plate, so to say!"

And the shop shook under his heavy fist which he banged on the counter; he made the umbrellas and the parasols dance again. Denise, bewildered, could not get in a word. She stood there, motionless, waiting for the end of his tirade; whilst Pépé, very tired, had fallen asleep on a chair. At last, when Bourras became a little calmer, she resolved to deliver Mouret's message.

No doubt the old man was irritated, but the excess even of his anger, the blind alley in which he found himself, might deter-mine an abrupt acceptance.

"I've just met someone," she commenced. "Yes, a person from The Paradise, very well informed. It appears that they are going to offer you eighty thousand francs tomorrow."

"Eighty thousand francs!" interrupted he, in a terrible voice; "eighty thousand francs! Not for a million now!"

She tried to reason with him. But at that moment the shop door opened, and she suddenly drew back, pale and silent. It was her uncle Baudu, with his yellow face and aged look. Bourras seized his neighbor by the button-hole, and roared out in his face without allowing him to say a word, as if goaded on by his presence:

"What do you think they have the cheek to offer me? Eighty thousand francs! They've got so far, the brigands! they think I'm going to sell myself like a prostitute. Ah! they've bought the house, and think they've now got me. Well! it's all over, they sha'n't have it! I might have given way, perhaps; but now it be-longs to them, let them try and take it!"

"So the news is true?" said Baudu in his slow voice. "I had heard of it, and came over to know if it was so."

"Eighty thousand francs!" repeated Bourras. "Why not a hun-dred thousand at once? It's this immense sum of money that makes me indignant. Do they think they can make me commit a knavish trick with their money! They sha'n't have it, by heavens! Never, never, you hear me?"

Denise gently observed, in her calm, quiet way: "They'll have it in nine years' time, when your lease expires."

And, notwithstanding her uncle's presence, she begged of the old man to accept. The struggle was becoming impossible, he was fighting against a superior force; he would be mad to refuse the fortune offered him. But he still replied no. In nine years' time he hoped to be dead, so as not to see it.

"You hear, Monsieur Baudu," resumed he, "your niece is on their side, it's her they have employed to corrupt me. She's with the brigands, my word of honor!"

Baudu, who up to then had appeared not to notice Denise, now raised his head, with the morose movement that he affected when standing at his shop door, every time she passed. But, slowly, he turned round and looked at her, and his thick lips trembled.

"I know it," replied he in a half-whisper, and he continued to look at her.

Denise, affected almost to tears, thought him greatly changed by trouble. Perhaps he was stricken with remorse for not having assisted her during the time of misery she had just passed through. Then the sight of Pépé sleeping on the chair, amidst the noise of the discussion, seemed to suddenly inspire him with compassion.

"Denise," said he simply, "come tomorrow and have dinner with us and bring the little one. My wife and Geneviève asked me to invite you if I met you."

She turned very red, and went up and kissed him. And as he was going away, Bourras, delighted at this reconciliation, cried out to him again: "Just talk to her, she isn't a bad sort. As for me, the house may fall, I shall be found in the ruins."

"Our houses are already falling, neighbor," said Baudu with a sombre air. "We shall all be crushed under them."

CHAPTER VIII.

At this time the whole neighborhood was talking of the great thoroughfare to be opened from the Bourse to the new Opera House, under the name of the Rue du Dix-Décembre. The expropriation judgments had just been delivered, two gangs of demolishers were already attacking the opening at the two ends, the first pulling down the old mansions in the Rue Louis-le-Grand, the other destroying the thin walls of the old Vaudeville; and one could hear the picks getting closer. The Rue de Choiseul and the Rue de la Michodière got quite excited over their condemned houses. Before a fortnight passed, the opening would make a great hole in these streets, letting in the sun and air.

But what stirred up the district still more, was the work going on at The Ladies' Paradise. Considerable enlargements were talked of, gigantic shops having frontages in the Rue de la Michodière, the Rue Neuve-Saint-Augustin, and the Rue Monsigny. Mouret, it was said, had made arrangements with Baron Hartmann, chairman of the Crédit Immobilier, and he would occupy the whole block, except the future frontage in the Rue du Dix-Décembre, on which the baron wished to construct a rival to the Grand Hôtel. The Paradise people were buying up leases on all sides, the shops were closing, the tenants moving; and in the empty buildings an army of workmen were commencing the various alterations under a cloud of plaster. In the midst of this disorder, old Bourras's narrow hovel was the only one that remained standing and intact, obstinately sticking between the high walls covered with masons.

When, the next day, Denise went with Pépé to her uncle Baudu's, the street was just at that moment blocked up by a line of tumbrels discharging bricks before the Hôtel Duvillard. Baudu was standing at his shop door looking on with a gloomy air. As The Ladies' Paradise became larger, The Old Elbeuf seemed to get smaller. The young girl thought the windows looked blacker than ever, and more and more crushed beneath the low first storey, with its prison-like bars; the damp had still further discolored the old green sign-board, a sort of distress oozed from the whole frontage, livid in hue, and, as it were, grown thinner.

"Here you are, then!" said Baudu. "Take care! they would run right over you."

Inside the shop, Denise experienced the same heart-broken sensation; she found it darker, invaded more than ever by the somnolence of approaching ruin; empty corners formed dark and gloomy holes, the dust was invading the counters and drawers, whilst an odor of saltpetre rose from the bales of cloth that were no longer moved about. At the desk Madame Baudu and Geneviève were standing mute and motionless, as in some solitary spot, where no one would come to disturb them. The mother was hemming some dusters. The daughter, her hands spread on her knees, was gazing at the emptiness before her.

"Good evening, aunt," paid Denise; "I'm delighted to see you again, and if I have hurt your feelings, I hope you will forgive me."

Madame Baudu kissed her, greatly affected. "My poor child," said she, "if I had no other troubles, you would see me gayer than this."

"Good evening, cousin," resumed Denise, kissing Geneviève on the cheeks.

The latter woke up with a sort of start, and returned her kisses, without finding a word to say. The two women then took up Pépé, who was holding out his little arms, and the reconciliation was complete.

"Well! it's six o'clock, let's go to dinner," said Baudu. "Why haven't you brought Jean?"

"But he was to come," murmured Denise, embarrassed. "I saw him this morning, and he faithfully promised me. Oh! we must

not wait for him; his master has kept him, I dare say." She suspected some extraordinary adventure, and wished to apologize
for him in advance.

"In that case, we will commence," said her uncle. Then turning
towards the obscure depths of the shop, he added:

"Come on, Colomban, you can dine with us. No one will
come."

Denise had not noticed the shopman. Her aunt explained to
her that they had been obliged to get rid of the other salesman
and the young lady. Business was getting so bad that Colomban
sufficed; and even he spent many idle hours, drowsy, falling off
to sleep with his eyes open. The gas was burning in the dining
room, although they were enjoying long summer days. Denise
slightly shivered on entering, seized by the dampness falling
from the walls. She once more beheld the round table, the places
laid on the American cloth, the window drawing its air and light
from the dark and fetid back yard. And these things appeared to
her to be gloomier than ever, and tearful like the shop.

"Father," said Geneviève, uncomfortable for Denise's sake,
"shall I close the window? There's rather a bad smell."

He smelt nothing, and seemed surprised. "Shut the window if
you like," replied he at last. "But we sha'n't get any air then."

And indeed they were almost stifled. It was a family dinner,
very simple. After the soup, as soon as the servant had served the
boiled beef, the old man as usual commenced about the people
opposite. At first he showed himself very tolerant, allowing his
niece to have a different opinion.

"Dear me! you are quite free to support these great hair-
brained houses. Each one has his ideas, my girl. If you were not
disgusted at being so disgracefully chucked out you must have
strong reasons for liking them; and even if you went back again,
I should think none the worse of you. No one here would be offended, would they?"

"Oh, no!" murmured Madame Baudu.

Denise quietly gave her reasons, as she had at Robineau's: the
logical evolution in business, the necessities of modern times,
the greatness of these new creations, in short, the growing well-

being of the public. Baudu, his eyes opened, and his mouth clamming, listened with a visible tension of intelligence. Then, when she had finished, he shook his head.

"That's all phantasmagoria, you know. Business is business, there's no getting over that. I own that they succeed, but that's all. For a long time I thought they would smash up; yes, I expected that, waiting patiently—you remember? Well, no, it appears that now-a-days thieves make fortunes, whilst honest people die of hunger. That's what we've come to. I'm obliged to bow to facts. And I do bow, on my word, I do bow!" A deep anger was gradually rising within him. All at once he flourished his fork. "But The Old Elbeuf will never give way! I said as much to Bourras, you know, Neighbor, you're going over to the cheapjacks; your paint and your varnish are a disgrace."

"Eat your dinner!" interrupted Madame Baudu, feeling anxious, on seeing him so excited.

"Wait a bit, I want my niece thoroughly to understand my motto. Just listen, my girl: I'm like this decanter, I don't budge. They succeed, so much the worse for them! As for me, I protest—that's all!"

The servant brought in a piece of roast veal. He cut it up with his trembling hands; but he no longer had his correct glance, his skill in weighing the portions. The consciousness of his defeat deprived him of the confidence he used to have as a respected employer. Pépé thought his uncle was getting angry, and they had to pacify him, by giving him some dessert, some biscuits which were near his plate. Then Baudu, lowering his voice, tried to talk of something else. For a moment he spoke of the demolitions going on, approving of the Rue du Dix-Décembre, the cutting of which would certainly improve the business of the neighborhood. But then again he returned to The Ladies' Paradise; everything brought him back to it, it was a kind of complaint. They were covered with plaster, and business was stopped since the builders' carts had commenced to block up the street. It would soon be really ridiculous, in its immensity; the customers would lose themselves. Why not have the central markets at once? And, in spite of his wife's supplicating looks, notwithstanding his own effort, he went on from the works to the amount of business done in the big shop. Was it not inconceivable? In less than four years they had increased their figures five-fold; the annual receipts, formerly eight million francs, now attained the sum of forty millions, according to the last balance-sheet. In fact it was a piece of folly, a thing that had never been seen before, and against which it was perfectly useless to struggle. They were always increasing, they had now a thousand employees and twenty-eight departments. These twenty-eight departments enraged him more than anything else. No doubt they had duplicated a few, but others were quite new; for instance a furniture department, and a department for fancy goods. The idea! Fancy goods! Really these people were not at all proud, they would end by selling fish. Baudu, though affecting to respect Denise's opinions, attempted to convert her.

"Frankly, you can't defend them. What would you say were I to add a hardware department to my cloth business? You would say I was mad. Confess, at least, that you don't esteem them."

And as the young girl simply smiled, feeling uncomfortable, understanding the uselessness of good reasons, he resumed: "In short, you are on their side. We won't talk about it any more, for it's useless to let that part us again. It would be too much to see them come between me and my family! Go back with them, if you like; but pray don't worry me with any more of their stories!"

A silence ensued. His former violence was reduced to this feverish resignation. As they were suffocating in the narrow room, heated by the gas-burner, the servant had to open the window again; and the damp, pestilential air from the yard blew into the apartment. A dish of stewed potatoes appeared, and they helped themselves slowly, without a word.

"Look at those two," recommended Baudu, pointing with his knife to Geneviève and Colomban. "Ask them if they like your Ladies' Paradise."

Side by side in the usual place where they had found themselves twice a-day for the last twelve years, the engaged couple were eating in moderation, and without uttering a word. He, exaggerating the coarse good-nature of his face, seemed to be concealing, behind his drooping eyelashes, the inner flame which was devouring him; whilst she, her head bowed lower beneath her too heavy hair, seemed to be giving way entirely, as if ravaged by a secret grief.

"Last year was very disastrous," explained Baudu, "and we have been obliged to postpone the marriage, not for our own pleasure; ask them what they think of your friends."

Denise, in order to pacify him, interrogated the young people.

"Naturally I can't be very fond of them," replied Geneviève. "But never fear, everyone doesn't detest them."

And she looked at Colomban, who was rolling up some breadcrumbs with an absorbed air. When he felt the young girl's gaze directed towards him, he broke out into a series of violent exclamations: "A rotten shop! A lot of rogues, every man-jack of them! A regular pest in the neighborhood!"

"You hear him! You hear him!" exclaimed Baudu, delighted. "There's one they'll never get hold of! Ah! my boy, you're the last of the old stock, we sha'n't see any more!"

But Geneviève, with her severe and suffering look, still kept her eyes on Colomban, diving into the depths of his heart. And he felt troubled, he redoubled his invectives. Madame Baudu was watching them with an anxious air, as if she foresaw another misfortune in this direction. For some time her daughter's sadness had frightened her, she felt her to be dying. "The shop is left to take care of itself," said she at last, quitting the table, desirous of putting an end to the scene. "Go and see, Colomban; I fancy I heard someone."

They had finished, and got up. Baudu and Colomban went to speak to a traveler, who had come for orders. Madame Baudu carried Pépé off to show him some pictures. The servant had quickly cleared the table, and Denise was lounging by the window, looking into the little back yard, when turning round she saw Geneviève still in her place, her eyes fixed on the American cloth, which was still damp from the sponge having been passed over it.

"Are you suffering, cousin?" she asked.

The young girl did not reply, obstinately studying a rent in the cloth, too preoccupied by the reflections passing through her mind. Then she raised her head with pain, and looked at the sympathizing face bent over hers. The others had gone, then? What was she doing on this chair? And suddenly a flood of sobs stifled her, her head fell forward on the edge of the table. She wept on, wetting her sleeve with her tears.

"Good heavens! what's the matter with you?" cried Denise in dismay. "Shall I call someone?"

Geneviève nervously seized her by the arm, and held her back, stammering: "No, no, stay. Don't let mamma know! With you I don't mind; but not the others—not the others! It's not my fault, I assure you. It was on finding myself all alone. Wait a bit; I'm better, and I'm not crying now."

But sudden attacks kept seizing her, causing her frail body to tremble. It seemed as though the weight of her hair was weighing down her head. As she was rolling her poor head on her folded arms, a hair-pin came out, and her hair fell over her neck, burying it in its folds. Denise, quietly, for fear of attracting attention, tried to console her. She undid her dress, and was heart-broken on seeing how fearfully thin she was. The poor girl's bosom was as hollow as that of a child. Denise took the hair by handfuls, that superb head of hair which seemed to be absorbing all her life, and twisted it up, to clear it away, and give her a little air.

"Thanks, you are very kind," said Geneviève. "Ah! I'm not very stout, am I? I used to be stouter, but it's all gone away. Do up my dress or mamma might see my shoulders. I hide them as much as I can. Good heavens! I'm not at all well, I'm not at all well."

However, the attack passed away, and she sat there completely worn out, looking fixedly at her cousin. After a pause she abruptly asked: "Tell me the truth: does he love her?"

Denise felt a blush rising to her cheek. She was perfectly well aware that Geneviève referred to Colomban and Clara; but she pretended to be surprised.

"Who, dear?"

Geneviève shook her head with an incredulous air. "Don't tell falsehoods, I beg of you. Do me the favor of setting my doubts at rest. You must know, I feel it. Yes, you have been this girl's comrade, and I've seen Colomban run after you, and talk to you in a low voice. He was giving you messages for her, wasn't he? Oh! for pity's sake, tell me the truth; I assure you it will do me good."

Never had Denise been in such an awkward position. She lowered her eyes before this almost dumb girl, who yet guessed all. However, she had the strength to deceive her still. "But it's you he loves!"

Geneviève turned away in despair. "Very well, you won't tell me anything. However, I don't care, I've seen them. He's continually going outside to look at her. She, upstairs, laughs like a bad woman. Of course they meet out of doors."

"As for that, no, I assure you!" exclaimed Denise, forgetting herself, carried away by the desire to give her, at least, that consolation.

The young girl drew a long breath, and smiled feebly. Then with the weak voice of a convalescent: "I should like a glass of water. Excuse me if I trouble you. Look, over there in the sideboard."

When she got hold of the bottle, she drank a large glassful right off, keeping Denise away with one hand, the latter being afraid Geneviève might do herself harm.

"No, no, let me be; I'm always thirsty. In the night I get up to drink." There was a fresh silence. Then she went on again quietly: "If you only knew, I've been accustomed to the idea of this marriage for the last ten years. I was still wearing short dresses, when Colomban was courting me. I hardly remember how things have come about. By always living together, being shut up here together, without any other distractions between us, I must have ended by believing him to be my husband before he really was. I didn't know whether I loved him. I was his wife, and that's all. And now he wants to go off with another girl! Oh, heavens! my heart is breaking! You see, it's a grief that I've never felt before. It hurts me in the bosom, and in the head; then it spreads everywhere, and is killing me."

Her eyes filled with tears. Denise, whose eyelids were also wet with pity, asked her: "Does my aunt suspect anything?"

"Yes, mamma has her suspicions, I think. As to papa, he is too worried, and does not know the pain he is causing me by postponing this marriage. Mamma has questioned me several times, greatly alarmed to see me pining away. She has never been very strong herself, and has often said: 'My poor child, I've not made you very strong.' Besides, one doesn't grow much in these shops. But she must find me getting really too thin now. Look at my arms; would you believe it?"

And with a trembling hand she again took up the water bottle. Her cousin tried to prevent her drinking.

"No, I'm so thirsty, let me drink."

They could hear Baudu talking in a loud voice. Then yielding to an inspiration of her tender heart, Denise knelt down before Geneviève, throwing her arms round her neck, kissing her, and assuring her that everything would turn out all right, that she would marry Colomban, that she would get well, and live happily. But she got up quickly, her uncle was calling her.

"Jean is here. Come along."

It was indeed Jean, looking rather scared, who had come to dinner. When they told him it was striking eight, he looked amazed. Impossible! He had only just left his master's. They chaffed him. No doubt he had come by way of the Bois de Vincennes. But as soon as he could get near his sister, he whispered to her: "It's a little laundry-girl who was taking back some linen. I've got a cab outside by the hour. Give me five francs."

He went out a minute, and then returned to dinner, for Madame Baudu would not hear of his going away without taking, at least, a plate of soup. Geneviève had reappeared in her usual silent and retiring manner. Colomban was half asleep behind the counter. The evening passed away, slow and melancholy, only animated by Baudu's step, as he walked from one end of the empty shop to the other. A single gas-burner was alight—the shadow of the low ceiling fell in large masses, like black earth from a ditch.

Several months passed away. Denise came in nearly every evening to cheer up Geneviève a bit, but the house became more

melancholy than ever. The works opposite were a continual torment, which intensified their bad luck. Even when they had an
hour of hope—some unexpected joy—the falling of a tumbrel-
load of bricks, the sound of the saw of a stonecutter, or the simple call of a mason, sufficed at once to mar their pleasure. In fact,
the whole neighborhood felt the shock. From the boarded enclo-
sure, running along and blocking up the three streets, there issued a movement of feverish activity. Although the architect
used the existing building, he altered them in various ways to
adapt them to their new uses; and right in the centre at the opening caused by the courtyards, he was building a central gallery
as big as a church, which was to terminate with a grand entrance
in the Rue Neuve-Saint-Augustin right in the middle of the
frontage. They had, at first, experienced great difficulty in laying
the foundations, for they had come on to some sewer deposits
and loose earth, full of human bones. Besides that, the boring of
the well had made the neighbors very anxious—a well three hundred feet deep, destined to give two hundred gallons a minute.
They had now got the walls up to the first storey; the entire
block was surrounded by scaffolding, regular towers of timber
work. There was an incessant noise from the grinding of the
windlasses hoisting up the stone, the abrupt discharge of iron
bars, the clamor of this army of workmen, accompanied by the
noise of picks and hammers. But above all, what deafened the
people was the sound of the machinery. Everything went by
steam, screeching whistles rent the air; whilst, at the slightest
gust of wind, clouds of plaster flew about and covered the neighboring roofs like a fall of snow. The Baudus in despair looked on
at this implacable dust penetrating everywhere—getting through
the closest woodwork, soiling the goods in their shop, even gliding into their beds; and the idea that they must continue to
breathe it—that it would finish by killing them—empoisoned
their existence.

The situation, however, was destined to become worse still,
for in September, the architect, afraid of not being ready, decided to carry on the work at night also. Powerful electric lamps
were established, and the uproar became continuous. Gangs of

men relieved each other; the hammers never stopped, the engines whistled night and day; the everlasting clamor seemed to raise and scatter the white dust. The Baudus now had to give up the idea of sleeping even; they were shaken in their beds; the noises changed into nightmare as soon as they fell off to sleep. Then, if they got up to calm their fever, and went, with bare feet, to look out of the window, they were frightened by the vision of The Ladies' Paradise flaring in the darkness like a colossal forge, where their ruin was being forged. Along the half-built walls, dotted with open bays, the electric lamps threw a large blue flood of light, of a blinding intensity. Two o'clock struck—then three, then four; and during the painful sleep of the neighborhood, the works, increased by this lunar brightness, became colossal and fantastic, swarming with black shadows, noisy workmen, whose profiles gesticulated on the crude whiteness of the new plastering.

Baudu was quite right. The small traders in the neighboring streets were receiving another mortal blow. Every time The Ladies' Paradise created new departments there were fresh failures among the shopkeepers of the district. The disaster spread, one could hear the cracking of the oldest houses. Mademoiselle Tatin, at the under-linen shop in the Passage Choiseul, had just been declared bankrupt; Quinette, the glover, could hardly hold out another six months; the furriers, Vanpouille, were obliged to sub-let a part of their premises; and if the Bédorés, brother and sister, the hosiers, still kept on in the Rue Gaillon, they were evidently living on money saved formerly. And now more smashes were going to be added to those long since foreseen; the department for fancy goods threatened a toy-shopkeeper in the Rue Saint-Roch, Deslignières, a big, full-blooded man; whilst the furniture department attacked Messrs. Piot and Rivoire, whose shops were sleeping in the shadow of the Passage Sainte-Anne. It was even feared that an attack of apoplexy would carry off the toy-man, who had gone into a terrible rage on seeing The Ladies' Paradise mark up purses at thirty per cent, reduction. The furniture dealers, who were much calmer, affected to joke at these counter-jumpers who wanted to meddle with such articles as chairs and tables; but customers were already leaving them, the success of the department had every appearance of being a formidable one. It was all over, they were obliged to bow their heads. After these others would be swept off, and there was no reason why every business should not be driven away. One day The Ladies' Paradise alone would cover the neighborhood with its roof.

At present, morning and evening, when the thousand employees went in and came out, they formed such a long procession in the Place Gaillon that people stopped to look at them as they would at a passing regiment. For ten minutes they blocked up all the streets; and the shopkeepers at their doors thought bitterly of their single assistant, whom they hardly knew how to find food for. The last balance-sheet of the big shop, the forty millions turned over, had also caused a revolution in the neighborhood. The figure passed from house to house amid cries of surprise and anger. Forty millions! Think of that! No doubt the net profit did not exceed more than four per cent, with their heavy general expenses, and system of low prices; but sixteen hundred thousand francs was a jolly sum, one could be satisfied with four per cent, when one operated on such a scale as that. It was said that Mouret's starting capital of five hundred thousand francs, augmented each year by the total profits, a capital which must at that moment have amounted to four millions, had thus passed ten times over the counters in the form of goods. Robineau, when he made this calculation before Denise, after dinner, was overcome for a moment, his eyes fixed on his empty plate. She was right, it was this incessant renewal of the capital that constituted the invincible force of the new system of business. Bourras alone denied the facts, refusing to understand, superb and stupid as a mile-stone. A pack of thieves and nothing more! A lying set! Cheap-jacks who would be picked up out of the gutter one fine morning!

The Baudus, however, notwithstanding their wish not to change anything in the way of The Old Elbeuf, tried to sustain the competition. The customers no longer coming to them, they forced themselves to go to the customers, through the agency of travellers. There was at that time, in the Paris market, a traveler connected with all the great tailors, who saved the little cloth and flannel houses when he condescended to represent them. Naturally they all tried to get hold of him; he assumed the importance of a personage; and Baudu, having haggled with him, had the misfortune of seeing him come to terms with the Matignons, in the Rue Croix-des-Petits-Champs. One after the other, two other travellers robbed him; a third, an honest man, did no business. It was a slow death, without any shock, a continual decrease of business, customers lost one by one. A day came when the bills fell very heavily. Up to that time they had lived on their former savings; but now they began to contract debts. In December, Baudu, terrified by the amount of the bills he had accepted, resigned himself to a most cruel sacrifice: he sold his country-house at Rambouillet, a house which cost him a lot of money in continual repairs, and for which the tenants had not even paid the rent when he decided to get rid of it. This sale killed the only dream of his life, his heart bled as for the loss of some dear one. And he had to sell for seventy thousand francs that which had cost him more than two hundred thousand, considering himself fortunate to have met the Lhommes, his neighbors, who were desirous of adding to their property. The seventy thousand francs would keep the business going a little longer; for notwithstanding the repulses already encountered, the idea of struggling sprang up again; perhaps with great care they might conquer even now.

The Sunday on which the Lhommes paid the money, they were good enough to dine at The Old Elbeuf. Madame Aurélie was the last to arrive; they had to wait for the cashier, who came late, scared by a whole afternoon's music: as for young Albert, he had accepted the invitation, but did not put in an appearance. It was, moreover, a somewhat painful evening. The Baudus, living without air in their narrow dining room, suffered from the gust of wind brought in by the Lhommes, with their scattered family and taste for a free existence. Geneviève, wounded by Madame Aurélie's imperial airs, did not open her mouth; whilst Colomban was admiring her with a shiver, on reflecting that she reigned over Clara. Before retiring to rest, in the evening, Madame Baudu being already in bed, Baudu walked about the room for a long time. It was a mild night, thawing and damp. Outside, notwithstanding the closed windows, and drawn curtains, one could hear the machinery roaring on the opposite side of the way.

"Do you know what I'm thinking of, Elisabeth?" said he at last. "Well! these Lhommes may earn as much money as they like, I'd rather be in my shoes than theirs. They get on well, it's true. The wife said, didn't she? That she had made nearly twenty thousand francs this year, and that has enabled her to take my poor house. Never mind! I've no longer, the house, but I don't go playing music in one direction, whilst you are gadding about in the other. No, look you, they can't be happy."

He was still laboring under the grief of his sacrifice, nourishing a certain rancor against those people who had bought up his darling dream. When he came near the bed, he gesticulated, leaning over his wife; then, returning to the window, he stood silent for a minute, listening to the noise of the works. And he resumed his old accusations, his despairing complaints about the new times; nobody had ever seen such things, a shop-assistant earning more than a tradesman, cashiers buying up the employers' property. Everything was going to the dogs; family ties no longer existed, people lived at hotels instead of eating their meals at home in a respectable manner. He ended by prophesying that young Albert would later on swallow up the Rambouillet property with a lot of actresses.

Madame Baudu listened to him, her head flat on the pillow, so pale that her face was the color of the sheets. "They've paid you," at length said she, softly.

At this Baudu became dumb. He walked about for an instant with his eyes on the ground. Then he resumed: "They've paid me, 'tis true; and, after all, their money is as good as another's. It would be funny if we revived the business with this money. Ah! if I were not so old and worn out!"

A long silence ensued. The draper was full of vague projects. Suddenly his wife spoke again, her eyes fixed on the ceiling, without moving her head: "Have you noticed your daughter lately?"

"No," replied he.

"Well! she makes me rather anxious. She's getting pale, she seems to be pining away."

He stood before the bed, full of surprise. "Really! whatever for? If she's ill she should say so. Tomorrow we must send for the doctor."

Madame Baudu still remained motionless. After a short time, she declared with her meditative air: "This marriage with Colomban, I think it would be better to get it over."

He looked at her, then began walking about again. Certain things came back to his mind. Was it possible that his daughter was falling ill over the shopman? Did she love him so much that she could not wait? Here was another misfortune! It worried him all the more from the fact that he himself had fixed ideas about this marriage. He could never consent to it in the present state of affairs. However, his anxiety softened him.

"Very good," said he at last, "I'll speak to Colomban."

And without saying another word he continued his walk. Soon afterwards his wife fell off to sleep, quite white, as if dead; but he still kept on walking about. Before getting into bed he drew aside the curtains and glanced outside; on the other side of the street, the gaping windows of the old Hôtel Duvillard showed the workmen moving about in the dazzling glare of the electric light.

The next morning Baudu took Colomban to the further end of the store-room on the upper floor, having made up his mind over night what he should say to him. "My boy," said he, "you know I've sold my property at Rambouillet. That will enable us to show good fight. But I should like beforehand to have a talk with you."

The young man, who seemed to dread the interview, waited with an awkward air. His small eyes twinkled in his large face, and he stood there with his mouth open—a sign with him of profound agitation.

"Just listen to me," resumed the draper. "When old Hauche-corne left me The Old Elbeuf, the house was prosperous; he himself had received it from old Finet in a satisfactory state. You know my ideas; I should consider it wrong if I passed this family trust to my children in a diminished state; and that's why I've always postponed your marriage with Geneviève. Yes, I was obstinate; I hoped to bring back our former prosperity; I wanted to hand you the books, saying: "'Look here! the year I commenced we sold so much cloth, and this year, the year I retire, we have sold ten thousand or twenty thousand francs' worth more.' In short, you understand, it was a vow I had made to myself, the very natural desire I had to prove that the house had not lost anything in my hands. Otherwise it would seem to me I was robbing you." His voice was stifled with emotion. He blew his nose to recover a bit, and asked, "You don't say anything?"

But Colomban had nothing to say. He shook his head, and waited, more and more troubled, thinking he could guess what the governor was aiming at. It was the marriage without further delay. How could he refuse? He would never have the strength. And the other girl, of whom he dreamed at night, devoured by such a flame that he frequently threw himself quite naked on the floor, in the fear of dying of it.

"Now," continued Baudu, "there's a sum of money that may save us. The situation becomes worse every day, and perhaps by making a supreme efforts—In short, I thought it right to warn ou. We are going to venture our last stake. If we are beaten, why that will entirely ruin us! But, my poor boy, your marriage must be again postponed, for I don't wish to throw you two all alone into the struggle. That would be too cowardly, wouldn't it?"

Colomban, greatly relieved, had seated himself on a pile of swan-skin flannel. His legs were still trembling. He was afraid of showing his joy, he held down his head, rolling his fingers on his knees.

"You don't say anything?" repeated Baudu.

No, he said nothing, he could find nothing to say. The draper then slowly continued: "I was sure this would grieve you. You must muster up courage. Pull yourself together a bit, don't let yourself be crushed in this way. Above all, understand my position. Can I hang such a weight on your neck? Instead of leaving you a good business, I should leave you a bankruptcy perhaps. No, it's only a scoundrel who would play such a trick! No doubt, I desire nothing but your happiness, but no one shall ever make me go against my conscience."

And he went on for a long time in this way, swaying about in a maze of contradictions, like a man who would have liked to be understood at half a word and finds himself obliged to explain everything. As he had promised his daughter and the shop, strict probity forced him to deliver both in good condition, without defects or debts. But he was tired, the burden seemed to be too much for him, his stammering voice was one of supplication. He got more entangled than ever in his words, he was still expecting a sudden rally from Colomban, some heartfelt cry, which came not.

"I know," murmured he, "that old men are wanting in ardour. With young ones, things light up. They are full of fire, it's natural. But, no, no, I can't, my word of honor! If I gave it up to you, you would blame me later on."

He stopped, trembling, and as the young man still kept his head down, he asked him for the third time, after a painful silence: "You don't say anything?" At last, but without looking at him, Colomban replied: "There's nothing to say. You are the master, you know better than all of us. As you wish it we'll wait, we'll try and be reasonable."

It was all over. Baudu still hoped he was going to throw himself into his arms, exclaiming: "Father, do you take a rest, we'll fight in our turn; give us the shop as it is, so that we may work a miracle and save it!" Then he looked at him, and was seized with shame, accusing himself of having wished to dupe his children. The deep-rooted maniacal honesty of the shopkeeper was awakened in him; it was this prudent fellow who was right, for in business there is no such thing as sentiment, it is only a question of figures.

"Give me your hand, my boy," said he in conclusion. "It's settled we won't speak about the marriage for another year. One must think of the business before everything."

That evening, in their room, when Madame Baudu questioned her husband as to the result of the conversation, the latter had resumed his obstinate wish to fight in person to the bitter end. He gave Colomban high praise, calling him a solid fellow, firm in his ideas, brought up with the best principles, incapable, for instance, of joking with the customers like those puppies at The Paradise. No, he was honest, he belonged to the family, he didn't speculate on the business as though he were a stock-jobber.

"Well, then, when's the marriage to take place?" asked Madame Baudu.

"Later on," replied he, "when I am able to keep to my promises."

She made no gestures, she simply observed: "It will be our daughter's death."

Baudu restrained himself, stirred up with anger. He was the one whom it would kill, if they continually upset him like this! Was it his fault? He loved his daughter—would lay down his life for her; but he could not make the business prosper when it obstinately refused to do so. Geneviève ought to have a little more sense, and wait patiently for a better balance-sheet. The deuce! Colomban was there, no one would run away with him!

"It's incredible!" repeated he; "such a well-trained girl!"

Madame Baudu said no more. No doubt she had guessed Geneviève's jealous agony; but she did not dare to inform her husband. A singular womanly modesty always prevented her approaching certain tender, delicate subjects with him. When he saw her so silent, he turned his anger against the people opposite, stretching his fists out in the air, towards the works, where they were setting up large iron girders, with a great noise of hammers.

Denise had decided to return to The Ladies' Paradise, having understood that the Robineaus, though forced to cut down their staff, did not like to dismiss her. To maintain their position, now, they were obliged to do everything themselves. Gaujean, obstinate in his rancor, renewed their bills, even promised to find them funds; but they were frightened, they wanted to go in for economy and order. During a whole fortnight Denise had felt uneasy with them, and she had to speak first, saying she had found a situation elsewhere. This was a great relief. Madame Robineau embraced her, deeply affected, saying she should always miss her. Then when, in reply to a question, the young girl said she was going back to Mouret's, Robineau turned pale.

"You are right!" he exclaimed violently.

It was not so easy to tell the news to old Bourras. However, Denise had to give him notice, and she trembled, for she was full of gratitude towards him. Bourras just at this time was in a continual fever of rage—full of invectives against the works going on next door. The builder's carts blocked up his doorway; the picks tapped on his walls; everything in his place, the umbrellas and the sticks, danced about to the noise of the hammers. It seemed that the hovel, obstinately remaining amid all these demolitions, was going to give way. But the worst of all was that the architect, in order to connect the existing shops with those about to be opened in the Hôtel Duvillard, had conceived the idea of boring a passage under the little house that separated them. This house belonged to the firm of Mouret & Co., and the lease stipulating that the tenant should submit to all necessary repairs, the workmen appeared on the scene one morning. At this Bourras nearly went into a fit. Wasn't it enough to strangle him on all sides, on the right, the left, and behind, without attacking him underfoot as well, taking the ground from under him! And he drove the masons away, and went to law. Repairs, yes! but this was rather a work of embellishment. The neighborhood thought he would carry the day, without, however, being sure of anything. The case, however, threatened to be a long one, and people became very excited over this interminable duel. The day Denise resolved to give him notice, Bourras had just returned from his lawyer.

"Would you believe it!" exclaimed he, "they now say the house is not solid; they pretend that the foundations must be strengthened. Confound it! they have shaken it up so with their infernal machines, that it isn't astonishing if it gives way!"

Then, when the young girl announced she was going away,

and that she was going back to The Ladies' Paradise at a salary of a thousand francs, he was so amazed that he simply raised his trembling hands in the air. The emotion made him drop into a chair.

"You! you!" he stammered. "Ah, I'm the only one—I'm the only one left!" After a pause, he asked: "And the youngster?"

"He'll go back to Madame Gras's," replied Denise. "She was very fond of him."

They again remained silent. She would have rather seen him furious, shearing and banging with his fist; this old man, speechless, crushed, made her heart bleed. But he gradually recovered, and cried out: "A thousand francs! that can't be refused. You'll all go. Go, then, leave me here alone. Yes, alone—you understand! There shall be one who will never bow his head. And tell them I'll win my lawsuit, if I have to sell my last shirt for it!"

Denise was not to leave Robineau's till the end of the month. She had seen Mouret again; everything was settled. One evening as she was going up to her room, Deloche, who was watching for her in a doorway, stopped her. He was delighted, having just heard the good news; they were all talking about it in the shop, he said. And he told her the gossip of the counters.

"You know, the young ladies in the dress department are pulling long faces!" Then, interrupting himself, he added: "By the way, you remember Clara Prunaire? Well, it appears the governor has—You understand?"

He had turned quite red. She, very pale, exclaimed: "Monsieur Mouret!"

"Funny taste—eh?" he resumed. "A woman who looks like a horse. The little girl from the under-linen department, whom he had twice last year, was, at least, good-looking. However, that's his business."

Denise, once upstairs, almost fainted away. It was surely through coming up too quick. Leaning out of the window she had a sudden vision of Valognes, the deserted street and grassy pavement, which she used to see from her room as a child; and she was seized with a desire to go and live there—to seek refuge in the peace and forgetfulness of the country. Paris irritated her, she hated The Ladies' Paradise, she hardly knew why she had consented to go back. She would certainly suffer as much as ever there; she was already suffering from an unknown uneasiness since Deloche's stories. Suddenly, without any notice, a flood of tears forced her to leave the window. She wept on for some time, and found a little courage to live on still. The next day at breakfast-time, as Robineau had sent her on an errand, and she was passing The Old Elbeuf, she pushed open the door on seeing Colomban alone in the shop. The Baudus were breakfasting; she could hear the clatter of the knives and forks in the little room.

"You can come in," said the shopman. "They are at breakfast."

But she motioned him to be silent, and drew him into a corner. Then, lowering her voice, she said: "It's you I want to speak to. Have you no heart? Don't you see that Geneviève loves you, and that it's killing her."

She was trembling, the previous night's fever had taken possession of her again. He, frightened, surprised at this sudden attack, stood looking at her, without a word.

"Do you hear?" she continued. "Geneviève knows you love another. She told me so. She wept like a child. Ah, poor girl! she isn't very strong now, I can tell you! If you had seen her thin arms! It's heart-breaking. You can't leave her to die like this!"

At last he spoke, quite overcome. "But she isn't ill—you exaggerate! I don't see anything myself. Besides, it's her father who is postponing the marriage."

Denise sharply corrected this falsehood, certain that the least persistence on the part of the young man would decide her uncle. As to Colomban's surprise, it was not feigned; he had really never noticed Geneviève's slow agony. For him it was a very disagreeable revelation; for while he remained ignorant of it, he had no great blame to tax himself with.

"And who for?" resumed Denise. "For a worthless girl! You can't know who you are loving! Up to the present I have not wanted to hurt your feelings, I have often avoided answering your continual questions. Well! she goes with everybody, she laughs at you, you will never have her, or you may have her, like others, just once in a way."

He listened to her, very pale; and at each of the sentences she threw into his face, his lips trembled. She, in a cruel fit, yielded to a transport of anger of which she had no consciousness. "In short," said she in a final cry, "she's with Monsieur Mouret, if you want to know!"

Her voice was stifled, she turned paler than Colomban himself. Both stood looking at each other. Then he stammered out: "I love her!"

Denise felt ashamed of herself. Why was she talking in this way to this young fellow? Why was she getting so excited? She stood there mute, the simple reply he had just given resounded in her heart like the clang of a bell, which deafened her. "I love her, I love her!" and it seemed to spread. He was right, he could not marry another woman. And as she turned round, she observed Geneviève on the threshold of the dining room.

"Be quiet!" she said rapidly.

But it was too late, Geneviève must have heard, for her face was white and bloodless. Just at that moment a customer opened the door—Madame Bourdelais, one of the last faithful customers of The Old Elbeuf, where she found solid goods for her money; for a long time past Madame de Boves had followed the fashion, and gone over to The Ladies' Paradise; Madame Marty herself no longer came, entirely captivated by the seductions of the display opposite. And Geneviève was forced to go forward, and say in her weak voice:

"What do you desire, madame?"

Madame Bourdelais wished to see some flannel. Colomban took down a roll from a shelf. Geneviève showed the article; and both of them, their hands cold, found themselves brought together behind the counter. Meanwhile Baudu came out of the dining room last, behind his wife, who had gone and seated herself at the pay-desk. At first he did not meddle with the sale, but stood up, looking at Madame Bourdelais.

"It is not good enough," said the latter. "Show me the strongest you have."

Colomban took down another bundle. There was a silence. Madame Bourdelais examined the stuff.

"How much?"

"Six francs, madame," replied Geneviève. The lady made an abrupt movement. "Six francs!" said she. "But they have the same opposite at five francs."

A slight contraction passed over Baudu's face. He could not help interfering politely. No doubt madame made a mistake, the stuff ought to have been sold at six francs and a half; it was impossible to give it at five francs. It must be another quality she was referring to.

"No, no," she repeated, with the obstinacy of a lady who could not be deceived. "The quality is the same. It may even be a little thicker."

And the discussion got very warm. Baudu, his face getting bilious, made an effort to continue smiling. His bitterness against The Ladies' Paradise was bursting in his throat.

"Really," said Madame Bourdelais at last, "you must treat me better, otherwise I shall go opposite, like the others."

He then lost his head, and cried out, shaking with a passion he could not repress: "Well! go opposite!"

At this she got up, greatly annoyed, and went away without turning round, saying: "That's what I am going to do, sir."

A general stupor ensued. The governor's violence had frightened all of them. He was himself scared, and trembled at what he had just said. The phrase had escaped against his will in the explosion of a long pent-up rancor. And the Baudus now stood there motionless, following Madame Bourdelais with their looks, watching her cross the street. She seemed to be carrying off their fortune. When she slowly passed under the high door of The Ladies' Paradise, when they saw her disappear in the crowd, they felt a sort of sudden wrench.

"There's another they've taken from us!" murmured the draper. Then turning towards Denise, of whose re-engagement he was aware, he said: "You as well, they've taken you back. Oh, I don't blame you for it. As they have the money, they are naturally the strongest."

Just then, Denise, still hoping that Geneviève had not overheard Colomban, was saying to her: "He loves you. Try and cheer up."

But the young girl replied to her in a very low and heartbroken voice: "Why do you tell me a falsehood? Look! he can't help it, he's always glancing up there. I know very well they've stolen him from me, as they've robbed us of everything else."

Geneviève went and sat down on the seat at the desk near her mother. The latter had doubtless guessed the fresh blow received by her daughter, for her anxious eyes wandered from her to Colomban, and then to The Ladies' Paradise. It was true, they had stolen everything from them: from the father, a fortune; from the mother, her dying child; from the daughter, a husband, waited for for ten years. Before this condemned family, Denise, whose heart was overflowing with pity, felt for an instant afraid of being wicked. Was she not going to assist this machine which was crushing the poor people? But she felt herself carried away as it were by an invisible force, and knew that she was doing no wrong.

"Bah!" resumed Baudu, to give himself courage; "we sha'n't die over it, after all. For one customer lost we shall find two others. You hear, Denise, I've got over seventy thousand francs there, which will certainly trouble your Mouret's rest. Come, come, you others, don't look so glum!"

But he could not enliven them. He himself relapsed into a pale consternation; and they all stood with their eyes on the monster, attracted, possessed, full of their misfortune. The work was nearly finished, the scaffolding had been removed from the front, a whole side of the colossal edifice appeared, with its white walls and large light windows. Along the pavement, at last open to circulation, stood eight vans that the messengers were loading one after the other before the parcels-office. In the sunshine, a ray of which ran along the street, the green panels, picked out with red and yellow, sparkled like so many mirrors, sending blinding reflections right into The Old Elbeuf. The drivers, dressed in black, of a correct appearance, were holding the horses well in, superb pairs, shaking their silvered bits. And each time a van was loaded, there was a sonorous, rolling noise, which made the neighboring small shops tremble. And before this triumphal procession, which they were destined to submit to twice a day, the Baudus' hearts broke. The father half fainted away, asking himself where this continual flood of goods could go to; whilst the mother, tormented to death about her daughter, continued to gaze into the street, her eyes drowned in a flood of tears.

CHAPTER IX.

It was on a Monday, the 14th of March, that The Ladies' Paradise inaugurated its new buildings by a great exhibition of summer novelties, which was to last three days. Outside, a sharp wind was blowing, the passers-by, surprised by this return of winter, spun along, buttoned up in their overcoats. However, behind the closed doors of the neighboring shops, quite an agitation was fermenting; and one could see, against the windows, the pale faces of the small tradesmen, occupied in counting the first carriages which stopped before the new grand entrance in the Rue Neuve-Saint-Augustin. This door, lofty and deep like a church porch, surmounted by a group—Industry and Commerce hand-in-hand amidst a complication of symbols—was sheltered by a vast awning, the fresh gilding of which seemed to light up the pavement with a ray of sunshine. To the right and left stretched the shop fronts, barely dry and of a blinding whiteness, running along the Rue Monsigny and the Rue de la Michodière, occupying the whole island, except on the Rue du Dix-Décembre side, where the Crédit Immobilier intended to build. Along this barrack-like development, the small tradesmen, when they raised their heads, perceived the piles of goods through the large plate-glass windows which, from the ground floor up to the second storey, opened the house to the light of day. And this enormous cube, this colossal bazaar, shut out the sky from them, seeming to cause the cold which was making them shiver behind their frozen counters.

As early as six o'clock, Mouret was on the spot, giving his final orders. In the centre, starting from the grand entrance, a large

gallery ran from end to end, flanked right and left by two nar-
rower galleries, the Monsigny Gallery and the Michodière Gallery. The court-yards had been glazed and turned into halls, iron
staircases rose from the ground floor, iron bridges were thrown
from one end to the other on the two storeys. The architect, who
happened to be a young man of talent, with modern ideas, had
only used stone for the underground floor and the corner pillars,
constructing the whole carcase of iron, the assemblage of beams
and rafters being supported by columns. The arches of the flooring and the partitions were of brickwork. Space had been gained
everywhere, light and air entered freely, and the public circulated with the greatest ease under the bold flights of the far-
stretching girders. It was the cathedral of modern commerce,
light but solid, made for a nation of customers. Below, in the central gallery, after the door bargains, came the cravat, the glove,
and the silk departments; the Monsigny Gallery was occupied by
the linen and the Rouen goods; the Michodière Gallery by the
mercery, the hosiery, the drapery, and the woollen departments.
Then, on the first floor were installed the ready-made, the under-
linen, the shawl, the lace, and other new departments, whilst the
bedding, the carpets, the furnishing materials, all the cumbersome articles difficult to handle, had been relegated to the second floor. The number of departments was now thirty-nine, with
eighteen hundred employees, of whom two hundred were
women. Quite a little world operated there, in the sonorous life
of the high metallic naves.

Mouret's unique passion was to conquer woman. He wished
her to be queen in his house, and he had built this temple to get
her completely at his mercy. His sole aim was to intoxicate her
with gallant attentions, and traffic on her desires, work on her
fever. Night and day he racked his brain to invent fresh attrac-
tions. He had already introduced two lifts lined with velvet for
the upper storeys, in order to spare delicate ladies the trouble of
mounting the stairs. Then he had just opened a bar where the
customers could find, gratis, some light refreshment, syrups and
biscuits, and a reading-room, a monumental gallery, decorated
with excessive luxury, in which he had even ventured on an exhi-

bition of pictures. But his most profound idea was to conquer the mother through the child, when unable to do so through her coquetry; he neglected no means, speculated on every sentiment, created departments for little boys and girls, arresting the passing mothers by distributing pictures and air-balls to the children. A stroke of genius this idea of distributing to each buyer a red air-ball made of fine gutta-percha, bearing in large letters the name of the shop, and which, held by a string, floated in the air, parading in the streets a living advertisement.

But the greatest power of all was the advertising. Mouret spent three hundred thousand francs a year in catalogues, advertisements, and bills. For his summer sale he had launched forth two hundred thousand catalogues, of which fifty thousand went abroad, translated into every language. He now had them illustrated with engravings, even accompanying them with samples, gummed between the leaves. It was an overflowing display; The Ladies' Paradise became a household word all over the world, invading the walls, the newspapers, and even the curtains at the theatres. He declared that woman was powerless against advertising, that she was bound to follow the crowd. Not only that, he laid still more seductive traps for her, analyzing her like a great moralist. Thus he had discovered that she could not resist a bargain, that she bought without necessity when she thought she saw a cheap line, and on this observation he based his system of reductions in price, progressively lowering the price of unsold articles, preferring to sell them at a loss, faithful to his principle of the continual renewal of the goods. He had penetrated still further into the heart of woman, and had just thought of the "returns," a masterpiece of Jesuitical seduction. "Take whatever you like, madame; you can return the article if you don't like it." And the woman who hesitated was provided with the last excuse, the possibility of repairing an extravagant folly, she took the article with an easy conscience. The returns and the reduction of prices now formed part of the classical working of the new style of business.

But where Mouret revealed himself as an unrivalled master was in the interior arrangement of the shops. He laid down as a law that not a corner of The Ladies' Paradise ought to remain deserted, requiring everywhere a noise, a crowd, evidence of life; for life, said he, attracts life, increases and multiplies. From this law he drew all sorts of applications. In the first place, there ought always to be a crush at the entrance, so that the people in the street should mistake it for a riot; and he obtained this crush by placing a lot of bargains at the doors, shelves and baskets overflowing with very low-priced articles; so that the common people crowded there, stopping up the doorway, making the shop look as if it were crammed with customers, when it was often only half full. Then, in the galleries, he had the art of concealing the departments in which business was slack; for instance, the shawl department in summer, and the printed calico department in winter, he surrounded them with busy departments, drowning them with a continual uproar. It was he alone who had been inspired with the idea of placing on the second floor the carpet and furniture counters, counters where the customers were less frequent, and which if placed on the ground floor would have canoed empty, cold spaces. If he could have managed it, he would have had the street running through his shop.

Just at that moment, Mouret was a prey to an attack of inspiration. On the Saturday evening, as he was giving a last look at the preparations for the Monday's great sale, he was suddenly struck with the idea that the arrangement of the departments adopted by him was wrong and stupid; and yet it seemed a perfectly logical arrangement: the stuffs on one side, the made-up articles on the other, an intelligent order of things which would enable the customers to find their way themselves. He had thought of this orderly arrangement formerly, in Madame Hédouin's narrow shop; and now he felt his faith shaken, just as he carried out his idea. Suddenly he cried out that they would "have to alter all that." They had forty-eight hours, and half what had been done had to be changed. The staff, frightened, bewildered, had been obliged to work two nights and the entire Sunday, amidst a frightful disorder. On the Monday morning even, an hour before the opening, there was still some goods to be placed.

Decidedly the governor was going mad, no one understood, a general consternation prevailed.

"Come, look sharp!" cried Mouret, with the quiet assurance of his genius. "There are some more costumes to be taken upstairs. And the Japan goods, are they placed on the central landing? A last effort, my boys, you'll see the sale by-and-by."

Bourdoncle had also been there since daybreak. He did not understand any more than the others, and he followed the governor's movements with an anxious eye. He hardly dared to ask him any questions, knowing how Mouret received people in those critical moments. However, he at last made up his mind, and gently asked:

"Was it really necessary to upset everything like that, on the eve of our sale?"

At first Mouret shrugged his shoulders without replying. Then as the other persisted, he burst out: "So that all the customers should heap themselves into one corner—eh? A nice idea of mine! I should never have got over it! Don't you see that it would have localized the crowd. A woman would have come in, gone straight to the department she wished, passed from the petticoat counter to the dress one, from the dress to the mantle, then retired, without having even lost herself for a moment! Not one would have thoroughly seen the establishment!"

"But," remarked Bourdoncle, "now that you have disarranged everything, and thrown the goods all over the place, the employees will wear out their legs in guiding the customers from department to department."

Mouret gave a look of superb contempt. "I don't care a hang for that! They're young, it'll make them grow! So much the better if they do walk about! They'll appear more numerous, and increase the crowd. The greater the crush the better; all will go well!" He laughed, and deigned to explain his idea, lowering his voice: "Look here, Bourdoncle, listen to the result. Firstly, this continual circulation of customers disperses them all over the shop, multiplies them, and makes them lose their heads; secondly, as they must be conducted from one end of the establishment to the other, if they want, for instance, a lining after having bought a dress, these journeys in every direction triple the size of the house in their eyes; thirdly, they are forced to traverse departments where they would never have set foot otherwise, temptations present themselves on their passage, and they succumb; fourthly—" Bourdoncle was now laughing with him. At this Mouret, delighted, stopped to call out to the messengers: "Very good, my boys! now for a sweep, and it'll be splendid!"

But on turning round he perceived Denise. He and Bourdoncle were opposite the ready-made department, which he had just dismembered by sending the dresses and costumes up on the second floor at the other end of the building. Denise, the first down, was opening her eyes with astonishment, quite bewildered by the new arrangements.

"What is it?" murmured she; "are we going to move?"

This surprise appeared to amuse Mouret, who adored these sensational effects. Early in February Denise had returned to The Ladies' Paradise, where she had been agreeably surprised to find the staff polite, almost respectful. Madame Aurélie especially was very kind; Marguerite and Clara seemed resigned; even down to old Jouve, who also bowed his head, with an awkward embarrassed air, as if desirous of effacing the disagreeable memory of the past. It sufficed that Mouret had said a few words, everybody was whispering, following her with their eyes. And in this general amiability, the only things that wounded her were Deloche's singularly melancholy looks, and Pauline's inexplicable smiles. However, Mouret was still looking at her in his delighted way.

"What is it you want, mademoiselle?" asked he at last. Denise had not noticed him. She blushed slightly. Since her return she had received marks of kindness from him which greatly touched her. Pauline, without her knowing why, had given her a full account of the governor's and Clara's love affairs: where he saw her, and what he paid her; and she often returned to the subject, even adding that he had another mistress, that Madame Desforges, well known by all the shop. Such stories stirred up Denise, she felt in his presence all her former fears, an uneasiness in which her gratitude was struggling against her anger.

"It's all this confusion going on in the place," she murmured. Mouret then approached her and said in a lower voice:

"Have the goodness to come to my office this evening after business. I wish to speak to you."

Greatly agitated, she bowed her head without saying a word. And she went into the department where the other saleswomen were now arriving. But Bourdoncle had overheard Mouret, and he looked at him with a smile. He even ventured to say when they were alone:

"That girl again! Be careful; it will end by being serious!"

Mouret hastily defended himself, concealing his emotion beneath an air of superior indifference. "Never fear, it's only a joke! The woman who'll catch me isn't born, my dear fellow!"

And as the shop was opening at last, he rushed off to give a final look at the various counters. Bourdoncle shook his head. This Denise, so simple and quiet, began to make him uneasy. The first time, he had conquered by a brutal dismissal. But she had reappeared, and he felt she had become so strong that he now treated her as a redoubtable adversary, remaining mute before her, patiently waiting. Mouret, whom he caught up, was shouting out downstairs, in the Saint-Augustin Hall, opposite the entrance door:

"Are you playing with me? I ordered the blue parasols to be put as a border. Just pull all that down, and be quick about it!"

He would listen to nothing; a gang of messengers had to come and re-arrange the exhibition of parasols. Seeing the customers arriving, he even had the doors closed for a moment, declaring that he would not open them, rather than have the blue parasols in the centre. It ruined his composition. The renowned dressers, Hutin, Mignot, and others, came to look, and opened their eyes; but they affected not to understand, being of a different school.

At last the doors were opened again, and the crowd flowed in. From the first, before the shop was full, there was such a crush at the doorway that they were obliged to call the police to re-establish the circulation on the pavement. Mouret had calculated correctly; all the housekeepers, a compact troop of middle-class women and workmen's wives, swarmed around the bargains and remnants displayed in the open street. They felt the "hung" goods at the entrance; a calico at seven sous, a wool and cotton grey stuff at nine sous, and, above all, an Orleans cloth at seven sous and a half, which was emptying the poorer purses. There was an elbowing, a feverish crushing around the shelves and baskets containing the articles at reduced prices, lace at two sous, ribbon at five, garters at three the pair, gloves, petticoats, cravats, cotton socks, and stockings, were all tumbled about, and disappearing, as if swallowed up by the voracious crowd. Notwithstanding the cold, the shopmen who were selling in the open street could not serve fast enough. A woman in the family way cried out with pain; two little girls were nearly stifled.

All the morning this crush went on increasing. Towards one o'clock there was a crowd waiting to enter; the street was blocked as in a time of riot. Just at that moment, as Madame de Boves and her daughter Blanche were standing on the pavement opposite, hesitating, they were accosted by Madame Marty, also accompanied by her daughter Valentine.

"What a crowd—eh?" said the former. "They're killing themselves inside. I ought not to have come, I was in bed, but got up to get a little fresh air."

"Just like me," said the other. "I promised my husband to go and see his sister at Montmartre. Then just as I was passing, I thought of a piece of braid I wanted. I may as well buy it here as anywhere else, mayn't I? Oh, I sha'n't spend a sou! in fact I don't want anything."

However, they did not take their eyes off the door, seized and carried away as it were by the force of the crowd.

"No, no, I'm not going in, I'm afraid," murmured Madame de Boves. "Blanche, let's go away, we should be crushed."

But her voice failed, she was gradually yielding to the desire to follow the others; and her fear dissolved in the irresistible affection of the crush. Madame Marty was also giving way repeating:

"Keep hold of my dress, Valentine. Ah, well! I've never seen such a thing before. You are lifted off your feet. What will it be inside?"

The ladies, seized by the current, could not now go back. As streams attract to themselves the fugitive waters of a valley, so it seemed that the wave of customers, flowing into the vestibule, was absorbing the passers-by, drinking in the population from the four corners of Paris. They advanced but slowly, squeezed almost to death, kept upright by the shoulders and bellies around them, of which they felt the close heat; and their satisfied desire enjoyed the painful entrance which incited still further their curiosity. There was a pell-mell of ladies arrayed in silk, of poorly dressed middle-class women, and of bare-headed girls, all excited and carried away by the same passion. A few men buried beneath the overflow of bosoms were casting anxious glances around them. A nurse, in the thickest of the crowd, held her baby above her head, the youngster crowing with delight. The only one to get angry was a skinny woman, who broke out into bad words, accusing her neighbor of digging right into her.

"I really think I shall lose my skirts in this crowd," remarked Madame de Boves.

Mute, her face still fresh from the open air, Madame Marty was standing on tip-toe to see above the others' heads into the depths of the shop. The pupils of her grey eyes were as contracted as those of a cat coming out of the broad daylight; she had the reposed flesh, and the clear expression of a person just waking up.

"Ah, at last!" said she, heaving a sigh. The ladies had just extricated themselves. They were in the Saint-Augustin Hall, which they were greatly surprised to find almost empty. But a feeling of comfort invaded them, they seemed to be entering into springtime after emerging from the winter of the street. Whilst outside, the frozen wind, laden with rain and hail, was still blowing, the fine season, in The Paradise galleries, was already budding forth with the light stuffs, the flowery brilliancy of the tender shades, the rural gaiety of the summer dresses and the parasols.

"Do look there!" exclaimed Madame de Boves, standing motionless, her eyes in the air.

It was the exhibition of parasols. Wide-open, rounded off like shields, they covered the whole hall, from the glazed roof to the varnished oak moldings below. They described festoons round the semi-circular arches of the upper storeys; they descended in garlands along the slender columns; they ran along in close lines on the balustrades of the galleries and the staircases; and everywhere, ranged symmetrically, speckling the walls with red, green, and yellow, they looked like great Venetian lanterns, lighted up for some colossal entertainment. In the corners were more complicated patterns, stars composed of parasols at thirty-nine sous, the light shades of which, pale-blue, cream-white, and blush rose, seemed to burn with the sweetness of a night-light; whilst up above, immense Japanese parasols, on which golden-colored cranes soared in a purple sky, blazed forth with the reflections of a great conflagration.

Madame Marty endeavored to find a phrase to express her rapture, but could only exclaim, "It's like fairyland!" Then trying to find out where she was she continued: "Let's see, the braid is in the mercery department. I shall buy my braid and be off."

"I will go with you," said Madame de Boves. "Eh? Blanche, we'll just go through the shop, nothing more."

But they had hardly left the door before they lost themselves. They turned to the left, and as the mercery department had been moved, they dropped right into the middle of the one devoted to collarettes, cuffs, trimmings, &c. It was very warm under the galleries, a hot-house heat, moist and close, laden with the insipid odor of the stuffs, and in which the stamping of the crowd was stifled. They then returned to the door, where an outward current was already established, an interminable line of women and children, over whom floated a multitude of red air-balls. Forty thousand of these were ready; there were men specially placed for their distribution. To see the customers who were going out, one would have thought there was a flight of enormous soap-bubbles above them, at the end of the almost invisible strings, reflecting the fiery glare of the parasols. The whole place was illuminated by them.

"There's quite a world here!" declared Madame de Boves. "You hardly know where you are."

However, the ladies could not remain in the eddy of the door, right in the crush of the entrance and exit. Fortunately, Jouve, the inspector, came to their assistance. He stood in the vestibule, grave, attentive, eyeing each woman as she passed. Specially charged with the inside police, he was on the lookout for thieves, and especially followed women in the family way, when the fever of their eyes became too alarming.

"The mercery department, ladies?" said he obligingly. "Turn to the left; look! just there behind the hosiery department."

Madame de Boves thanked him. But Madame Marty, turning round, no longer saw her daughter Valentine beside her. She was beginning to feel frightened, when she caught sight of her, already a long way off, at the end of the Saint-Augustin Hall, deeply absorbed before a table covered with a heap of women's cravats at nineteen sous. Mouret practiced the system of offering articles to the customers, hooking and plundering them as they passed: for he used every sort of advertisement, laughing at the discretion of certain fellow-tradesmen who thought the articles should be left to speak for themselves. Special salesmen, idle and smooth-tongued Parisians, thus got rid of considerable quantities of small trashy things.

"Oh, mamma!" murmured Valentine, "just look at these cravats. They have a bird embroidered at the corners."

The shopman cracked up the article, swore it was all silk, that the manufacturer had become bankrupt, and that they would never have such a bargain again.

"Nineteen sous—is it possible?" said Madame Marty, tempted as well as her daughter. "Well! I can take a couple, that won't ruin us."

Madame de Boves disdained this style of thing, she detested things being offered. A shopman calling her made her run away. Madame Marty, surprised, could not understand this nervous horror of commercial quackery, for she was of another nature; she was one of those fortunate women who delight in being thus violated, in bathing in the caress of this public offering, with the enjoyment of plunging one's hands in everything, and wasting one's time in useless talk.

"Now," she said, "I'm going for my braid. I don't wish to see anything else."

However, as she crossed the cravat and glove departments, her heart once more failed her. There was, under the diffuse light, a display made up of bright and gay colors, which produced a ravishing effect. The counters, symmetrically arranged, seemed like so many flower-borders, changing the hall into a French garden, in which smiled a tender gamut of blossoms. Lying on the bare wood, in open boxes, and protruding from the overflowing drawers, a quantity of silk handkerchiefs displayed the bright scarlet of the geranium, the creamy white of the petunia, the golden yellow of the chrysanthemum, the sky-blue of the verbena; and higher up, on brass stems, twined another florescence, fichus carelessly hung, ribbons unrolled, quite a brilliant cordon, which extended along, climbed up the columns, and were multiplied indefinitely by the mirrors. But what most attracted the crowd was a Swiss cottage in the glove department, made entirely of gloves, a chef d'oeuvre of Mignot's, which had taken him two days to arrange. In the first place, the ground floor was composed of black gloves; then came straw-colored, mignonette, and red gloves, distributed in the decoration, bordering the windows, forming the balconies, and taking the place of the tiles.

"What do you desire, madame?" asked Mignot, on seeing Madame Marty planted before the cottage. "Here are some Swedish kid gloves at one franc fifteen sous, first quality."

He offered his wares with furious energy, calling the passing customers from the end of his counter, dunning them with his politeness. As she shook her head in refusal he continued: "Tyrolian gloves, one franc five sous. Turin gloves for children, embroidered gloves in all colors."

"No, thanks; I don't want anything," declared Madame Marty.

But feeling that her voice was softening, he attacked her with greater energy than ever, holding the embroidered gloves before her eyes; and she could not resist, she bought a pair. Then, as Madame de Boves looked at her with a smile, she blushed.

"Don't you think me childish—eh? If I don't make haste and get my braid and be off, I shall be done for."

Unfortunately, there was such a crush in the mercery department that she could not get served. They had both been waiting for over ten minutes, and were getting annoyed, when the sudden meeting with Madame Bourdelais occupied their attention. The latter explained, with her quiet practical air, that she had just brought the little ones to see the show. Madeleine was ten, Edmond eight, and Lucien four years old; and they were laughing with joy, it was a cheap treat long promised.

"They are really too comical; I shall buy a red parasol," said Madame Marty all at once, stamping with impatience at being there doing nothing.

She chose one at fourteen francs and a half. Madame Bourdelais, after having watched the purchase with a look of blame, said to her amicably: "You are very wrong to be in such a hurry. In a month's time you could have had it for ten francs. They won't catch me like that."

And she developed quite a theory of careful housekeeping. As the shops lowered their prices, it was simply a question of waiting. She did not wish to be taken in by them, preferred to take advantage of their real bargains. She even showed a feeling of malice in the struggle, boasting that she had never left them a sou profit.

"Come," said she at last, "I've promised my little ones to show them the pictures upstairs in the reading-room. Come up with us, you have plenty of time."

And the braid was forgotten. Madame Marty yielded at once, whilst Madame de Boves refused, preferring to take a turn on the ground floor first. Besides, they were sure to meet again upstairs. Madame Bourdelais was looking for a staircase when she perceived one of the lifts; and she pushed her children in to complete their pleasure. Madame Marty and Valentine also entered the narrow cage, where they were closely packed; but the mirrors, the velvet seats, and the polished brass work took up their attention so much that they arrived at the first storey without having felt the gentle ascent of the machine. Another pleasure was in store for them, in the first gallery. As they passed before the refreshment bar, Madame Bourdelais did not fail to gorge her little family with syrup. It was a square room with a large marble counter; at the two ends there were silvered fountains from which flowed a small stream of water; whilst rows of bottles stood on small shelves behind. Three waiters were continually engaged wiping and filling the glasses. To restrain the thirsty crowd, they had been obliged to establish a system of turns, as at theatres and railway-stations, by erecting a barrier covered with velvet. The crush was terrific. Some people, losing all shame before these gratuitous treats, made themselves ill.

"Well! where are they?" exclaimed Madame Bourdelais when she extricated herself from the crowd, after having wiped the children's faces with her handkerchief.

But she caught sight of Madame Marty and Valentine at the further end of another gallery, a long way off. Both buried beneath a heap of petticoats, were still buying. They were conquered, the mother and daughter were rapidly disappearing in the fever of spending which was carrying them away. When she at last arrived in the reading-room Madame Bourdelais installed Madeleine, Edmond, and Lucien before the large table; then taking from one of the shelves some photographic albums she brought them to them. The ceiling of the long apartment was covered with gold; at the two extremities, monumental chimney-pieces faced each other; some rather poor pictures, very richly framed, covered the walls; and between the columns before each of the arched bays opening into the various shops, were tall green plants in majolica vases. Quite a silent crowd surrounded the table, which was littered with reviews and newspapers, with here and there some ink-stands and boxes of stationery. Ladies took off their gloves, and wrote their letters on the paper stamped with the name of the house, which they crossed out with a dash of the pen. A few men, lolling back in the armchairs, were reading the newspapers. But a great many people sat there doing nothing: husbands waiting for their wives, let loose in the various departments, discreet young women looking out for their lovers, old relations left there as in a cloak-room, to be taken away when time to leave. And this little society, comfortably installed, quietly reposed itself there, glancing through the open bays into the depths of the galleries and the halls, from which a distant murmur ascended above the grating of the pens and the rustling of the newspapers.

"What! you here!" said Madame Bourdelais. "I didn't know you."

Near the children was a lady concealed behind the pages of a review. It was Madame Guibal. She seemed annoyed at the meeting; but quickly recovering herself, related that she had come to sit down for a moment to escape the crush. And as Madame Bourdelais asked her if she was going to make any purchases, she replied with her languorous air, hiding behind her eyelashes the egotistical greediness of her looks:

"Oh! no. On the contrary, I have come to return some goods. Yes, some door-curtains which I don't like. But there is such a crowd that I am waiting to get near the department."

She went on talking, saying how convenient this system of returns was; formerly she never bought anything, but now she sometimes allowed herself to be tempted. In fact, she returned four articles out of five, and was getting known at all the counters for her strange system of buying, and her eternal discontent which made her bring back the articles one by one, after having kept them several days. But, whilst speaking, she did not take her eyes off the doors of the reading-room; and she appeared greatly relieved when Madame Bourdelais rejoined her children, to explain the photographs to them. Almost at the same moment Monsieur de Boves and Paul de Vallagnosc came in. The count, who affected to be showing the young man through the new buildings, exchanged a rapid glance with Madame Guibal; and she then plunged into her review again, as if she had not seen him.

"Hullo, Paul!" suddenly exclaimed a voice behind these gentlemen.

It was Mouret, on his way round to give a look at the various departments. They shook hands, and he at once asked: "Has Madame de Boves done us the honor of coming?"

"Well, no," replied the husband, "and she very much regrets it. She's not very well. Oh! nothing dangerous!"

But suddenly he pretended to catch sight of Madame Guibal,

and ran off, going up to her bareheaded, whilst the others merely bowed to her from a distance. She also pretended to be surprised. Paul smiled; he now understood the affair, and he related to Mouret in a low voice how Monsieur de Boves, whom he had met in the Rue Richelieu, had tried to get away from him, and had finished by dragging him into The Ladies' Paradise, under the pretext that he must show him the new buildings. For the last year the lady had drawn from Monsieur de Boves all the money and pleasure she could, never writing to him, making appointments with him in public places, churches, museums, and shops, to arrange their affairs.

"I fancy that at each meeting they change their hotel," murmured the young man. "Not long ago, he was on a tour of inspection; he wrote to his wife every day from Blois, Libourne, and Tarbes; and yet I feel convinced I saw them going into a family boarding-house at Batignolles. But look at him, isn't he splendid before her with his military correctness! The old French gallantry, my dear fellow, the old French gallantry!"

"And your marriage?" asked Mouret.

Paul, without taking his eyes off the count, replied that they were still waiting for the death of the aunt. Then, with a triumphant air: "There, did you see him? He stooped down, and slipped an address into her hand. She's now accepting with the most virtuous air. She's a terrible woman, that delicate red-haired creature with her careless ways. Well! there are some fine things going on in your place!"

"Oh!" said Mouret, smiling, "these ladies are not in my house, they are at home here."

He then began to joke. Love, like the swallows, always brought good luck to a house. No doubt he knew the girls who wandered about from counter to counter, the ladies who accidentally met a friend in the shop; but if they bought nothing, they filled up a place, and helped to crowd and warm the shop. Still continuing his gossip, he carried his old comrade off, and planted him on the threshold of the reading-room, opposite the grand central gallery, the successive halls of which ran along at their feet. Behind them, the reading-room still retained its quiet air, only disturbed by the scratching of the pens and the rustling of the newspapers. One old gentleman had gone to sleep over the *Moniteur*. Monsieur de Boves was looking at the pictures, with the evident intention of losing his future son-in-law in the crowd as soon as possible. And, alone, amid this calmness, Madame Bourdelais was amusing her children, talking very loud, as in a conquered place.

"You see they are quite at home," said Mouret, who pointed with a broad gesture to the multitude of women with which the departments were overflowing.

Just at that moment Madame Desforges, after having nearly had her mantle carried away in the crowd, at last came in and crossed the first hall. Then, on reaching the principal gallery, she raised her eyes. It was like a railway span, surrounded by the balustrades of the two storeys, intersected by hanging staircases, crossed by flying bridges. The iron staircases developed bold curves, multiplying the landings; the iron bridges suspended in space, ran straight along, very high up; and all this iron formed, beneath the white light of the windows, an excessively light architecture, a complicated lace-work through which the daylight penetrated, the modern realization of a dreamed of palace, of a Babel-like heaping up of the storeys, enlarging the rooms, opening up glimpses on to other floors and into other rooms without end. In fact, iron reigned every where; the young architect had had the honesty and courage not to disguise it under a coating of paint imitating stone or wood. Down below, in order not to outshine the goods, the decoration was sober, with large regular spaces in neutral tints; then as the metallic work ascended, the capitals of the columns became richer, the rivets formed ornaments, the shoulder-pieces and corbels were loaded with sculptured work; up above, there was a mass of painting, green and red, amidst a prodigality of gold, floods of gold, heaps of gold, even to the glazed-work, the glass of which was enameled and inlaid with gold. Under the covered galleries, the bare brickwork of the arches was also decorated in bright colors. Mosaics and earthenware also formed part of the decoration, enlivening the friezes, lighting up with their fresh notes the severity of the whole; whilst the stairs, with their red velvet covered hand-rails, were edged with a band of carved polished iron, which shone like the steel of a piece of armour.

Although she had already seen the new establishment Madame Desforges stood still, struck by the ardent life which was this day animating the immense nave. Below, around her, continued the eddying of the crowd, of which the double current of those entering and those going out made itself felt as far as the silk department; a crowd still very mixed in its elements, though the afternoon was bringing a greater number of ladies amongst the shopkeepers and house-wives; a great many women in mourning, with their flowing veils, and the inevitable wet nurses straying about, protecting their babies with their outstretched arms. And this sea of faces, these many-colored hats, these bare heads, both dark and light, rolled from one end of the gallery to the other, confused and discolored amidst the loud glare of the stuffs. Madame Desforges could see nothing but large price tickets bearing enormous figures everywhere, their white patches standing out on the bright printed cottons, the shining silks, and the sombre woolens. Piles of ribbons curtailed the heads, a wall of flannel threw out a promontory; on all sides the mirrors carried the departments back into infinite space, reflecting the displays with portions of the public, faces reversed, and halves of shoulders and arms; whilst to the right and to the left the lateral galleries opened up other vistas, the snowy background of the linen department, the speckled depth of the hosiery one, distant views illuminated by the rays of light from some glazed bay, and in which the crowd appeared nothing but a mass of human dust. Then, when Madame Desforges raised her eyes, she saw, along the staircases, on the flying bridges, around the balustrade of each storey, a continual humming ascent, an entire population in the air, travelling in the cuttings of the enormous ironwork construction, casting black shadows on the diffused light of the enameled windows. Large gilded lustres hung from the ceiling; a decoration of rugs, embroidered silks, stuffs worked with gold, hung down, draping the balustrade with gorgeous banners; and, from one end to the other, there were clouds of lace, palpitations of muslin, trophies of silks, apotheoses of half-dressed dummies; and right at the top, above all this confusion, the bedding department, suspended as it were, displayed little iron bedsteads with their mattresses, hung with their white curtains, a sort of school dormitory sleeping amidst the stamping of the customers, rarer and rarer as the departments ascended.

"Does madame require a cheap pair of garters?" asked a salesman of Madame Desforges, seeing her standing still. "All silk, twenty-nine sous."

She did not deign to answer. Things were being offered around her more feverishly than ever. She wanted, however, to find out where she was. Albert Lhomme's pay-desk was on her left; he knew her by sight and ventured to give her an amiable smile, not in the least hurry in the midst of the heaps of bills by which he was besieged; whilst, behind him, Joseph, struggling with the string-box, could not pack up the articles fast enough. She then saw where she was; the silk department must be in front of her. But it took her ten minutes to get there, the crowd was becoming so immense. Up in the air, at the end of their invisible strings, the red air-balls had become more numerous than ever; they now formed clouds of purple, gently blowing towards the doors, continuing to scatter themselves over Paris; and she had to bow her head beneath the flight of air-balls, when very young children held them, the string rolled round their little fingers.

"What! you have ventured here, madame?" exclaimed Bouthemont gaily, as soon as he caught sight of Madame Desforges.

The manager of the silk department, introduced to her by Mouret himself, was now in the habit of sometimes calling on her at her five o'clock tea. She thought him common, but very amiable, of a fine sanguine temper, which surprised and amused her. Besides, about two days before he had openly related to her the affair between Mouret and Clara, without any calculation, out of stupidity, like a fellow who loves a joke; and, stung with jealousy, concealing her wounded feelings beneath an appearance of disdain, she had come to try and discover her rival, a young lady in the dress department he had merely said, refusing to name her.

"Do you require anything today?" he asked her.

"Of course, or else I should not have come. Have you any silk for morning gowns?"

She hoped to obtain the name of the young lady from him, for she was full of a desire to see her. He immediately called Favier; and resumed talking to her, whilst waiting for the salesman, who was just finishing serving a customer who happened to be "the pretty lady," that beautiful blonde of whom the whole department occasionally spoke, without knowing anything of her life or even her name. This time the pretty lady was in deep mourning. Ah, who had she lost—her husband or her father? Not her father, or she would have appeared more melancholy. What had they been saying? She was not a gay woman then; she had a real husband. Unless, however, she should be in mourning for her mother. For a few minutes, notwithstanding the press of business, the department exchanged these various speculations.

"Make haste! it's intolerable!" cried Hutin to Favier, who had just returned from showing his customer to the pay-desk. "When that lady is here you never seem to finish. She doesn't care a fig for you!"

"She cares a deuced sight more for me than I do for her!" replied the vexed salesman.

But Hutin threatened to report him to the directors if he did not show more respect for the customers. He was getting terrible, of a morose severity, since the department had conspired together to get him into Robineau's place. He even showed himself so intolerable, after the promises of good-fellowship, with which he had formerly warmed his colleagues, that the latter were now secretly supporting Favier against him.

"Now, then, no back answers," replied Hutin sharply. "Monsieur Bouthemont wishes you to show some light designs in silks."

In the middle of the department, an exhibition of summer silks lighted up the hall with an aurora-like brilliancy, like the rising of a star, in the most delicate tints possible: pale rose, tender yellow, limpid blue, the entire gamut of iris. There were silks of a cloudy fineness, surahs lighter than the down falling from the trees, satined pekins soft and supple as a Chinese virgin's skin. There were, moreover, Japanese pongees, Indian tussores and corahs, without counting the light French silks, the thousand stripes, the small checks, the flowered patterns, all the most fanciful designs, which made one think of ladies in furbelows, walking about, in the sweet May mornings, under the immense trees of some park.

"I'll take this, the Louis XIV. with figured roses," said Madame Desforges at last.

And whilst Favier was measuring it, she made a last attempt with Bouthemont, who had remained near her.

"I'm going up to the ready-made department to see if there are any travelling cloaks. Is she fair, the young lady you were talking about?"

The manager, who felt rather anxious on finding her so persistent, merely smiled. But, just at that moment, Denise went by. She had just passed on to Liénard, who had charge of the merinoes, Madame Boutarel, that provincial lady who came up to Paris twice a year, to scatter all over The Ladies' Paradise the money she scraped together out of her housekeeping. And as Favier was about to take up Madame Desforges's silk, Hutin, thinking to annoy him, interfered.

"It's quite unnecessary, Mademoiselle Denise will have the kindness to conduct this lady."

Denise, quite confused, at once took charge of the parcel and the debit-note. She could never meet this young man face to face without experiencing a feeling of shame, as if he reminded her of a former fault; and yet she had only sinned in her dreams.

"But, tell me," said Madame Desforges, in a low tone, to Bouthemont, "isn't it this awkward girl? He has taken her back, then? But it is she, the heroine of the adventure!"

"Perhaps," replied the head of department, still smiling, and fully decided not to tell the truth.

Madame Desforges then slowly ascended the staircase, preceded by Denise; but she had to stop every two or three steps to avoid being carried away by the descending crowd. In the living vibration of the whole building, the iron supports seemed to stagger beneath the weight, as if continually trembling from the breath of the crowd. On each stair was a dummy, strongly fixed, displaying some garment: a costume, cloak, or dressing-gown; and it was like a double row of soldiers for some triumphal march-past, with the little wooden arm like the handle of a poniard, stuck into the red swan-skin, which gave a bloody appearance to the stump of a neck crowning the whole.

Madame Desforges was at last reaching the first storey, when a still greater surging of the crowd forced her to stop once more. She had now, beneath her, the departments on the ground floor, with the press of customers she had just passed through. It was a new spectacle, a sea of heads fore-shortened, concealing the bodices, swarming with a busy agitation. The white price tickets now appeared but so many thin lines, the promontory of flannels cut through the gallery like a narrow wall; whilst the carpets and the embroidered silks which decked the balustrades hung at her feet like processional banners suspended from the gallery of a church. In the distance, she could perceive the angles of the lateral galleries, as from the top of a steeple one perceives the corners of the neighboring streets, with the black spots of the passers-by moving about. But what surprised her above all, in the fatigue of her eyes blinded by the brilliant pell-mell of colours, was, when she lowered her lids, to feel the crowd more than ever, by its dull noise like the rising tide, and by the human warmth that it exhaled. A fine dust rose from the floor, laden with the odor of woman, the odor of her linen and her bust, of her skirts and her hair, an invading, penetrating odor, which seemed to be the incense of this temple raised for the worship of her body.

Meanwhile Mouret, still standing up before the reading-room with Vallagnosc, was inhaling this odor, intoxicating himself with it, and repeating: "They are quite at home. I know some who spend the whole day here, eating cakes and writing their letters. There's only one thing more to do, and that is, to find them beds."

This joke made Paul smile, he who, in the *ennui* of his pessimism, continued to think the crowd stupid in thus running after a lot of gew-gaws. Whenever he came to give his old comrade a look up, he went away almost vexed to see him so full of life amidst his people of coquettes. Would not one of them, with shallow brain and empty heart, teach him one day the stupidity and uselessness of existence? That very day Octave seemed to lose some of his admirable equilibrium; he who generally inspired his customers with a fever, with the tranquil grace of an operator, was as though seized by the passion with which the establishment was gradually burning. Since he had caught sight of Denise and Madame Desforges coming up the grand staircase, he had been talking louder, gesticulating against his will; and, whilst affecting not to turn his face towards them, he became more and more animated as he felt them drawing nearer. His face got redder, his eyes had a little of that rapture with which the eyes of his customers ultimately vacillated.

"You must be robbed fearfully," murmured Vallagnosc, who thought the crowd looked very criminal.

Mouret threw his arms out. "My dear fellow, it's beyond all imagination."

And, nervously, delighted at having something to talk about, he gave a number of details, related cases, and classified the subjects. In the first place, there were the professional thieves; these women did the least harm of all, for the police knew everyone of them. Then came the kleptomaniacs, who stole from a perverse desire, a new sort of nervous affection which a mad doctor had classed, proving the results of the temptation provided by the big shops. In the last place must be counted the women in an interesting condition, whose robberies were of a special order. For instance, at the house of one of them, the superintendent of police had found two hundred and forty-eight pairs of pink gloves stolen from every shop in Paris.

"That's what makes the women have such funny eyes here, then," murmured Vallagnosc; "I've been watching them with their greedy, shameful looks, like mad creatures. A fine school for honesty!"

"Hang it!" replied Mouret, "though we make them quite at

home, we can't let them take away the goods under their mantles. And sometimes they are very respectable people. Last week
we had the sister of a chemist, and the wife of a councillor. We
try and settle these matters."

He stopped to point out Jouve, the inspector, who was just
then looking sharp after a woman in the family way, down below
at the ribbon counter. This woman, whose enormous belly suffered a great deal from the pushing of the crowd, was accompanied by a friend, whose mission appeared to be to defend her
against the heavy shocks, and each time she stopped in a department, Jouve did not take his eyes off her, whilst her friend near
her ransacked the card-board boxes at her ease.

"Oh! he'll catch her!" resumed Mouret; "he knows all their
tricks."

But his voice trembled, he laughed in an awkward manner.
Denise and Henriette, whom he had ceased to watch, were at
last passing behind him, after having had a great deal of trouble
to get out of the crowd. He turned round suddenly, and bowed
to his customer with the discreet air of a friend who does not
wish to compromise a woman by stopping her in the middle of a
crowd of people. But the latter, on the alert, had at once perceived the look with which he had first enveloped Denise. It
must be this girl, this was the rival she had had the curiosity to
come and see.

In the ready-made department, the young ladies were losing
their heads. Two of them had fallen ill, and Madame Frédéric,
the second-hand, had quietly given notice the previous day, and
gone to the cashier's office to take her money, leaving The Ladies' Paradise all in a minute, as The Ladies' Paradise itself discharged its employees. Ever since the morning, in spite of the
feverish rush of business, everyone had been talking of this adventure. Clara, maintained in the department by Mouret's caprice, thought it grand. Marguerite related how exasperated
Bourdoncle was; whilst Madame Aurélie, greatly vexed, declared
that Madame Frédéric ought at least to have informed her, for
such hypocrisy had never before been heard of.

Although the latter had never confided in anyone, she was suspected of having given up the drapery business to marry the proprietor of some baths in the neighborhood of the Halles.

"It's a travelling cloak that madame desires, I believe?" asked Denise of Madame Desforges, after having offered her a chair.

"Yes," replied the latter, curtly, decided on being rude.

The new decorations of the department were of a rich severity: high carved oak cupboards, mirrors filling the whole space of the panels, and a red Wilton carpet, which stifled the continued movement of the customers. Whilst Denise was gone for the cloaks, Madame Desforges, who was looking round, perceived herself in a glass; and she continued contemplating herself. She must be getting old to be cast aside for the first-comer. The glass reflected the entire department with its commotion, but she only beheld her own pale face; she did not hear Clara behind her relating to Marguerite instances of Madame Frédéric's mysterious ways, the manner in which she went out of her way night and morning to go through the Passage Choiseul, in order to make believe that she perhaps lived over the water.

"Here are our latest designs," said Denise. "We have them in several colors."

She laid out four or five cloaks. Madame Desforges looked at them with a scornful air, and became harsher at each fresh one she examined. Why those frillings which made the garment look so scanty? And the other one, square across the shoulders, one would have thought it had been cut out with a hatchet. Though it was for travelling she could not dress like a sentry-box.

"Show me something else, mademoiselle."

Denise unfolded and folded the garments without the slightest sign of ill temper. And it was just this calm, serene patience which exasperated Madame Desforges still further. Her looks continually returned to the glass in front of her. Now that she saw herself there, close to Denise, she made a comparison. Was it possible that he should prefer this insignificant creature to herself? She now remembered that this was the girl she had formerly seen making her debut with such a silly figure, awkward as a peasant girl just arrived from her village. No doubt she looked better now, stiff and correct in her silk dress. But how puny, how common-place!

"I will show you some other models, madame," said Denise, quietly.

When she returned, the scene began again. Then it was the cloth that was heavy and no good whatever. Madame Desforges turned round, raised her voice, endeavoring to attract Madame Aurélie's attention, in the hope of getting the young girl a scolding. But Denise, since her return, had gradually conquered the department, and now felt quite at home in it; the first-hand had even recognized in her some rare and valuable qualities as a saleswoman—an obstinate sweetness, a smiling conviction. Therefore Madame Aurélie simply shrugged her shoulders, taking care not to interfere.

"Would you kindly tell me the kind of garment you require, madame?" asked Denise, once more, with her polite persistence, which nothing could discourage.

"But you've got nothing!" exclaimed Madame Desforges.

She stopped, surprised to feel a hand laid on her shoulder. It was Madame Marty, carried right through the establishment by her fever for spending. Her purchases had increased to such an extent, since the cravats, the embroidered gloves, and the red parasol, that the last salesman had just decided to place the whole on a chair, for it would have broken his arm; and he walked in front of her, drawing the chair along, on which was heaped up a pile of petticoats, napkins, curtains, a lamp, and three straw hats.

"Ah!" said she, "you are buying a travelling cloak."

"Oh! dear, no," replied Madame Desforges; "they are frightful."

But Madame Marty had just noticed a striped cloak which she rather liked. Her daughter Valentine was already examining it. So Denise called Marguerite to clear the article out of the department, it being a model of the previous year, and the latter, at a glance from her comrade, presented it as an exceptional bargain. When she had sworn that they had lowered the price twice, that from a hundred and fifty francs, they had reduced it to a hundred and thirty, and that it was now at a hundred and ten, Madame Marty could not withstand the temptation of its cheapness. She bought it, and the salesman who accompanied her left the chair and the parcel, with the debit-notes attached to the goods.

Meanwhile, behind the ladies' backs, and amidst the jostlings of the sale, the gossip of the department about Madame Frédéric still went on.

"Really! she had someone?" asked a little saleswoman, fresh in the department.

"The bath-man, of course!" replied Clara. "Mustn't trust those sly, quiet windows."

Then whilst Marguerite was debiting the cloak, Madame Marty turned her head, and designating Clara by a slight movement of the eyebrows, she whispered to Madame Desforges: "Monsieur Mouret's caprice, you know!"

The other, surprised, looked at Clara; then, turning her eyes towards Denise, replied: "But it isn't the tall one; the little one!"

And as Madame Marty could not be sure which, Madame Desforges resumed aloud, with the scorn of a lady for chambermaids: "Perhaps the tall one and the little one; all those who like!"

Denise had heard everything. She turned pale, and raised her big, pure eyes on this lady who was thus wounding her, and whom she did not know. No doubt it was the lady of whom they had spoken to her, the lady whom the governor saw outside. In the look that was exchanged between them, Denise displayed such a melancholy dignity, such a frank innocence, that Henriette felt quite awkward.

"As you have nothing presentable to show me here, conduct me to the dress and costume department," said she, abruptly.

"I'll go with you as well," exclaimed Madame Marty, "I wanted to see a costume for Valentine."

Marguerite took the chair by its back, and dragged it along on its hind feet, that were getting worn by this species of cartage. Denise only carried a few yards of silk, bought by Madame Desforges. It was quite a journey, now that the robes and costumes were on the second floor, at the other end of the establishment.

And the long journey commenced along the crowded galleries. Marguerite walked in front, drawing the chair along, like a little carriage, slowly opening herself a passage. As soon as she reached the under-linen department, Madame Desforges began to complain: wasn't it ridiculous, a shop where one was obliged to walk a couple of leagues to find the least thing! Madame Marty also said she was tired to death, yet she did not the less enjoy this fatigue, this slow exhaustion of her strength, amidst the inexhaustible treasures displayed on every side. Mouret's idea, full of genius, seized upon her, stopping her at each department. She made a first halt before the trousseaux, tempted by some chemises that Pauline sold her; and Marguerite found herself relieved from the burden of the chair, which Pauline had to take, with the debit-notes. Madame Desforges could have gone on her road, and thus have liberated Denise quicker, but she seemed happy to feel her behind her, motionless and patient, whilst she was lingering there, advising her friend. In the baby-linen department the ladies went into ecstasies, without buying anything. Then Madame Marty's weakness commenced anew; she succumbed successively before a black silk corset, a pair of fur cuffs, sold at a reduction on account of the lateness of the season, and some Russian lace much in vogue at that time for trimming table-linen. All these things were heaped up on the chair, the parcels still increased, making the chair creak; and the salesmen who succeeded each other, found it more and more difficult to drag along as the load became heavier.

"This way, madame," said Denise without a murmur, after each halt.

"But it's absurd!" exclaimed Madame Desforges. "We shall never get there. Why not have put the dresses and costumes near the ready-made department? It is a jumble!"

Madame Marty, whose eyes were sparkling, intoxicated by this succession of riches dancing before her, repeated in a half whisper:

"Oh, dear! What will my husband say? You are right, there is no order in this place. You lose yourself, and commit all sorts of follies."

On the great central landing, the chair could barely pass. Mouret had just blocked the space with a lot of fancy goods, drinking-cups mounted on gilded zinc, trashy dressing-cases and liqueur stands, being of opinion that the crowd was not sufficiently great, and that circulation was too easy. He had authorized one of his shopmen to exhibit there on a small table Chinese and Japanese curiosities, knick-knacks at a low price, which the customers eagerly snatched up. It was an unexpected success, and he already thought of extending this business. Whilst two messengers carried the chair up to the second storey, Madame Marty bought six ivory studs, some silk mice, and an enameled match-box.

On the second floor the journey was continued. Denise, who had been showing customers about in this way since the morning, was dropping with fatigue; but she still continued correct, amiable, and polite. She had to wait for the ladies again in the furnishing materials department, where a ravishing cretonne had tempted Madame Marty. Then, in the furniture department, it was a work-table that took her fancy. Her hands trembled, she jokingly entreated Madame Desforges to prevent her spending any more, when a meeting with Madame Guibal furnished her with an excuse. It was in the carpet department, where the latter had gone to return a lot of Oriental door-curtains bought by her five days before. And she was standing, talking to the salesman, a brawny fellow, who, with his sinewy arms handled from morning to night loads heavy enough to kill a bullock. Naturally he was quite astounded at this "return," which deprived him of his commission. He did his best to embarrass his customer, suspecting some queer adventure, no doubt a ball given with these curtains, bought at The Ladies' Paradise, and then returned, to avoid hiring at an upholsterer's: he knew this was frequently done by the needy portion of society. In short, she must have some reason for returning them; if she did not like the designs or the colors, he would show her others, he had a most complete assortment. To all these insinuations Madame Guibal replied in the quietest, most unconcerned manner possible, with a queenly assurance that the curtains did not suit her, without deigning to add any explanation. She refused to look at any others, and he was obliged to give way, for the salesmen had orders to take back the goods, even if they saw they had been used.

As the three ladies went off together, and Madame Marty referred with remorse to the work-table for which she had no earthly need, Madame Guibal said in her calm voice: "Well! you can return it. You saw it was quite easy. Let them send it home. You can put it in your drawing-room, keep it for a time, then if you don't like it, return it."

"Ah! that's a good idea!" exclaimed Madame Marty. "If my husband makes too much fuss, I'll send everything back." This was for her the supreme excuse, she calculated no longer, but went on buying, with the secret wish to keep everything, for she was not a woman to give anything back.

At last they arrived in the dress and costume department. But as Denise was about to deliver to another young lady the silk bought by Madame Desforges, the latter seemed to change her mind, and declared that she would decidedly take one of the travelling cloaks, the light grey one with the hood; and Denise had to wait complacently to bring her back to the ready-made department. The young girl felt herself being treated like a servant by this imperious, whimsical customer; but she had sworn to herself to do her duty, and retained her calm attitude, notwithstanding the rising of her heart and the shock to her pride. Madame Desforges bought nothing in the dress and costume department.

"Oh! mamma," said Valentine, "if that little costume should fit me!"

In a low tone, Madame Guibal was explaining her tactics to Madame Marty. When she saw a dress she liked in a shop, she had it sent home, took the pattern of it, and then sent it back. And Madame Marty bought the costume for her daughter remarking: "A good idea! You are very practical, my dear madame."

They had been obliged to abandon the chair. It had been left in distress, in the furniture department, with the work-table. The weight was too much, the hind legs threatened to break off; and it was arranged that all the purchases should be centralized at one pay-desk, and from there sent down to the delivery department. The ladies, still accompanied by Denise, then began wandering all about the establishment, making a second appearance in nearly every department. They seemed to take up all the space on the stairs and in the galleries. Every moment some fresh meeting brought them to a standstill. Thus, near the reading-room, they once more came across Madame Bourdelais and her three children. The youngsters were loaded with parcels: Madeline had a dress for herself, Edmond was carrying a collection of little shoes, whilst the youngest, Lucien, was wearing a new cap.

"You as well!" said Madame Desforges, laughingly, to her old school-fellow.

"Pray, don't speak of it!" cried out Madame Bourdelais. "I'm furious. They get hold of us by the little ones now! You know what a little I spend on myself! But how can you expect me to resist the voices of these young children, who want everything? I had come just to show them round, and here am I plundering the whole establishment!"

Mouret, who happened to be there still, with Vallagnosc and Monsieur de Boves, was listening to her with a smile. She observed it, and gaily complained, with a certain amount of real irritation, of these traps laid for a mother's tenderness; the idea that she had just yielded to the fevers of advertising raised her indignation, and he, still smiling, bowed, fully enjoying this triumph. Monsieur de Boves had maneuvered so as to get near Madame Guibal, whom he ultimately followed, trying for the second time to lose Vallagnosc; but the latter, tired of the crush, hastened to rejoin him. Denise was again brought to a standstill, obliged to wait for the ladies. She turned her back, and Mouret himself affected not to see her. Madame Desforges, with the delicate scent of a jealous woman, had no further doubt. Whilst he was complimenting her and walking beside her, like a gallant host, she was deep in thought, asking herself how she could convince him of his treason.

Monsieur de Boves and Vallagnosc, who went on in front with Madame Guibal, had reached the lace department, a luxurious room, near the ready-made department, surrounded with stocks of carved oak drawers, which were constantly being opened and shut. Around the columns, covered with red velvet, were spirals of white lace; and from one end of the department to the other, hung lengths of Maltese; whilst on the counters there were quantities of large cards, wound round with Valenciennes, Malines, and handmade point. At the further end two ladies were seated before a mauve silk skirt, on which Deloche was placing pieces of Chantilly, the ladies looking on silently, without making up their minds.

"Hallo!" said Vallagnosc, quite surprised, "you said Madame de Boves was unwell. But there she is standing over there near that counter, with Mademoiselle Blanche."

The count could not help starting back, and casting a side glance at Madame Guibal.

"Dear me! so she is," said he.

It was very warm in this room. The customers, half stifled, had pale faces with flaming eyes. It seemed as if all the seductions of the shop had converged into this supreme temptation, that it was the secluded alcove where the customers were doomed to fall, the corner of perdition where the strongest must succumb. Hands were plunged into the overflowing heaps, retaining an intoxicating trembling from the contact.

"I fancy those ladies are ruining you," resumed Vallagnosc, amused at the meeting.

Monsieur de Boves assumed the look of a husband perfectly sure of his wife's discretion, from the simple fact that he did not give her a sou to spend. The latter, after having wandered through all the departments with her daughter, without buying anything, had just stranded in the lace department in a rage of unsated desire. Half dead with fatigue, she was leaning up against the counter. She dived about in a heap of lace, her hands became soft, a warmth penetrated as far as her shoulders. Then suddenly, just as her daughter turned her head and the salesman went away, she was thinking of slipping a piece of point d'Alençon under her mantle. But she shuddered, and dropped it, on hearing Vallagnosc's voice saying gaily:

"Ah! we've caught you, madame."

For several seconds she stood there speechless and pale. Then she explained that, feeling much better, she thought she would take a stroll. And on noticing that her husband was with Madame Guibal, she quite recovered herself, and looked at them with such a dignified air that the other lady felt obliged to say:

"I was with Madame Desforges when these gentlemen met us."

The other ladies came up just at that moment, accompanied by Mouret, who again detained them to point out Jouve the inspector, who was still following the woman in the family way and her lady friend. It was very curious, they could not form any idea of the number of thieves that were arrested in the lace department. Madame de Boves, who was listening, fancied herself between two gendarmes, with her forty-six years, her luxury, and her husband's fine position; but yet she felt no remorse, thinking she ought to have slipped the lace up her sleeve. Jouve, however, had just decided to lay hold of the woman in the family way, despairing of catching her in the act, but fully suspecting her of having filled her pockets, with a sleight of hand which had escaped him. But when he had taken her aside and searched her, he was wild to find nothing on her—not a cravat, not a button. Her friend had disappeared. All at once he understood: the woman in the family way was only there as a blind; it was the friend who did the trick.

This affair amused the ladies. Mouret, rather vexed, merely said: "Old Jouve has been floored this time. He'll have his revenge."

"Oh!" replied Vallagnosc, "I don't think he's equal to it. Besides, why do you display such a quantity of goods? It serves you right, if you are robbed. You ought not to tempt these poor, defenseless women so."

This was the last word, which sounded like the sharp note of the day, in the growing fever of the establishment. The ladies then separated, crossing the crowded departments for the last time. It was four o'clock, the rays of the setting sun were darting through the large windows in the front, lighting up crossways the glazed roofs of the halls, and in this red, fiery light sprung up, like a golden vapor, the thick dust raised by the circulation of the crowd. A broad ray ran along the grand central gallery, showing up on a flaming ground the staircases, the flying bridges, all the network of suspended iron. The mosaics and the terra-cotta of the friezes sparkled, the green and red paint were lighted up by the fire of the masses of gold scattered everywhere. It was like a red-hot furnace, in which the displays were now burning, the palaces of gloves and cravats, the clusters of ribbons and lace, the lofty piles of linen and calico, the diapered parterres in which flourished the light silks and foulards. The exhibition of parasols, with their shield-like roundness, threw out a sort of metallic reflection. In the distance were a lot of lost counters, sparkling, swarming with a moving crowd, ablaze with sunshine.

And at this last moment, amidst this over-warmed air, the women reigned supreme. They had taken the whole place by storm, camping there as in a conquered country, like an invading horde installed amongst the overhauling of the goods. The salesmen, deafened, knocked up, were now nothing but their slaves, of whom they disposed with a sovereign's tyranny. Fat women elbowed their way through the crowd. The thinnest ones took up a lot of space, and became quite arrogant. They were all there, with heads high and abrupt gestures, quite at home, without the slightest politeness one for the other, using the house as much as they could, even carrying away the dust from the walls. Madame Bourdelais, desirous of making up for her expenditure, had again taken her children to the refreshment bar; the crowd was now pushing about there in a furious way, even the mothers were gorging themselves with Malaga; they had drunk since the opening eighty quarts of syrup and seventy bottles of wine. After having bought her travelling cloak, Madame Desforges had managed to secure some pictures at the pay-desk; and she went away

scheming to get Denise into her house, where she could humiliate her before Mouret himself, so as to see their faces and arrive
at a conclusion. Whilst Monsieur de Boves succeeded in losing
himself in the crowd and disappearing with Madame Guibal,
Madame de Boves, followed by Blanche and Vallagnosc, had had
the fancy to ask for a red air-ball, although she had bought nothing. It was always something, she would not go away empty-
handed, she would make a friend of her doorkeeper's little girl
with it. At the distributing counter they were just commencing
the fortieth thousand: forty thousand red air-balls which had
taken flight in the warm air of the shop, quite a cloud of red air-
balls which were now floating from one end of Paris to the other,
bearing upwards to the sky the name of The Ladies' Paradise!

Five o'clock struck. Of all the ladies, Madame Marty and her
daughter were the only ones to remain, in the final crisis of the
sale. She could not tear herself away, although ready to drop
with fatigue, retained by an attraction so strong that she was
continually retracing her steps, though wanting nothing, wandering about the departments out of a curiosity that knew no
bounds. It was the moment in which the crowd, goaded on by
the advertisements, completely lost itself; the sixty thousand
francs paid to the newspapers, the ten thousand bills posted on
the walls, the two hundred thousand catalogues distributed all
over the world, after having emptied their purses, left in the
women's minds the shock of their intoxication; and the customers still remained, shaken by Mouret's other inventions, the reduction of prices, the "returns," the endless gallantries. Madame
Marty lingered before the various stalls, amidst the hoarse cries
of the salesmen, the chinking of the gold at the pay-desks, and
the rolling of the parcels down into the basement; she again traversed the ground floor, the linen, the silk, the glove, and the
woollen departments; then she went upstairs again, abandoning
herself to the metallic vibrations of the suspended staircases and
the flying-bridges, returning to the ready-made, the under-linen,
and the lace departments; she even ascended to the second floor,
into the heights of the bedding and furniture department; and
everywhere the employees. Hutin and Favier, Mignot and Lié-

nard, Deloche, Pauline and Denise, nearly dead with fatigue, were making a last effort, snatching victories from the expiring fever of the customers. This fever had gradually increased since the morning, like the intoxication arising from the tumbling of the stuffs. The crowd shone forth under the fiery glare of the five o'clock sun. Madame Marty's face was now animated and nervous, like that of an infant after drinking pure wine. Arrived with clear eyes and fresh skin from the cold of the street, she had slowly burnt her sight and complexion, at the spectacle of this luxury, of these violent colors, the continued gallop of which irritated her passion. When she at last went away, after saying she would pay at home, terrified by the amount of her bill, her features were drawn up, her eyes were like those of a sick person. She was obliged to fight her way through the crowd at the door, where the people were almost killing each other, amidst the struggle for the bargains. Then, when she got into the street, and found her daughter, whom she had lost for a moment, the fresh air made her shiver, she stood there frightened in the disorder of this neurosis of the immense establishments.

In the evening, as Denise was returning from dinner, a messenger called her: "You are wanted at the director's office, mademoiselle."

She had forgotten the order Mouret had given her in the morning, to go to his office after the sale. He was standing waiting for her. On going in she did not close the door, which remained wide open.

"We are very pleased with you, mademoiselle," said he, "and we have thought of proving our satisfaction. You know in what a shameful manner Madame Frédéric has left us. From tomorrow you will take her place as second-hand."

Denise listened to him immovable with surprise. She murmured in a trembling voice: "But, sir, there are saleswomen in the department who are much my seniors."

"What does that matter?" resumed he. "You are the most capable, the most trustworthy. I choose you; it's quite natural. Are you not satisfied?"

She blushed, feeling a delicious happiness and embarrassment, in which her first fright vanished. Why had she at once thought of the suppositions with which this unhoped-for favor would be received? And she stood filled with her confusion, notwithstanding her sudden burst of gratitude. He was looking at her with a smile, in her simple silk dress, without a single piece of jewelry, nothing but the luxury of her royal, blonde head of hair. She had become more refined, her skin was whiter, her manner delicate and grave. Her former puny insignificance was developing into a charm of a penetrating discretion.

"You are very kind, sir," she stammered. "I don't know how to tell you."

But she was cut short by the appearance of Lhomme in the doorway. In his hand he was holding a large leather bag, and with his mutilated arm he was pressing an enormous notecase to his chest; whilst, behind him, his son Albert was carrying a load of bags, which were weighing him down.

"Five hundred and eighty-seven thousand two hundred and ten francs thirty centimes!" cried out the cashier, whose flabby, used-up face seemed to be lighted up with a ray of sunshine, in the reflection of such a sum.

It was the day's receipts, the highest The Ladies' Paradise had ever done. In the distance, in the depths of the shop that Lhomme had just passed through slowly, with the heavy gait of an overloaded beast of burden, one could hear the uproar, the ripple of surprise and joy, left by this colossal sum which passed.

"But it's superb!" said Mouret, enchanted. "My good Lhomme, put it down there, and take a rest, for you look quite done up. I'll have this money taken to the central cashier's office. Yes, yes, put it all on my table, I want to see the heap."

He was full of a childish gaiety. The cashier and his son laid down their burdens. The leather bag gave out a clear, golden ring, two of the other bags bursting let out a stream of silver and copper, whilst from the notecase peeped forth corners of bank notes. One end of the large table was entirely covered; it was like the tumbling of a fortune picked up in ten hours.

When Lhomme and Albert had retired, mopping their faces, Mouret remained for a moment motionless, lost, his eyes fixed on the money. Then, raising his head, he perceived Denise, who had drawn back. He began to smile again, forced her to come forward, and finished by saying he would give her all she could take in her hand; and there was a sort of love-bargain beneath his playfulness.

"Look! out of the bag. I bet it would be less than a thousand francs, your hand is so small!"

But she drew back again. He loved her, then? Suddenly she understood, she felt the growing flame of desire with which he had enveloped her since her return to the shop. What overcame her more than anything else was to feel her heart beating violently. Why did he wound her with all this money, when she was overflowing with gratitude, and he could have done anything with her by a friendly word? He was coming closer to her, continuing to joke, when, to his great annoyance, Bourdoncle appeared, under the pretence of informing him of the number of entries— the enormous number of seventy thousand customers had entered The Ladies' Paradise that day. And she hastened away, after having again thanked him.

CHAPTER X.

The first Sunday in August everyone was busy with the stock-taking, which had to be finished by the evening. Early in the morning all the employees were at their posts, as on a week-day, and the work commenced with closed doors, in the immense establishment, entirely free from customers.

Denise, however, had not come down with the other young ladies at eight o'clock. Confined to her room for the last five days by a sprained ankle, caused when going up stairs to the work-rooms, she was going on much better; but, sure of Madame Aurélie's indulgence, she did not hurry down, and sat putting her boots on with difficulty, resolved, however, to show herself in the department. The young ladies' bedrooms now occupied the entire fifth storey of the new buildings, along the Rue Monsigny; there were sixty of them, on either side of a corridor, and they were much more comfortable than formerly, although still furnished with the iron bedstead, large wardrobe, and little mahogany toilet-table. The private life of the saleswomen became more refined and elegant there, they displayed a taste for scented soap and fine linen, quite a natural ascent towards middle-class ways as their positions improved, although high words and banging doors were still sometimes heard amidst the hotel-like gust that carried them away, morning and evening. Denise, being second-hand in her department, had one of the largest rooms, the two attic windows of which looked into the street. Being much better off now, she indulged in several little luxuries, a red eider-down coverlet for the bed, covered with Maltese lace, a small carpet in front of the wardrobe, and two blue-glass vases containing a few faded roses on the toilet table.

When she got her boots on she tried to walk across the room; but was obliged to lean against the furniture, being still rather lame. But that would soon come right again, she thought. At the same time, she had been quite right in refusing the invitation to dine at uncle Baudu's that evening, and in asking her aunt to take Pépé out for a walk, for she had placed him with Madame Gras again. Jean, who had been to see her the previous day, was to dine at his uncle's also. She continued to try to walk, resolved to go to bed early, in order to rest her leg, when Madame Cabin, the housekeeper, knocked and gave her a letter, with an air of mystery.

The door closed. Denise, astonished by this woman's discreet smile, opened the letter. She dropped on to a chair; it was a letter from Mouret, in which he expressed himself delighted at her recovery, and begged her to go down and dine with him that evening, as she could not go out. The tone of this note, at once familiar and paternal, was in no way offensive; but it was impossible for her to mistake its meaning. The Ladies' Paradise well knew the real signification of these invitations, which were legendary: Clara had dined, others as well, all those the governor had specially remarked. After dinner, as the witlings were wont to say, came the dessert. And the young girl's white cheeks were gradually invaded by a flow of blood.

The letter slipped on to her knees, and Denise, her heart beating violently, remained with her eyes fixed on the blinding light of one of the windows. This was the confession she must have made to herself, in this very room, during her sleepless moments: if she still trembled when he passed, she now knew it was not from fear; and her former uneasiness, her old terror, could have been nothing but the frightened ignorance of love, the disorder of her growing affections, in her youthful wildness. She did not argue with herself, she simply felt that she had always loved him from the hour she had shuddered and stammered before him. She had loved him when she had feared him as a pitiless master;

she had loved him when her distracted heart was dreaming of Hutin, unconsciously yielding to a desire for affection. Perhaps she might have given herself to another, but she had never loved any but this man, whose mere look terrified her. And her whole past life came back to her, unfolding itself in the blinding light of the window: the hardships of her start, that sweet walk under the shady trees of the Tuileries Gardens, and, lastly, the desires with which he had enveloped her ever since her return. The letter dropped on the ground, Denise still gazed at the window, dazzled by the glare of the sun.

Suddenly there was a knock. She hastened to pick up the letter and conceal it in her pocket. It was Pauline, who, having slipped away under some pretext, had come for a little gossip.

"How are you, my dear? We never meet now—"

But as it was against the rules to go up into the bedrooms, and, above all, for two to be shut in together, Denise took her to the end of the passage, into the ladies' drawing-room, a gallant present from Mouret to the young ladies, who could spend their evenings there till eleven o'clock. The apartment, decorated in white and gold, of the vulgar nudity of a hotel room, was furnished with a piano, a central table, and some arm-chairs and sofas protected with white covers. But, after a few evenings spent together, in the first novelty of the thing, the saleswomen never went into the place without coming to high words at once. They required educating to it, the little trading city was wanting in accord. Meanwhile, almost the only one that went there in the evening was the second-hand in the corset department, Miss Powell, who strummed away at Chopin on the piano, and whose coveted talent ended by driving the others away.

"You see my ankle's better now," said Denise, "I was going downstairs."

"Well!" exclaimed the other, "what zeal! I'd take it easy if I had the chance!"

They both sat down on a sofa. Pauline's attitude had changed since her friend had been promoted to be second-hand in the ready-made department. With her good-natured cordiality was mingled a shade of respect, a sort of surprise to feel the puny

little saleswoman of former days on the road to fortune. Denise
liked her very much, and confided in her alone, amidst the continual gallop of the two hundred women that the firm now employed.

"What's the matter?" asked Pauline, quickly, when she remarked the young girl's troubled looks.

"Oh! nothing," replied the latter, with an awkward smile.

"Yes, yes; there's something the matter with you. Have you no
faith in me, that you have given up telling me your troubles?"

Then Denise, in the emotion that was swelling her bosom—an
emotion she could not control—abandoned herself to her feelings. She gave her friend the letter, stammering: "Look! he has
just written to me."

Between themselves, they had never openly spoken of Mouret.
But this very silence was like a confession of their secret pre-
occupations. Pauline knew everything. After having read the letter, she clasped Denise in her arms, and softly murmured: "My
dear, to speak frankly, I thought it was already done. Don't be
shocked; I assure you the whole shop must think as I do. Naturally! he appointed you as second-hand so quickly, then he's always after you. It's obvious!" She kissed her affectionately, and
then asked her: "You will go this evening, of course?"

Denise looked at her without replying. All at once she burst
into tears, her head on Pauline's shoulder. The latter was quite
astonished.

"Come, try and calm yourself; there's nothing in the affair to
upset you like this."

"No, no; let me be," stammered Denise. "If you only knew
what trouble I am in! Since I received that letter, I have felt beside myself. Let me have a good cry, that will relieve me."

Full of pity, though not understanding, Pauline endeavored
to console her. In the first place, he had thrown up Clara. It was
said he still visited a lady outside, but that was not proved.
Then she explained that one could not be jealous of a man in
such a position. He had too much money; he was the master,
after all. Denise listened to her, and had she been ignorant of
her love, she could no longer have doubted it after the suffering

she felt at the name of Clara and the allusion to Madame Desforges, which made her heart bleed. She could hear Clara's disagreeable voice, she could see Madame Desforges dragging her
about the different departments with the scorn of a rich lady
for a poor shop-girl.

"So you would go yourself?" asked she.

Pauline, without pausing to think, cried out: "Of course, how
can one do otherwise!" Then reflecting, she added: "Not now,
but formerly, because now I am going to marry Baugé, and it
would not be right."

In fact, Baugé, who had left the Bon Marché for The Ladies'
Paradise, was going to marry her about the middle of the month.
Bourdoncle did not like these married couples; they had managed, however, to get the necessary permission, and even hoped
to obtain a fortnight's holiday for their honeymoon.

"There you are," declared Denise, "when a man loves a girl he
ought to marry her. Baugé is going to marry you."

Pauline laughed heartily. "But my dear, it isn't the same thing.
Baugé is going to marry me because he is Baugé. He's my equal,
that's a natural thing. Whilst Monsieur Mouret! Do you think
Monsieur Mouret can marry his saleswomen?"

"Oh! No, oh! no," exclaimed the young girl, shocked by the ab-
surdity of the question, "and that's why he ought not to have
written to me."

This argument completely astonished Pauline. Her coarse
face, with her small tender eyes, assumed quite an expression of
maternal compassion. Then she got up, opened the piano, and
softly played with one finger, "King Dagobert," to enliven the
situation, no doubt. Into the nakedness of the drawing-room,
the white coverings of which seemed to increase the emptiness,
came the noises from the street, the distant melopoeia of a
woman crying out green peas. Denise had thrown herself back
on the sofa, her head against the wood-work, shaken by a fresh
flood of sobs, which she stifled in her handkerchief.

"Again!" resumed Pauline, turning round. "Really you are not
reasonable. Why did you bring me here? We ought to have
stopped in your room."

She knelt down before her, and commenced lecturing her again. How many others would like to be in her place! Besides, if the thing did not please her, it was very simple: she had only to say no, without worrying herself like this. But she should reflect before risking her position by a refusal which was inexplicable, considering she had no engagement elsewhere. Was it such a terrible thing after all? And the reprimand was finishing up by some pleasantries, gaily whispered, when a sound of footsteps was heard in the passage. Pauline ran to the door and looked out.

"Hush! Madame Aurélie!" she murmured. "I'm off, and just you dry your eyes. She need not know what's up."

When Denise was alone, she got up, and forced back her tears; and, her hands still trembling, with the fear of being caught there doing nothing, she closed the piano, which her friend had left open. But on hearing Madame Aurélie knocking at her door, she left the drawing-room.

"What! you are up!" exclaimed the first-hand. "It's very thoughtless of you, my dear child. I was just coming up to see how you were, and to tell you that we did not require you downstairs."

Denise assured her that she felt very much better, that it would do her good to do something to amuse herself.

"I sha'n't tire myself, madame. You can place me on a chair, and I'll do some writing."

Both then went downstairs. Madame Aurélie, who was most attentive, insisted on Denise leaning on her shoulder. She must have noticed the young girl's red eyes, for she was stealthily examining her. No doubt she was aware of a great deal of what was going on.

It was an unexpected victory: Denise had at last conquered the department. After struggling for six months, amidst her torments as drudge and fag, without disarming her comrades' ill-will, she had in a few weeks entirely overcome them, and now saw them around her submissive and respectful. Madame Aurélie's sudden affection had greatly assisted her in this ungrateful task of softening her comrades' hearts towards her. It was whispered that the first-hand was Mouret's obliging factotum, that she rendered him many delicate services; and she took the young girl under her protection with such warmth that the latter must have been recommended to her in a very special manner. But Denise had also brought all her charm into play in order to disarm her enemies. The task was all the more difficult from the fact that she had to obtain their pardon for her appointment to the situation of second-hand. The young ladies spoke of this as an injustice, accused her of having earned it at dessert, with the governor; and even added a lot of abominable details. But in spite of their revolt, the title of second-hand influenced them, Denise assumed a certain authority which astonished and over-awed the most hostile spirits. Soon after, she even found flatterers amongst the new hands; and her sweetness and modesty finished the conquest. Marguerite came over to her side. Clara was the only one to continue her ill-natured ways, still venturing on the old insult of the "unkempt girl," which no one now saw the fun of. During her short intimacy with Mouret, she had taken advantage of it to neglect her work, being of a wonderfully idle, gossiping nature; then, as he had quickly tired of her, she did not even recriminate, incapable of jealousy in the disorderly abandon of her existence, perfectly satisfied to have profited from it to the extent of being allowed to stand about doing nothing. But, at the same time, she considered that Denise had robbed her of Madame Frédéric's place. She would never have accepted it, on account of the worry; but she was vexed at the want of politeness, for she had the same claims as the other one, and prior claims too.

"Hullo! there's the young mother being trotted out after her confinement," murmured she, on seeing Madame Aurélie bringing Denise in on her arm.

Marguerite shrugged her shoulders, saying, "I dare say you think that's a good joke!"

Nine o'clock struck. Outside, an ardent blue sky was warming the streets, cabs were rolling towards the railway stations, the whole population, dressed out in Sunday clothes, was streaming in long rows towards the suburban woods. Inside the building, inundated with sun through the large open bays, the cooped-up staff had just commenced the stocktaking. They had closed the doors; people stopped on the pavement, looking through the windows, astonished at this shutting-up when an extraordinary activity was going on inside. There was, from one end of the galleries to the other, from the top floor to the bottom, a continual movement of employees, their arms in the air, and parcels flying about above their heads; and all this amidst a tempest of cries and a calling out of prices, the confusion of which ascended and became a deafening roar. Each of the thirty-nine departments did its work apart, without troubling about its neighbor. At this early hour the shelves had hardly been touched, there were only a few bales of goods on the floors; the machine would have to get up more steam if they were to finish that evening.

"Why have you come down?" asked Marguerite of Denise, good-naturedly. "You'll only make yourself worse, and we are quite enough to do the work."

"That's what I told her," declared Madame Aurélie, "but she insisted on coming down to help us."

All the young ladies flocked round Denise. The work was interrupted even for a time. They complimented her, listening with various exclamations to the story of her sprained ankle. At last Madame Aurélie made her sit down at a table; and it was understood that she should merely write down the articles as they were called out. On such a day as this they requisitioned any employee capable of holding a pen: the inspectors, the cashiers, the clerks, even down to the shop messengers; and the various departments divided amongst themselves these assistants of a day to get the work over quicker. It was thus that Denise found herself installed near Lhomme the cashier and Joseph the messenger, both bending over large sheets of paper.

"Five mantles, cloth, fur trimming, third size, at two hundred and forty francs!" cried Marguerite. "Four ditto, first size, at two hundred and twenty!"

The work once more commenced. Behind Marguerite three saleswomen were emptying the cupboards, classifying the articles, giving them to her in bundles; and, when she had called them out, she threw them on the table, where they were gradually heaping up in enormous piles. Lhomme wrote down the articles, Joseph kept another list for the clearinghouse. Whilst this was going on, Madame Aurélie herself, assisted by three other saleswomen, was counting the silk garments, which Denise entered on the sheets. Clara was employed in looking after the heaps, to arrange them in such a manner that they should occupy the least space possible on the tables. But she was not paying much attention to her work, for the heaps were already tumbling down.

"I say," asked she of a little saleswoman who had joined that winter, "are they going to give you a rise? You know the second-hand is to have two thousand francs, which, with her commission, will bring her in nearly seven thousand."

The little saleswoman, without ceasing to pass some cloaks down, replied that if they didn't give her eight hundred francs she would take her hook. The rises were always given the day after the stock-taking; it was also the epoch at which, the amount of business done during the year being known, the managers of the departments drew their commission on the increase of this figure, compared with that of the preceding year. Thus, notwithstanding the bustle and uproar of the work, the impassioned gossiping went on everywhere. Between two articles called out, they talked of nothing but money. The rumor ran that Madame Aurélie would exceed twenty-five thousand francs; and this immense sum greatly excited the young ladies. Marguerite, the best saleswoman after Denise, had made four thousand five hundred francs, fifteen hundred francs salary, and about three thousand francs commission; whilst Clara had not made two thousand five hundred francs altogether.

"I don't care a button for their rises!" resumed the latter, still talking to the little saleswoman. "If papa were dead, I would jolly soon clear out of this! But what exasperates me is to see seven thousand francs given to that strip of a girl! What do you say?"

Madame Aurélie violently interrupted the conversation, turning round with her imperial air. "Be quiet, young ladies. We can't hear ourselves speak, my word of honor!"

Then she resumed calling out: "Seven mantles, old style, Sicilian, first size, at a hundred and thirty! Three pelisses, surah, second size, at a hundred and fifty! Have you got that down, Mademoiselle Baudu?"

"Yes, madame."

Clara then had to look after the armfuls of garments piled on the tables. She pushed them about, and made more room. But she soon left them again to reply to a salesman, who was looking for her. It was the glover, Mignot, escaped from his. He whispered a request for twenty francs; he already owed her thirty, a loan effected the day after a race, after having lost his week's salary on a horse; this time he had squandered his commission, drawn over night, and had not ten sous for his Sunday. Clara had only ten francs about her, which she lent him with a fairly good grace. And they went on talking, spoke of a party of six, indulged in at a restaurant at Bougival, where the women had paid their share: it was much better, they all felt perfectly at their ease like that. Then Mignot, who wanted his twenty francs, went and bent over Lhomme's shoulder. The latter, stopped in his writing, appeared greatly troubled. However, he dared not refuse, and was looking for the money in his purse, when Madame Aurélie, astonished not to hear Marguerite's voice, which had been interrupted, perceived Mignot, and understood at once. She roughly sent him back to his department, saying she didn't want anyone to come and distract her young ladies from their work. The truth is, she dreaded this young man, a bosom friend of Albert's, the accomplice of his doubtful tricks, which she trembled to see turn out badly some day. Therefore, when Mignot had got his ten francs, and had run away, she could not help saying to her husband:

"Is it possible! to let a fellow like that get over you!"

"But, my dear, I really could not refuse the young man." She closed his mouth with a shrug of her substantial shoulders. Then, as the saleswomen were slyly grinning at this family explanation, she resumed with severity: "Now, Mademoiselle Vadon, don't let's go to sleep."

"Twenty cloaks, cashmere extra, fourth size, at eighteen francs and a half," resumed Marguerite in her sing-song voice. Lhomme, with his head bowed down, had resumed writing. They had gradually raised his salary to nine thousand francs a year; and he was very humble before Madame Aurélie, who still brought nearly triple as much into the family.

For a while the work pushed forward. Figures flew about, the parcels of garments rained thick and fast on the tables. But Clara had invented another amusement: she was teasing the messenger, Joseph, about a passion that he was said to nourish for a young lady in the pattern-room. This young lady, already twenty-eight years old, thin and pale, was a protégée of Madame Desforges, who had wanted to make Mouret engage her as a saleswoman, backing up her recommendation with a touching story: an orphan, the last of the De Fontenailles, an old and noble family of Poitou, thrown into the streets of Paris with a drunken father, but yet virtuous amidst this misfortune, with an education too limited, unfortunately, to take a place as governess or music-mistress. Mouret generally got angry when anyone recommended to him these broken-down gentlewomen; there was not, said he, a class of creatures more incapable, more insupportable, more narrow-minded than these gentlewomen; and, besides, a saleswoman could not be improvised, she must serve an apprenticeship, it was a complicated and delicate business. However, he took Madame Desforges's protégée, but put her in the pattern-room, in the same way as he had already found places, to oblige friends, for two countesses and a baroness in the advertising department, where they addressed envelopes, etc. Mademoiselle de Fontenailles earned three francs a day, which just enabled her to live in her modest room, in the Rue d'Argenteuil. It was on seeing her, with her sad look and such shabby clothes, that Joseph's heart, very tender under his rough soldier's manner, had been touched. He did not confess, but he blushed, when the young ladies in the ready-made department chaffed him; for the pattern-room was not far off, and they had often observed him prowling about the doorway.

"Joseph is somewhat absent-minded," murmured Clara. "His nose is always turned towards the under-linen department."

They had requisitioned Mademoiselle de Fontenailles there, and she was assisting at the outfitting counter. As the messenger was continually glancing in that direction, the saleswomen began to laugh. He became very confused, and plunged into his accounts; whilst Marguerite, in order to arrest the flood of gaiety which was tickling her throat, cried out louder still: "Fourteen jackets, English cloth, second size, at fifteen francs!"

At this, Madame Aurélie, who was engaged in calling out some cloaks, could not make herself heard. She interfered with a wounded air, and a majestic slowness: "A little softer, mademoiselle. We are not in a market. And you are all very unreasonable, to be amusing yourselves with these childish matters, when our time is so precious."

Just at that moment, as Clara was not paying any attention to the parcels, a catastrophe took place. Some mantles tumbled down, and all the heaps on the tables, dragged down with them, fell one after the other, so that the carpet was strewn with them.

"There! what did I say!" cried the first-hand, beside herself. "Pray be more careful, Mademoiselle Prunaire; it's intolerable!"

But a hum ran along: Mouret and Bourdoncle, making their round of inspection, had just appeared. The voices started again, the pens sputtered along, whilst Clara hastened to pick up the garments. The governor did not interrupt the work. He stood there several minutes, mute, smiling; and it was on his lips alone that a slight feverish shivering was visible in his gay and victorious face of stock-taking days. When he perceived Denise, he nearly gave way to a gesture of astonishment. She had come down, then? His eyes met Madame Aurélie's. Then, after a moment's hesitation, he went away into the under-linen department.

However, Denise, warned by the slight noise, had raised her head. And, after having recognized Mouret, she had immediately bent over her work again, without ostentation. Since she had been writing in this mechanical way, amidst the regular calling-out of the articles, a peaceful feeling had stolen over her. She had always yielded thus to the first excesses of her sensitiveness: the tears suffocated her, her passion doubled her torments;

then she regained her self-command, finding a grand, calm courage, a strength of will, quiet but inexorable. Now, with her limpid eyes, and pale complexion, she was free from all agitation, entirely given up to her work, resolved to crush her heart and to do nothing but her will.

Ten o'clock struck, the uproar of the stock-taking was increasing in the activity of the departments. And amidst the cries incessantly raised, crossing each other on all sides, the same news was circulating with surprising rapidity: every salesman knew that Mouret had written that morning inviting Denise to dinner. The indiscretion came from Pauline. On going downstairs, still excited, she had met Deloche in the lace department, and, without noticing that Liénard was talking to the young man, she immediately relieved her mind of the secret.

"It's done, my dear fellow. She's just received a letter. He invites her for this evening."

Deloche turned very pale. He had understood, for he often questioned Pauline; they spoke of their common friend every day, of Mouret's love for her, of the famous invitation which would finish by bringing the adventure to an issue. She frequently scolded him for his secret love for Denise, with whom he would never succeed, and she shrugged her shoulders whenever he expressed his approval of the girl's conduct in resisting the governor.

"Her foot's better, she's coming down," continued Pauline. "Pray don't put on that funeral face. It's a piece of good luck for her, this invitation." And she hastened back to her department.

"Ah! good!" murmured Liénard, who had heard all, "you're talking about the young girl with the sprain. You were quite right to be so quick in defending her last night at the café!"

He also ran off; but before he had returned to the woollen department, he had already related the story to four or five fellows. In less than ten minutes, it had gone the round of the whole shop.

Liénard's last remark referred to a scene which had taken place the previous evening, at the Café Saint-Roch. Deloche and he were now constantly together. The former had taken Hutin's room at the Hôtel de Smyrne, when that gentleman, appointed second-hand, had hired a suite of three rooms; and the two shopmen came to The Ladies' Paradise together in the morning, and waited for each other in the evening in order to go away together. Their rooms, which were next door to each other, looked into the same black yard, a narrow well, the odor from which poisoned the hotel. They got on very well together, notwithstanding then: difference of character, the one carelessly squandering the money he drew from his father, the other penniless, perpetually tortured by ideas of saving, both having, however, a point in common, their unskilfulness as salesmen, which left them to vegetate at their counters, without any increase of salary. After leaving the shop, they spent the greater part of their time at the Café Saint-Roch. Quite free from customers during the day, this café filled up about half-past eight with an overflowing crowd of employees, that crowd of shopmen disgorged into the street from the great door in the Place Gaillon. Then burst forth a deafening uproar of clinking dominoes, bursts of laughter and yelping voices, amidst the thick smoke of the pipes. Beer and coffee were in great demand. Seated in the left-hand corner, Liénard went in for the dearest drinks, whilst Deloche contented himself with a glass of beer, which he would take four hours to drink. It was there that the latter had heard Favier, at a neighboring table, relate some abominable things about Denise, the way in which she had "hooked" the governor, by pulling her dress up whenever she went upstairs in front of him. He had with difficulty restrained himself from striking him. Then, as the other went on, saying that the young girl went down every night to join her lover, he called him a liar, feeling mad with rage.

"What a blackguard! It's a lie, it's a lie, I tell you!"

And in the emotion which was agitating him, he let out too much, with a stammering voice, entirely opening his heart.

"I know her, and it isn't true. She has never had any affection except for one man; yes, for Monsieur Hutin, and even he has never noticed it, he can't even boast of ever having as much as touched her."

The report of this quarrel, exaggerated, misconstrued, was

already affording amusement for the whole shop, when the story of Mouret's letter was circulated. In fact, it was to a salesman in the silk department that Liénard first confided the news. With the silk-vendors the stock-taking was going on rapidly. Favier and two shopmen, mounted on stools, were emptying the shelves, passing the pieces of stuff to Hutin as they went on, the latter, standing on a table, calling out the figures, after consulting the tickets; and he then dropped the pieces, which, rising slowly like an autumn tide, were gradually encumbering the floor. Other men were writing, Albert Lhomme was also helping them, his face pale and heavy after a night spent in a low public-house at La Chapelle. A ray of sun fell from the glazed roof of the hall, through which could be seen the ardent blue of the sky.

"Draw those blinds!" cried out Bouthemont, very busy superintending the work. "The sun is unbearable!"

Favier, who was stretching to reach a piece, grumbled under his breath: "A nice thing to shut people up a lovely day like this! No fear of it raining on a stock-taking day! And they keep us under lock and key like a lot of convicts when all Paris is outdoors!"

He passed the piece to Hutin. On the ticket was the measurement, diminished at each sale by the quantity sold, which greatly simplified the work. The second-hand cried out: "Fancy silk, small check, twenty-one yards, at six francs and a half."

And the silk went to increase the heap on the floor. Then he continued a conversation commenced, by saying to Favier: "So he wanted to fight you?"

"Yes, I was quietly drinking my glass of beer. It was hardly worthwhile contradicting me, she has just received a letter from the governor inviting her to dinner. The whole shop is talking about it."

"What! it wasn't done!"

Favier handed him another piece.

"A caution, isn't it? One would have staked his life on it. It seemed like an old connection."

"Ditto, twenty-five yards!" cried Hutin.

The dull thud of the piece was heard, whilst he added in a

lower tone: "She carried on fearfully, you know, at that old fool Bourras's."

The whole department was now joking about the affair, without, however, allowing the work to suffer. The young girl's name passed from mouth to mouth, the fellows arched their backs and winked. Bouthemont himself, who took a rare delight in such gay stories, could not help adding his joke, the bad taste of which filled his heart with joy. Albert, waking up a bit, swore he had seen Denise with two soldiers at the Gros-Caillou. At that moment Mignot came down, with the twenty francs he had just borrowed, and he stopped to slip ten francs into Albert's hand, making an appointment with him for the evening; a projected lark, restrained for want of money, but still possible, notwithstanding the smallness of the sum. But handsome Mignot, when he heard about the famous letter, made such an abominable remark, that Bouthemont was obliged to interfere.

"That's enough, gentlemen. It isn't our business. Go on, Monsieur Hutin."

"Fancy silk, small check, thirty-two yards, at six francs and a half," cried out the latter.

The pens started off again, the parcels fell regularly, the flood of stuffs still increased, as if the overflow of a river had emptied itself there. And the calling out of the fancy silks never ceased. Favier, in a half whisper, remarked that the stock was in a nice state; the governors would be enchanted; that big stupid of a Bouthemont might be the best buyer in Paris, but as a salesman he was not worth his salt. Hutin smiled, delighted, approving by a friendly look; for after having himself introduced Bouthemont into The Ladies' Paradise, in order to drive out Robineau, he was now undermining him also, with the firm intention of robbing him of his place. It was the same war as formerly, treacherous insinuations whispered in the partners' ears, an excessive display of zeal in order to push one's self forward, a regular campaign carried on with affable cunning. However, Favier, towards whom Hutin was displaying some fresh condescension, took a look at the latter, thin and cold, with his bilious face, as if to count the mouthfuls in this short, squat little man, and looking as though he were waiting till his comrade had swallowed up Bouthemont, in order to eat him afterwards. He, Favier, hoped to get the second-hand's place, should his friend be appointed manager. Then, they would see. And both, consumed by the fever which was raging from one end of the shop to the other, talked of the probable rises of salary, without ceasing to call out the stock of fancy silks; they felt sure Bouthemont would reach thirty thousand francs that year; Hutin would exceed ten thousand; Favier estimated his pay and commission at five thousand five hundred. The amount of business in the department was increasing yearly, the salesmen were promoted and their salaries doubled, like officers in time of war.

"Won't those fancy silks soon be finished?" asked Bouthemont suddenly, with an annoyed air. "What a miserable spring, always raining! People have bought nothing but black silks."

His fat, jovial face became cloudy; he looked at the growing heap on the floor, whilst Hutin called out louder still, in a sonorous voice, not free from triumph—"Fancy silks, small check, twenty-eight yards, at six francs and a half."

There was still another shelf-full. Favier, whose arms were beginning to feel tired, was now going very slowly. As he handed Hutin the last pieces he resumed in a low tone—"Oh! I say, I forgot. Have you heard that the second-hand in the ready-made department once had a regular fancy for you?"

The young man seemed greatly surprised. "What! How do you mean?"

"Yes, that great booby Deloche let it out to us. I remember her casting sheep's eyes at you some time back."

Since his appointment as second-hand Hutin had thrown up his music-hall singers and gone in for governesses. Greatly flattered at heart, he replied with a scornful air, "I like them a little better stuffed, my boy; besides, it won't do to take up with anybody, as the governor does." He stopped to call out—

"White Poult silk, thirty-five yards, at eight francs fifteen sous."

"Oh! at last!" murmured Bouthemont, greatly relieved.

But a bell rang, it was the second table, to which Favier belonged. He got off the stool, another salesman took his place, and he was obliged to step over the mountain of pieces of stuff with which the floor was encumbered. Similar heaps were scattered about in very department; the shelves, the boxes, the cupboards were being gradually emptied, whilst the goods were overflowing on every side, under-foot, between the counters and the tables, in a continual rising. In the linen department was heard the heavy falling of the bales of calico; in the mercery department there was a clicking of boxes; and distant rumbling sounds came from the furniture department. Every sort of voice was heard together, shrill voices, thick voices; figures whizzed through the air, a rustling clamor reigned in the immense nave— the clamor of the forests in January when the wind is whistling through the branches.

Favier at last got clear and went up the dining room staircase. Since the enlargement of The Ladies' Paradise the refectories had been shifted to the fourth storey in the new buildings. As he hurried up he came upon Deloche and Liénard, so he fell back on Mignot, who was following on his heels.

"The deuce!" said he, in the corridor leading to the kitchen, opposite the blackboard on which the bill of fare was inscribed, "you can see it's stock-taking day. A regular feast! Chicken, or leg of mutton, and artichokes! Their mutton won't be much of a success!"

Mignot sniggered, murmuring, "Everyone's going in for chicken, then!"

However, Deloche and Liénard had taken their portions and had gone away. Favier then leant over at the wicket and called out—"Chicken!"

But he had to wait; one of the kitchen helps had cut his finger in carving, and this caused some confusion. Favier stood there, with his face to the opening, looking into the kitchen with its giant appliances—the central range, over which two rails fixed to the ceiling brought forward, by a system of chains and pulleys, the colossal coppers, which four men could not have lifted. Several cooks, quite white in the sombre red of the furnace, were attending to the evening soup coppers, mounted on iron ladders, armed with skimmers fixed on long handles. Then against the wall were grills large enough to roast martyrs on, saucepans big enough to cook a whole sheep in, a monumental plate-warmer, and a marble well kept full by a continual stream of water. To the left could be seen a washing-up place, stone sinks as large as ponds; whilst on the other side to the right, was an immense meat-safe, in which some large joints of red meat were hanging on steel hooks. A machine for peeling potatoes was working with the tic-tac of a mill. Two small trucks laden with freshly-picked salad were being wheeled along by some kitchen helps into the fresh air under a fountain.

"Chicken," repeated Favier, getting impatient. Then, turning round, he added in a lower tone, "There's one fellow cut himself. It's disgusting, it's running over the food."

Mignot wanted to see. Quite a string of shopmen had now arrived; there was a good deal of laughing and pushing. The two young men, their heads at the wicket, exchanged their remarks before this phalansterian kitchen, in which the least utensils, even the spits and larding pins, assumed gigantic proportions. Two thousand luncheons and two thousand dinners had to be served, and the number of employees was increasing every week. It was quite an abyss, into which was thrown daily something like forty-five bushels of potatoes, one hundred and twenty pounds of butter, and sixteen hundred pounds of meat; and at each meal they had to broach three casks of wine, over a hundred and fifty gallons were served out at the wine counter.

"Ah! at last!" murmured Favier when the cook reappeared with a large pan, out of which he handed him the leg of a fowl.

"Chicken," said Mignot behind him.

And with their plates in their hands they both entered the refectory, after having taken their wine at the counter; whilst behind them the word "Chicken" was repeated without ceasing, regularly, and one could hear the cook picking up the pieces with his fork with a rapid and measured sound.

The men's dining room was now an immense apartment, where places for five hundred at each of the three dinners could easily be laid. There were long mahogany tables, placed parallel across the room, and at either end were similar tables reserved for the managers of departments and the inspectors; whilst in the centre was a counter for the extras. Large windows, right and left, lighted up with a white light this gallery, of which the ceiling, notwithstanding its being four yards high, seemed very low, crushed by the enormous development of the other dimensions. The sole ornament on the walls, painted a light yellow, were the napkin cupboards. After this first refectory came that of the messengers and car-men, where the meals were served irregularly, according to the necessities of the work.

"What! you've got a leg as well, Mignot?" said Favier, as he took his place at one of the tables opposite his companion.

Other young men now sat down around them. There was no tablecloth, the plates gave out a cracked sound on the bare mahogany, and everyone was crying out in this particular corner, for the number of legs was really prodigious.

"These chickens are all legs!" remarked Mignot.

Those who had pieces of the carcase were greatly discontented. However, the food had been much better since the late improvements. Mouret no longer treated with a contractor at a fixed sum; he had taken the kitchen into his own hands, organizing it like one of the departments, with a head-cook, under-cooks, and an inspector; and if he spent more he got more work out of the staff—a practical humane calculation which long terrified Bourdoncle.

"Mine is pretty tender, all the same," said Mignot. "Pass over the bread!"

The big loaf was sent round, and after cutting a slice for himself he dug the knife into the crust. A few dilatory ones now hurried in, taking their places; a ferocious appetite, increased by the morning's work, ran along the immense tables from one end to the other. There was an increasing clatter of forks, a sound of bottles being emptied, the noise of glasses laid down too violently, the grinding rumble of five hundred pairs of powerful jaws working with wonderful energy. And the talk, still very rare, was stifled in the mouths full of food.

Deloche, however, seated between Baugé and Liénard, found

himself nearly opposite Favier. They had glanced at each other with a rancorous look. The neighbors whispered, aware of their quarrel the previous day. Then they laughed at poor Deloche's ill-luck, always famishing, always falling on to the worst piece at table, by a sort of cruel fatality. This time he had come in for the neck of a chicken and bits of the carcase. Without saying a word he let them joke away, swallowing large mouthfuls of bread, and picking the neck with the infinite art of a fellow who entertains a great respect for meat.

"Why don't you complain?" asked Baugé.

But he shrugged his shoulders. What would be the good? It was always the same. When he ventured to complain things went worse than ever.

"You know the Bobbin fellows have got their club now," said Mignot, all at once. "Yes, my boy, the 'Bobbin Club.' It's held at a tavern in the Rue Saint-Honoré, where they hire a room on Saturdays."

He was speaking of the mercery salesmen. The whole table began to joke. Between two mouthfuls, with his voice still thick, each one made some remark, added a detail; the obstinate readers alone remained mute, absorbed, their noses buried in some newspapers. It could not be denied; shop-men were gradually assuming a better style; nearly half of them now spoke English or German. It was no longer good form to go and kick up a row at Bullier, to prowl about the music-halls for the pleasure of hissing ugly singers. No; a score of them got together and formed a club.

"Have they a piano like the linen-drapers?" asked Liénard.

"I should rather think they have a piano!" exclaimed Mignot. "And they play, my boy, and sing! There's even one of them, little Bavoux, who recites verses."

The gaiety redoubled, they chaffed little Bavoux, but still beneath this laughter there lay a great respect. They then spoke of a piece at the Vaudeville, in which a counter-jumper played a nasty part, which annoyed several of them, whilst others were anxiously wondering what time they would get away, having invitations to pass the evening at friends' houses; and from all points were heard similar conversations amidst the increasing noise of the crockery. To drive out the odour of the food—the warm steam which rose from the five hundred plates—the windows had been opened, while the lowered blinds were scorching in the heavy August sun. An ardent breath came in from the street, golden reflections yellowed the ceiling, bathing in a reddish light the perspiring eaters.

"A nice thing to shut people up such a fine Sunday as this!" repeated Favier.

This reflection brought them back to the stock-taking. It was a splendid year. And they went on to speak of the salaries—the rises—the eternal subject, the stirring question which occupied them all. It was always thus on chicken days, a wonderful excitement declared itself, the noise at last became insupportable. When the waiters brought the artichokes one could not hear one's self speak. The inspector on duty had orders to be indulgent.

"By the way," cried out Favier, "you've heard the news?"

But his voice was drowned. Mignot was asking: "Who doesn't like artichoke, I'll sell my dessert for an artichoke."

No one replied. Everybody liked artichoke. This lunch would be counted amongst the good ones, for peaches were to be given for dessert.

"He has invited her to dinner, my dear fellow," said Favier to his right-hand neighbor, finishing his story. "What! you didn't know it?"

The whole table knew it, they were tired of talking about it since the first thing, in the morning. And the same poor jokes passed from mouth to mouth. Deloche had turned pale again. He looked at them, his eyes finishing by resting on Favier, who was persisting in repeating:

"If he's not had her, he's going to. And he won't be the first; oh! no, he won't be the first."

He was also looking at Deloche. He added with a provoking air: "Those who like bones can have her for a crown!"

Suddenly, he ducked his head. Deloche, yielding to an irresistible movement, had just thrown his last glass of wine into his tormentor's face, stammering: "Take that, you infernal liar! I ought to have drenched you yesterday!"

It caused quite a scandal. A few drops had spurted on Favier's neighbors, whilst he only had his hair slightly wetted: the wine, thrown by an awkward hand, had fallen the other side of the table. But the others got angry, asking if she was his mistress that he defended her in this way? What a brute! he deserved a good sound drubbing to teach him manners. However, their voices fell, an inspector was observed coming along, and it was useless to introduce the management into the quarrel. Favier contented himself with saying:

"If it had caught me, you would have seen some sport!"

Then the affair wound up in jeers. When Deloche, still trembling, wished to drink to hide his confusion, and seized his empty glass mechanically, they burst out laughing. He laid his glass down again awkwardly, and commenced sucking the leaves of the artichoke he had already eaten.

"Pass Deloche the water bottle," said Mignot, quietly; "he's thirsty."

The laughter increased. The young men took their clean plates from the piles standing on the table, at equal distances, whilst the waiters handed round the dessert, which consisted of peaches, in baskets. And they all held their sides when Mignot added, with a grin:

"Each man to his taste. Deloche takes wine with his peaches."

The latter sat motionless, with his head hanging down, as if deaf to the joking going on around him: he was full of a despairing regret for what he had just done. These fellows were right—what right had he to defend her? They would now think all sorts of villainous things: he could have killed himself for having thus compromised her, in attempting to prove her innocence. This was always his luck, he might just as well kill himself at once, for he could not even yield to the promptings of his heart without doing some stupid thing. And the tears came into his eyes. Was it not always his fault if the whole shop was talking of the letter written by the governor? He heard them grinning and making abominable remarks about this invitation, of which Liénard alone had been informed; and he accused himself, he ought not to have let Pauline speak before the latter; he was really responsible for the annoying indiscretion committed.

"Why did you go and relate that?" he murmured at last, in a voice full of grief. "It's very bad."

"I?" replied Liénard. "But I only told it to one or two persons, enjoining secrecy. One never knows how these things get about!"

When Deloche made up his mind to drink a glass of water the whole table burst out laughing again. They had finished and were lolling back on their chairs waiting for the bell recalling them to work. They had not asked for many extras at the great central counter, the more so as the firm treated them to coffee that day. The cups were steaming, perspiring faces shone under the light vapors, floating like the blue clouds from cigarettes. At the windows the blinds hung motionless, without the slightest flapping. One of them, drawn up, admitted a ray of sunshine which traversed the room and gilded the ceiling. The uproar of the voices beat on the walls with such force that the bell was at first only heard by those at the tables near the door. They got up, and the confusion of the departure filled the corridors for a long time. Deloche, however, remained behind to escape the malicious remarks that were still being made. Baugé even went out before him, and Baugé was, as a rule, the last to leave, going a circuitous way so as to meet Pauline as she went to the ladies' dining room; a maneuver arranged between them—the only chance of seeing each other for a minute during business hours. But this time, just as they were indulging in a loving kiss in a corner of the passage they were surprised by Denise, who was also going up to lunch. She was walking slowly on account of her foot.

"Oh! my dear," stammered Pauline, very red, "don't say anything, will you?"

Baugé, with his big limbs and giant proportions, was trembling like a little boy. He murmured, "They'd very soon pitch us out. Though our marriage may be announced, they don't allow any kissing, the animals!"

Denise, greatly agitated, affected not to have seen them; and Baugé disappeared just as Deloche, who was going the longest way round, appeared in his turn. He tried to apologize, stammering out phrases that Denise did not at first catch. Then, as he blamed Pauline for having spoken before Liénard, and she stood there looking very embarrassed, Denise at last understood the whispered phrases she had heard around her all the morning. It was the story of the letter that was circulating. She was again seized by the shudder with which this letter had agitated her; she felt herself disrobed by all these men.

"But I didn't know," repeated Pauline. "Besides, there's nothing bad in the letter. Let them gossip; they're jealous, of course!"

"My dear," said Denise at last, with her prudent air, "I don't blame you in any way! You've spoken nothing but the truth. I *have* received a letter, and it is my duty to answer it."

Deloche went away heart-broken, having understood that the young girl accepted the situation and would keep the appointment that evening. When the two young ladies had lunched in a small room adjoining the large dining room, and in which the women were served much more comfortably, Pauline had to assist Denise downstairs, for the latter's foot was worse.

Down below in the afternoon warmth the stock-taking was roaring louder than ever. The moment for the supreme effort had arrived, when before the work, behindhand since the morning, every force was put forth in order to finish that evening. The voices got louder still, one saw nothing but the waving of arms continually emptying the shelves, throwing the goods down, and it was impossible to get along, the tide of the bales and piles of goods on the floor rose as high as the counters. A sea of heads, of brandished fists, of limbs flying about, seemed to extend to the very depths of the departments, like the distant confusion of a riot. It was the last fever of the clearance, the machine nearly ready to burst; whilst along the plate-glass windows, round the closed shop, a few rare pedestrians continued to pass, pale with the stifling boredom of a summer Sunday. On the pavement in the Rue Neuve-Saint-Augustin were planted three tall girls, bareheaded and sluttish looking, impudently sticking their faces against the windows, trying to see the curious work going on inside.

When Denise returned to the ready-made department Madame Aurélie left Marguerite to finish calling out the garments. There was still a lot of checking to be done, for which, desirous of silence, she retired into the pattern-room, taking the young girl with her.

"Come with me, we'll do the checking; then you can add up the totals."

But as she wished to leave the door open, in order to look after the young ladies, the noise came in, and they could not hear much better. It was a large, square room, furnished simply with some chairs and three long tables. In one corner were the great machine knives, for cutting up the patterns. Entire pieces were consumed; they sent away every year more than sixty thousand francs' worth of material, cut up in strips. From morning to night, the knives were cutting up silk, wool, and linen, with a scythe-like noise. Then the books had to be got together, gummed or sewn. And there was also between the two windows, a little printing-press for the tickets.

"Not so loud, please!" cried Madame Aurélie, now and again, quite unable to hear Denise reading out the articles.

When the checking of the first lists was finished, she left the young girl at one of the tables, absorbed in the adding up. But she returned almost immediately, and placed Mademoiselle de Fontenailles near her; the under-linen department not wanting her any longer, had sent her to Madame Aurélie. She could also do some adding-up, it would save time. But the appearance of the marchioness, as Clara ill-naturedly called her, had disturbed the department. They laughed and joked at poor Joseph, their ferocious sallies could be heard in the pattern-room.

"Don't draw back, you are not at all in my way," said Denise, seized with pity for the poor girl. "My inkstand will suffice, we'll dip together."

Mademoiselle de Fontenailles, dulled and stultified by her unfortunate position, could not even find a word of gratitude. She appeared to be a woman who drank, her thinness had a livid appearance, and her hands alone, white and delicate, attested the distinction of her birth.

The laughter ceased all at once, and the work resumed its regular roar. It was Mouret who was once more going through the departments. But he stopped and looked round for Denise, surprised not to see her there. He made a sign to Madame Aurélie; and both drew aside, talking in a low tone for a moment. He must be questioning her. She indicated with her eyes the pattern-room, then seemed to be making a report. No doubt she was relating that the young girl had been weeping that morning.

"Very good!" said Mouret, aloud, coming nearer. "Show me the lists."

"This way, sir," said the first-hand. "We have run away from the noise."

He followed her into the next room. Clara was not duped by this maneuver, and said they had better go and fetch a bed at once. But Marguerite threw her the garments at a quicker rate, in order to take up her attention and close her mouth. Wasn't the second-hand a good comrade? Her affairs did not concern anyone. The department was becoming an accomplice, the young ladies got more agitated than ever, Lhomme and Joseph affected not to see or hear anything. And Jouve, the inspector, who, passing by, had remarked Madame Aurélie's tactics, commenced walking up and down before the pattern-room door, with the regular step of a sentry guarding the will and pleasure of a superior.

"Give Monsieur Mouret the lists," said the first-hand.

Denise gave them, and sat there with her eyes raised. She had slightly started, but had conquered herself, and retained a fine calm look, although her cheeks were pale. For a moment, Mouret appeared to be absorbed in the list of articles, without a look for the young girl. A silence reigned, Madame Aurélie then went up to Mademoiselle de Fontenailles, who had not even turned her head, appeared dissatisfied with her counting, and said to her in a half whisper:

"Go and help with the parcels. You are not used to figures."

The latter got up, and returned to the department, where she was greeted by a whispering on all sides. Joseph, exposed to the laughing eyes of these young minxes, was writing anyhow. Clara, delighted with this assistant who arrived, was yet very rough with her, hating her as she hated all the women in the shop. What an idiotic thing to yield to the love of a workman, when one was a marchioness! And yet she envied her this love.

"Very good!" repeated Mouret, still affecting to read.

However, Madame Aurélie hardly knew how to get away in her turn in a decent fashion. She stamped about, went to look at the knives, furious with her husband for not inventing a pretext for calling her; but he was never any good for serious matters, he would have died of thirst close to a pond. It was Marguerite who was intelligent enough to go and ask the first-hand a question.

"I'm coming," replied the latter.

And her dignity being now protected, having a pretext in the eyes of the young ladies who were watching her, she at last left Denise and Mouret alone together, going out with her imperial air, her profile so noble, that the saleswomen did not even dare to smile. Mouret had slowly laid the lists on the table, and stood looking at the young girl, who had remained seated, pen in hand. She did not avert her gaze, but she had turned paler.

"You will come this evening?" asked he.

"No, sir, I cannot. My brothers are to be at uncle's tonight, and I have promised to dine with them."

"But your foot! You walk with such difficulty."

"Oh, I can get so far very well. I feel much better since the morning."

He had now turned pale in his turn, before this quiet refusal. A nervous revolt agitated his lips. However, he restrained himself, and resumed with the air of a good-natured master simply interesting himself in one of his young ladies: "Come now, if I begged of you—You know what great esteem I have for you."

Denise retained her respectful attitude. "I am greatly touched, sir, by your kindness to me, and I thank you for this invitation. But I repeat, I cannot; my brothers expect me."

She persisted in not understanding. The door remained open, and she felt that the whole shop was pushing her on to yield.

Pauline had amicably called her a great simpleton, the others would laugh at her if she refused the invitation. Madame Aurélie, who had gone away, Marguerite, whose rising voice she could hear, Lhomme, with his motionless, discreet attitude, all these people were wishing for her fall, throwing her into the governor's arms. And the distant roar of the stock-taking, the millions of goods called out on all sides, thrown about in every direction, were like a warm wind, carrying the breath of passion straight towards her. There was a silence. Now and again, Mouret's voice was drowned by the noise which accompanied him, with the formidable uproar of a kingly fortune gained in battle.

"When will you come, then?" asked he again. "Tomorrow?"

This simple question troubled Denise. She lost her calmness for a moment, and stammered: "I don't know—I can't—"

He smiled, and tried to take her hand, which she withheld. "What are you afraid of?"

But she quickly raised her head, looked him straight in the face, and said, smiling, with her sweet, brave look: "I am afraid of nothing, sir. I can do as I like, can't I? I don't wish to, that's all!"

As she finished speaking, she was surprised by hearing a creaking noise, and on turning round saw the door slowly closing. It was Jouve, the inspector, who had taken upon himself to pull it to. The doors were a part of his duty, none should ever remain open. And he gravely resumed his position as sentinel. No one appeared to have noticed this door being closed in such a simple manner. Clara alone risked a strong remark in Mademoiselle de Fontenailles's ear, but the latter's face remained expressionless.

Denise, however, had got up. Mouret was saying to her in a low and trembling voice: "Listen, Denise, I love you. You have long known it, pray don't be so cruel as to play the ignorant. And don't fear anything. Many a time I've thought of calling you into my office. We should have been alone, I should only have had to lock the door. But I did not wish to; you see I speak to you here, where anyone can enter. I love you, Denise!" She was standing up, very pale, listening to him, still looking straight into his face.

"Tell me. Why do you refuse? Have you no wants? Your brothers are a heavy burden. Anything you might ask me, anything you might require of me."

With a word, she stopped him: "Thanks, I now earn more than I want."

"But it's perfect liberty that I am offering you, an existence of pleasure and luxury. I will set you up in a home of your own. I will assure you a little fortune."

"No, thanks; I should soon get tired of doing nothing. I earned my own living before I was ten years old."

He was almost mad. This was the first one who did not yield. He had only had to stoop to pick up the others, they all awaited his pleasure like submissive slaves; and this one said no, without even giving a reasonable pretext. His desire, long restrained, goaded by resistance, became stronger than ever. Perhaps he had not offered enough, he thought, and he doubled his offers; he pressed her more and more.

"No, no, thanks," replied she each time, without faltering.

Then he allowed this cry from his heart to escape him: "But don't you see that I am suffering! Yes, it's stupid, but I am suffering like a child!"

Tears came into his eyes. A fresh silence reigned. They could still hear behind the closed door the softened roar of the stock-taking. It was like a dying note of triumph, the accompaniment became more discreet, in this defeat of the master.

"And yet if I liked—" said he in an ardent voice, seizing her hands. She left them in his, her eyes turned pale, her whole strength was deserting her. A warmth came from this man's burning hands, filling her with a delicious cowardice. Good heavens! how she loved him, and with what delight she could have hung on his neck and remained there!

"I will! I will!" repeated he, in his passionate excitement. "I expect you tonight, otherwise I will take measures."

He was becoming brutal. She set up a low cry; the pain she felt at her wrists restored her courage. With an angry shake she disengaged herself. Then, very stiff, looking taller in her weakness: "No, leave me alone! I am not a Clara, to be thrown over in a day.

Besides, you love another; yes, that lady who comes here. Stay with her. I do not accept half an affection."

He was struck with surprise. What was she saying, and what did she want? The girls he had picked up in the shop had never asked to be loved. He ought to have laughed at such an idea, and this attitude of tender pride completely conquered his heart.

"Now, sir, please open the door," resumed she. "It is not proper to be shut up together in this way."

He obeyed; and with his temples throbbing, hardly knowing how to conceal his anguish, he recalled Madame Aurélie, and broke out angrily about the stock of cloaks, saying that the prices must be lowered, until everyone had been got rid of. Such was the rule of the house—a clean sweep was made every year, they sold at sixty per cent loss rather than keep an old model or any stale material. At that moment, Bourdoncle, seeking Mouret, was waiting for him outside, stopped before the closed door by Jouve, who had said a word in his ear with a grave air. He got very impatient, without, however, summoning up the courage to interrupt the governor's tête-à-tête. Was it possible? Such a day too, and with that puny creature! And when Mouret at last came out Bourdoncle spoke to him about the fancy silks, of which the stock left on hand would be enormous. This was a relief for Mouret, who could now cry out at his ease. What the devil was Bouthemont thinking about? He went off, declaring that he could not allow a buyer to display such a want of sense as to buy beyond the requirements of the business.

"What is the matter with him?" murmured Madame Aurélie, quite overcome by his reproaches.

And the young ladies looked at each other with a surprised air. At six o'clock the stock-taking was finished. The sun was still shining—a blonde summer sun, of which the golden reflection streamed through the glazed roofs of the halls. In the heavy air of the streets, tired families were already returning from the suburbs, loaded with bouquets, dragging their children along. One by one, the departments had become silent. Nothing was now heard in the depths of the galleries but the lingering calls of a few men clearing a last shelf. Then even these voices ceased, and there remained of the bustle of the day nothing but a shivering, above the formidable piles of goods. The shelves, cupboards, boxes, and band-boxes, were now empty: not a yard of stuff, not an object of any sort had remained in its place. The vast establishment presented nothing but the carcase of its usual appearance, the wood-work was absolutely bare, as on the day of entering into possession. This nakedness was the visible proof of the complete and exact taking of the stock. And on the ground was sixteen million francs' worth of goods, a rising sea, which had finished by submerging the tables and counters. The shopmen, drowned up to the shoulders, had commenced to put each article back into its place. They expected to finish about ten o'clock.

When Madame Aurélie, who went to the first dinner, returned to the dining room, she announced the amount of business done during the year, which the totals of the various departments had just given. The figure was eighty million francs, ten millions more than the preceding year. The only real decrease was on the fancy silks.

"If Monsieur Mouret is not satisfied, I should like to know what more he wants," added the first-hand. "See! he's over there, at the top of the grand staircase, looking furious."

The young ladies went to look at him. He was standing alone, with a sombre countenance, above the millions scattered at his feet.

"Madame," said Denise, at this moment, "would you kindly let me go away now? I can't do any more good on account of my foot, and as I am to dine at my uncle's with my brothers."

They were all astonished. She had not yielded, then! Madame Aurélie hesitated, and seemed inclined to prohibit her going out, her voice sharp and disagreeable; whilst Clara shrugged her shoulders, full of incredulity. That wouldn't do! it was very simple—the governor no longer wanted her! When Pauline learnt this, she was in the baby-linen department with Deloche, and the sudden joy exhibited by the young man made her very angry. That did him a lot of good, didn't it? Perhaps he was pleased to see that his friend had been stupid enough to miss a fortune? And Bourdoncle, who did not dare to approach Mouret in his ferocious isolation, marched up and down amidst these rumors, in despair also, and full of anxiety. However, Denise went downstairs. As she arrived at the bottom of the left-hand staircase, slowly, supporting herself by the banister, she came upon a group of grinning salesmen. Her name was pronounced, and she felt that they were talking about her adventure. They had not noticed her.

"Oh! all that's put on, you know," Favier was saying. "She's full of vice! Yes, I know someone she wanted to take by force."

And he looked at Hutin, who, in order to preserve his dignity as second-hand, was standing a certain distance apart, without joining in their conversation. But he was so flattered by the air of envy with which the others were contemplating him, that he deigned to murmur: "She was a regular nuisance to me, that girl!"

Denise, wounded to the heart, clung to the banister. They must have seen her, for they all disappeared, laughing. He was right, she thought, and she accused herself of her former ignorance, when she used to think about him. But what a coward he was, and how she scorned him now! A great trouble had seized her: was it not strange that she should have found the strength just now to repulse a man whom she adored, when she used to feel herself so feeble in bygone days before this worthless fellow, whom she had only dreamed of? Her sense of reason and her bravery foundered before these contradictions of her being, in which she could not read clearly. She hastened to cross the hall. Then a sort of instinct prompted her to raise her head, whilst an inspector opened the door, closed since the morning. And she perceived Mouret, who was still at the top of the stairs, on the great central landing, dominating the gallery. But he had forgotten the stock-taking, he did not see his empire, this building bursting with riches. Everything had disappeared, his former glorious victories, his future colossal fortune. With a desponding look he was watching Denise's departure, and when she had passed the door everything disappeared, a darkness came over the house.

CHAPTER XI.

That day Bouthemont was the first to arrive at Madame Desforges's four o'clock tea. Still alone in her large Louis XVI. drawing-room, the brasses and brocatelle of which shone out with a clear gaiety, the latter rose with an air of impatience, saying, "Well?"

"Well," replied the young man, "when I told him I should doubtless call on you he formally promised me to come."

"You made him thoroughly understand that I counted on the baron today?"

"Certainly. That's what appeared to decide him."

They were speaking of Mouret, who the year before had suddenly taken such a liking to Bouthemont that he had admitted him to share his pleasures, and had even introduced him to Henriette, glad to have an agreeable fellow always at hand to enliven an intimacy of which he was getting tired. It was thus that Bouthemont had ultimately become the confidant of his governor and of the handsome widow; he did their little errands, talked of the one to the other, and sometimes reconciled them. Henriette, in her jealous fits, abandoned herself to a familiarity which sometimes surprised and embarrassed him, for she lost all her lady-like prudence, using all her art to save appearances.

She resumed violently, "You ought to have brought him. I should have been sure then."

"Well," said he, with a good-natured laugh, "it isn't my fault if he escapes so frequently now. Oh! he's very fond of me, all the same. Were it not for him I should be in a bad way at the shop."

His situation at The Ladies' Paradise was really menaced since the last stock-taking. It was in vain that he adduced the rainy season; one could not overlook the considerable stock of fancy silks; and as Hutin was improving the occasion, undermining him with the governors with an increase of sly rage, he felt the ground cracking under him. Mouret had condemned him, weary, no doubt, of this witness who prevents him breaking with Henriette, tired of a familiarity which was profitless. But, in accordance with his usual tactics, he was pushing Bourdoncle forward; it was Bourdoncle and the other partners who insisted on his dismissal at each board-meeting; whilst he resisted still, according to his account, defending his friend energetically, at the risk of getting into serious trouble with the others.

"Well, I shall wait," resumed Madame Desforges. "You know that girl is coming here at five o'clock, I want to see them face to face. I must discover their secret."

And she returned to this long-meditated plan. She repeated in her fever that she had requested Madame Aurélie to send her Denise to look at a mantle which fitted badly. When she had once got the young girl in her room, she would find a means of calling Mouret, and could then act. Bouthemont, who had sat down opposite her, was gazing at her with his fine laughing eyes, which he endeavored to render grave. This jovial, dissipated fellow, with his coal-black beard, whose warm Gascon blood empurpled his cheeks, was thinking that these fine ladies were not much good, and that they let out a nice lot of secrets, when they opened their hearts. His friend's mistresses, simple shop-girls, certainly never made more complete confessions.

"Come," he ventured to say at last, "what does that matter to you? I swear to you there is nothing whatever between them."

"Just so," cried she, "because he loves her! I don't care in the least for the others, chance acquaintances, friends of a day!"

She spoke of Clara with disdain. She was well aware that Mouret, after Denise's refusal, had fallen back on this tall, red-haired girl, with the horse's head, doubtless by calculation; for he maintained her in the department, loading her with presents. Not only that, for the last three months he had been leading a terrible life, squandering his money with a prodigality which caused a great many remarks; he had bought a mansion for a worthless actress, and was being ruined by two or three other jades, who seemed to be struggling to outdo each other in costly, stupid caprices.

"It's this creature's fault," repeated Henriette. "I feel sure he's ruining himself with the others because she repulses him. Besides, what's his money to me? I should have loved him better poor. You know how I love him, you who have become our friend."

She stopped, choked, ready to burst into tears; and with a movement of abandon she held out her two hands to him. It was true, she adored Mouret for his youth and his triumphs, never had any man thus conquered her so entirely in a quiver of her flesh and of her pride; but at the thought of losing him, she also heard the knell of her fortieth year, and she asked herself with terror how she should replace this great love.

"I'll have my revenge," murmured she. "I'll have my revenge, if he behaves badly!"

Bouthemont continued to hold her hands in his. She was still handsome. But she would be a very awkward mistress, thought he, and he did not like that style of woman. The thing, however, deserved thinking over; perhaps it would be worthwhile risking certain annoyances.

"Why don't you set up for yourself?" she asked all at once, drawing her hands away.

He was astonished. Then he replied: "But it would require an immense sum. Last year I had an idea in my head. I feel convinced that there are customers enough in Paris for one or two more big shops; but the district would have to be chosen. The Bon Marché has the left side of the river; the Louvre occupies the centre; we monopolize, at The Paradise, the rich west-end district. There remains the north, where a rival to the Place Clichy could be created. And I had discovered a splendid position, near the Opera House."

"Well?"

He set up a noisy laugh. "Just fancy. I was stupid enough to go and talk to my father about it. Yes, I was simple enough to ask him to find some shareholders at Toulouse."

And he gaily described the anger of the old man, enraged against the great Parisian bazaars, in his little country shop. Old Bouthemont, suffocated by the thirty thousand francs a year earned by his son, had replied that he would give his money and that of his friends to the hospitals rather than contribute a sou to one of those shops which were the pests of the drapery business.

"Besides," continued the young man, "it would require millions."

"Suppose they were found?" observed Madame Desforges, simply.

He looked at her, serious all at once. Was it not merely a jealous woman's word? But she did not give him time to question her, adding: "In short, you know what a great interest I take in you. We'll talk about it again."

The outer bell had rung. She got up, and he, himself, with an instinctive movement, drew back his chair, as if they might have been surprised. A silence reigned in the drawing-room, with its pretty hangings, and decorated with such a profusion of green plants that there was quite a small wood between the two windows. She stood there waiting, with her ear towards the door.

"There he is," she murmured.

The footman announced Monsieur Mouret and Monsieur de Vallagnosc. Henriette could not restrain a movement of anger. Why had he not come alone? He must have gone after his friend, fearful of a tête-à-tête with her. However, she smiled and shook hands with the two men.

"What a stranger you are getting. I may say the same for you, Monsieur de Vallagnosc."

Her great grief was to be becoming stout, and she squeezed herself into tight black silk dresses, to conceal her increasing obesity. However, her pretty face, with her dark hair, preserved its amiable expression. And Mouret could familiarly tell her, enveloping her with a look:

"It's useless to ask how you are. You are as fresh as a rose."

"Oh! I'm almost too well," replied she. "Besides, I might have died; you would have known nothing about it."

She was examining him also, and thought him looking tired and nervous, his eyes heavy, his complexion livid.

"Well," she resumed, in a tone which she endeavored to render agreeable, "I cannot return the compliment; you don't look at all well today."

"Overwork!" remarked Vallagnosc.

Mouret shrugged his shoulders, without replying. He had just perceived Bouthemont, and nodded to him in a friendly way. During the time of their close intimacy he used to take him away direct from the department, bringing him to Henriette's during the busiest moments of the afternoon. But times had changed; he said to him in a half whisper:

"You went away rather early. They noticed your departure, and are furious about it."

He referred to Bourdoncle and the other persons who had an interest in the business, as if he were not himself the master.

"Ah!" murmured Bouthemont, rather anxious.

"Yes, I want to talk to you. Wait for me, we'll leave together."

Meanwhile, Henriette had sat down again; and while listening to Vallagnosc, who was announcing that Madame de Boves would probably pay her a visit, she did not take her eyes off Mouret. The latter, silent again, gazed at the furniture, seemed to be looking for something on the ceiling. Then as she laughingly complained that she had only gentlemen at her four o'clock tea, he so far forgot himself as to blurt out:

"I expected to find Baron Hartmann here."

Henriette turned pale. No doubt she knew he came to her house solely to meet the baron; but he might have avoided throwing his indifference in her face like this. At that moment the door had opened and the footman was standing behind her. When she had interrogated him by a sign, he leant over her and said in a very low tone:

"It's for that mantle. You wished me to let you know. The young lady is there."

Then Henriette raised her voice, so as to be heard. All her jealous suffering found relief in the following words, of a scornful harshness: "She can wait!"

"Shall I show her into your dressing-room?"

"No, no. Let her stay in the ante-room!"

And when the servant had gone out she quietly resumed her conversation with Vallagnosc. Mouret, who had relapsed into his former lassitude, had listened with a careless, distracted air, without understanding. Bouthemont, preoccupied by the adventure, was reflecting. But almost immediately after the door was opened again, and two ladies were shown in.

"Just fancy," said Madame Marty, "I was alighting at the door, when I saw Madame de Boves coming under the arcade."

"Yes," explained the latter, "it's a fine day, and my doctor says I must take walking exercise."

Then, after a general hand-shaking, she asked Henriette: "You're engaging a new maid, then?"

"No," replied the other, astonished. "Why?"

"Because I've just seen a young girl in the ante-room."

Henriette interrupted her, laughing. "It's true; all these shop-girls look like ladies' maids, don't they? Yes, it's a young person come to alter a mantle."

Mouret looked at her intently, a suspicion crossing his mind. She went on with a forced gaiety, explaining that she had bought this mantle at The Ladies' Paradise the previous week.

"What!" asked Madame Marty, "have you deserted Sauveur, then?"

"No, dear, but I wished to make an experiment. Besides, I was pretty well satisfied with a first purchase, a travelling cloak. But this time it has not succeeded at all. You may say what you like, one is horribly trussed up in the big shops. I speak out plainly, even before you, Monsieur Mouret; you will never know how to dress a woman with the slightest claim to distinction."

Mouret did not defend his house, still keeping his eyes on her, thinking to himself that she would never have dared to do such a thing. And it was Bouthemont who had to plead the cause of The Ladies' Paradise.

"If all the aristocratic ladies who patronize us announced the fact," replied he, gaily, "you would be astonished at our customers. Order a garment to measure at our place, it will equal one from Sauveur's, and will cost but half the money. But there, just because it's cheaper it's not so good."

"So it doesn't fit, this mantle you speak of?" resumed Madame de Boves. "Ah! now I remember the young person. It's rather dark in your ante-room."

"Yes," added Madame Marty, "I was wondering where I had seen that figure. Well, go, my dear, don't stand on ceremony with us."

Henriette assumed a look of disdainful unconcern. "Oh, presently, there is no hurry."

The ladies continued to discuss the articles from the big shops. Then Madame de Boves spoke of her husband, who, she said, had gone to inspect the breeding depot at Saint-Lô; and just then Henriette was relating that through the illness of an aunt Madame Guibal had been suddenly called into Franche-Comté. Moreover, she did not reckon that day on Madame Bourdelais, who at the end of every month shut herself up with a needlewoman to look over her young people's under-linen. But Madame Marty seemed agitated with some secret trouble. Her husband's position at the Lycée Bonaparte was menaced, in consequence of lessons given by the poor man in certain doubtful institutions where a regular trade was carried on with the B.A. diplomas; the poor fellow picked up a pound where he could, feverishly, in order to meet the ruinous expenses which pillaged his household; and his wife, on seeing him weeping one evening in the fear of a dismissal, had conceived the idea of getting her friend Henriette to speak to a director at the Ministry of Public Instruction with whom she was acquainted. Henriette finished by quieting her with a few words. It was understood that Monsieur Marty was coming himself to know his fate and to thank her.

"You look ill, Monsieur Mouret," observed Madame de Boves.

"Overwork!" repeated Vallagnosc, with his ironical phlegm.

Mouret quickly got up, as if ashamed at forgetting himself

thus. He went and took his accustomed place in the midst of the ladies, summoning up all his agreeable talent. He was now occupied with the winter novelties, and spoke of a considerable arrival of lace; and Madame de Boves questioned him as to the price of Bruges lace: she felt inclined to buy some. She had now got so far as to economize the thirty sous for a cab, often going home quite ill from the effects of stopping before the windows. Draped in a mantle which was already two years old she tried, in imagination, on her queenly shoulders all the dearest things she saw; and it was like tearing her flesh away when she awoke and found herself dressed in her patched, old dresses, without the slightest hope of ever satisfying her passion.

"Baron Hartmann," announced the man-servant.

Henriette observed with what pleasure Mouret shook hands with the new arrival. The latter bowed to the ladies and looked at the young man with that subtle expression which sometimes illumined his big Alsatian face.

"Always plunged in dress!" murmured he, with a smile. Then, like a friend of the house, he ventured to add, "There's a charming young girl in the ante-room. Who is it?"

"Oh, nobody," replied Madame Desforges, in her ill-natured voice. "Only a shop-girl waiting to see me."

But the door remained half open, the servant was bringing in the tea. He went out, came in again, placed the china service on the table, then some plates of sandwiches and biscuits. In the vast room, a bright light, softened by the green plants, illuminated the brass-work, bathing the silk hangings in a tender flame; and each time the door was opened one could perceive an obscure corner of the ante-room, which was only lighted by two ground-glass windows. There, in the darkness, appeared a sombre form, motionless and patient. It was Denise, still standing up; there was a leather-covered form there, but a feeling of pride prevented her sitting down on it. She felt the insult keenly. She had been there for the last half-hour, without a gesture, without a word. The ladies and the baron had taken stock of her in passing; she could now hear the voices from the drawing-room. All this amiable luxury wounded her with its indifference, and still she did not move. Suddenly, through the half-open door, she perceived Mouret, and he, on his side, had at last guessed it to be her.

"Is it one of your saleswomen?" asked Baron Hartmann.

Mouret had succeeded in concealing his great agitation; but his voice trembled somewhat with emotion: "No doubt; but I don't know which."

"It's the little fair girl from the ready-made department," replied Madame Marty, obligingly, "the second-hand, I believe."

Henriette looked at Mouret in her turn.

"Ah!" said he, simply.

And he tried to change the conversation, speaking of the fetes given to the King of Prussia then passing through Paris. But the baron returned maliciously to the young ladies in the big establishments. He affected to be desirous of gaining information, and put several questions: Where did they come from in general? Was their conduct as bad as it was said to be? Quite a discussion ensued.

"Really," he repeated, "you think them well behaved."

Mouret defended their virtue with a conviction which made Vallagnosc smile. Bouthemont then interfered, to save his chief. Of course there were some of all sorts, bad and good. Formerly they had nothing but the refuse of the trade, a poor, vague class of girls drifted into the drapery business; whilst now, such respectable families as those living in the Rue de Sevres, for instance, positively brought up their girls for the Bon Marché. In short, when they liked to conduct themselves well, they could, for they were not, like the work-girls of Paris, obliged to board and lodge themselves; they had bed and board, their existence was provided for, an existence excessively hard, no doubt. The worst of all was their neutral, badly-defined position, between the shopwoman and the lady. Thrown into the midst of luxury, often without any previous instruction, they formed a singular, nameless class. Their misfortunes and vices sprung from that.

"I," said Madame de Boves, "I don't know any creatures more disagreeable. Really, one could slap them sometimes."

And the ladies vented their spite. They devoured each other

before the shop-counters; it was a question of woman against woman in the sharp rivalry of money and beauty. It was an ill-natured jealousy felt by the saleswomen towards the well-dressed customers, the ladies whose manners they tried to imitate, and a still stronger feeling on the part of the poorly-dressed customers, the lower-class ones, against the saleswomen, those girls dressed in silk, from whom they would have liked to exact a servant's humility when serving a ten sou purchase.

"Don't speak of them," said Henriette, by way of conclusion, "a wretched lot of beings ready to sell themselves the same as their goods."

Mouret had the strength to smile. The baron was looking at him, so touched by his graceful command over himself that he changed the conversation, returning to the fetes to be given to the King of Prussia, saying they would be superb, the whole trade of Paris would profit by them. Henriette remained silent and thoughtful, divided between the desire to forget Denise in the ante-room, and the fear that Mouret, now aware of her presence, might go away. At last she quitted her chair.

"You will allow me?"

"Certainly, my dear," replied Madame Marty. "I'll do the honors of the house for you."

She got up, took the teapot, and filled the cups. Henriette turned towards Baron Hartmann, saying: "You'll stay a few minutes, won't you?"

"Yes; I want to speak to Monsieur Mouret. We are going to invade your little drawing-room."

She went out, and her black silk dress, rustling against the door, produced a noise like that of a snake wriggling through the brushwood. The baron at once maneuvered to carry Mouret off, leaving the ladies to Bouthemont and Vallagnosc. Then they stood talking before the window of the other room in a low tone. It was quite a fresh affair. For a long time Mouret had cherished a desire to realize his former project, the invasion of the whole block by The Ladies' Paradise, from the Rue Monsigny to the Rue de la Michodière and from the Rue Neuve-Saint-Augustin to the Rue du Dix-Décembre. There was still a vast piece of ground, in the latter street, remaining to be acquired, and that sufficed to spoil his triumph, he was tortured with the desire to complete his conquest, to erect there a sort of apotheosis, a monumental façade. As long as his principal entrance should remain in the Rue Neuve-Saint-Augustin, in a dark street of old Paris, his work would be incomplete, wanting in logic. He wished to set it up before new Paris, in one of these modern avenues through which passed the busy crowd of the latter part of the nineteenth century. He saw it dominating, imposing itself as the giant palace of commerce, casting a greater shadow over the city than the old Louvre itself. But up to the present he had been baulked by the obstinacy of the Crédit Immobilier, which still held to its first idea of building a rival to the Grand Hôtel on this land. The plans were ready, they were only waiting for the clearing of the Rue du Dix-Décembre to commence the work. At last, by a supreme effort, Mouret had almost convinced Baron Hartmann.

"Well!" commenced the latter, "we had a board-meeting yesterday, and I came today, thinking I should meet you, and being desirous of keeping you informed. They still resist."

The young man gave way to a nervous gesture. "But it's ridiculous. What do they say?"

"Dear me! they say what I have said to you myself, and what I am still inclined to think. Your façade is only an ornament, the new buildings would only extend by about a tenth the surface of your establishment, and it would be throwing away immense sums on a mere advertisement."

At this Mouret burst out. "An advertisement! an advertisement! In any case this will be in stone and outlive all of us. Just consider that it would increase our business tenfold! We should see our money back in two years. What matters about what you call the wasted ground, if this ground returns you an enormous interest! You will see the crowd, when our customers are no longer obliged to struggle through the Rue Neuve-Saint-Augustin, but can freely pass down a thoroughfare large enough for six carriages abreast."

"No doubt," replied the baron, laughing. "But you are a poet in your way, let me tell you once more. These gentlemen think it would be dangerous to further extend your business. They want to be prudent for you."

"What do they mean? Prudent! I don't understand. Don't the figures show the constant progression of our business? At first, with a capital of five hundred thousand francs, I did business to the extent of two millions, turning the capital over four times. It then became four million francs, which, turned over ten times, has produced business to the extent of forty millions. In short, after successive increases, I have just learnt, from the last stock-taking, that the amount of business done now amounts to a total of eighty millions; thus the capital, only slightly increased—for it does not exceed six millions—has passed over our counters in the form of more than twelve times."

He raised his voice, tapping the fingers of his right hand on the palm of his left hand, knocking down these millions as he would have cracked a few nuts. The baron interrupted him.

"I know, I know. But you don't hope to keep on increasing in this way, do you?"

"Why not?" asked Mouret, ingenuously. "There's no reason why it should stop. The capital can be turned over as often as fifteen times. I predicted as much long ago. In certain departments it can be turned over twenty-five or thirty times. And after? Well! after, we'll find a means of turning it over more than that."

"So you'll finish by drinking up all the money in Paris, as you'd drink a glass of water?"

"Most decidedly. Doesn't Paris belong to the women, and don't the women belong to us?"

The baron laid his hands on Mouret's shoulders, looking at him with a paternal air. "Listen, you're a fine fellow, and I am really fond of you. There's no resisting you. We'll go into the matter seriously, and I hope to make them listen to reason. Up to the present, we are perfectly satisfied with you. Your dividends astonish the Bourse. You must be right; it will be better to put more money into your business, than to risk this competition with the Grand Hôtel, which is hazardous."

Mouret's excitement subsided at once; he thanked the baron,

but without any of his usual enthusiasm; and the latter saw him turn his eyes towards the door of the next room, again seized with the secret anxiety which he was concealing. However, Vallagnosc had come up, understanding that they had finished talking business. He stood close to them, listening to the baron, who was murmuring with the gallant air of an old man who had seen life:

"I say, I fancy they're taking their revenge."

"Who?" asked Mouret, embarrassed.

"Why, the women. They're getting tired of belonging to you; you now belong to them, my dear fellow; it's only just!"

He joked him, well aware of the young man's notorious love affairs: the mansion bought for the actress, the enormous sums squandered with girls picked up in private supper rooms, amused him as an excuse for the follies he had formerly committed himself. His old experience rejoiced.

"Really, I don't understand," repeated Mouret.

"Oh! you understand well enough. They always get the last word. In fact, I said to myself: It isn't possible, he's boasting, be can't be so strong as that! And there you are! Bleed the women, work them as you would a coal mine, and what for? In order that they may work you afterwards, and force you to refund at last! Take care, for they'll draw more blood and money from you than you have ever sucked from them."

He laughed louder still; and Vallagnosc was also grinning, without, however, saying a word.

"Dear me! one must have a taste of everything," confessed Mouret, at last, pretending to laugh as well. "Money is so stupid, if it isn't spent."

"As for that, I agree with you," resumed the baron. "Enjoy yourself, my dear fellow, I'll not be the one to preach to you, nor to tremble for the great interests we have confided to your care. Everyone must sow his wild oats, and his head is generally clearer afterwards. Besides, there's nothing unpleasant in ruining one's self when one feels capable of building up another fortune. But if money is nothing, there are certain sufferings—"

He stopped, his smile became sad, former sufferings presented themselves amid the irony of his skepticism. He had watched the duel between Henriette and Mouret with the curiosity of one who still felt greatly interested in other people's love battles; and he felt that the crisis had arrived, he guessed the drama, well acquainted with the story of this Denise, whom he had seen in the ante-room.

"Oh! as for suffering, that's not in my line," said Mouret, in a tone of bravado. "It's quite enough to pay."

The baron looked at him for a moment without speaking. Without wishing to insist on his discreet allusion he added, slowly—"Don't make yourself worse than you are! You'll lose something else besides your money at that game. Yes, you'll lose a part of yourself, my dear fellow." He stopped, again laughing, to ask, "That often happens, doesn't it, Monsieur de Vallagnosc?"

"So they say, baron," the young man simply replied. Just at this moment the door was opened. Mouret, who was going to reply, slightly started. The three men turned round. It was Madame Desforges, looking very gay, putting her head through the doorway to call, in a hurried voice—

"Monsieur Mouret! Monsieur Mouret!" Then, when she perceived the three men, she added, "Oh! you'll excuse me, won't you, gentlemen? I'm going to take Monsieur Mouret away for a minute. The least he can do, as he has sold me a frightful mantle, is to give me the benefit of his experience. This girl is a stupid, without the least idea. Come, come! I'm waiting for you."

He hesitated, undecided, flinching before the scene he could foresee. But he had to obey. The baron said to him, with his air at once paternal and mocking, "Go, my dear fellow, go, madame wants you."

Mouret followed her. The door closed, and he thought he could hear Vallagnosc's grin stifled by the hangings. His courage was entirely exhausted. Since Henriette had quitted the drawing-room, and he knew Denise was alone in the house in jealous hands, he had experienced a growing anxiety, a nervous torment, which made him listen from time to time as if suddenly startled by a distant sound of weeping. What could this woman invent to torture her? And his whole love, this love which surprised him even now, went out to the young girl like a support and a consolation. Never had he loved her so strongly, with that charm so powerful in suffering. His former affections, his love for Henriette herself—so delicate, so handsome, the possession of whom was so flattering to his pride—had never been more than agreeable pastimes, frequently a calculation, in which he sought nothing but a profitable pleasure. He used quietly to leave his mistresses and go home to bed, happy in his bachelor liberty, without a regret or a care on his mind; whilst now his heart beat with anguish, his life was taken, he no longer enjoyed the forgetfulness of sleep in his great, solitary bed. Denise was his only thought. Even at this moment she was the sole object of his anxiety, and he was telling himself that he preferred to be there to protect her, notwithstanding his fear of some regrettable scene with the other one.

At first, they both crossed the bedroom, silent and empty. Then Madame Desforges, pushing open a door, entered the dressing-room, followed by Mouret. It was a rather large room, hung with red silk, furnished with a marble toilet table and a large wardrobe with three compartments and great glass doors. As the window looked into the yard, it was already rather dark, and the two nickel-plated gas burners on either side of the wardrobe had been lighted.

"Now, let's see," said Henriette, "perhaps we shall get on better."

On entering, Mouret had found Denise standing upright, middle of the bright light. She was very pale, modestly dressed in a cashmere jacket, and a black hat, and was holding on one arm the mantle bought at The Ladies' Paradise. When she saw the young man her hands slightly trembled.

"I wish Monsieur Mouret to judge," resumed Henriette. "Just help me, mademoiselle."

And Denise, approaching, had to give her the mantle. She had already placed some pins on the shoulders, the part that did not fit. Henriette turned round to look at herself in the glass.

"Is it possible? Speak frankly."

"It really is a failure, madame," said Mouret, to cut the matter short. "It's very simple; the young lady will take your measure, and we will make you another."

"No, I want this one, I want it immediately," resumed she, with vivacity. "But it's too narrow across the chest, and it forms a ruck at the back between the shoulders." Then, in her sharpest voice, she added: "It's no use you standing looking at me, mademoiselle, that won't make it any better! Try and find a remedy. It's your business."

Denise again commenced to place the pins, without saying a word. That went on for some time: she had to pass from one shoulder to the other, and was even obliged to go almost on her knees, to pull the mantle down in front. Above her placing herself entirely in Denise's hands, Madame Desforges gave her face the harsh expression of a mistress exceedingly difficult to please. Delighted to lower the young girl to this servant's work, she gave her sharp and brief orders, watching for the least sign of suffering on Mouret's face.

"Put a pin here! No! not there, here, near the sleeve. You don't seem to understand! That isn't it, there's the ruck showing again. Take care, you're pricking me now!"

Twice had Mouret vainly attempted to interfere, to put an end to this scene. His heart was beating violently from this humiliation of his love; and he loved Denise more than ever, with a deep tenderness, in the presence of her admirably silent and patient attitude. If the young girl's hands still trembled somewhat, at being treated in this way before his face, she accepted the necessities of her position with the proud resignation of a courageous girl. When Madame Desforges found they were not likely to betray themselves, she tried another way, she commenced to smile on Mouret, treating him openly as her lover. The pins having run short, she said to him:

"Look, my dear, in the ivory box on the dressing-table. Really! it's empty? Kindly see on the chimney-piece in the bedroom; you know, at the corner of the looking-glass."

She spoke as if he were quite at home, in the habit of sleeping there, and knew where to find everything, even the brushes and combs. When he brought back a few pins, she took them one by one, and forced him to stay near her, looking at him and speaking low.

"I don't fancy I'm hump-backed. Give me your hand, feel my shoulders, just to please me. Am I really made like that?"

Denise slowly raised her eyes, paler than ever, and set about placing the pins in silence. Mouret could only see her blonde tresses, twisted at the back of her delicate neck; but by the slight shudder which was raising them, he thought he could perceive the uneasiness and shame of her face. Now, she would certainly repulse him, and send him back to this woman, who did not conceal her connection even before strangers. Brutal thoughts came into his head, he could have struck Henriette. How was he to stop her talk? How should he tell Denise that he adored her, that she alone existed for him at this moment, and that he was ready to sacrifice for her all his former affections? The worst of women would not have indulged in the equivocal familiarities of this well-born lady. He took his hand away, and drew back, saying:

"You are wrong to go so far, madame, since I myself consider the garment to be a failure."

One of the gas-burners was hissing, and in the stuffy, moist air of the room, nothing else was heard but this ardent breath. The looking-glasses threw large sheets of light on the red silk hangings, on which were dancing the shadows of the two women. A bottle of verbena, of which the cork had been left out, spread a vague odor, something like that of a fading bouquet.

"There, madame, I can do no more," said Denise, at last, rising up.

She felt thoroughly worn out. Twice she had run the pins in her fingers, as if blinded, her eyes in a mist. Was he in the plot? Had he sent for her, to avenge himself for her refusal, by showing that other women loved him? And this thought chilled her; she never remembered to have stood in need of so much courage, not even during the terrible hours of her life when she wanted for bread. It was comparatively nothing to be humiliated, but to see him almost in the arms of another woman, as if she had not been there! Henriette looked at herself in the glass, and once more broke out into harsh words.

"But it's absurd, mademoiselle. It fits worse than ever. Just look how tight it is across the chest. I look like a wet nurse."

Denise, losing all patience, made a rather unfortunate remark. "You are slightly stout, madame. We cannot make you thinner than you are."

"Stout! stout!" exclaimed Henriette, who now turned pale in her turn. "You're becoming insolent, mademoiselle. Really, I should advise you to criticize others!"

They both stood looking at each other, face to face, trembling. There was now neither lady or shop-girl. They were simply two women, made equal by their rivalry. The one had violently taken off the mantle and cast it on a chair, whilst the other was throwing on the dressing-table the few pins she had in her hands.

"What astonishes me," resumed Henriette," is that Monsieur Mouret should tolerate such insolence. I thought, sir, that you were more particular about your employees."

Denise had again assumed her brave, calm manner. She gently replied: "If Monsieur Mouret keeps me, it's because he has no fault to find. I am ready to apologize to you, if he wishes it."

Mouret was listening, excited by this quarrel, unable to find a word to put a stop to it. He had a great horror of these explanations between women, their asperity wounding his sense of elegance and gracefulness. Henriette wished to force him to say something in condemnation of the young girl; and, as he remained mute, still undecided, she stung him with a final insult:

"Very good, sir. It seems that I must suffer the insolence of your mistresses in my own house even! A girl you've picked up out of the gutter!"

Two big tears gushed from Denise's eyes. She had kept them back for some time, but her whole being succumbed beneath this last insult. When he saw her weeping like that, without the slightest attempt at retaliation, with a silent, despairing dignity, Mouret no longer hesitated, his heart went out towards her in an immense burst of tenderness. He took her hands in his and stammered:

"Go away immediately, my child, and forget this house!"

Henriette, perfectly amazed, choking with anger, stood looking at them.

"Wait a minute," continued he, folding up the mantle himself, "take this garment away. Madame can buy another elsewhere. And pray don't cry any more. You know how much I esteem you."

He went with her to the door, which he closed after her. She had not said a word; but a pink flame had colored her cheeks, whilst her eyes were wet with fresh tears, tears of a delicious sweetness. Henriette, who was suffocating, had taken out her handkerchief and was crushing her lips with it. This was a total overthrowing of her calculations, she herself had been caught in the trap she had laid. She was mortified with herself for having pushed the matter too far, tortured with jealousy. To be abandoned for such a creature as that! To see herself disdained before her! Her pride suffered more than her love.

"So, it's that girl that you love?" said she, painfully, when they were alone.

Mouret did not reply at once; he was walking about from the window to the door, as if absorbed by some violent emotion. At last he stopped, and very politely, in a voice which he tried to render cold, he replied with simplicity: "Yes, madame."

The gas-burner was still hissing in the stifling air of the dressing-room. But the reflex of the glasses were no longer traversed by dancing shadows, the room seemed bare, of a heavy dullness. Henriette suddenly dropped on a chair, twisting her handkerchief in her febrile fingers, repeating amidst her sobs:

"Good heavens! How miserable I am!"

He stood looking at her for several seconds, and then went away quietly. She, left all alone, wept on in silence, before the pins scattered over the dressing-table and the floor.

When Mouret returned to the little drawing-room, he found Vallagnosc alone, the baron having gone back to the ladies. As he felt himself very agitated still, he sat down at the further end of the room, on a sofa; and his friend, seeing him turn pale, charitably came and stood before him, to conceal him from curious eyes. At first, they looked at each other without saying a word. Then Vallagnosc, who seemed to be inwardly amused at Mouret's confusion, finished by asking in his bantering voice:

"Are you still enjoying yourself?"

Mouret did not appear to understand him at first. But remembered their former conversations on the empty and the useless torture of life, he replied: "Of course, I've never before lived so much. Ah! my boy, don't you laugh, the hours that make one die of grief are by far the shortest." He lowered his voice, continuing gaily, beneath his half-wiped tears: "Yes, you know all, don't you? Between them they have rent my heart. But yet it's nice, as nice as kisses, the wounds they make. I am thoroughly worn out; but, no matter, you can't think how I love life! Oh! I shall win her at last, this little girl who still says no!"

Vallagnosc simply said: "And after?"

"After? Why, I shall have her! Isn't that enough? If you think yourself strong, because you refuse to be stupid and to suffer, you make a great mistake! You are merely a dupe, my boy, nothing more! Try and long for a woman and win her at last: that pays you in one minute for all your misery."

But Vallagnosc once more trotted out his pessimism. What was the good of working so much if money could not buy everything? He would very soon have shut up shop and given up work forever, the day he found out that his millions could not even buy the woman he wanted! Mouret, listening to him, became grave. Then he set off violently, he believed in the all-powerfulness of his will.

"I want her, and I'll have her! And if she escapes me, you'll see what a place I shall have built to cure myself. It will be splendid, all the same. You don't understand this language, old man, otherwise you would know that action contains its own recompense. To act, to create, to struggle against facts, to overcome them or be overthrown by them, all human health and joy consists in that!"

"Simple method of diverting one's self," murmured the other.

"Well, I prefer diverting myself. As one must die, I would rather die of passion than boredom!"

They both laughed, this reminded them of their old discussions at college. Vallagnosc, in an effeminate voice, then commenced to parade his theories of the insipidity of things, investing with a sort of fanfaronade the immobility and emptiness of his existence. Yes, he dragged on from day to day at the office, in three years he had had a rise of six hundred francs; he was now receiving three thousand six hundred, barely enough to pay for his cigars; it was getting worse than ever, and if he did not kill himself, it was simply from a dislike of all trouble. Mouret having spoken of his marriage with Mademoiselle de Boves, he replied that notwithstanding the obstinacy of the aunt in refusing to die, the matter was going to be concluded; at least, he thought so, the parents were agreed, and he was ready to do anything they might tell him to do. What was the use of wishing or not wishing, since things never turned out as one desired? He quoted as an example his future father-in-law, who expected to find in Madame Guibal an indolent blonde, the caprice of an hour, but who was now led by her with a whip, like an old horse on its last legs. Whilst they supposed him to be busy inspecting the stud at Saint-Lô, she was squandering his last resources in a little house hired by him at Versailles.

"He's happier than you," said Mouret, getting up.

"Oh! rather!" declared Vallagnosc. "Perhaps it's only doing wrong that's somewhat amusing."

Mouret had now recovered his spirits. He was thinking about getting away; but not wishing his departure to resemble a flight he resolved to take a cup of tea, and went into the other drawing-room with his friend, both in high spirits. The baron asked him if the mantle had been made to fit, and Mouret replied, carelessly, that he gave it up as far as he was concerned. They all seemed astonished. Whilst Madame Marty hastened to serve him, Madame de Boves accused the shops of always keeping their garments too narrow. At last, he managed to sit down near Bouthemont, who had not stirred. They were forgotten for a moment, and, in reply to anxious questions put by Bouthemont, desirous of knowing what he had to say to him, Mouret did not wait to get into the street, but abruptly informed him that the board of directors had decided to deprive themselves of his services. Between each phrase he drank a drop of tea, protesting all the while that he was in despair. Oh! a quarrel that he had not even then got over, for he had left the meeting beside himself with rage. But what could he do? He could not break with these gentlemen about a simple question of staff. Bouthemont, very pale, had to thank him once more.

"What a terrible mantle," observed Madame Marty. "Henriette can't get over it."

And really, this prolonged absence began to make everyone feel awkward. But, at that very moment, Madame Desforges appeared.

"So you've given it up as well?" cried Madame de Boves, gaily.

"How do you mean?"

"Why, Monsieur Mouret told us you could do nothing with it." Henriette affected the greatest surprise. "Monsieur was joking. The mantle will fit splendidly."

She appeared very calm and smiling. No doubt she had bathed her eyes, for they were quite fresh, without the slightest trace of redness. Whilst her whole being was still trembling and bleeding, she managed to conceal her torture beneath the mask of her smiling, well-bred elegance. And she offered the sandwiches to Vallagnosc with her usual graceful smile. The baron alone, who knew her so well, remarked, the slight contraction of her lips, and the sombre fire, which she had not been able to extinguish in her eyes. He guessed the whole scene.

"Dear me! each one to his taste," said Madame de Boves, also accepting a sandwich. "I know some women who would never buy a ribbon except at the Louvre. Others only swear by the Bon Marché. It's a question of temperament, no doubt."

"The Bon Marché is very provincial," murmured Madame Marty, "and one gets so crushed at the Louvre."

They had again returned to the big shops. Mouret had to give his opinion; he came up to them and affected to be very just. The

Bon Marché was an excellent house, solid, respectable; but the Louvre certainly had a more aristocratic class of customers.

"In short, you prefer The Ladies' Paradise," said the baron, smiling.

"Yes," replied Mouret, quietly. "There we really love our customers."

All the women present were of his opinion. It was just that, they were at a sort of private party at The Ladies' Paradise, they felt there a continual caress of flattery, an overflowing adoration which detained the most dignified and virtuous woman. The enormous success of the establishment sprung from this gallant seduction.

"By the way," asked Henriette, who wished to appear entirely at her ease, "what have you done with my protégée, Monsieur Mouret? You know—Mademoiselle de Fontenailles." And turning towards Madame Marty she explained, "A marchioness, my dear, a poor girl fallen into poverty."

"Oh," said Mouret, "she earns three francs a day stitching pattern-books, and I fancy I shall be able to marry her to one of my messengers."

"Oh! fie! what a horror!" exclaimed Madame de Boves. He looked at her, and replied in his calm voice: "Why madame? Isn't it better for her to marry an honest, hard-working messenger than to run the risk of being picked up by some good-for-nothing fellow outside?"

Vallagnosc wished to interfere for a joke. "Don't push him too far, madame, or he'll tell you that all the old families of France ought to sell calico."

"Well," declared Mouret, "it would at least be an honorable end for a great many of them."

They set up a laugh, the paradox seemed rather strong. He continued to sing the praises of what he called the aristocracy of work. A slight flush had colored Madame de Boves's cheeks, she was wild at the shifts she was put to by her poverty; whilst Madame Marty on the contrary approved, stricken with remorse on thinking of her poor husband. The footman had just ushered in the professor, who had called to take her home. He was drier, more emaciated than ever by his hard labor, and still wore his thin shining frock coat. When he had thanked Madame Desforges for having spoken for him at the Ministry, he cast at Mouret the timid glance of a man meeting the evil that is to kill him. And he was quite confused when he heard the latter asking him:

"Isn't it true, sir, that work leads to everything?"

"Work and economy," replied he, with a slight shivering of his whole body. "Add economy, sir."

Meanwhile, Bouthemont had not moved from his chair, Mouret's words were still ringing in his ears. He at last got up, and went and said to Henriette in a low tone: "You know, he's given me notice; oh! in the kindest possible manner. But may I be hanged if he sha'n't repent it! I've just found my sign, The Four Seasons, and shall plant myself close to the Opera House!"

She looked at him with a gloomy expression. "Reckon on me, I'm with you. Wait a minute." And she immediately drew Baron Hartmann into the recess of a window, and boldly recommended Bouthemont to him, as a fellow who was going to revolutionize Paris, in his turn, by setting up for himself. When she spoke of an advance of funds for her new protégé, the baron, though now astonished at nothing, could not suppress a gesture of bewilderment. This was the fourth fellow of genius she had confided to him, and he began to feel himself ridiculous. But he did not directly refuse, the idea of starting a competitor to The Ladies' Paradise even pleased him somewhat; for he had already invented, in banking matters, this sort of competition, to keep off others. Besides, the adventure amused him, and he promised to look into the matter.

"We must talk it over tonight," whispered Henriette, returning to Bouthemont. "Don't fail to call about nine o'clock. The baron is with us."

At this moment the vast room was full of voices. Mouret still standing up, in the midst of the ladies, had recovered his habitual elegant gracefulness, and was gaily defending himself from the charge of ruining them in dress, offering to prove by the figures that he enabled them to save thirty per cent on their purchases. Baron Hartmann watched him, seized with the fraternal admiration of a former man about town. Come! the duel was finished, Henriette was decidedly beaten, she certainly was not the coming woman. And he thought he could see the modest profile of the young girl whom he had observed on passing through the ante-room. She was there, patient, alone, redoubtable in her sweetness.

CHAPTER XII.

It was on the 25th of September that the building of the new façade of The Ladies' Paradise was commenced. Baron Hartmann, according to his promise, had had the matter settled at the last general meeting of the Crédit Immobilier. And Mouret was at length going to enjoy the realization of his dreams; this façade, about to arise in the Rue du Dix-Décembre, was like the very blossoming of his fortune. He wished, therefore, to celebrate the laying of the first stone, to make a ceremony of the work, and he distributed gratuities amongst his employees, and gave them game and champagne for dinner in the evening. Everyone noticed his wonderfully good humor during the ceremony, his victorious gesture as he laid the first stone, with a flourish of the trowel. For weeks he had been anxious, agitated by a nervous torment that he did not always succeed in concealing; and his triumph served as a respite, a distraction in his suffering. During the afternoon he seemed to have returned to his former healthy gaiety. But, after dinner, when he went through the refectory to drink a glass of champagne with his staff, he appeared feverish again, smiling with a painful look, his features drawn up by the unavowed pain that was devouring him. He was once more mastered by it.

The next day, in the ready-made department, Clara tried to be disagreeable with Denise. She had noticed Colomban's bashful passion, and took it into her head to joke about the Baudus. As Marguerite was sharpening her pencil while waiting for customers, she said to her, in a loud voice:

"You know my lover opposite. It really grieves me to see him in that dark shop, where no one ever enters."

"He's not so badly off," replied Marguerite, "he's going to marry the governor's daughter."

"Oh! oh!" replied Clara, "it would be good fun to lead him astray, then! I'll try the game on, my word of honor!"

And she continued in the same strain, happy to feel Denise was shocked. The latter forgave her everything else; but the idea of her dying cousin Geneviève, finished by this cruelty, threw her into an indignant rage. At that moment a customer came in, and as Madame Aurélie had just gone downstairs, she took the direction of the counter, and called Clara.

"Mademoiselle Prunaire, you had better attend to this lady instead of gossiping there."

"I wasn't gossiping."

"Have the kindness to hold your tongue, and attend to this lady immediately."

Clara gave in, conquered. When Denise showed her authority, quietly, without raising her voice, not one of them resisted. She had acquired absolute authority by her very moderation and sweetness. For a moment she walked up and down in silence, amidst the young ladies, who had become very serious. Marguerite had resumed sharpening her pencil, the point of which was always breaking. She alone continued to approve of Denise's resistance to Mouret, shaking her head, not acknowledging the baby she had had, but declaring that if they had any idea of the consequences of such a thing, they would prefer to remain virtuous.

"What! you're getting angry?" said a voice behind Denise.

It was Pauline, who was crossing the department. She had noticed the scene, and spoke in a low tone, smiling.

"But I'm obliged to," replied Denise in the same tone, "I can't manage them otherwise."

Pauline shrugged her shoulders. "Nonsense, you can be queen over all of us whenever you like."

She was still unable to understand her friend's refusal. Since the end of August, Pauline had been married to Baugé, a most stupid affair, she would sometimes gaily remark. The terrible Bourdoncle treated her anyhow, now, considering her as lost for trade. Her only terror was that they might one fine day send them to love each other elsewhere, for the managers had decreed love to be execrable and fatal to business. So great was her fear, that, when she met Baugé in the galleries, she affected not to know him. She had just had a fright—old Jouve had nearly caught her talking to her husband behind a pile of dusters.

"See! he's followed me," added she, after having hastily related the adventure to Denise. "Just look at him scenting me out with his big nose!"

Jouve, in fact, was then coming from the lace department, correctly arrayed in a white tie, his nose on the scent for some delinquent. But when he saw Denise he assumed a knowing air, and passed by with an amiable smile.

"Saved!" murmured Pauline. "My dear, you made him swallow that! I say, if anything should happen to me, you would speak for me, wouldn't you! Yes, yes, don't put on that astonished air, we know that a word from you would revolutionize the house."

And she ran off to her counter. Denise had blushed, troubled by these amicable allusions. It was true, however. She had a vague sensation of her power by the flatteries with which she was surrounded. When Madame Aurélie returned, and found the department quiet and busy under the surveillance of the second-hand, she smiled at her amicably. She threw over Mouret himself, her amiability increased daily for this young girl who might one fine morning desire her situation as first-hand. Denise's reign was commencing.

Bourdoncle along still stood out. In the secret war which he continued to carry on against the young girl, there was in the first place a natural antipathy. He detested her for her gentleness and her charm. Then he fought against her as a fatal influence which would place the house in peril the day when Mouret should succumb. The governor's commercial genius seemed bound to sink amidst this stupid affection: what they had gained by women would be swallowed up by this woman. None of them touched his heart, he treated them with the disdain of a man without passion, whose trade is to live on them, and who had had his last illusions dispelled by seeing them too closely in the miseries of his traffic. Instead of intoxicating him, the odor of these seventy thousand customers gave him frightful headaches: and so soon as he reached home he beat his mistresses. And what made him especially anxious in the presence of this little saleswoman, who had gradually become so redoubtable, was that he did not in the least believe in her disinterestedness, in the genuineness of her refusals. For him she was playing a part, the most skilful of parts; for if she had yielded at once, Mouret would doubtless have forgotten her the next day; whilst by refusing, she had goaded his desires, rendering him mad, capable of any folly. An artful jade, a woman learned in vice, would not have acted any different to this pattern of innocence.

Thus Bourdoncle could never catch sight of her, with her clear eyes, sweet face, and simple attitude, without being seized with a real fear, as if he had before him some disguised female flesh-eater, the sombre enigma of woman, Death in the guise of a virgin. In what way could he confound the tactics of this false novice? He was now only anxious to penetrate her artful ways, in the hope of exposing them to the light of day. She would certainly commit some fault, he would surprise her with one of her lovers, and she should again be dismissed. The house would then resume its regular working like a well wound-up machine.

"Keep a good look-out, Monsieur Jouve," repeated Bourdoncle to the inspector, "I'll take care that you shall be rewarded."

But Jouve was somewhat lukewarm, he knew something about women, and was asking himself whether he had not better take the part of this young girl, who might be the future sovereign mistress of the place. Though he did not now dare to touch her, he still thought her bewitchingly pretty. His colonel in bygone days had killed himself for a similar little thing, with an insignificant face, delicate and modest, one look from whom ravaged all hearts.

"I do," replied he. "But, on my word, I cannot discover anything."

And yet stories were circulating, there was quite a stream of abominable tittle-tattle running beneath the flattery and respect Denise felt arising around her. The whole house now declared that she had formerly had Hutin for a lover; no one could swear that the intimacy still continued, but they were suspected of meeting from time to time. Deloche also was said to sleep with her, they were continually meeting in dark corners, talking for hours together. It was quite a scandal!

"So, nothing about the first-hand in the silk department, nor about the young man in the lace one?" asked Bourdoncle.

"No, sir, nothing yet," replied the inspector.

It was with Deloche especially that Bourdoncle expected to surprise Denise. One morning he himself had caught them laughing together downstairs. In the meantime, he treated her on a footing of perfect equality, for he no longer disdained her, he felt her to be strong enough to overthrow even him, notwithstanding his ten years' service, if he lost the game.

"Keep your eye on the young man in the lace department," concluded he each time. "They are always together. If you catch them, call me, I'll manage the rest."

Mouret, however, was living in anguish. Was it possible that this child could torture him in this manner? He could always recall her arriving at The Ladies' Paradise, with her big shoes, thin black dress, and savage airs. She stammered, they all used to laugh at her, he himself had thought her ugly at first. Ugly! and now she could have brought him on his knees by a look, he thought her nothing less than an angel! Then she had remained the last in the house, repulsed, joked at, treated by him as a curious specimen of humanity. For months he had wanted to see how a girl sprung up, and had amused himself at this experiment, without understanding that he was risking his heart. She, little by little grew up, became redoubtable. Perhaps he had loved her from the first moment, even at the time he thought he felt nothing but pity for her. And yet he had only really begun to feel this love the evening of their walk under the chestnut trees of the Tuileries. His life started from there, he could still hear the laughing of a group of little girls, the distant fall of a jet of water, whilst in the warm shade she walked on beside him in silence.

After that he knew no more, his fever had increased hour by hour; all his blood, his whole being, in fact, was sacrificed. And for such a child—was it possible? When she passed him now, the slight wind from her dress seemed so powerful that he staggered.

For a long time he had struggled, and even now he frequently became indignant, endeavoring to extricate himself from this idiotic possession. What secret had she to be able to bind him in this way? Had he not seen her without boots? Had she not been received almost out of charity? He could have understood it had it been a question of one of those superb creatures who charm the crowd! but this little girl; this nobody! She had, in short, one of those insignificant faces which excite no remark. She could not even be very intelligent, for he remembered her bad beginning as a saleswoman. But, after every explosion of anger, he had experienced a relapse of passion, like a sacred terror at having insulted his idol. She possessed everything that renders a woman good—courage, gaiety, simplicity; and there exhaled from her gentleness, a charm of a penetrating, perfume-like subtlety. One might at first ignore her, or elbow her like any other girl; but the charm soon began to act, with a slow invincible force; one belonged to her forever, if she deigned to smile. Everything then smiled in her white face, her pretty eyes, her cheeks and chin full of dimples; whilst her heavy blonde hair seemed to light up also, with a royal and conquering beauty. He acknowledged himself vanquished; she was as intelligent as she was beautiful, her intelligence came from the best part of her being. Whilst the other saleswomen had only a superficial education, the varnish which scales off from girls of that class, she, without any false elegance, retained her native grace, the savor of her origin. The most complete commercial ideas sprang up from her experience, under this narrow forehead, the pure lines of which clearly announced the presence of a firm will and a love of order. And he could have clasped his hands to ask her pardon for having blasphemed her during his hours of revolt.

Why did she still refuse with such obstinacy. Twenty times had he entreated her, increasing his offers, offering money and more money. Then, thinking she must be ambitious, he had promised to appoint her first-hand, as soon as there should be a vacant department. And she refused, and still she refused! For him it was a stupor, a struggle in which his desire became enraged. Such an adventure appeared to him impossible, this child would certainly finish by yielding, for he had always regarded a woman's virtue as a relative matter. He could see no other object, everything disappeared before this necessity: to have her at last in his room, to take her on his knees, and kiss her on her lips; and at this vision, the blood of his veins ran quick and strong, he trembled, distracted by his own powerlessness.

His days now passed in the same grievous obsession, Denise's image rose with him; after having dreamed of her all night, it followed him before the desk in his office, where he signed his bills and orders from nine to ten o'clock: a work which he accomplished mechanically, never ceasing to feel her present, still saying no, with her quiet air. Then, at ten o'clock, came the board-meeting, a meeting of the twelve directors, at which he had to preside; they discussed matters affecting the in-door arrangements, examined the purchases, settled the window displays; and she was still there, he heard her soft voice amidst the figures, he saw her bright smile in the most complicated financial situations. After the board-meeting, she still accompanied him, making with him the daily inspection of the counters, returned with him to his office in the afternoon, remaining close to his chair from two till four o'clock, whilst he received a crowd of important business men, the principal manufacturers of all France, bankers, inventors; a continual come-and-go of the riches and intelligence of the land, an excited dance of millions, rapid interviews during which were hatched the biggest affairs on the Paris market. If he forgot her for a moment whilst deciding on the ruin or the prosperity of an industry, he found her again at a twitch of his heart; his voice died away, he asked himself what was the use of this princely fortune when she still refused. At last, when five o'clock struck, he had to sign the day's correspondence, the mechanical working of his hand again commenced, whilst she rose up before him more dominating than ever, seizing him entirely, to possess him during the solitary and ardent hours of the night. And the morrow was the same day over again, those days so active, so full of a colossal labor, which the slight shadow of a child sufficed to ravage with anguish.

But it was especially during his daily inspection of the departments that he felt his misery. To have built up this giant machine, to reign over such a world of people, and to be dying of grief because a little girl would not accept him! He scorned himself, dragging the fever and shame of his pain about with him everywhere. On certain days he became disgusted with his power, feeling a nausea at the very sight of the long galleries. At other times he would have wished to extend his empire, and make it so vast that she would perhaps yield out of sheer admiration and fear.

He first of all stopped in the basement opposite the chute. It was still in the Rue Neuve-Saint-Augustin; but it had been necessary to enlarge it, and it was now as wide as the bed of a river, down which the continual flood of goods rolled with the loud noise of rushing water; it was a constant succession of arrivals from all parts of the world, rows of wagons from all railways, a ceaseless discharging of merchandise, a stream of boxes and bales running underground, absorbed by the insatiable establishment. He gazed at this torrent flowing into his house, thought of his position as one of the masters of the public fortune, that he held in his hands the fate of the French manufacturers, and that he was unable to buy a kiss from one of his saleswomen.

Then he passed on to the receiving department, which now occupied that part of the basement running along the Rue Monsigny. Twenty tables were ranged there, in the pale light of the air-holes; dozens of shopmen were bustling about, emptying the cases, checking the goods, and marking them in plain figures, amidst the roar of the chute, which almost drowned their voices. Various managers of departments stopped him, he had to resolve difficulties and confirm orders. This cellar was filled with the tender glimmer of the satin, the whiteness of the linen, a prodigious unpacking in which the furs were mingled with the lace, the fancy goods with the Eastern curtains. With a slow step he made his way amongst all these riches thrown about in disorder, heaped up in their state. Above, they were destined to ornament the window displays, letting loose the race after money across the counters, no sooner shown than carried off, in the furious current of business which traversed the place. He thought of his having offered the young girl silks, velvets, anything she liked to take in any quantities, from these enormous heaps, and that she had refused by a shake of her fair head.

After that, he passed on to the other end of the basement, to pay his usual visit to the delivery department. Interminable corridors ran along, lighted up with gas; to the right and to the left, the reserves, closed in with gratings, were like so many subterranean stores, a complete commercial quarter, with its haberdashery, under-clothing, glove, and other shops, sleeping in the shade. Further on was placed one of the three stoves; further still, a fireman's post guarding the gas-meter, enclosed in its iron cage. He found, in the delivery department, the sorting tables already blocked with loads of parcels, bandboxes, and cases, continually arriving in large baskets; and Campion, the superintendent, gave him some particulars about the current work, whilst the twenty men placed under his orders distributed the parcels into large compartments, each bearing the name of a district of Paris, and from whence the messengers took them up to the vans, ranged along the pavement. One heard a series of cries, names of streets, and recommendations shouted out; quite an uproar, an agitation such as on board a mail boat about to start. And he stood there for a moment, motionless, looking at this discharge of goods which he had just seen absorbed by the house, at the opposite extremity of the basement: the enormous current there discharged itself into the street, after having filled the tills with gold. His eyes became misty, this colossal business no longer had any importance; he had but one idea, that of going away to some distant land, and abandoning everything, if she persisted in saying no.

He then went upstairs, continuing his inspection, talking, and agitating himself more and more, without finding any respite. On the second floor he entered the correspondence department, picking quarrels, secretly exasperated against the perfect regularity of this machine that he had himself built up. This department was the one that was daily assuming the most considerable importance; it now required two hundred employees—some opening, reading, and classifying the letters coming from the provinces and abroad, whilst others gathered into compartments the goods ordered by the correspondents. And the number of letters was increasing to such an extent that they no longer counted them; they weighed them, receiving as much as a hundred pounds per day. He, feverish, went through the three offices, questioning Levasseur as to the weight of the correspondence; eighty pounds, ninety pounds, sometimes, on a Monday, a hundred pounds. The figure increased daily, he ought to have been delighted. But he stood shuddering, in the noise made by the neighboring squad of packers nailing down the cases. Vainly he roamed about the house; the fixed idea remained fast in his mind, and as his power unfolded itself before him, as the mechanism of the business and the army of employees passed before his gaze, he felt more profoundly than ever the insult of his powerlessness. Orders from all Europe were flowing in, a special post-office van was required for his correspondence; and yet she said no, always no.

He went downstairs again, visiting the central cashier's office, where four clerks guarded the two giant safes, in which there had passed the previous year forty-eight million francs. He glanced at the clearing-house, which now occupied twenty-five clerks, chosen from amongst the most trustworthy. He went into the next office, where twenty-five young men, junior clerks, were engaged in checking the debit-notes, and calculating the salesmen's commission. He returned to the chief cashier's office, exasperated at the sight of the safes, wandering amidst these millions, the uselessness of which drove him mad. She said no, always no.

And it was always no, in all the departments, in the galleries, in the saloons, and in every part of the establishment! He went from the silk to the drapery department, from the linen to the lace department, he ascended to the upper floors, stopping on the flying bridges, prolonging his inspection with a maniacal, grievous minuteness. The house had grown out of all bounds, he had created this department, then this other; he governed this fresh domain, he extended his empire into this industry, the last one conquered; and it was no, always no, in spite of everything. His staff would now have sufficed to people a small town: there were fifteen hundred salesmen, and a thousand other employees of every sort, including forty inspectors and seventy cashiers; the kitchens alone gave occupation to thirty-two men; ten clerks were set apart for the advertising; there were three hundred and fifty shop messengers, all wearing livery, and twenty-four firemen living on the premises. And, in the stables, royal buildings situated in the Rue Monsigny, opposite the warehouse, were one hundred and forty-five horses, a luxurious establishment which was already celebrated in Paris. The first four conveyances which used formerly to stir up the whole neighborhood, when the house occupied only the corner of the Place Gaillon, had gradually increased to sixty-two trucks, one-horse vans, and heavy two-horse ones. They were continually scouring Paris, driven with knowing skill by drivers dressed in black, promenading the gold and purple sign of The Ladies' Paradise. They even went beyond the fortifications, into the suburbs; they were to be met on the dusty roads of Bicêtre, along the banks of the Marne, even in the shady drives of the Forest of Saint-Germain. Sometimes one would spring up from the depths of some sunny avenue, where all was silent and deserted, the superb animals trotting along, throwing into the mysterious peacefulness of this grand nature the loud advertisement of its varnished panels. He was even dreaming of launching them further still, into the neighboring departments; he would have liked to hear them rolling along every road in France, from one frontier to the other. But he no longer even troubled to visit his horses, though he was passionately fond of them. Of what good was this conquest of the world, since it was no, always no?

At present, in the evening, when he arrived at Lhomme's desk, he still looked through habit at the amount of the takings written on a card, which the cashier stuck on an iron file at his side;

this figure rarely fell below a hundred thousand francs, sometimes it ran up to eight and nine hundred thousand on big sale days; but these figures no longer sounded in his ears like a trumpet-blast, he regretted having looked at them, going away full of bitterness and scorn for money.

But Mouret's sufferings were destined to increase, for he became jealous. One morning, in the office, before the board-meeting commenced, Bourdoncle ventured to hint that the little girl in the ready-made department was playing with him.

"How?" asked he, very pale.

"Yes! she has lovers in this very building."

Mouret found strength to smile. "I don't think any more about her, my dear fellow. You can speak freely. Who are her lovers?"

"Hutin, they say, and then a salesman in the lace department— Deloche, that tall awkward fellow. I can't speak with certainty, never having seen them together. But it appears that it's notorious."

There was a silence. Mouret affected to arrange the papers on his desk, to conceal the trembling of his hands. At last, he observed, without raising his head: "We must have proofs, try and bring me some proofs. As for me, I assure you I don't care in the least, for I'm quite sick of her. But we can't allow such things to go on here."

Bourdoncle simply replied: "Never fear, you shall have proofs one of these days. I'm keeping a good look out."

This news deprived Mouret of all rest. He no longer had the courage to return to this conversation, but lived in the continual expectation of a catastrophe, in which his heart would be crushed. And this torment rendered him terrible, the whole house trembled before him. He now disdained to conceal himself behind Bourdoncle, but performed the executions in person, feeling a nervous desire for revenge, solacing himself by an abuse of his power, of that power which could do nothing for the contentment of his sole desire. Each one of his inspections became a massacre, his appearance caused a panic to run along from counter to counter. The dead winter season was just then approaching, and he made a clean sweep in the departments, multiplying the victims and pushing them into the streets. His first idea had been to dismiss Hutin and Deloche; then he had reflected that if he did not keep them, he would never discover anything; and the others suffered for them: the whole staff trembled. In the evening, when he found himself alone again, his eyes swelled up, big with tears.

One day especially terror reigned supreme. An inspector had the idea that Mignot was stealing. There were always a lot of strange-looking girls prowling around his counter; and one of them had just been arrested, her thighs and bosom padded with sixty pairs of gloves. From that moment a watch was kept, and the inspector caught Mignot in the act, facilitating the sleight of hand of a tall fair girl, formerly a saleswoman at the Louvre, but since gone wrong: the maneuver was very simple, he affected to try some gloves on her, waited till she had padded herself, and then conducted her to the pay-desk, where she paid for a single pair only. Mouret happened to be there, just at that moment. As a rule, he preferred not to mix himself up with these sort of adventures, which were pretty frequent; for notwithstanding the regular working of the well-arranged machine, great disorder reigned in certain departments of The Ladies' Paradise, and scarcely a week passed without some employee being dismissed for theft. The authorities preferred to hush up such matters as far as possible, considering it useless to set the police at work, and thus expose one of the fatal plague-spots of these great bazaars. But, that day, Mouret felt a real need of getting angry with someone, and he treated the handsome Mignot with such violence, and the latter stood there trembling with fear, his face pale and discomposed.

"I ought to call a policeman," cried Mouret, before all the other salesmen. "But why don't you answer? Who is this woman? I swear I'll send for the police, if you don't tell me the truth."

They had taken the woman away, and two saleswomen were undressing her. Mignot stammered out: "I don't know her, sir. She's the one who came."

"Don't tell lies!" interrupted Mouret, in a violent rage. "And there's nobody here to warn us! You are all in the plot, on my word! We are in a regular wood, robbed, pillaged, plundered. It's enough to make us have the pockets of each one searched before going out!"

Murmurs were heard. The three or four customers buying gloves stood looking on, frightened.

"Silence!" resumed he, furiously, "or I'll clear the place!"

But Bourdoncle came running up, anxious at the idea of the scandal. He whispered a few words in Mouret's ear, the affair was assuming an exceptional gravity; and he prevailed on him to take Mignot into the inspectors' office, a room on the ground floor near the entrance in the Rue Gaillon. The woman was there, quietly putting on her stays again. She had just mentioned Albert Lhomme's name. Mignot, again questioned, lost his head, and commenced to sob; he wasn't in fault, it was Albert who sent him his mistresses; at first he had merely afforded them certain advantages, enabling them to profit by the bargains; then, when they at last took to stealing, he was already too far compromised to report the matter. The principals now discovered a series of extraordinary robberies; goods taken away by girls, who went into the neighboring W.Cs, built near the refreshment bar and surrounded by evergreen plants, to hide the goods under their petticoats; purchases that a salesman neglected to call out at a pay-desk, when he accompanied a customer there, the price of which he divided with the cashier; even down to false returns, articles which they announced as brought back to the house, pocketing the money thus repaid; without even mentioning the classical robbery, parcels taken out under their coats in the evening, rolled round their bodies, and sometimes even hung down their legs. For the last fourteen months, thanks to Mignot and other salesmen, no doubt, whom they refused to name, this pilfering had been going on at Albert's desk, quite an impudent trade, for sums of which no one ever knew the exact total.

Meanwhile the news had spread into the various departments, causing the guilty consciences to tremble, and the most honest ones to quake at the general sweep that seemed imminent. Albert had disappeared into the inspectors' office. Next his father had passed, choking, his face full of blood, showing signs of apoplexy. Madame Aurélie herself was then called; and she, her head high beneath the affront, had the fat, puffed up appearance of a wax mask. The explanation lasted some time, no one knew the exact details; but it was said the first-hand had slapped her son's face, and that the worthy old father wept, whilst the governor, contrary to all his elegant habits, swore like a trooper, absolutely wanting to deliver the offenders up to justice. However, the scandal was hushed up. Mignot was the only one dismissed there and then. Albert did not disappear till two days later; no doubt his mother had begged that the family should not be dishonored by an immediate execution. But the panic lasted several days longer, for after this scene Mouret had wandered from one end of the establishment to the other, with a terrible expression, venting his anger on all those who dared even to raise their eyes.

"What are you doing there, sir, looking at the flies? Go and be paid!"

At last, the storm burst one day on the head of Hutin himself. Favier, appointed second-hand, was undermining the first-hand, in order to dislodge him from his position. This was always the way; he addressed crafty reports to the directors, taking advantage of every occasion to have the first-hand caught doing something wrong. Thus, one morning, as Mouret was going through the silk department, he stopped, surprised to see Favier engaged in altering the price tickets of a stock of black velvet.

"Why are you lowering the prices?" asked he. "Who gave you the order to do so?"

The second-hand, who was making a great noise over this work, as if he wished to attract the governor's attention, foreseeing the result, replied with an innocent, surprised air: "Why, Monsieur Hutin told me, sir."

"Monsieur Hutin! Where is Monsieur Hutin?"

And when the latter came upstairs, called by a salesman, an animated explanation ensued. What! he undertook to lower the prices himself now! But he appeared greatly astonished in his turn, having merely talked over the matter with Favier, without giving any positive orders. The latter then assumed the sorrowful air of an employee who finds himself obliged to contradict his superior. However, he was quite willing to accept the blame, if it would get the latter out of a scrape. Things began to look very bad.

"Understand, Monsieur Hutin!" cried Mouret, "I have never tolerated these attempts at independence. We alone decide about the prices."

He continued, with a sharp voice, and wounding intentions, which surprised the salesmen, for as a rule these discussions were carried on quietly, and the case might really have resulted from a misunderstanding. One could feel he had some unavowed spite to satisfy. He had at last caught that Hutin at fault, that Hutin who was said to be Denise's lover! He could now solace himself, by making him feel that he was the master! And he exaggerated matters, even insinuating that this reduction of price appeared to conceal very questionable intentions.

"Sir," repeated Hutin, "I meant to consult you about it. It is really necessary, as you know, for these velvets have not succeeded."

Mouret cut him short with a final insult. "Very good, sir; we will look into the matter. But don't do such a thing again, if you value your place."

And he walked off. Hutin, bewildered, furious, finding no one but Favier to confide in, swore he would go and throw his resignation at the brute's head. But he soon left off talking of going away, and began to stir up all the abominable accusations which were current amongst the salesmen against their chiefs. And Favier, his eye sparkling, defended himself with a great show of sympathy. He was obliged to reply, wasn't he? Besides, could anyone have foreseen such a row for so trifling a matter? What had come to the governor lately, that he should be so unbearable?

"We all know what's the matter with him," replied Hutin. "Is it my fault if that little jade in the dress-department is turning his head? My dear fellow, you can see the blow comes from there. He's aware I've slept with her, and he doesn't like it; or perhaps it's she herself who wants to get me pitched out, because I'm in her way. But I swear she shall hear from me, if ever she crosses my path."

Two days after, as Hutin was going up into the work-room, up-stairs, under the roof, to recommend a person, he started on perceiving at the end of a passage Denise and Deloche leaning out of a window, and plunged so deeply in private conversation that they did not even turn round. The idea of having them caught occurred to him suddenly, when he perceived with astonishment that Deloche was weeping. He at once went away without making any noise; and meeting Bourdoncle and Jouve on the stairs, told them some story about one of the *extincteurs* the door of which seemed to be broken; in this way they would go upstairs and drop on to the two others. Bourdoncle discovered them first. He stopped short, and told Jouve to go and fetch the governor, whilst he remained there. The inspector had to obey, greatly annoyed at being forced to compromise himself in such a matter.

This was a lost corner of the vast world in which the people of The Ladies' Paradise worked. One arrived there by a complication of stairs and passages. The work-rooms occupied the top of the house, a succession of low sloping rooms, lighted by large windows cut in the zinc roof, furnished solely with long tables and enormous iron stoves; and right along were a crowd of work-girls of all sorts, for the under-clothing, the lace, the dressmaking, and the house furnishing; living winter and summer in a stifling heat, amidst the odor special to the business; and one had to go straight through the wing, and turn to the right on passing the dressmakers, before coming to this solitary end of the corridor. The rare customers, that a salesman occasionally brought here for an order, gasped for breath, tired out, frightened, with the sensation of having been turning round for hours and hours, and of being a hundred leagues above the street.

Denise had often found Deloche waiting for her. As second-hand she had charge of the arrangements between her department and the work-room where only the models and alterations were done, and was always going up and down to give the necessary orders. He watched for her, inventing any pretext to run after her; then he affected to be surprised when he met her at the work-room door. She got to laugh about the matter, it became quite an understood thing. The corridor ran alongside the cistern, and enormous iron tank containing twelve thousand gallons of water; and there was another one of equal size on the roof, reached by an iron ladder. For an instant, Deloche would stand talking, leaning with one shoulder against the cistern in the continual abandonment of his long body, bent with fatigue. The noise of the water was heard, a mysterious noise of which the iron tank ever retained the musical vibration. Notwithstanding the deep silence, Denise would turn round anxiously, thinking she had seen a shadow pass on the bare, yellow-painted walls. But the window would soon attract them, they would lean out, and forget themselves in a pleasant gossip, in endless souvenirs of their native place. Below them, extended the immense glass roof of the central gallery, a lake of glass bounded by the distant housetops, like a rocky coast. Beyond, they saw nothing but the sky, a sheet of sky, which reflected in the sleeping water of the glazed work the flight of its clouds and the tender blue of its azure.

It so happened that Deloche was speaking of Valognes that day. "I was six years old; my mother took me to Valognes market in a cart. You know it's ten miles away; we had to leave Bricquebec at five o'clock. It's a fine country down our way. Do you know it?"

"Yes, yes," replied Denise, slowly, her looks lost in the distance. "I was there once, but was very little then. Nice roads with grass on each side, aren't there? And now and again sheep browsing in couples, dragging their clog along by the rope." She stopped, then resumed with a vague smile: "Our roads run as straight as an arrow for miles between rows of trees which afford a lot of shade. We have meadows surrounded with hedges taller than I am, where there are horses and cows feeding. We have a little river, and the water is very cold, under the brushwood, in a spot I know well."

"It is the same with us, exactly!" cried Deloche, delighted. "There's grass everywhere, each one encloses his plot with thorns and elms, and is at once at home; and it's quite green, a green far different to what we see in Paris. Dear me! what fun I've had at the bottom of the road, to the left, coming down from the mill!"

And their voices died away, they stopped with their eyes fixed and lost on the sunny lake of the glazed work. A mirage rose up before them from this blinding water, they saw an endless succession of meadows, the Cotentin bathed in the balmy breath of the ocean, a luminous vapor, which melted the horizon into a delicate pearly grey. Below, under the colossal iron framework, in the silk hall, roared the business, the trepidation of the machine at work; the entire house vibrated with the trampling of the crowd, the bustle of the shopmen, and the life of the thirty thousand persons elbowing each other there; and they, carried away by their dreams, on feeling this profound and dull clamor with which the roofs were resounding, thought they heard the wind passing over the grass, shaking the tall trees.

"Ah! Mademoiselle Denise," stammered Deloche, "why aren't you kinder to me? I love you so much!" Tears had come into his eyes, and as she tried to interrupt him with a gesture, he continued quickly: "No—let me tell you these things once more. We should get on so well together! People always find something to talk about when they come from the same place."

He was choking, and she at last managed to say kindly: "You're not reasonable; you promised me never to speak of that again. It's impossible. I have a good friendship for you, because you're a nice fellow; but I wish to remain free."

"Yes, yes. I know it," replied he in a broken voice, "you don't love me. Oh! you may say so, I quite understand it. There's nothing in me to make you love me. Listen, I've only had one sweet moment in my life, and that was when I met you at Joinville, do you remember? For a moment under the trees, when it was so dark, I thought your arm trembled, and was stupid enough to imagine——"

But she again interrupted him. Her quick ear had just caught Bourdoncle's and Jouve's steps at the end of the corridor.

"Hark, there's someone coming."

"No," said he, preventing her leaving the window, "it's in the cistern: all sorts of extraordinary noises come up from it, as if there were someone inside."

And he continued his timid, caressing complaints. She was no longer listening to him, rocked into dreamland by this declaration of love, her looks wandering over the roofs of The Ladies' Paradise. To the right and the left of the glazed gallery, other galleries, other halls, were glistening in the sun, between the tops of the houses, pierced with windows and running along symmetrically, like the wings of a barracks. Immense metallic works rose up, ladders, bridges, describing a lacework of iron in the air; whilst the kitchen chimneys threw out an immense volume of smoke like a factory, and the great square cistern, supported in the air on wrought-iron pillars, assumed a strange, barbarous profile, hoisted up to this height by the pride of one man. In the distance, Paris was roaring.

When Denise returned from this dreamy state, from this fanciful development of The Ladies' Paradise, in which her thoughts floated as in a vast solitude, she found that Deloche had seized her hand. And he appeared so woe-begone, so full of grief, that she had not the heart to draw it away.

"Forgive me," he murmured. "It's all over now; I should be quite too miserable if you punished me by withdrawing your friendship. I assure you I intended to say something else. Yes, I had determined to understand the situation and be very good." His tears again began to flow, he tried to steady his voice. "For I know my lot in life. It is too late for my luck to turn. Beaten at home, beaten in Paris, beaten everywhere. I've now been here four years and am still the last in the department. So I wanted to tell you not to trouble on my account. I won't annoy you any longer. Try to be happy, love someone else; yes, that would really be a pleasure for me. If you are happy, I shall be also. That will be my happiness."

He could say no more. As if to seal his promise he raised the young girl's hand to his lips—kissing it with the humble kiss of a slave. She was deeply affected, and said simply, in a tender, sisterly tone, which attenuated somewhat the pity of the words:

"My poor boy!"

But they started, and turned round; Mouret was standing before them.

For the last ten minutes, Jouve had been searching for the governor all over the place; but the latter was looking at the works going on for the new façade in the Rue du Dix-Décembre. He spent long hours there every day, trying to interest himself in this work, of which he had so long dreamed. This was his refuge against his torments, amidst the masons laying the immense corner-stones, and the engineers setting up the great iron frame-work. The façade already appeared above the level of the street, indicating the vast porch, and the windows of the first storey, a palace-like development in its crude state. He scaled the ladders, discussing with the architect the ornamentation which was to be something quite new, scrambled over the heaps of brick and iron, and even went down into the cellar; and the roar of the steam-engine, the tic-tac of the trowels, the noise of the ham-mers, the clamor of this people of workmen, all over this im-mense cage surrounded by sonorous planks, really distracted him for an instant. He came out white with plaster, black with iron-filings, his feet splashed by the water from the pumps, his pain so far from being cured that his anguish returned and his heart beat stronger than ever, as the noise of the works died away behind him. It so happened, on the day in question, a slight distraction had restored him his gaiety, and he was deeply inter-ested in an album of drawings of the mosaics and enameled terra-cottas which were to decorate the friezes, when Jouve came up to fetch him, out of breath, annoyed at being obliged to dirty his coat amongst all this building material. At first Mouret had cried out that they must wait; then, at a word spoken in a low tone by the inspector, he had immediately followed him, shivering, a prey again to his passion. Nothing else existed, the façade crumbled away before being built; what was the use of this supreme triumph of his pride, if the simple name of a woman whispered in his ear tortured him to this extent.

Upstairs, Bourdoncle and Jouve thought it prudent to vanish. Deloche had already run away, Denise alone remained to face Mouret, paler than usual, but looking straight into his eyes.

"Have the kindness to follow me, mademoiselle," said he in a harsh voice.

She followed him, they descended the two storeys, and crossed the furniture and carpet departments without saying a word. When he arrived at his office, he opened the door wide, saying, "Walk in, mademoiselle."

And, closing the door, he went to his desk. The new director's office was fitted up more luxuriously than the old one, the reps hangings had been replaced by velvet ones, and a book-case, incrusted with ivory, occupied one whole side; but on the walls there was still no picture but the portrait of Madame Hédouin, a young woman with a handsome calm face, smiling in its gold frame.

"Mademoiselle," said he at last, trying to maintain a cold, severe air, "there are certain things that we cannot tolerate. Good conduct is absolutely necessary here."

He stopped, choosing his words, in order not to yield to the furious anger which was rising up within him. What! she loved this fellow, this miserable salesman, the laughingstock of his counter! and it was the humblest, the most awkward of all that she preferred to him, the master! for he had seen them, she leaving her hand in his, and he covering that hand with kisses.

"I've been very good to you, mademoiselle," continued he, making a fresh effort. "I little expected to be rewarded in this way."

Denise, immediately on entering, had been attracted by Madame Hédouin's portrait; and, notwithstanding her great trouble, was still pre-occupied by it. Every time she came into the director's office her eyes were sure to meet those of this lady. She felt almost afraid of her, although she knew her to have been very good. This time, she felt her to be a protection.

"You are right, sir," she said, softly, "I was wrong to stop and talk, and I beg your pardon for doing so. This young man comes from my part of the country."

"I'll dismiss him!" cried Mouret, putting all his suffering into this furious cry.

And, completely overcome, entirely forgetting his position as a director lecturing a saleswoman guilty of an infraction of the rules, he broke out into a torrent of violent words. Had she no shame in her? A young girl like her abandoning herself to such a being! and he even made most atrocious accusations, introducing Hutin's name into the affair, and then others, in such a flood of words, that she could not even defend herself. But he would make a clean sweep, and kick them all out. The severe explanation he had promised himself, when following Jouve, had degenerated into the shameful violence of a scene of jealousy.

"Yes, your lovers! They told me about it, and I was stupid enough to doubt it. But I was the only one! I was the only one!"

Denise, suffocating, bewildered, stood listening to these frightful charges, which she had not at first understood. Did he really suppose her to be as bad as this? At another remark, harsher than all the rest, she silently turned towards the door. And, in reply to a movement he made to stop her, said:

"Let me alone, sir, I'm going away. If you think me what you say, I will not remain in the house another second."

But he rushed in front of the door, exclaiming: "Why don't you defend yourself? Say something!"

She stood there very stiff, maintaining an icy silence. For a long time he pressed her with questions, with a growing anxiety; and the mute dignity of this innocent girl once more appeared to be the artful calculation of a woman learned in all the tactics of passion. She could not have played a game better calculated to bring him to her feet, tortured by doubt, desirous of being convinced.

"Come, you say he is from your part of the country? Perhaps you've met there formerly. Swear that there has been nothing between you and this fellow."

And as she obstinately remained silent, as if still wishing to open the door and go away, he completely lost his head, and broke out into a supreme explosion of grief.

"Good heavens! I love you! I love you! Why do you delight in tormenting me like this? You can see that nothing else exists, that the people of whom I speak only touch me through you, and you alone can occupy my thoughts. Thinking you were jealous, I gave up all my pleasures. You were told I had mistresses; well! I have them no longer; I hardly set foot outside. Did I not prefer you at that lady's house? Have I not broken with her to belong solely to you? And I am still waiting for a word of thanks, a little gratitude. And if you fear that I should return to her, you may feel quite easy: she is avenging herself by helping one of our former salesmen to found a rival establishment. Tell me, must I go on my knees to touch your heart?"

He had come to this. He, who did not tolerate the slightest peccadillo with the shopwomen, who turned them out for the least caprice, found himself reduced to imploring one of them not to go away, not to abandon him in his misery. He held the door against her, ready to forgive her everything, to shut his eyes, if she merely deigned to lie. And it was true, he had got thoroughly sick of girls picked up at theatres and night-houses; he had long since given up Clara and now ceased to visit at Madame Desforges's house, where Bouthemont reigned supreme, while waiting for the opening of the new shop, The Four Seasons, which was already filling the newspapers with its advertisements.

"Must I go on my knees?" repeated he, almost choked by suppressed tears.

She stopped him, herself quite unable to conceal her emotion, deeply affected by this suffering passion. "You are wrong, sir, to agitate yourself in this way," replied she, at last. "I assure you that all these wicked reports are untrue. This poor fellow you have just seen is no more guilty than I am."

She said this with her brave, frank air, looking with her bright eyes straight into his face.

"Very good, I believe you," murmured he. "I'll not dismiss any of your comrades, since you take all these people under your protection. But why, then, do you repulse me, if you love no one else?"

A sudden constraint, an anxious bashfulness seized the young girl.

"You love someone, don't you?" resumed he, in a trembling voice. "Oh! you may speak out; I have no claim on your affections. Do you love anyone?"

She turned very red, her heart was in her mouth, and she felt all falsehood impossible before this emotion which was betraying her, this repugnance for a lie which made the truth appear in her face in spite of all.

"Yes," she at last confessed, feebly. "But I beg you to let me go away, sir, you are torturing me."

She was now suffering in her turn. Was it not enough to have to defend herself against him? Was she to be obliged to fight against herself, against the breath of tenderness which sometimes took away all her courage? When he spoke to her thus, when she saw him so full of emotion, so overcome, she hardly knew why she still refused; and it was only afterwards that she found, in the depths of her healthy, girlish nature, the pride and the prudence which maintained her intact in her virtuous resolution. It was by a sort of instinct of happiness that she still remained so obstinate, to satisfy her need of a quiet life, and not from any idea of virtue. She would have fallen into this man's arms, her heart seduced, her flesh overpowered if she had not experienced a sort of revolt, almost a feeling of repulsion before the definite bestowal of her being, ignorant of her future fate. The lover made her afraid, inspiring her with that fear that all women feel at the approach of the male.

Mouret gave way to a gesture of gloomy discouragement. He could not understand her. He turned towards his desk, took up some papers and then laid them down again, saying: "I will retain you no longer, mademoiselle; I cannot keep you against your will."

"But I don't wish to go away," replied she, smiling. "If you believe me to be innocent, I will remain. One ought always to believe a woman to be virtuous, sir. There are numbers who are so, I assure you."

Denise's eyes had involuntarily wandered towards Madame Hédouin's portrait: that lady so wise and so beautiful, whose blood, they said, had brought good fortune to the house. Mouret followed the young girl's look with a start, for he thought he heard his dead wife pronounce this phrase, one of her own sayings which he at once recognized. And it was like a resurrection, he discovered in Denise the good sense, the just equilibrium of her he had lost, even down to the gentle voice, sparing of useless words. He was struck by this resemblance, which rendered him sadder still.

"You know I am yours," murmured he in conclusion. "Do what you like with me."

Then she resumed gaily: "That is right, sir. The advice of a woman, however humble she may be, is always worth listening to when she has a little intelligence. If you put yourself in my hands, be sure I'll make nothing but a good man of you!"

She smiled, with that simple unassuming air which had such a charm. He also smiled in a feeble way, and escorted her as far as the door, as he would a lady.

The next day Denise was appointed first-hand. The dress and costume department was divided, the management creating especially for her one for children's costumes, which was installed close to the ready-made one. Since her son's dismissal, Madame Aurélie had been trembling, for she found the directors getting cool towards her, and saw the young girl's power increasing daily. Would they not shortly sacrifice her in favor of this latter, by taking advantage of the first pretext? Her emperor's mask, puffed up with fat, seemed to have got thinner from the shame which now stained the whole Lhomme dynasty; and she made a show of going away every evening on her husband's arm, for they were brought nearer together by misfortune, and felt vaguely that the evil came from the disorder of their home; whilst the poor old man, more affected than her, in a sickly fear of being himself suspected of robbery, counted over the receipts, again and again, noisily, performing miracles with his amputated arm. So that, when she saw Denise appointed first-hand in the children's costume department, she experienced such joy that she paraded the most affectionate feeling towards the young girl, really grateful to her for not having taken her place away. And she overwhelmed her with attentions, treating her as an equal, often going to talk to her in the neighboring department, with a stately air, like a queen-mother paying a visit to a young queen.

In fact, Denise was now at the summit. Her appointment as first-hand had destroyed the last resistance. If some still babbled, from that itching of the tongue which ravages every assemblage of men and women, they bowed very low before her face. Marguerite, now second-hand, was full of praise for her. Clara, herself, inspired with a secret respect before this good fortune, which she felt herself incapable of achieving, had bowed her head. But Denise's victory was more complete still over the gentlemen; over Jouve, who now bent almost double whenever he addressed her; over Hutin, seized with anxiety on feeling his position giving way under him; and over Bourdoncle, reduced at last to powerlessness. When the latter saw her coming out of the director's office, smiling, with her quiet air, and that the next day Mouret had insisted on the board creating this new department, he had yielded, vanquished by a sacred terror of woman. He had always given in thus before Mouret, recognizing him to be his master, notwithstanding his escapades and his idiotic love affairs. This time the woman had proved the stronger, and he was expecting to be swept away by the disaster.

However, Denise bore her triumph in a peaceable, charming manner, happy at these marks of consideration, even affecting to see in them a sympathy for the miseries of her debut and the final success of her patient courage. Thus she received with a laughing joy the slightest marks of friendship, and this caused her to be really loved by some, she was so kind, sympathetic, and full of affection. The only person for whom she still showed an invincible repugnance was Clara, having learned that this girl had amused herself by taking Colomban home with her one night as she had said she would do for a joke; and he, carried away by his passion, was becoming more dissipated every day, whilst poor Geneviève was slowly dying. The adventure was talked of at The Ladies' Paradise, and thought very droll.

But this trouble, the only one she had outside, did not in any way change Denise's equable temper. It was especially in her department that she was seen at her best, in the midst of her little world of babies of all ages. She was passionately fond of children, and she could not have been placed in a better position. Sometimes there were fully fifty girls and as many boys there, quite a turbulent school, let loose in their growing coquettish desires. The mothers completely lost their heads. She, conciliating, smiling, had the little ones placed in a line, on chairs; and when there happened to be amongst the number a rosy-cheeked little angel, whose pretty face tempted her, she would insist on serving her herself, bringing the dress and trying it on the child's dimpled shoulders, with the tender precaution of an elder sister. There were fits of laughter, cries of joy, amidst the scolding voices of the mothers. Sometimes a little girl, already a grand lady, nine or ten years old, having a cloth jacket to try on, would stand studying it before a glass, turning round, with an absorbed air, her eyes sparkling with a desire to please. The counters were encumbered with the things unpacked, dresses in pink and blue Asian linen for children of from one to five years, blue sailor costumes, with plaited skirt and blouse, trimmed with fine cambric muslin, Louis XV. costumes, mantles, jackets, a pell-mell of narrow garments, stiffened in their infantine grace, something like the cloak-room of a regiment of big dolls, taken out of the wardrobes and given up to pillage. Denise had always a few sweets in her pockets, to appease the tears of some youngster in despair at not being able to carry off a pair of red trousers; and she lived there amongst these little ones as in her own family, feeling quite young again herself from the contact of all this innocence and freshness incessantly renewed around her skirts.

She now had frequent friendly conversations with Mouret. When she went to the office to take orders and furnish information, he kept her talking, enjoying the sound of her voice. It was what she laughingly called "making a good man of him." In her prudent, cautious Norman head there sprang up all sorts of projects, ideas about the new business which she had already ventured to hint at when at Robineau's, and some of which she had expressed on the evening of their walk in the Tuileries Gardens. She could not be occupied in any matter, see any work going on, without being moved with a desire to introduce some improvement in the mechanism. Then, since her entry into The Ladies' Paradise, she was especially pained by the precarious position of the employees; the sudden dismissals shocked her, she thought them iniquitous and stupid, hurtful to all, to the house as much as to the staff. Her former sufferings were still fresh in her mind, and her heart was seized with pity every time she saw a new-comer, her feet bruised, her eyes dim with tears, dragging herself along in her misery in her silk dress, amidst the spiteful persecution of the old hands. This dog's life made the best of them bad; and the sad work of destruction commenced: all eaten up by the trade before the age of forty, disappearing, falling into unknown places, a great many dying in harness, some of consumption and exhaustion, others of fatigue and bad air, a few thrown on the street, the happiest married, buried in some little provincial shop. Was it humane, was it just, this frightful consumption of human life that the big shops carried on every year? And she pleaded the cause of the wheel-work of the colossal machine, not from any sentimental reasons, but by arguments appealing to the very interests of the employers. To make a machine solid and strong, it is necessary to use good iron; if the iron breaks or is broken, there is a stoppage of work, repeated expenses of starting, quite a loss of power.

Sometimes she would become quite animated, she would picture an immense ideal bazaar, the phalansterium of modern commerce, in which each one should have his exact share of the profits, according to his merits, with the certainty of the future, assured to him by a contract. Mouret would feel amused at this, notwithstanding his fever. He accused her of socialism, embarrassed her by pointing out the difficulties of carrying out these schemes; for she spoke in the simplicity of her soul, bravely trusting in the future, when she perceived a dangerous hole underlying her tender-hearted plans. He was, however, shaken, captivated by this young voice, still trembling from the evils endured, so convinced and earnest in pointing out the reforms which would tend to consolidate the house; yet he listened while joking with her; the salesmen's position gradually improved, the wholesale dismissals were replaced by a system of holidays granted during the dead seasons, and there was also about to be created a sort of benefit club which would protect the employees against bad times and ensure them a pension. It was the embryo of the vast trades' unions of the twentieth century.

Denise did not confine her attention solely to healing the wounds from which she had herself bled; she conceived various delicate feminine ideas, which, communicated to Mouret, delighted the customers. She also caused Lhomme's happiness by supporting a scheme he had long nourished, that of creating a band of music, in which all the executants should be chosen from amongst the staff. Three months later Lhomme had a hundred and twenty musicians under his direction, the dream of his whole life was realized. And a grand fête was given on the premises, a concert and a ball, to introduce the band of The Ladies' Paradise to the customers and the whole world. The newspapers took the matter up, Bourdoncle himself, frightened by these innovations, was obliged to bow before this immense advertisement. Afterwards, a recreation room for the men was established, with two billiard tables and backgammon and chess boards. Then classes were held in the house of an evening; there were lessons in English and German, in grammar, arithmetic, and geography; they even had lessons in riding and fencing. A library was formed, ten thousand volumes were placed at the disposal of the employees. And a resident doctor giving consultations gratis was also added, together with baths, and hair-dressing and refreshment saloons. Every want in life was provided for, everything was to be obtained without going outside—board, lodging, and clothing. The Ladies' Paradise sufficed entirely for all its own wants and pleasures, in the very heart of Paris, taken up by all this clatter, by this working city which was springing up so vigorously out of the ruins of the old streets, at last opened to the rays of the sun.

Then a fresh movement of opinion took place in Denise's favor. As Bourdoncle, vanquished, repeated with despair to his friends that he would give a great deal to put Denise into Mouret's arms himself, it was concluded that she had not yielded, that her all-powerfulness resulted from her refusal. From that moment she became immensely popular. They knew for what indulgences they were indebted to her, and they admired her for the force of her will. There was one, at least, who could master the governor, who avenged all the others, and knew how to get something else besides promises out of him! So she had come at last, she who was to make him treat the poor devils with a little respect! When she went through the shop, with her delicate, self-willed head, her tender, invincible air, the salesmen smiled at her, were proud of her, and would willingly have exhibited her to the crowd. Denise, in her happiness, allowed herself to be carried along by this increasing sympathy. Was it all possible? She saw herself arrive in a poor dress, frightened, lost amidst the mechanism of the terrible machine; for a long time she had had the sensation of being nothing, hardly a grain of seed beneath these millstones which were crushing a whole world; and now today she was the very soul of this world, she alone was of consequence, able at a word to increase or slacken the pace of the colossus lying at her feet. And yet she had not wished for these things, she had simply presented herself, without calculation, with the sole charm of her sweetness. Her sovereignty sometimes caused her an uneasy surprise; why did they all obey her? She was not pretty, she did nothing wrong. Then she smiled, her heart at rest, feeling within herself nothing but goodness and prudence, a love of truth and logic which constituted all her strength.

One of Denise's greatest joys was to be able to assist Pauline. The latter, being about to become a mother, was trembling, aware that two other saleswomen in the same condition had been sent away. The principals did not tolerate these accidents, maternity being suppressed as cumbersome and indecent; they occasionally allowed marriage, but would admit of no children. Pauline had, it was true, her husband in the house; but still she felt anxious, it being almost impossible for her to appear at the counter; and in order to postpone a probable dismissal, she laced herself very tightly, resolved to conceal her state as long as she could. One of the two saleswomen who had been dismissed, had just been delivered of a still-born child, through having laced herself up in this way; and it was not certain that she herself would recover. Meanwhile, Bourdoncle had observed that Pauline's complexion was getting very livid, and that she had a painfully stiff way of walking. One morning he was standing near her, in the under-linen department, when a messenger, taking away a bundle, ran up against her with such force that she cried out with pain. Bourdoncle immediately took her on one side, made her confess, and submitted the question of her dismissal to the board, under the pretext that she stood in need of country air: the story of this accident would spread, and would have a disastrous effect on the public if she should have a miscarriage, as had already taken place in the baby-linen department the year before. Mouret, who was not at the meeting, could only give his opinion in the evening. But Denise having had time to interfere, he closed Bourdoncle's mouth, in the interest of the house itself. Did they wish to frighten the heads of families and the young mothers amongst their customers? And it was decided, with great pomp, that every married saleswoman should, when in the family way, be sent to a special midwife's as soon as her presence at the counter became offensive to the customers.

The next day when Denise went up into the infirmary to see Pauline, who had been obliged to take to her bed on account of the blow she had received, the latter kissed her violently on both cheeks. "How kind you are! Had it not been for you I should have been turned away. Pray don't be anxious about me, the doctor says it's nothing."

Baugé, who had slipped away from his department, was also there, on the other side of the bed. He likewise stammered his thanks, troubled before Denise, whom he now treated as an important person, of a superior class. Ah! if he heard any more nasty remarks about her, he would soon close the mouths of the jealous ones! But Pauline sent him away with a good-natured shrug of the shoulders.

"My poor darling, you're always saying something stupid. Leave us to talk together."

The infirmary was a long, light room, containing twelve beds, with their white curtains. Those who did not wish to go home to their families were nursed here. But on the day in question, Pauline was the only occupant, in a bed near one of the large windows which looked on to the Rue Neuve-Saint-Augustin. And they immediately commenced to exchange whispered words, tender confidences, in the calm air, perfumed with a vague odor of lavender.

"So he does just what you wish him to? How cruel you are, to make him suffer so! Come, just explain it to me, now I've ventured to approach the subject. Do you detest him?"

Pauline had retained hold of Denise's hand, as the latter sat near the bed, with her elbow on the bolster; and overcome by a sudden emotion, her cheeks invaded with color, she had a moment of weakness at this direct and unexpected question. Her secret escaped her, she buried her head in the pillow, murmuring:

"I love him!"

Pauline was astonished. "What! you love him? But it's very simple: say yes."

Denise, her face still concealed, replied "No" by an energetic shake of the head. And she did so, simply because she loved him, without being able to explain the matter. No doubt it was ridiculous; but she felt like that, she could not change her nature. Her friend's surprise increased, and she at length asked: "So it's all to make him marry you?"

At this the young girl sprung up, quite confused: "Marry me! Oh! no! Oh! I assure you that I have never wished for anything of the kind! No, never has such an idea entered my head; and you know what a horror I have of all falsehood!"

"Well, dear," resumed Pauline, kindly, "you couldn't have acted otherwise, if such had been your intention. All this must come to an end, and it is very certain that it can only finish by a marriage, as you won't let it be otherwise. I must tell you that everyone has the same idea; yes, they feel persuaded that you are riding the high horse, in order to make him take you to church. Dear me! what a funny girl you are!"

And she had to console Denise, who had again dropped her head on to the bolster, sobbing, declaring that she would certainly go away, since they attributed all sorts of things to her that had never crossed her mind. No doubt, when a man loved a woman he ought to marry her. But she asked for nothing, she had made no calculations, she simply begged to be allowed to live quietly, with her joys and her sorrows, like other people. She would go away.

At the same moment Mouret was going through the premises below. He had wanted to forget his thoughts by visiting the works once more. Several months had elapsed, the façade now reared its monumental lines behind the vast hoardings which concealed it from the public. Quite an army of decorators were at work: marble-cutters, mosaic-workers, and others. The central group above the door was being gilded; whilst on the acroteria were being fixed the pedestals destined to receive the statues of the manufacturing cities of France. From morning to night, in the Rue du Dix-Décembre, lately opened to the public, a crowd of idlers stood gaping about, their noses in the air, seeing nothing, but pre-occupied by the marvels that were related of this façade, the inauguration of which was going to revolutionize Paris. And it was on this feverish working-ground, amidst the artists putting the finishing touches to the realization of his dream commenced by the masons, that Mouret felt more bitterly than ever the vanity of his fortune. The thought of Denise had suddenly arrested him, this thought which incessantly pierced him with a flame, like the shooting of an incurable pain. He had run away, unable to find a word of satisfaction, fearful lest he should show his tears, leaving behind him the disgust of his triumph. This façade, which was at last erected, seemed little in his eyes, very much like one of those walls of sand that children build, and it might have been extended from one end of the city to the other, elevated to the starry sky, yet it would not have filled the emptiness of his heart, that the "yes" of a mere child could alone fill.

When Mouret entered his office he was almost choking with sobs. What did she want? He dared not offer her money now; and the confused idea of a marriage presented itself amidst his young widower's revolts. And, in the debility of his powerlessness, his tears began to flow. He was very miserable.

CHAPTER XIII.

One morning in November, Denise was giving her first orders in the department when the Baudus' servant came to tell her that Mademoiselle Geneviève had passed a very bad night, and wished to see her cousin immediately. For some time the young girl had been getting weaker and weaker, and she had been obliged to take to her bed two days before.

"Say I am coming at once," replied Denise, very anxious.

The blow which was finishing Geneviève was Colomban's sudden disappearance. At first, chaffed by Clara, he had stopped out several nights; then, yielding to the mad desires of a quiet, chaste fellow, he had become her obedient slave, and had not returned one Monday, but had simply sent a farewell letter to Baudu, written in the studied terms of a man about to commit suicide. Perhaps, at the bottom of this passion, there was also the crafty calculation of a fellow delighted at escaping a disastrous marriage. The draper's business was in as bad a way as his betrothed; the moment was propitious to break with them through any stupidity. And everyone cited him as an unfortunate victim of love.

When Denise arrived at The Old Elbeuf, Madame Baudu was there alone, sitting motionless behind the pay-desk, with her small white face, eaten up by anaemia, silent and quiet in the cold, deserted shop. There were no assistants now. The servant dusted the shelves, and it was even a question of replacing her by a charwoman. A dreary cold fell from the ceiling, hours passed away without a customer coming to disturb this silence, and the goods, no longer touched, became mustier and mustier every day.

"What's the matter?" asked Denise, anxiously. "Is Geneviève in danger?"

Madame Baudu did not reply at first. Her eyes filled with tears. Then she stammered: "I don't know; they don't tell me anything. Ah, it's all over, it's all over."

And she cast a sombre glance around the dark old shop, as if she felt her daughter and the shop disappearing together. The seventy thousand francs, produce of the sale of their Rambouillet property, had melted away in less than two years in this gulf of competition. In order to struggle against The Ladies' Paradise, which now kept men's cloths and materials for hunting and livery suits, the draper had made considerable sacrifices. At last he had been definitely crushed by the swan-skin cloth and flannels sold by his rival, an assortment that had not its equal in the market. Little by little his debts had increased, and, as a last resource, he had resolved to mortgage the old building in the Rue de la Michodière, where Finet, their ancestor, had founded the business; and it was now only a question of days, the crumbling away had commenced, the very ceilings seemed to be falling down and turning into dust, like an old worm-eaten structure carried away by the wind.

"Your uncle is upstairs," resumed Madame Baudu in her broken voice. "We stay with her two hours each. Someone must look out here; oh! but only as a precaution, for to tell the truth—"

Her gesture finished the phrase. They would have put the shutters up had it not been for their old commercial pride, which still propped them up in the presence of the neighborhood.

"Well, I'll go up, aunt," said Denise, whose heart was bleeding, amidst this resigned despair that even the pieces of cloth themselves exhaled.

"Yes, go upstairs quick, my girl. She's waiting for you. She's been asking for you all night. She has something to tell you."

But just at that moment Baudu came down. The rising bile gave his yellow face a greenish tinge, and his eyes were bloodshot. He was still walking with the muffled step with which he had quitted the sick room, and murmured, as if he might be heard upstairs, "She's asleep."

And, thoroughly worn out, he sat down on a chair, wiping his forehead with a mechanical gesture, puffing like a man who has just finished some hard work. A silence ensued, but at last he said to Denise: "You'll see her presently. When she is sleeping, she seems to me to be all right again."

There was again a silence. Face to face, the father and mother stood looking at each other. Then, in a half whisper, he went over his grief again, naming no one, addressing no one directly: "My head on the block, I wouldn't have believed it! He was the last one. I had brought him up as a son. If anyone had come and said to me, 'They'll take him away from you as well; he'll fall as well,' I would have replied, 'Impossible, it could not be.' And he has fallen all the same! Ah! the scoundrel, he who was so well up in real business, who had all my ideas! And all for a young monkey, one of those dummies that parade at the windows of bad houses! No! really, it's enough to drive one mad!"

He shook his head, his eyes fell on the damp floor worn away by generations of customers. Then he continued in a lower voice, "There are moments when I feel myself the most culpable of all in our misfortune. Yes, it's my fault if our poor girl is upstairs devoured by fever. Ought not I to have married them at once, without yielding to my stupid pride, my obstinacy in refusing to leave them the house less prosperous than before? Had I done that she would now have the man she loved, and perhaps their united youthful strength would have accomplished the miracle that I have failed to work. But I am an old fool, and saw through nothing; I didn't know that people fell ill over such things. Really he was an extraordinary fellow: with such a gift for business, and such probity, such simplicity of conduct, so orderly in every way—in short, my pupil."

He raised his head, still defending his ideas, in the person of the shopman who had betrayed him. Denise could not bear to hear him accuse himself, and she told him so, carried away by her emotion, on seeing him so humble, with his eyes full of tears, he who used formerly to reign as absolute master.

"Uncle, pray don't apologize for him. He never loved Geneviève, he would have run away sooner if you had tried to hasten the marriage. I have spoken to him myself about it; he was perfectly well aware that my cousin was suffering on his account, and you see that did not prevent him leaving. Ask aunt."

Without opening her lips, Madame Baudu confirmed these words by a nod. The draper turned paler still, blinded by his tears. He stammered out: "It must be in the blood, his father died last year through having led a dissolute life."

And he once more looked round the obscure shop, his eyes wandering from the empty counters to the full shelves, then resting on Madame Baudu, who was still at the pay-desk, waiting in vain for the customers who did not come.

"Come," said he, "it's all over. They've ruined our business, and now one of their hussies is killing our daughter."

No one spoke. The rolling of the vehicles, which occasionally shook the floor, passed like a funereal beating of drums in the still air, stifled under the low ceiling. Suddenly, amidst this gloomy sadness of the old dying shop, could be heard several heavy knocks, struck somewhere in the house. It was Geneviève, who had just awoke, and was knocking with a stick they had left near her bed.

"Let's go up at once," said Baudu, rising with a start. "Try and be cheerful, she mustn't know."

He himself rubbed his eyes to efface the trace of his tears. As soon as he had opened the door, on the first storey, they heard a frightened, feeble voice crying: "Oh, I don't like to be left alone. Don't leave me; I'm afraid to be left alone." Then, when she perceived Denise, Geneviève became calmer, and smiled joyfully. "You've come, then! How I've been longing to see you since yesterday. I thought you also had abandoned me!"

It was a piteous sight. The young girl's room looked out on to the yard, a little room lighted by a livid light. At first her parents had put her in their own room, in the front; but the sight of The Ladies' Paradise opposite affected her so much, that they had been obliged to bring her back to her own again. And there she lay, so very thin, under the bed-clothes, that one hardly suspected the form and existence of a human body. Her skinny arms, consumed by a burning fever, were in a perpetual movement of anxious, unconscious searching; whilst her black hair seemed thicker still, and to be eating up her poor face with its voracious vitality, that face in which was agonizing the final degenerateness of a family sprung up in the shade, in this cellar of old commercial Paris. Denise, her heart bursting with pity, stood looking at her. She did not at first speak, for fear of giving way to tears. At last she murmured:

"I came at once. Can I be of any use to you? You asked for me. Would you like me to stay?"

"No, thanks. I don't want anything. I only wanted to embrace you."

Tears filled her eyes. Denise quickly leant over, and kissed her on both cheeks, trembling to feel on her lips the flame of those hollow cheeks. But Geneviève, stretching out her arms, seized and kept her in a desperate embrace. Then she looked towards her father.

"Would you like me to stay?" repeated Denise. "Perhaps there is something I can do for you."

Geneviève's glance was still obstinately fixed on her father, who remained standing, with a stolid air, almost choking. He at last understood, and went away, without saying a word; and they heard his heavy footstep on the stairs.

"Tell me, is he with that woman?" asked the sick girl immediately, seizing her cousin's hand, and making her sit on the side of the bed. "I want to know, and you are the only one can tell me. They're living together, aren't they?"

Denise, surprised by these questions, stammered, and was obliged to confess the truth, the rumors that were current in the shop. Clara, tired of this fellow, who was getting a nuisance to her, had already broken with him, and Colomban, desolated, was pursuing her everywhere, trying to obtain a meeting from time to time, with a sort of canine humility. They said that he was going to take a situation at the Grands Magasins du Louvre.

"If you still love him, he may return," said Denise, to cheer the dying girl with this last hope. "Get well quick, he will acknowledge his errors, and marry you."

Geneviève interrupted her. She had listened with all her soul, with an intense passion that raised her in the bed. But she fell back almost immediately. "No, I know it's all over! I don't say anything, because I see papa crying, and I don't wish to make mamma worse than she is. But I am going, Denise, and if I called for you last night it was for fear of going off before the morning. And to think that he is not happy after all!"

And Denise having remonstrated, assuring her that she was not so bad as all that, she cut her short again, suddenly throwing off the bed-clothes with the chaste gesture of a virgin who has nothing to conceal in death. Naked to the waist, she murmured: "Look at me! Is it possible?"

Trembling, Denise quitted the side of the bed, as if she feared to destroy this fearful nudity with a breath. It was the last of the flesh, a bride's body used up by waiting, returned to the first infantile slimness of her young days. Geneviève slowly covered herself up again, saying: "You see I am no longer a woman. It would be wrong to wish for him still!"

There was a silence. Both continued to look at each other, unable to find a word to say. It was Geneviève who resumed: "Come, don't stay any longer, you have your own affairs to look after. And thanks, I was tormented by the wish to know, and am now satisfied. If you see him, tell him I forgive him. Adieu, dear Denise. Kiss me once more, for it's the last time."

The young girl kissed her, protesting: "No, no, don't despair, all you want is loving care, nothing more."

But the sick girl, shaking her head in an obstinate way, smiled, quite sure of what she said. And as her cousin was making for the door, she exclaimed: "Wait a minute, knock with this stick, so that papa may come up. I'm afraid to stay alone."

Then, when Baudu arrived in that small, gloomy room, where he spent hours seated on a chair, she assumed an air of gaiety, saying to Denise—"Don't come tomorrow, I would rather not. But on Sunday I shall expect you; you can spend the afternoon with me."

The next morning, at six o'clock, Geneviève expired after four hours' fearful agony. The funeral took place on a Saturday, a fearfully black, gloomy day, under a sooty sky which hung over the shivering city. The Old Elbeuf, hung with white linen, lighted up the street with a bright spot, and the candles burning in the fading day seemed so many stars drowned in the twilight. The coffin was covered with wreaths and bouquets of white roses; it was a narrow child's coffin, placed in the obscure passage of the house on a level with the pavement, so near the gutter that the passing carriages had already splashed the coverings. The whole neighborhood exhaled a dampness, a cellar-like moldy odor, with its continual rush of pedestrians on the muddy pavement.

At nine o'clock Denise came over to stay with her aunt. But as the funeral was starting, the latter—who had ceased weeping, her eyes burnt with tears—begged her to follow the body and look after her uncle, whose mute affliction and almost idiotic grief filled the family with anxiety. Below, the young girl found the street full of people, for the small traders in the neighborhood were anxious to show the Baudus a mark of sympathy, and in this eagerness there was also a sort of manifestation against The Ladies' Paradise, whom they accused of causing Geneviève's slow agony. All the victims of the monster were there—Bédoré and sister from the hosier's shop in the Rue Gaillon, the furriers, Vanpouille brothers, and Deslignières the toyman, and Piot and Rivoire the furniture dealers; even Mademoiselle Tatin from the under-clothing shop, and the glover Quinette, long since cleared off by bankruptcy, had made it a duty to come, the one from Batignolles, the other from the Bastille, where they had been obliged to take situations. Whilst waiting for the hearse, which was late, these people, tramping about in the mud, cast glances of hatred towards The Ladies' Paradise, the bright windows and gay displays of which seemed an insult in face of The Old Elbeuf, which, with its funeral trappings and glimmering candles, cast a gloom over the other side of the street. A few curious faces appeared at the plate-glass windows; but the colossus maintained the indifference of a machine going at full speed, unconscious of the deaths it may cause on the road.

Denise looked round for her brother Jean, whom she at last perceived standing before Bourras's shop, and she went and asked him to walk with his uncle, to assist him if he could not get along. For the last few weeks Jean had been very grave, as if tormented by some worry. Today, buttoned up in his black frock-coat, a full grown man, earning his twenty francs a day, he seemed so dignified and so sad that his sister was surprised, for she had no idea he loved his cousin so much as that. Desirous of sparing Pépé this needless grief, she had left him with Madame Gras, intending to go and fetch him in the afternoon to see his uncle and aunt.

The hearse had still not arrived, and Denise, greatly affected, was watching the candles burn, when she was startled by a well-known voice behind her. It was Bourras. He had called the chestnut-seller opposite, in his little box, against the public-house, and said to him:

"I say, Vigouroux, just keep a look-out for me a bit, will you? You see I've closed the door. If anyone comes tell them to call again. But don't let that disturb you, no one will come."

Then he took his stand on the pavement, waiting like the others. Denise, feeling rather awkward, glanced at his shop. He entirely abandoned it now; there was nothing left but a disorderly array of umbrellas eaten up by the damp air, and canes blackened by the gas. The embellishments that he had made, the delicate green paint work, the glasses, the gilded sign, were all cracking, already getting dirty, presenting that rapid and lamentable decrepitude of false luxury laid over ruins. But though the old crevices were reappearing, though the spots of damp had sprung up over the gildings, the house still held its ground obstinately, hanging on to the flanks of The Ladies' Paradise like a dishonoring wart, which, although cracked and rotten, refused to fall off.

"Ah! the scoundrels," growled Bourras, "they won't even let her be carried away."

The hearse, which had at last arrived, had just got into collision with one of The Ladies' Paradise vans, which was spinning along, shedding in the mist its starry radiance, with the rapid trot of two superb horses. And the old man cast on Denise an oblique glance, lighted up under his bushy eyebrows. Slowly, the funeral started off, splashing through the muddy pools, amid the silence of the omnibuses and carriages suddenly pulled up. When the coffin, draped with white, crossed the Place Gaillon, the sombre looks of the cortege were once more plunged into the windows of the big shop, where two saleswomen alone had run up to look on, pleased at this distraction. Baudu followed the hearse with a heavy mechanical step, refusing by a sign the arm offered by Jean, who was walking with him. Then, after a long string of people, came three mourning coaches. As they passed the Rue Neuve-des-Petits-Champs, Robineau ran up to join the cortege, very pale, and looking much older.

At Saint-Roch, a great many women were waiting, the small traders of the neighborhood, who had been afraid of the crowd at the house. The manifestation was developing into quite a riot; and when, after the service, the procession started off back, all the men followed, although it was a long walk from the Rue Saint-Honoré to the Montmartre Cemetery. They had to go up the Rue Saint-Roch, and once more pass The Ladies' Paradise. It was a sort of obsession; this poor young girl's body was paraded round the big shop like the first victim fallen in time of revolution. At the door some red flannels were flapping like so many flags, and a display of carpets blazed forth in a florescence of enormous roses and full-blown peonies. Denise had got into one of the coaches, being agitated by some smarting doubts, her heart oppressed by such a feeling of grief that she had not the strength to walk. At that moment there was a stop, in the Rue du Dix-Décembre, before the scaffolding of the new façade which still obstructed the thoroughfare. And the young girl observed old Bourras, left behind, dragging along with difficulty, close to the wheels of the coach in which she was riding alone. He would never get as far as the cemetery, she thought. He raised his head, looked at her, and all at once got into the coach.

"It's my confounded knees," exclaimed he. "Don't draw back! Is it you that we detest?"

She felt him to be friendly and furious as in former days. He grumbled, declared that Baudu must be fearfully strong to be able to keep up after such blows as he had received. The procession had resumed its slow pace; and on leaning out, Denise saw her uncle walking with his heavy step, which seemed to regulate the rumbling and painful march of the cortege. She then threw herself back into the corner, listening to the endless complaints of the old umbrella maker, rocked by the melancholy movement of the coach.

"The police ought to clear the public thoroughfare, my word! They've been blocking up our street for the last eighteen months with the scaffolding of their façade, where a man was killed the other day. Never mind! When they want to enlarge further they'll have to throw bridges over the street. They say there are now two thousand seven hundred employees, and that the business will amount to a hundred millions this year. A hundred millions! Just fancy, a hundred millions!"

Denise had nothing to say in reply. The procession had just turned into the Rue de la Chaussée d'Antin, where it was stopped by a block of vehicles. Bourras went on, with a vague expression in his eyes, as if he were dreaming aloud. He still failed to understand the triumph achieved by The Ladies' Paradise, but he acknowledged the defeat of the old-fashioned traders.

"Poor Robineau's done for, he's got the face of a drowning man. And the Bédorés and the Vanpouilles, they can't keep going; they're like me, played out. Deslignières will die of apoplexy. Piot and Rivoire have the yellow jaundice. Ah! we're a fine lot; a pretty cortege of skeletons to follow the poor child. It must be comical for those looking on to see this string of bankrupts pass. Besides, it appears that the clean sweep is to continue. The scoundrels are creating departments for flowers, bonnets, perfumery, shoemaking, all sorts of things. Grognet, the perfumer in the Rue de Grammont, can clear out, and I wouldn't give ten francs for Naud's shoeshop in the Rue d'Antin. The cholera has spread as far as the Rue Sainte-Anne, where Lacassagne, at the feather and flower shop, and Madame Chadeuil, whose bonnets are so well-known, will be swept away before long. And after those, others; it will still go on! All the businesses in the neighborhood will suffer. When counter-jumpers commence to sell soap and goloshes, they are quite capable of dealing in fried potatoes. My word, the world is turning upside down!"

The hearse was just then crossing the Place de la Trinité to ascend the steep Rue Blanche, and from the corner of the gloomy coach Denise, who, broken-hearted, was listening to the endless complaints of the old man, could see the coffin as they issued from the Rue de la Chausseé d'Antin. Behind her uncle, marching along with the blind, mute face of an ox about to be poleaxed, she seemed to hear the tramping of a flock of sheep led to the slaughter-house, the discomfiture of the shops of a whole district, the small traders dragging along their ruin, with the thud of damp shoes, through the muddy streets of Paris. Bourras still went on, in a deeper voice, as if slackened by the difficult ascent of the Rue Blanche.

"As for me, I am settled. But I still hold on all the same, and won't let go. He's just lost his appeal case. Ah! that's cost me something, what with nearly two years' pleading, and the solicitors and the barristers! Never mind, he won't pass under my shop, the judges have decided that such a work could not be considered as a legitimate case of repairing. Fancy, he talked of creating underneath a light saloon to judge the colors of the stuffs by gas-light, a subterranean room which would have united the hosiery to the drapery department! And he can't get over it; he can't swallow the fact that an old humbug like me should stop his progress, when everybody are on their knees before his money. Never! I won't! that's understood. Very likely I may be worsted. Since I have had to go to the money-lenders, I know the villain is looking after my paper, in the hope to play me some villainous trick, no doubt. But that doesn't matter. He says 'yes,' and I say 'no,' and shall still say 'no,' even when I get between two boards like this poor little girl who has just been nailed up."

When they reached the Boulevard de Clichy, the coach went at a quicker pace; one could hear the heavy breathing of the mourners, the unconscious haste of the cortege, anxious to get the sad ceremony over. What Bourras did not openly mention, was the frightful misery into which he had fallen, bewildered amidst the confusion of the small trader who is on the road to ruin and yet remains obstinate, under a shower of protested bills. Denise, well acquainted with his situation, at last interrupted the silence by saying, in a voice of entreaty:

"Monsieur Bourras, pray don't stand out any longer. Let me arrange matters for you."

But he interrupted her with a violent gesture. "You be quiet. That's nobody's business. You're a good little girl, and I know you lead him a hard life, this man who thought you were for sale like my house. But what would you answer if I advised you to say 'yes?' You'd send me about my business. Therefore, when I say 'no,' don't you interfere in the matter."

And the coach having stopped at the cemetery gate, he got out with the young girl. The Baudus' vault was situated in the first alley on the left. In a few minutes the ceremony was terminated. Jean had drawn away his uncle, who was looking into the grave with a gaping air. The mourners wandered about amongst the neighboring tombs, and the faces of all these shopkeepers, their blood impoverished by living in their unhealthy shops, assumed an ugly suffering look under the leaden sky. When the coffin slipped gently down, their blotched and pimpled cheeks paled, and their bleared eyes, blinded with figures, turned away.

"We ought all to jump into this hole," said Bourras to Denise, who had kept close to him. "In burying this poor girl they are burying the whole district. Oh! I know what I am saying, the old-fashioned business may go and join the white roses they are throwing on to her coffin."

Denise brought back her uncle and brother in a mourning coach. The day was for her exceedingly dull and melancholy. In the first place, she began to get anxious at Jean's paleness, and when she understood that it was on account of another woman, she tried to quiet him by opening her purse, but he shook his head and refused, saying it was serious this time, the niece of a very rich pastry-cook, who would not accept even a bunch of violets. Afterwards, in the afternoon, when Denise went to fetch Pépé from Madame Gras's, the latter declared that he was getting too big for her to keep any longer; another annoyance, for she would be obliged to find him a school, perhaps send him away. And to crown all she was thoroughly heart-broken, on bringing Pépé back to kiss his aunt and uncle, to see the gloomy sadness of The Old Elbeuf. The shop was closed, and the old couple were at the further end of the little room, where they had forgotten to light the gas, notwithstanding the complete obscurity of this winter's day. They were now quite alone, face to face, in the house, slowly emptied by ruin; and the death of their daughter deepened the shady corners, and was like the supreme cracking which was soon to break up the old rafters, eaten away by the damp. Beneath this destruction, her uncle, unable to stop himself, still kept walking round the table, with his funeral-like step, blind and silent; whilst her aunt said nothing, she had fallen into a chair, with the white face of a wounded person, whose blood was running away drop by drop. They did not even weep when Pépé covered their cold cheeks with kisses. Denise was choked with tears.

That same evening Mouret sent for the young girl to speak of a child's garment he wished to launch forth, a mixture of the Scotch and Zouave costumes. And still trembling with pity, shocked at so much suffering, she could not contain herself; she first ventured to speak of Bourras, of that poor old man whom they were about to ruin. But, on hearing the umbrella maker's name, Mouret flew into a rage at once. The old madman, as he called him, was the plague of his life, and spoilt his triumph by his idiotic obstinacy in not giving up his house, that ignoble hovel which was a disgrace to The Ladies' Paradise, the only little corner of the vast block that escaped his conquest. The matter was becoming a regular nightmare; anyone else but Denise speaking in favor of Bourras would have run the risk of being dismissed immediately, so violently was Mouret tortured by the sickly desire to kick the house down. In short, what did they wish him to do? Could he leave this heap of ruins sticking to The Ladies' Paradise? It would be got rid of, the shop was to pass through it. So much the worse for the old fool! And he spoke of his repeated proposals; he had offered him as much as a hundred thousand francs. Wasn't that fair? He never haggled, he gave the money required; but in return he expected people to be reasonable, and allow him to finish his work! Did anyone ever try to stop the locomotives on a railway? She listened to him, with drooping eyes, unable to find any but purely sentimental reasons. The old man was so old, they might have waited till his death; a failure would kill him. Then he added that he was no longer able to prevent things going their course. Bourdoncle had taken the matter up, for the board had resolved to put an end to it. She had nothing more to add, notwithstanding the grievous pity she felt for her old friend.

After a painful silence, Mouret himself commenced to speak of the Baudus, by expressing his sorrow at the death of their daughter. They were very worthy people, very honest, but had been pursued by the worst of luck. Then he resumed his arguments; at bottom, they had really caused their own misfortune by obstinately sticking to the old ways in their worm-eaten place; it was not astonishing that the place should be falling about their heads. He had predicted it scores of times; she must remember that he had charged her to warn her uncle of a fatal disaster, if the latter still clung to his old-fashioned stupid ways. And the catastrophe had arrived; no one in the world could now prevent it. They could not reasonably expect him to ruin himself to save the neighborhood. Besides, if he had been foolish enough to close The Ladies' Paradise, another big shop would have sprung up of itself next door, for the idea was now starting from the four corners of the globe; the triumph of these manufacturing and industrial cities was sown by the spirit of the times, which was sweeping away the tumbling edifice of former ages. Little by little Mouret warmed up, and found an eloquent emotion with which to defend himself against the hatred of his involuntary victims, the clamor of the small dying shops that was heard around him. They could not keep their dead, he continued, they must bury them; and with a gesture he sent down into the grave, swept away and threw into the common hole the corpse of old-fashioned business, the greenish, poisonous remains of which were becoming a disgrace to the bright, sunlighted streets of new Paris. No, no, he felt no remorse, he was simply doing the work of his age, and she knew it; she, who loved life, who had a passion for big affairs, concluded in the full glare of publicity. Reduced to silence, she listened to him for some time, and then went away, her soul full of trouble.

That night Denise slept but little. A sleeplessness, traversed by nightmare, kept her turning over and over in her bed. It seemed to her that she was quite little, and she burst into tears, in their garden at Valognes, on seeing the blackcaps eat up the spiders, which themselves devoured the flies. Was it then really true, this necessity for the world to fatten on death, this struggle for existence which drove people into the charnel-house of eternal destruction? Afterwards she saw herself before the vault into which they had lowered Geneviève, then she perceived her uncle and aunt in their obscure dining room. In the profound silence, a heavy voice, as of something tumbling down, traversed the dead air; it was Bourras's house giving way, as if undermined by a high tide. The silence recommenced, more sinister than ever, and a fresh rumbling was heard, then another, then another; the Robineaus, the Bédorés, the Vanpouilles, cracked and fell down in their turn, the small shops of the neighborhood were disappearing beneath an invisible pick, with a brusque, thundering noise, as of a tumbrel being emptied. Then an immense pity awoke her with a start. Heavens! what tortures! There were families weeping, old men thrown out into the street, all the poignant dramas that ruin conjures up. And she could save nobody; and she felt that it was right, that all this misery was necessary for the health of the Paris of the future. When day broke she became calmer, a feeling of resigned melancholy kept her awake, turned towards the windows through which the light was making its way. Yes, it was the meed of blood that every revolution exacted from its martyrs, every step forward was made over the bodies of the dead. Her fear of being a wicked girl, of having assisted in the ruin of her fellow-creatures, now melted into a heartfelt pity, in the face of these evils without remedy, which are the painful accompaniment of each generation's birth. She finished by seeking some possible comfort in her goodness, she dreamed of the means to be employed in order to save her relations at least from the final crash.

Mouret now appeared before her with his passionate face and

caressing eyes. He would certainly refuse her nothing; she felt sure he would accord her all reasonable compensation. And her thoughts went astray in trying to judge him. She knew his life, was aware of the calculating nature of his former affections, his continual exploitation of woman, mistresses taken up to further his own ends, and his intimacy with Madame Desforges solely to get hold of Baron Hartmann, and all the others, such as Clara and the rest, pleasure bought, paid for, and thrown out on the pavement. But these beginnings of a love adventurer, which were the talk of the shop, were gradually effaced by the strokes of genius of this man, his victorious grace. He was seduction itself. What she could never have forgiven was his former deception, his lover's coldness under the gallant comedy of his attentions. But she felt herself to be entirely without rancor, now that he was suffering through her. This suffering had elevated him. When she saw him tortured by her refusal, atoning so fully for his former disdain for woman, he seemed to have made amends for all his faults.

That morning Denise obtained from Mouret the compensation she might judge legitimate the day the Baudus and old Bourras should succumb. Weeks passed away, during which she went to see her uncle nearly every afternoon, escaping from her counter for a few minutes, bringing her smiling face and brave courage to enliven the sombre shop. She was especially anxious about her aunt, who had fallen into a dull stupor since Geneviève's death; it seemed that her life was quitting her hourly; and when people spoke to her she would reply with an astonished air that she was not suffering, but that she simply felt as if overcome by sleep. The neighbors shook their heads, saying she would not live long to regret her daughter.

One day Denise was coming out of the Baudus', when, on turning the corner of the Place Gaillon, she heard a loud cry. The crowd rushed forward, a panic arose, that breath of fear and pity which so suddenly seizes a crowd. It was a brown omnibus, belonging to the Bastille-Batignolles line, which had run over a man, coming out of the Rue Neuve-Saint-Augustin, opposite the fountain. Upright on his seat, with furious gestures, the driver was pulling in his two kicking horses, and crying out, in a great passion:

"Confound you! Why don't you look out, you idiot!"

The omnibus had now stopped, and the crowd had surrounded the wounded man, and, strange to say, a policeman was soon on the spot. Still standing up, invoking the testimony of the people on the knife-board, who had also got up, to look over and see the wounded man, the coachman was explaining the matter, with exasperated gestures, choked by his increasing anger.

"It's something fearful. This fellow was walking in the middle of the road, quite at home. I called out, and he at once threw himself under the wheels!"

A house-painter, who had run up, brush in hand, from a neighboring house, then said, in a sharp voice, amidst the clamor: "Don't excite yourself. I saw him, he threw himself under. He jumped in, head first. Another unfortunate tired of life, no doubt."

Others spoke up, and all agreed upon it being a case of suicide, whilst the policeman pulled out his book and made his entry. Several ladies, very pale, got out quickly, and ran away without looking back, filled with horror by the soft shaking which had stirred them up when the omnibus passed over the body. Denise approached, attracted by a practical pity, which prompted her to interest herself in all sorts of street accidents, wounded dogs, horses down, and tillers falling off roofs. And she immediately recognized the unfortunate fellow who had fainted away, his clothes covered with mud.

"It's Monsieur Robineau," cried she, in her grievous astonishment.

The policeman at once questioned the young girl, and she gave his name, profession, and address. Thanks to the driver's energy, the omnibus had twisted round, and thus only Robineau's legs had gone under the wheels, but it was to be feared that they were both broken. Four men carried the wounded draper to a chemist's shop in the Rue Gaillon, whilst the omnibus slowly resumed its journey.

"My stars!" said the driver, whipping up his horses, "I've done a famous day's work."

Denise followed Robineau into the chemist's. The latter, waiting for a doctor who could not be found, declared there was no immediate danger, and that the wounded man had better be taken home, as he lived in the neighborhood. A lad started off to the police-station to order a stretcher, and Denise had the happy thought of going on in front and preparing Madame Robineau for this frightful blow. But she had the greatest trouble in the world to get into the street through the crowd, which was struggling before the door. This crowd, attracted by death, was increasing every minute; men, women, and children stood on tip-toe, and held their own amidst a brutal pushing, and each new-comer had his version of the accident, so that at last it was said to be a husband pitched out of the window by his wife's lover.

In the Rue Neuve-des-Petits-Champs, Denise perceived Madame Robineau on the threshold of the silk warehouse. This gave her a pretext for stopping, and she talked on for a moment, trying to find a way of breaking the terrible news. The shop presented the disorderly, abandoned appearance of the last struggles of a dying business. It was the inevitable end of the great battle of the silks; the Paris Paradise had crushed its rival by a fresh reduction of a sou; it was now sold at four francs nineteen sous, Gaujean's silk had found its Waterloo. For the last two months Robineau, reduced to all sorts of shifts, had been leading a fearful life, trying to prevent a declaration of bankruptcy.

"I've just seen your husband pass through the Place Gaillon," murmured Denise, who had now entered the shop.

Madame Robineau, whom a secret anxiety seemed to be continually attracting towards the street, said quickly: "Ah, just now, wasn't it? I'm waiting for him, he ought to be back; Monsieur Gaujean came up this morning, and they have gone out together."

She was still charming, delicate, and gay; but her advanced state of pregnancy gave her a fatigued look, and she was more frightened, more bewildered than ever, by these business matters, which she did not understand, and which were all going wrong. As she often said, what was the use of it all? Would it not be better to live quietly in some small house, and be contented with modest fare?

"My dear child," resumed she with her smile, which was becoming sadder, "we have nothing to conceal from you. Things are not going on well, and my poor darling is worried to death. Today this Gaujean has been tormenting him about some bills overdue. I was dying with anxiety at being left here all alone."

And she was returning to the door when Denise stopped her, having heard the noise of the crowd and guessing that it was the wounded man being brought along, surrounded by a mob of idlers anxious to see the end of the affair. Then, with a parched throat, unable to find the consoling words she would have wished, she had to explain the matter.

"Don't be anxious, there's no immediate danger. I've seen Monsieur Robineau, he has met with an accident. They are just bringing him home, pray don't be frightened."

The poor woman listened to her, white as a sheet, without clearly understanding. The street was full of people, the drivers of the impeded cabs were swearing, the men had laid down the stretcher before the shop in order to open both glass doors.

"It was an accident," continued Denise, resolved to conceal the attempt at suicide. "He was on the pavement and slipped under the wheels of an omnibus. Only his feet were hurt. They've sent for a doctor. There's no need to be anxious."

A shudder passed over Madame Robineau. She set up an inarticulate cry, then ceased talking and ran to the stretcher, drawing the covering away with her trembling hands. The men who had brought Robineau were waiting to take him away as soon as the doctor arrived. They dared not touch him, who had come round again, and whose sufferings were frightful at the slightest movement. When he saw his wife his eyes filled with tears. She embraced him, and stood looking fixedly at him, and weeping. In the street the tumult was increasing; the people pressed forward as at a theatre, with glistening eyes; some work-girls, escaped from a shop, were almost pushing through the windows eager to see what was going on. In order to avoid this feverish curiosity, and thinking, besides, that it was not right to leave the shop open, Denise decided on letting the metallic shutters down. She went and turned the winch, the wheels of which gave out a plaintive cry, the sheets of iron slowly descended, like the heavy draperies of a curtain falling on the catastrophe of a fifth act. When she went in again, after closing the little round door in the shutters, she found Madame Robineau still clasping her husband in her arms, in the half-light which came from the two stars cut in the shutters. The ruined shop seemed to be gliding into nothingness, the two stars alone glittered on this sudden and brutal catastrophe of the streets of Paris.

At last Madame Robineau recovered her speech. "Oh, my darling!—oh, my darling! my darling!"

This was all she could say, and he, suffocated, confessed himself with a cry of remorse when he saw her kneeling thus before him. When he did not move he only felt the burning lead of his legs.

"Forgive me, I must have been mad. When the lawyer told me before Gaujean that the posters would be put up tomorrow, I saw flames dancing before me as if the walls were burning. After that I remember nothing else. I came down the Rue de la Michodière—it seemed that The Paradise people were laughing at me, that immense house seemed to crush me. So, when the omnibus came up, I thought of Lhomme and his arm, and threw myself underneath the omnibus."

Madame Robineau had slowly fallen on to the floor, horrified by this confession. Heavens! he had tried to kill himself. She seized the hand of her young friend, who leant over towards her quite overcome. The wounded man, exhausted by emotion, had just fainted away again; and the doctor not having arrived, two men went all over the neighborhood for him. The doorkeeper belonging to the house had gone off in his turn to look for him.

"Pray, don't be anxious," repeated Denise, mechanically, herself also sobbing.

Then Madame Robineau, seated on the floor, with her head against the stretcher, her cheek placed on the mattress where her husband was lying, relieved her heart. "Oh! I must tell you. It's all for me he wanted to die. He's always saying, 'I've robbed you; it was not my money.' And at night he dreams of this money, waking up covered with perspiration, calling himself an incapable fellow, saying that those who have no head for business ought not to risk other people's money. You know he has always been nervous, his brain tormented. He finished by conjuring up things that frightened me. He saw me in the street in tatters, begging, his darling wife, whom he loved so tenderly, whom he longed to see rich and happy." But on turning round, she noticed he had opened his eyes; and she continued in a trembling voice: "My darling, why have you done this? You must think me very wicked! I assure you, I don't care if we are ruined. So long as we are together, we shall never be unhappy. Let them take everything, and we will go away somewhere, where you won't hear any more about them. You can still work; you'll see how happy we shall be!"

She placed her forehead near her husband's pale face, and both were silent, in the emotion of their anguish. There was a pause. The shop seemed to be sleeping, benumbed by the pale night which enveloped it; whilst behind the thin shutters could be heard the noises of the street, the life of the busy city, the rumble of the vehicles, and the hustling and pushing of the passing crowd. At last Denise, who went every minute to glance through the hall door, came back, exclaiming: "Here's the doctor!"

He was a young fellow, with bright eyes, whom the doorkeeper had found and brought in. He preferred to examine the poor man before they put him to bed. Only one of his legs, the left one, was broken above the ankle; it was a simple fracture, no serious complication appeared likely to result from it. And they were about to carry the stretcher into the back-room when Gaujean arrived. He came to give them an account of a last attempt to settle matters, an attempt which had failed; the declaration of bankruptcy was definite.

"Dear me," murmured he, "what's the matter?"

In a few words, Denise informed him. Then he stopped, feeling rather awkward, while Robineau said, in a feeble voice: "I don't bear you any ill-will, but all this is partly your fault."

"Well, my dear fellow," replied Gaujean, "it wanted stronger men than us. You know I'm not in a much better state than you."

They raised the stretcher; Robineau still found strength to say: "No, no, stronger fellows than us would have given way as we have. I can understand such obstinate old men as Bourras and Baudu standing out, but you and I, who are young, who had accepted the new style of things! No, Gaujean, it's the last of a world."

They carried him off. Madame Robineau embraced Denise with an eagerness in which there was almost a feeling of joy, to have at last got rid of all those worrying business matters. And, as Gaujean went away with the young girl, he confessed to her that this poor devil of a Robineau was right. It was idiotic to try and struggle against The Ladies' Paradise. He personally felt himself lost, if he did not give in. Last night, in fact, he had secretly made a proposal to Hutin, who was just leaving for Lyons. But he felt very doubtful, and tried to interest Denise in the matter, aware, no doubt, of her powerfulness.

"My word," said he, "so much the worse for the manufacturers! Everyone would laugh at me if I ruined myself in fighting for other people's benefit, when these fellows are struggling who shall make at the cheapest price! As you said some time ago, the manufacturers have only to follow the march of progress by a better organization and new methods. Everything will come all right; it suffices that the public are satisfied."

Denise smiled and replied: "Go and say that to Monsieur Mouret himself. Your visit will please him, and he's not the man to display any rancor, if you offer him even a centime profit per yard."

Madame Baudu died in January, on a bright sunny afternoon. For some weeks she had been unable to go down into the shop that a charwoman now looked after. She was in bed, propped up by the pillows. Nothing but her eyes seemed to be living in her white face, and, her head erect, she kept them obstinately fixed on The Ladies' Paradise opposite, through the small curtains of the windows. Baudu, himself suffering from this obsession, from the despairing fixity of her gaze, sometimes wanted to draw the large curtains to. But she stopped him with an imploring gesture, obstinately desirous of seeing the monster shop till the last moment. It had now robbed her of everything, her business, her daughter; she herself had gradually died away with The Old Elbeuf, losing a part of her life as the shop lost its customers; the day it succumbed, she had no more breath left. When she felt she was dying, she still found the strength to insist on her husband opening the two windows. It was very mild, a bright ray of sun gilded The Ladies' Paradise, whilst the bedroom of their old house shivered in the shade. Madame Baudu lay with her fixed gaze, absorbed by the vision of the triumphal monument, the clear, limpid windows, behind which a gallop of millions was passing. Slowly her eyes grew dim, invaded by darkness; and when they at last sunk in death, they remained wide open, still looking, drowned in tears.

Once more the ruined traders of the district followed the funeral procession. There were the brothers Vanpouille, pale at the thought of their December bills, paid by a supreme effort which they would never be able to repeat. Bédoré, with his sister, leant on his cane, so full of worry and anxiety that his liver complaint was getting worse every day. Deslignières had had a fit, Piot and Rivoire walked on in silence, with downcast looks, like men entirely played out. They dared not question each other about those who had disappeared, Quinette, Mademoiselle Tatin, and others, who were sinking, ruined, swept away by this disastrous flood; without counting Robineau, still in bed, with his broken leg. But they pointed with an especial air of interest to the new tradesmen attacked by the plague; the perfumer Grognet, the milliner Madame Chadeuil, Lacassagne, the flower maker, and Naud, the bootmaker, still standing firm, but seized by the anxiety of the evil, which would doubtless sweep them away in their turn. Baudu walked along behind the hearse with the same heavy, stolid step as when he had followed his daughter; whilst at the back of a mourning coach could be seen Bourras's sparkling eyes under his bushy eyebrows, and his hair of a snowy white.

Denise was in great trouble. For the last fifteen days she had been worn out with fatigue and anxiety; she had been obliged to put Pépé to school, and had been running about for Jean, who was so stricken with the pastry-cook's niece, that he had implored his sister to go and ask her hand in marriage. Then her aunt's death, these repeated catastrophes had quite over-whelmed the young girl. Mouret again offered his services, giv-ing her leave to do what she liked for her uncle and the others. One morning she had an interview with him, at the news that Bourras was turned into the street, and that Baudu was going to shut up shop. Then she went out after breakfast in the hope of comforting these two, at least.

In the Rue de la Michodière, Bourras was standing on the pavement opposite his house, from which he had been expelled the previous day by a fine trick, a discovery of the lawyers; as Mouret held some bills, he had easily obtained an order in bankruptcy against the umbrella-maker; then he had given five hundred francs for the expiring lease at the sale ordered by the court; so that the obstinate old man had allowed himself to be deprived of, for five hundred francs, what he had refused to give up for a hundred thousand. The architect, who came with his gang of workmen, had been obliged to employ the police to get him out. The goods had been taken and sold; but he still kept himself obstinately in the corner where he slept, and from which they did not like to drive him, out of pity. The workmen even attacked the roofing over his head. They had taken off the rotten slates, the ceilings fell in, the walls cracked, and yet he stuck there, under the naked old beams, amidst the ruins of the shop. At last the police came, and he went away. But the follow-ing morning he again appeared on the opposite side of the street, after having spent the night in a lodging-house in the neighborhood.

"Monsieur Bourras!" said Denise, kindly.

He did not hear her, his flaming eyes were devouring the workmen who were attacking the front of the hovel with their picks. Through the empty window-frames could be seen the inside of the house, the miserable rooms, and the black staircase, where the sun had not penetrated for the last two hundred years.

"Ah! it's you," replied he, at last, when he recognized her. "A nice bit of work they're doing, eh? The robbers!"

She did not now dare to speak, stirred up by the lamentable sadness of the old place, herself unable to take her eyes off the moldy stones that were falling. Above, in a corner of the ceiling of her old room, she still perceived the name in black and shaky letters—Ernestine—written with the flame of a candle, and the remembrance of those days of misery came back to her, inspiring her with a tender sympathy for all suffering. But the workmen, in order to knock one of the walls down at a blow, had attacked it at its base. It was tottering.

"Should like to see it crush all of them," growled Bourras, in a savage voice.

There was a terrible cracking noise. The frightened workmen ran out into the street. In falling down, the wall tottered and carried all the house with it. No doubt the hovel was ripe for the fall—it could no longer stand, with its flaws and cracks; a push had sufficed to cleave it from top to bottom. It was a pitiful crumbling away, the razing of a mud-house soddened by the rains. Not a board remained standing; there was nothing on the ground but a heap of rubbish, the dung of the past thrown at the street corner.

"Oh, heavens!" exclaimed the old man, as if the blow had resounded in his very entrails.

He stood there gaping, never supposing it would have been over so quick. And he looked at the gap, the hollow space at last left free on the flanks of The Ladies' Paradise. It was like the crushing of a gnat, the final triumph over the annoying obstinacy of the infinitely small, the whole isle invaded and conquered. The passers-by lingered to talk to the workmen, who were crying out against these old buildings, only good for killing people.

"Monsieur Bourras," repeated Denise, trying to get him on

one side, "you know that you will not be abandoned. All your wants will be provided for."

He held up his head. "I have no wants. You've been sent by them, haven't you? Well, tell them that old Bourras still knows how to work, and that he can find work wherever he likes. Really, it would be a fine thing to offer charity to those they are assassinating!"

Then she implored him: "Pray accept, Monsieur Bourras; don't give me this grief."

But he shook his bushy head. "No, no, it's all over. Good-bye. Go and live happily, you who are young, and don't prevent old people sticking to their ideas."

He cast a last glance at the heap of rubbish, and then went away. She watched him disappear, elbowed by the crowd on the pavement. He turned the corner of the Place Gaillon, and all was over. For a moment, Denise remained motionless, lost in thought. At last she went over to her uncle's. The draper was alone in the dark shop of The Old Elbeuf. The charwoman only came morning and evening to do a little cooking, and to take down and put up the shutters. He spent hours in this solitude, often without being disturbed once during the whole day, bewildered, and unable to find the goods when a stray customer happened to venture in. And there in the half-light he marched about unceasingly, with that heavy step he had at the two funerals, yielding to a sickly desire, regular fits of forced marching, as if he were trying to rock his grief to sleep.

"Are you feeling better, uncle?" asked Denise. He only stopped for a second to glance at her. Then he started off again, going from the pay-desk to an obscure corner.

"Yes, yes. Very well, thanks."

She tried to find some consoling subject, some cheerful remark, but could think of nothing. "Did you hear the noise? The house is down."

"Ah! it's true," murmured he, with an astonished look, "that must have been the house. I felt the ground tremble. Seeing them on the roof this morning, I closed my door."

And he made a vague movement, to imitate that such things

no longer interested him. Every time he arrived before the pay-desk, he looked at the empty seat, that well-known velvet covered seat, where his wife and daughter had grown up. Then when his perpetual walking brought him to the other end, he gazed at the shelves drowned in shadow, in which a few pieces of cloth were gradually growing moldy. It was a widowed house, those he loved had disappeared, his business had come to a shameful end, and he was left alone to commune with his dead heart, and his pride brought low amidst all these catastrophes. He raised his eyes towards the black ceiling, overcome by the sepulchral silence which reigned in the little dining room, the family nook, of which he had formerly loved every part, even down to the stuffy odor. Not a breath was now heard in the old house, his regular heavy step made the ancient walls resound, as if he were walking over the tombs of his affections.

At last Denise approached the subject which had brought her. "Uncle, you can't stay like this. You must come to a decision."

He replied, without stopping his walk—"No doubt; but what would you have me do? I've tried to sell, but no one has come. One of these mornings I shall shut up shop and go off."

She was aware that a failure was no longer to be feared. The creditors had preferred to come to an understanding before such a long series of misfortunes. Everything paid, the old man would find himself in the street, penniless.

"But what will you do, then?" murmured she, seeking some transition in order to arrive at the offer she dared not make.

"I don't know," replied he. "They'll pick me up all right." He had changed his route, going from the dining room to the windows with their lamentable displays, looking at the latter, every time he came to them, with a gloomy expression. His gaze did not even turn towards the triumphal façade of The Ladies' Paradise, whose architectural lines ran as far as the eye could see, to the right and to the left, at both ends of the street. He was thoroughly annihilated, and had not even the strength to get angry.

"Listen, uncle," said Denise, greatly embarrassed; "perhaps there might be a situation for you." She stopped, and stammered. "Yes, I am charged to offer you a situation as inspector."

"Where?" asked Baudu.

"Opposite," replied she; "in our shop. Six thousand francs a year; a very easy place."

Suddenly he stopped in front of her. But instead of getting angry as she feared he would, he turned very pale, succumbing to a grievous emotion, a feeling of bitter resignation.

"Opposite, opposite," stammered he several times. "You want me to go opposite?"

Denise herself was affected by this emotion. She recalled the long struggle of the two shops, assisted at the funerals of Geneviève and Madame Baudu, saw before her The Old Elbeuf overthrown, utterly ruined by The Ladies' Paradise. And the idea of her uncle taking a situation opposite, and walking about in a white necktie, made her heart leap with pity and revolt.

"Come, Denise, is it possible?" said he, simply, wringing his poor trembling hands.

"No, no, uncle," exclaimed she, in a sudden burst of her just and excellent being. "It would be wrong. Forgive me, I beg of you."

He resumed his walk, his step once more broke the funereal silence of the house. And when she left him, he was still going on in that obstinate locomotion of great griefs, which turn round themselves without ever being able to get beyond.

Denise passed another sleepless night. She had just touched the bottom of her powerlessness. Even in favor of her own people she was unable to find any consolation. She had been obliged to assist to the bitter end at this invincible work of life which requires death as its continual seed. She no longer struggled, she accepted this law of combat; but her womanly soul was filled with a weeping pity, with a fraternal tenderness at the idea of suffering humanity. For years, she herself had been caught in the wheel-work of the machine. Had she not bled there? Had they not bruised her, dismissed her, overwhelmed her with insults? Even now she was frightened, when she felt herself chosen by the logic of facts. Why her, a girl so puny? Why should her small hand suddenly become so powerful amidst the monster's work? And the force which was sweeping everything away, carried her away in her turn, she, whose coming was to be a revenge. Mouret had invented this mechanism for crushing the world, and its brutal working shocked her; he had sown ruin all over the neighborhood, despoiled some, killed others; and yet she loved him for the grandeur of his work, she loved him still more at every excess of his power, notwithstanding the flood of tears which overcame her, before the sacred misery of the vanquished.

CHAPTER XIV.

The Rue du Dix-Décembre, looking quite new with its chalk-white houses and the final scaffoldings of some nearly finished buildings, stretched out beneath a clear February sun; a stream of carriages was passing at a rattling pace through this gleam of light, which traversed the damp shadow of the old Saint-Roch quarter; and, between the Rue de la Michodière and the Rue de Choiseul, there was a great tumult, the crushing of a crowd excited by a month's advertising, their eyes in the air, gaping at the monumental façade of The Ladies' Paradise, inaugurated that Monday, on the occasion of a grand show of white goods.

The bright new masonry displayed a vast development of polychromatic architecture, relieved by gildings, announcing the tumult and sparkle of the business inside, and attracting attention like a gigantic window-display all aglow with the liveliest colors. In order not to neutralize the show of goods, the decoration of the ground floor was of a sober description; the base of sea-green marble; the corner pillars and the supporting columns were covered with black marble, the severity of which was relieved by gilded medallions; and the rest of plate-glass, in iron sashes, nothing but glass, which seemed to open up the depths of the halls and galleries to the full light of day. But as the floors ascended, the tones became brighter. The frieze on the ground floor was decorated with a series of mosaics, a garland of red and blue flowers, alternating with marble slabs, on which were cut the names of goods, running all round, encircling the colossus. Then the base of the first floor, made of enameled bricks, supported the large windows, as high as the frieze, formed of gilded escutcheons, with the arms of the towns of France, and designs in terra-cotta, the enamel of which reproduced the bright colored flowers of the base. Then, right at the top, the entablature blossomed forth like the ardent florescence of the entire façade, the mosaics and the faience re-appeared with warmer colorings, the zinc gutters were carved and gilded, while along the acroteria ran a nation of statues, representing the great industrial and manufacturing cities, their delicate silhouettes standing out against the sky. The spectators were especially astonished at the sight of the central door, also decorated with a profusion of mosaics, faience, and terra-cotta, and surmounted by an allegorical group, the new gilding of which glittered in the sun: Woman dressed and kissed by a flight of laughing cupids.

About two o'clock the police were obliged to make the crowd move on, and to look after the carriages. The palace was built, the temple raised to the extravagant folly of fashion. It dominated everything, covering a whole district with its shadow. The scar left on its flank by the demolition of Bourras's hovel had already been so skillfully cicatrized that it would have been impossible to find the place formerly occupied by this old wart—the four façades now ran along the four streets, without a break in their superb isolation. Since Baudu's retirement, The Old Elbeuf, on the other side of the way, had been closed, walled up like a tomb, behind the shutters that were never now taken down; little by little the cab-wheels had splashed them, posters covered them up and pasted them together, a rising tide of advertising, which seemed like the last shovelful of earth thrown over the old-fashioned commerce; and, in the middle of this dead frontage, dirtied by the mud from the street, discolored by the refuse of Paris, was displayed, like a flag planted over a conquered empire, an immense yellow poster, quite wet, announcing in letters two feet high the great sale at The Ladies' Paradise. It was as if the colossus, after each enlargement, seized with shame and repugnance for the black old quarter, where it had modestly sprung up, and that it had later on slaughtered, had just turned its back to it, leaving the mud of the narrow streets in its track, presenting its upstart face to the noisy, sunny thoroughfare of new Paris.

As it was now represented in the engraving of the advertisements, it had grown bigger and bigger, like the ogre of the legend, whose shoulders threatened to pierce the clouds. In the first place, in the foreground of the engraving, were the Rue du Dix-Décembre, the Rue de la Michodière, and the Rue de Choiseul, filled with little black figures, and spread out immoderately, as if to make room for the customers of the whole world. Then came a bird's eye view of the buildings themselves, of an exaggerated immensity, with their roofings which described the covered galleries, the glazed courtyards in which could be recognized the halls, the endless detail of this lake of glass and zinc shining in the sun. Beyond, stretched forth Paris, but Paris diminished, eaten up by the monster: the houses, of a cottage-like humility in the neighborhood of the building, then dying away in a cloud of indistinct chimneys; the monuments seemed to melt into nothing, to the left two dashes for Notre-Dame, to the right a circumflex accent for the Invalides, in the background the Panthéon, ashamed and lost, no larger than a lentil. The horizon, crumbled into powder, became no more than a contemptible frame-work, as far as the heights of Châtillon, out into the open country, the vanishing expanse of which indicated how far reached the state of slavery.

Ever since the morning the crowd had been increasing. No shop had ever yet stirred up the city with such a profusion of advertisements. The Ladies' Paradise now spent nearly six hundred thousand francs a year in posters, advertisements, and appeals of all sorts; the number of catalogues sent away amounted to four hundred thousand, more than a hundred thousand francs' worth of stuff was cut up for patterns. It was a complete invasion of the newspapers, the walls, and the ears of the public, like a monstrous brass trumpet, which, blown incessantly, spread to the four corners of the earth the tumult of the great sales. And, for the future, this façade, before which people were now crowding, became a living advertisement, with its bespangled, gilded magnificence, its windows large enough to display the entire poem of woman's clothing, its profusion of signs, painted, engraved, and cut in stone, from the marble slabs on the ground floor to the sheets of iron rounded off in semicircles above the roof, unfolding their gilded streamers on which the name of the house could be read in letters bright as the sun, standing out against the azure blue of the sky.

To celebrate the inauguration, there had been added trophies and flags; each storey was gay with banners and standards bearing the arms of the principal cities of France; and right at the top, the flags of all nations, run up on masts, fluttered in the air, while the show of cotton and linen goods downstairs assumed in the windows a tone of blinding intensity. Nothing but white, a complete trousseau, and a mountain of sheets to the left, a lot of curtains forming a chapel, and pyramids of handkerchiefs to the right, fatigued the eyes; and, between the hung goods at the door, whole pieces of cotton, calico, and muslin in clusters, like snow-drifts, were planted some dressed engravings, sheets of bluish cardboard, on which a young bride, or a lady in ball costume, both life size and dressed in real lace and silk, smiled with their painted faces. A circle of idlers was constantly forming, a desire arose from the admiration of the crowd.

What caused an increase of curiosity around The Ladies' Paradise was a catastrophe of which all Paris was talking, the burning down of The Four Seasons, the big shop Bouthemont had opened near the Opera-house, hardly three weeks before. The newspapers were full of details, of the fire breaking out through an explosion of gas during the night, the hurried flight of the young ladies in their night-dresses, and the heroic conduct of Bouthemont, who had carried five of them out on his shoulders. The enormous losses were covered, and the people commenced to shrug their shoulders, saying what a splendid advertisement it was. But for the moment attention again flowed back to The Ladies' Paradise, excited by all these stories flying about, occupied to a wonderful extent by these colossal establishments, which by their importance took up such a large place in public life. Wonderfully lucky, this Mouret! Paris saluted her star, and crowded to see him still standing, since the very flames now undertook to sweep all competition from beneath his feet; and the profits of the season were already being calculated, people began to estimate the swollen flood of customers which would be sent into his shop by the forced closing of the rival house. For a moment he had felt anxious, troubled at feeling a jealous woman against him, that Madame Desforges, to whom he owed in a manner his fortune. Baron Hartmann's financial dilettantism, putting money into the two affairs, annoyed him also. Then he was exasperated at having missed a genial idea which had occurred to Bouthemont, who had artfully had his shop blessed by the vicar of the Madeleine, followed by all his clergy; an astonishing ceremony, a religious pomp paraded from the silk department to the glove department, and so on throughout the establishment. This imposing ceremony had not, it is true, prevented everything being destroyed, but had done as much good as a million francs' worth of advertisements, so great an impression had it produced on the fashionable world. From that day, Mouret dreamed of having the archbishop.

The clock over the door was striking three, and the afternoon crush had commenced, nearly a hundred thousand customers were struggling in the various galleries and halls. Outside, the carriages were stationed from one end of the Rue du Dix-Décembre to the other, and over against the Opera-house another compact mass occupied the *cul-de-sac,* where the future avenue was to commence. Common cabs were mingled with private broughams, the drivers waiting amongst the wheels, the rows of horses neighing and shaking their bits, which sparkled in the sun. The lines were incessantly reformed, amidst the calls of the messengers, the pushing of the animals which closed in of their own accord, whilst fresh vehicles were continually arriving and taking their places with the rest. The pedestrians flew on to the refuges in frightened bands, the pavements were black with people, in the receding perspective of the wide and straight thoroughfare. And a clamor arose from between the white houses, this human stream rolled along under the soul of overflowing Paris, a sweet and enormous breath, of which one could feel the giant caress.

Madame de Boves, accompanied by her daughter Blanche and Madame Guibal, was standing, at a window, looking at a display of half made up costumes.

"Oh! do look," said she, "at those print costumes at nineteen francs fifteen sous!"

In their square boxes, the costumes, tied round with a favor, were folded so as to present the trimmings alone, embroidered with blue and red; and, occupying the corner of each box, was an engraving showing the garment made up, worn by a young person looking like some princess.

"But they are not worth more," murmured Madame Guibal. "They fall into rags as soon as you handle them."

They had now become intimate since Monsieur de Boves had been confined to his arm-chair by an attack of gout. The wife put up with the mistress, preferring that things should take place in her own house, for in this way she picked up a little pocket money, sums that the husband allowed himself to be robbed of, having, himself, need of forbearance.

"Well! let's go in," resumed Madame Guibal. "We must see their show. Hasn't your son-in-law made an appointment with you inside?"

Madame de Boves did not reply, entirely absorbed by the string of carriages, which, one by one, opened their doors and let out more customers.

"Yes," said Blanche, at last, in her indolent voice. "Paul is to join us about four o'clock in the reading-room, on leaving the ministry."

They had been married about a month, and Vallagnosc, after a leave of absence of three weeks, spent in the South of France, had just returned to his post. The young woman had already her mother's portly look, and her flesh appeared puffed up and coarser since her marriage.

"But there's Madame Desforges over there!" exclaimed the countess, looking at a brougham that had just arrived.

"Do you think so?" murmured Madame Guibal. "After all those stories! She must still be weeping over the fire at The Four Seasons."

It was really Henriette. On perceiving her friends, she came up with a gay, smiling air, concealing her defeat beneath the fashionable ease of her manner.

"Dear me! yes, I wanted to have a look round. It's better to see for one's self, isn't it? Oh! we are still good friends with Monsieur Mouret, though he is said to be furious since I have interested myself in that rival house. Personally, there is only one thing I cannot forgive him, and that is, to have pushed on the marriage of my protégée, Mademoiselle de Fontenailles, with that Joseph—"

"What! it's done?" interrupted Madame de Boves. "What a horror!"

"Yes, my dear, and solely to annoy us. I know him; he wished to intimate that the daughters of our great families are only fit to marry his shop messengers."

She was getting quite animated. They had all four remained on the pavement, amidst the pushing at the entrance. Little by little, however, the stream carried them in; and they had only to abandon themselves to the current, they passed the door as if lifted up, without being conscious of it, talking louder to make themselves heard. They were now asking each other about Madame Marty; it was said that poor Monsieur Marty, after violent scenes at home, had gone quite mad; he was diving into all the treasures of the earth, exhausting mines of gold, loading tumbrels with diamonds and precious stones.

"Poor fellow!" said Madame Guibal, "he who was always so shabby, with his teacher's humility! And the wife?"

"She's ruining an uncle, now," replied Henriette, "a worthy old man who has gone to live with her, having lost his wife. But she must be here, we shall see her."

A surprise made the ladies stop short. Before them extended the shop, the largest drapery establishment in the world, as the advertisements said. The grand central gallery now ran from end to end, extending from the Rue du Dix-Décembre to the

Rue Neuve-Saint-Augustin; whilst to the right and to the left, like the aisles of a church, ran the Monsigny Gallery and the Michodière Gallery, right along the two streets, without a break. Here and there the halls crossed and formed open spaces amidst the metallic framework of the suspended stairs and flying bridges. The inside arrangements had been all changed: the bargains were now placed on the Rue du Dix-Décembre side, the silk department was in the centre, the glove department occupied the Saint-Augustin Hall at the back; and, from the new grand vestibule, one beheld, on looking up, the bedding department, moved from one end of the second floor to the other. The number of departments now amounted to the enormous figure of fifty; several, quite fresh, were to be inaugurated that very day; others, become too important, had been simply divided, in order to facilitate the sales; and, owing to this continual increase of business, the staff had been increased to three thousand and forty-five employees.

What caused the ladies to stop was the prodigious spectacle of the grand exhibition of white goods. In the first place, there was the vestibule, a hall with bright mirrors, paved with mosaics, where the low-priced goods detained the voracious crowd. Then there were the galleries, plunged in a glittering blaze of light, a borealistic vista, quite a country of snow, revealing the endless steppes hung with ermine, the accumulation of icebergs shimmering in the sun. One found there the whiteness of the outside windows, but vivified, colossal, burning from one end of the enormous building to the other, with the white flame of a fire in full swing. Nothing but white goods, all the white articles from each department, a riot of white, a white star, the twinkling of which was at first blinding, so that the details could not be distinguished amidst this unique whiteness. But the eye soon became accustomed to it; to the left, in the Monsigny Gallery, jutted out the white promontories of cotton and calico, the white rocks formed of sheets, napkins, and handkerchiefs; whilst to the right, in the Michodière Gallery, occupied by the mercery, the hosiery, and the woollen goods, were exposed constructions of mother of pearl buttons, a pretty decoration composed of white socks, one whole room covered with white swan-skin, traversed in the distance by a stream of light. But the brightness shone with especial brilliancy in the central gallery, amidst the ribbons and the cravats, the gloves and the silks. The counters disappeared beneath the whiteness of the silks, the ribbons, and the gloves.

Round the iron columns were twined flounces of white muslin, looped up now and again with white silk handkerchiefs. The staircases were decorated with white drapings, quiltings and dimities alternating along the balustrades, encircling the halls as high as the second storey; and this tide of white assumed wings, hurried off and lost itself, like a flight of swans. And the white hung from the arches, a fall of down, a snowy sheet of large flakes; white counterpanes, white coverlets floated about in the air, suspended like banners in a church; long jets of Maltese lace hung across, seeming to suspend swarms of white butterflies; other lace fluttered about on all sides, floating like fleecy clouds in a summer sky, filling the air with their clear breath. And the marvel, the altar of this religion of white was, above the silk counter, in the great hall, a tent formed of white curtains, which fell from the glazed roof. The muslin, the gauze, the lace flowed in light ripples, whilst very richly embroidered tulles, and pieces of oriental silk striped with silver, served as a background to this giant decoration, which partook of the tabernacle and of the alcove. It made one think of a broad white bed, awaiting in its virginal immensity the white princess, as in the legend, she who was to come one day, all powerful, with the bride's white veil.

"Oh! extraordinary!" repeated the ladies. "Wonderful!" They never tired of this song in praise of white that the goods of the entire establishment were singing. Mouret had never conceived anything more extraordinary; it was the master stroke of his genius for display. Beneath the flow of all this whiteness, in the apparent disorder of the tissues, fallen as if by chance from the open drawers, there was a harmonious phrase, the white followed up and developed in all its tones, springing into existence, growing, and blossoming forth with the complicated orchestration of a master's fugue, the continual development of which carries away the mind in an ever-increasing flight. Nothing but white, and never the same goods, all styles outvying with, opposing, and completing one another, attaining the very brilliancy of light itself. Starting from the dull shades of the calico and linen, and the heavy shades of the flannel and cloth, there then came the velvet, silk, and satin goods—quite an ascending gamut, the white gradually lighted up, finishing in little flames at the breaks of the folds; and the white flew away in the transparencies of the curtains, becoming free and clear with the muslin, the lace, and above all the tulle, so light and airy that it was like the extreme and last note; whilst the silver of the oriental silk sung higher than all in the depths of the giant alcove.

The place was full of life. The lifts were besieged with people, there was a crush at the refreshment-bar and in the reading-room, quite a nation was moving about in these regions covered with the snowy fabrics. And the crowd seemed to be black, like skaters on a Polish lake in December. On the ground floor there was a heavy swell, agitated by a reflux, in which could be distinguished nothing but the delicate and enraptured faces of the women. In the chisellings of the iron framework, along the staircases, on the flying bridges, there was an endless procession of small figures, as if lost amidst the snowy peaks of a mountain. A suffocating hot-house heat surprised one on these frozen heights. The buzz of voices made a great noise like a rushing stream. Up above, the profusion of gildings, the glazed work picked out with gold, and the golden roses seemed like a ray of the sun shining on the Alps of the grand exhibition of white goods.

"Come," said Madame de Boves, "we must go forward. It's impossible to stay here."

Since she came in, Jouve, the inspector, standing near the door, had not taken his eyes off her; and when she turned round she encountered his gaze. Then, as she resumed her walk, he let her get a little in front, but followed her at a distance, without, however, appearing to take any further notice of her.

"Ah!" said Madame Guibal, stopping again as she came to the first pay-desk, "it's a pretty idea, these violets!"

She referred to the new present made by The Ladies' Paradise, one of Mouret's ideas, which was making a great noise in the newspapers; small bouquets of white violets, bought by thousands at Nice and distributed to every customer buying the smallest article. Near each pay-desk were messengers in uniform, delivering the bouquets under the supervision of an inspector. And gradually all the customers were decorated in this way, the shop was filling with these white flowers, every woman becoming the bearer of a penetrating perfume of violets.

"Yes," murmured Madame Desforges, in a jealous voice, "it's not a bad idea."

But, just as they were going away, they heard two shopmen joking about these violets. A tall, thin fellow was expressing his astonishment: the marriage between the governor and the first-hand in the costume department was coming off, then? Whilst a short, fat fellow replied that he didn't know, but that the flowers were bought at any rate.

"What!" exclaimed Madame de Boves, "Monsieur Mouret is going to marry?"

"That's the latest news," replied Madame Desforges, affecting the greatest indifference. "Of course, he's sure to end like that."

The countess shot a quick glance at her new friend. They both now understood why Madame Desforges had come to The Ladies' Paradise notwithstanding her rupture with Mouret. No doubt she yielded to the invincible desire to see and to suffer.

"I shall stay with you," said Madame Guibal, whose curiosity was awakened. "We shall meet Madame de Boves again in the reading-room."

"Very good," replied the latter. "I want to go on the first floor. Come along, Blanche." And she went up followed by her daughter, whilst Jouve, the inspector, still on her track, ascended by another staircase, in order not to attract attention. The two other ladies were soon lost in the compact crowd on the ground floor.

All the counters were talking of nothing else but the governor's love affairs, amidst the press of business. The adventure, which had for months been occupying the employees, delighted

406 : ÉMILE ZOLA

at Denise's long resistance, had all at once come to a crisis; it had become known that the young girl intended to leave The Ladies' Paradise, notwithstanding all Mouret's entreaties, under the pretext of requiring rest. And the opinions were divided. Would she leave? Would she stay? Bets of five francs circulated from department to department that she would leave the following Sunday. The knowing ones staked a lunch on the final marriage; however, the others, those who believed in her departure, did not risk their money without good reasons. Certainly the little girl had the strength of an adored woman who refuses, but the governor, on his side, was strong in his wealth, his happy widowerhood, and his pride which a last exaction might exasperate. Nevertheless, they were all of opinion that this little saleswoman had carried on the business with the science of a *rouée*, full of genius, and that she was playing the supreme stake in thus offering him this bargain: Marry me or I go away.

Denise, however, thought but little of these things. She had never imposed any conditions or made any calculation. And the reason of her departure was the result of this very judgment of her conduct, which caused her continual surprise. Had she wished for all this? Had she shown herself artful, coquettish, ambitious? No, she had come simply, and was the first to feel astonished at inspiring this passion. And again, now, why did they ascribe her resolution to quit The Ladies' Paradise to craftiness? It was so natural! She began to feel a nervous uneasiness, an intolerable anguish, amidst this continual gossip which was going on in the house, Mouret's feverish pursuit of her, and the combats she was obliged to engage in against herself; and she preferred to go away, seized with fear lest she might one day yield and regret it forever afterwards. If there were in this any learned tactics, she was totally ignorant of it, and she asked herself in despair what was to be done to avoid appearing to be running after a husband. The idea of a marriage now irritated her, and she resolved to say no, and still no, in case he should push his folly to that extent. She alone ought to suffer. The necessity for the separation caused her tears to flow, but she told herself, with her great courage, that it was necessary, that she would have no rest or happiness if she acted in any other way.

When Mouret received her resignation, he remained mute and cold, in the effort which he made to contain himself. Then he replied that he granted her a week's reflection, before allowing her to commit such a stupid act. At the expiration of the week, when she returned to the subject, and expressed a strong wish to go away after the great sale, he said nothing further, but affected to talk the language of reason to her: she had little or no fortune, she would never find another position equal to that she was leaving. Had she another situation in view? If so, he was quite prepared to offer her the advantages she expected to obtain elsewhere. And the young girl having replied that she had not looked for any other situation, that she intended to take a rest at Valognes, thanks to the money she had already saved, he asked her what would prevent her returning to The Ladies' Paradise if her health alone were the reason of her departure. She remained silent, tortured by this cross-examination. He at once imagined that she was about to join a lover, a future husband perhaps. Had she not confessed to him one evening that she loved someone? From that moment he carried deep in his heart, like the stab of a knife, this confession wrung from her in an hour of trouble. And if this man was to marry her, she was giving up all to follow him: that explained her obstinacy. It was all over, and he simply added in his icy tones, that he would detain her no longer, since she could not tell him the real cause of her leaving. These harsh words, free from anger, affected her far more than the anger she had feared.

Throughout the week that Denise was obliged to spend in the shop, Mouret kept his rigid paleness. When he crossed the departments, he affected not to see her, never had he seemed more indifferent, more buried in his work; and the bets began again, only the brave ones dared to back the marriage. However, beneath this coldness, so unusual with him, Mouret concealed a frightful crisis of indecision and suffering. Fits of anger brought the blood to his head: he saw red, he dreamed of taking Denise in a close embrace, keeping her, and stifling her cries. Then he tried to reason with himself, to find some practical means of preventing her going away; but he constantly ran up against his powerlessness, the uselessness of his power and money. An idea, however, was growing amidst his mad projects, and gradually imposing itself, notwithstanding his revolt. After Madame Hédouin's death he had sworn never to marry again; deriving from a woman his first good fortune, he resolved in future to draw his fortune from all women. It was with him, as with Bourdoncle, a superstition that the head of a great drapery establishment should be single, if he wished to retain his masculine power over the growing desires of his world of customers; the introduction of a woman changed the air, drove away the others, by bringing her own odor. And he still resisted the invincible logic of facts, preferring to die rather than yield, seized with sudden bursts of fury against Denise, feeling that she was the revenge, fearing he should fall vanquished over his millions, broken like a straw by the eternal feminine force, the day he should marry her. Then he slowly became cowardly again, dismissing his repugnance; why tremble? She was so sweet-tempered, so prudent, that he could abandon himself to her without fear. Twenty times an hour the battle recommenced in his distracted mind. His pride tended to aggravate the wound, and he completely lost his reason when he thought that, even after this last submission, she might still say no, if she loved another. The morning of the great sale, he had still not decided on anything, and Denise was to leave the next day.

When Bourdoncle, on the day in question, entered Mouret's office about three o'clock, according to custom, he surprised him sitting with his elbows on the desk, his hands over his eyes, so greatly absorbed that he had to touch him on the shoulder. Mouret glanced up, his face bathed in tears; they both looked at each other, held out their hands, and a hearty grip was exchanged between these two men who had fought so many commercial battles side by side. For the past month Bourdoncle's attitude had completely changed; he now bowed before Denise, and even secretly pushed the governor on to a marriage with her.

No doubt he was thus maneuvering to save himself being swept away by a force which he now recognized as superior. But there could have been found at the bottom of this change the awakening of an old ambition, the timid and gradually growing hope to swallow up in his turn this Mouret, before whom he had so long bowed. This was in the air of the house, in this struggle for existence, of which the continued massacres warmed up the business around him. He was, carried away by the working of the machine, seized by the others' appetites, by that voracity which, from top to bottom, drove the lean ones to the extermination of the fat ones. But a sort of religious fear, the religion of chance, had up to that time prevented him making the attempt. And the governor was becoming childish, drifting into a ridiculous marriage, ruining his luck, destroying his charm with the customers. Why should he dissuade him from it, when he could so easily take up the business of this played-out man, fallen into the arms of a woman? Thus it was with the emotion of an adieu, the pity of an old friendship, that he shook his chief's hand, saying:

"Come, come, courage! Marry her, and finish the matter."

Mouret already felt ashamed of his moment of cowardice, and got up, protesting: "No, no, it's too stupid. Come, let's take our turn round the shop. Things are looking well, aren't they? I fancy we shall have a magnificent day."

They went out and commenced their afternoon inspection through the crowded departments. Bourdoncle cast oblique glances at him, anxious at this last display of energy, watching his lips to catch the least sign of suffering. The business was in fact throwing forth its fire, in an infernal roar, which made the house tremble with the violent shaking of a big steamer going at full speed. At Denise's counter were a crowd of mothers dragging along their little girls and boys, swamped beneath the garments they were trying on. The department had brought out all its white articles, and there, as everywhere else, was a riot of white, enough to dress in white a troop of shivering cupids, white cloth cloaks, white piques and cashmere dresses, sailor costumes, and even white Zouave costumes. In the centre, for the sake of the effect, and although the season had not arrived, was a display of communion costumes, the white muslin dress and veil, the white satin shoes, a light gushing florescence, which, planted there, produced the effect of an enormous bouquet of innocence and candid delight. Madame Bourdelais was there with her three children, Madeleine, Edmond, Lucien, seated according to their size, and was getting angry with the latter, the smallest, because he was struggling with Denise, who was trying to put a woollen muslin jacket on him.

"Keep still, Lucien! Don't you think it's rather tight, mademoiselle?" And with the sharp look of a woman difficult to deceive, she examined the stuff, studied the cut, and scrutinized the stitching. "No, it fits well," she resumed. "It's no trifle to dress all these little ones. Now I want a mantle for this young lady."

Denise had been obliged to assist in serving during the busy moments of the day. She was looking for the mantle required, when she set up a cry of surprise.

"What! It's you; what's the matter?"

Her brother Jean, holding a parcel in his hand, was standing before her. He had married a week before, and on the Saturday his wife, a dark little woman, with a provoking, charming face, had paid a long visit to The Ladies' Paradise to make some purchases. The young people were to accompany Denise to Valognes, a regular marriage trip, a month's holiday, which would remind them of old times.

"Just imagine," said he, "Therese has forgotten a lot of things. There are some articles to be changed, and others to be bought. So, as she was in a hurry, she sent me with this parcel. I'll explain—"

But she interrupted him on perceiving Pépé, "What; Pépé as well! and his school?"

"Well," said Jean, "after dinner on Sunday I had not the heart to take him back. He will go back this evening. The poor child is very downhearted at being shut up in Paris whilst we are enjoying ourselves at home."

Denise smiled on them, in spite of her suffering. She handed over Madame Bourdelais to one of her young ladies, and came back to them in a corner of the department, which was, fortunately, getting deserted. The little ones, as she still called them, had now grown to be big fellows. Pépé, twelve years old, was already taller and bigger than her, still silent and living on caresses, of a charming, cajoling sweetness; whilst Jean, broad-shouldered, was quite a head taller than his sister, and still possessed his feminine beauty, with his blonde hair blowing about in the wind. And she, always slim, no fatter than a sky-lark, as she said, still retained her anxious motherly authority over them, treating them as children wanting all her attention, buttoning up Jean's coat so that he should not look like a rake, and seeing that Pépé had got a clean handkerchief. When she saw the latter's swollen eyes, she gently chided him.

"Be reasonable, my boy. Your studies cannot be interrupted. I'll take you away at the holidays. Is there anything you want? But perhaps you prefer to have the money." Then she turned towards the other. "You, youngster, yet making him believe we are going to have wonderful fun. Just try and be a little more careful."

She had given Jean four thousand francs, half of her savings, to enable him to set up housekeeping. The younger one cost her a great deal for schooling, all her money went for them, as in for-mer days. They were her sole reason for living and working, for she had again declared she would never marry.

"Well, here are the things," resumed Jean. "In the first place, there's a cloak in this parcel that Therese—"

But he stopped, and Denise, on turning round to see what had frightened him, perceived Mouret behind them. For a moment he had stood looking at her in her motherly attitude between the two big boys, scolding and embracing them, turning them round as mothers do babies when changing their clothes. Bour-doncle had remained on one side, appearing to be interested in the business, but he did not lose sight of this little scene.

"They are your brothers, are they not?" asked Mouret, after a silence.

He had the icy tone and rigid attitude, which he now assumed with her. Denise herself made an effort to remain cold and un-concerned. Her smile died away, and she replied: "Yes, sir. I've married off the eldest, and his wife has sent him for some purchases."

Mouret continued looking at the three of them. At last he said: "The youngest has grown very much. I recognize him, I remember having seen him in the Tuileries Gardens one evening with you."

And his voice, which was becoming moderate, slightly trembled. She, suffocating, bent down, pretending to arrange Pépé's belt. The two brothers, who had turned scarlet, stood smiling on their sister's master.

"They're very much like you," said the latter.

"Oh!" exclaimed she, "they're much handsomer than I am!"

For a moment he seemed to be comparing their faces. How she loved them! And he walked a step or two; then returned and whispered in her ear: "Come to my office after business, I want to speak to you before you go away."

This time Mouret went off and continued his inspection. The battle was once more raging within him, for the appointment he had given caused him a sort of irritation. To what idea had he yielded on seeing her with her brothers? It was maddening to think he could no longer find the strength to assert his will. However, he could settle it by saying a word of adieu. Bourdoncle, who had rejoined him, seemed less anxious, though he was still examining him with stealthy glances.

Meanwhile, Denise had returned to Madame Bourdelais. "How are you getting on with the mantle, madame?"

"Oh, very well. I've spent enough for one day. These little ones are ruining me!"

Denise now being able to slip away, went and listened to Jean's explanations, then accompanied him to the various counters, where he would certainly have lost his head without her. First came the mantle, which Therese wished to change for a white cloth cloak, same size, same shape. And the young girl, having taken the parcel, went up to the ready-made department, followed by her two brothers.

The department had laid out its light colored garments, summer jackets and mantillas, of light silk and fancy woollens. But there was little doing here, the customers were but few and far between. Nearly all the young ladies were new-comers. Clara had disappeared a month before, some said she had eloped with the husband of one of the saleswomen, others that she had gone on the streets. As for Marguerite, she was at last about to take the management of the little shop at Grenoble, where her cousin was waiting for her. Madame Aurélie remained immutable, in the round cuirass of her silk dress, with her imperial mask which retained the yellowish puffiness of an antique marble. Her son Albert's bad conduct was a source of great trouble to her, and she would have retired into the country had it not been for the inroads made on the family savings by this scapegrace, whose terrible extravagance threatened to swallow up piece by piece their Rigolles property. It was a sort of punishment for their home broken up, for the mother had resumed her little excursions with her lady friends, and the father on his side continued his musical performances. Bourdoncle was already looking upon Madame Aurélie with a discontented air, surprised that she had not the tact to resign; too old for business! the knell was about to sound which would sweep away the Lhomme dynasty.

"Ah! it's you," said she to Denise, with an exaggerated amiability. "You want this cloak changed, eh? Certainly, at once. Ah! there are your brothers; getting quite men, I declare!"

In spite of her pride, she would have gone on her knees to pay her court to the young girl. Nothing else was being talked of in her department, as in the others, but Denise's departure; and the first-hand was quite ill over it, for she had been reckoning on the protection of her former saleswoman. She lowered her voice: "They say you're going to leave us. Really, it isn't possible?"

"But it is, though," replied Denise.

Marguerite was listening. Since her marriage had been decided on, she had marched about with her putty-looking face, assuming more disdainful airs than ever. She came up saying: "You are quite right. Self-respect above everything, I say. Allow me to bid you adieu, my dear."

Some customers arriving at that moment, Madame Aurélie requested her, in a harsh voice, to attend to business. Then, as Denise was taking the cloak to effect the "return" herself, she protested, and called an auxiliary. This, again, was an innovation suggested to Mouret by the young girl—persons charged with carrying the articles, which relieved the saleswomen of a great burden.

"Go with Mademoiselle Denise," said the first-hand, giving her the cloak. Then, returning to Denise: "Pray consider well. We are all heart-broken at your leaving."

Jean and Pépé, who were waiting, smiling amidst this over-flowing crowd of women, followed their sister. They now had to go to the under-linen department, to get four chemises like the half-dozen that Therese had bought on the Saturday. But there, where the exhibition of white goods was snowing down from every shelf, they were almost stifled, and found it very difficult to get past.

In the first place, at the stay counter a little scene was causing a crowd to collect. Madame Boutarel, who had arrived in Paris this time with her husband and daughter, had been wandering all about the shop since the morning collecting an outfit for the young lady, who was about to be married. The father was con-sulted every moment, and they never appeared likely to finish. At last the family had just stranded here; and whilst the young lady was absorbed in a profound study of some drawers, the mother had disappeared, having cast her coquettish eyes on a delicious pair of stays. When Monsieur Boutarel, a big, full-blooded man, left his daughter, bewildered, to go and look for his wife, he at last found her in a fitting-room, at the door of which he was politely invited to take a seat. These rooms were like narrow cells, glazed with ground glass, where the men, and even the husbands, were not allowed to enter, by an exaggerated sentiment of propriety on the part of the directors. Saleswomen came out and went in again quickly, allowing those outside to divine, by the rapid closing of the door, visions of ladies in their petticoats, with bare arms and shoulders—stout women with white flesh, and thin ones with flesh the color of old ivory. A row of men were waiting outside, seated on armchairs, and looking very weary. Monsieur Boutarel, when he understood, got really angry, crying out that he wanted his wife, that he insisted on knowing what was going on inside, that he certainly would not allow her to undress without him. It was in vain that they tried to calm him; he seemed to think there were some very queer things going on inside. Madame Boutarel was obliged to come out, to the delight of the crowd, who were discussing and laughing over the affair.

Denise and her brothers were at last able to get past. Every article of female linen, all those white under-things that are usually concealed, were here displayed, in a suite of rooms, classed in various departments. The corsets and dress-improvers occupied one counter, there were the stitched corsets, the Duchesse, the cuirass, and, above all, the white silk corsets, dove-tailed with colors, forming for this day a special display; an army of dummies without heads or legs, nothing but the bust, dolls' breasts flattened under the silk, and close by, on other dummies, were horse-hair and other dress improvers, prolonging these broomsticks into enormous, distended croups, of which the profile assumed a ludicrous unbecomingness. But afterwards commenced the gallant dishabille, a dishabille which strewed the vast rooms, as if an army of lovely girls had undressed themselves from department to department, down to the very satin of their skin. Here were articles of fine linen, white cuffs and cravats, white fichus and collars, an infinite variety of light gewgaws, a white froth which escaped from the drawers and ascended like so much snow. There were jackets, little bodices, morning dresses and peignoirs, linen, nansouck, lace, long white garments, roomy and thin, which spoke of the lounging in a lazy morning after a night of tenderness. Then appeared the undergarments, falling one by one; the white petticoats of all lengths, the petticoat that clings to the knees, and the long petticoat with which the gay ladies sweep the pavement, a rising sea of petticoats, in which the legs were drowned; cotton, linen, and cambric drawers, large white drawers in which a man could dance; lastly, the chemises, buttoned at the neck for the night, or displaying the bosom in the day, simply supported by narrow shoulder-straps; chemises in all materials, common calico, Irish linen, cambric, the last white veil slipping from the panting bosom and hips.

And, at the outfitting counter, there was an indiscreet unpacking, women turned round and viewed on all sides, from the small housewife with her common calicoes, to the rich lady drowned in laces, an alcove publicly open, of which, the concealed luxury, the plaitings, the embroideries, the Valenciennes lace, became a sort of sexual depravation, as it developed into costly fantasies. Woman was dressing herself again, the white wave of this fall of linen was returning again to the shivering mystery of the petticoats, the chemise stiffened by the fingers of the workwomen, the frigid drawers retaining the creases of the box, all this cambric and muslin, dead, scattered over the counters, thrown about, heaped up, was going to become living, with the life of the flesh, odorous and warm with the odor of love, a white cloud become sacred, bathed in night, and of which the least flutter, the pink of a knee disclosed through the whiteness, ravaged the world. Then there was another room devoted to the baby linen, where the voluptuous snowy whiteness of woman's clothing developed into the chaste whiteness of the infant: an innocence, a joy, the young wife become a mother, flannel garments, chemises and caps large as doll's things, baptismal dresses, cashmere pelisses, the white down of birth, like a fine shower of white feathers.

"They are embroidered chemises," said Jean, who was delighted with this display, this rising tide of feminine attire into which he was plunging.

Pauline ran up at once, when she perceived Denise; and before even asking what she wanted, began to talk in a low tone, stirred up by the rumors circulating in the shop. In her department, two saleswomen had even got quarrelling, one affirming and the other denying her departure.

"You'll stay with us, I'll stake my life. What would become of me?" And as Denise replied that she intended to leave the next day. "No, no, you think so, but I know better. You must appoint me second-hand, now that I've got a baby. Baugé is reckoning on it, my dear."

Pauline smiled with an air of conviction. She then gave the six chemises; and, Jean having said that he was now going to the handkerchief counter, she called an auxiliary to carry the chemises and the jacket left by the auxiliary from the ready-made department. The girl who happened to answer was Mademoiselle de Fontenailles, recently married to Joseph. She had just obtained this menial situation as a great favor, and she wore a long black blouse, marked on the shoulder with a number in yellow wool.

"Follow this young lady," said Pauline. Then returning, and again lowering her voice: "It's understood that I am to be appointed second-hand, eh?"

Denise, troubled, defended herself; but at last promised, with a laugh, joking in her turn. And she went away, going down with Jean and Pépé, and followed by the auxiliary. On the ground floor, they fell into the woollen department, a corner of a gallery entirely hung with white swan-skin cloth and white flannel. Liénard, whom his father had vainly recalled to Angers, was talking to the handsome Mignot, now a traveler, and who had boldly reappeared at The Ladies' Paradise. No doubt they were speaking of Denise, for they both stopped talking to bow to her with a ceremonious air. In fact, as she went along through the departments the salesmen appeared full of emotion and bent their heads before her, uncertain of what she might be the next day. They whispered, thought she looked triumphant, and the betting was again altered; they began to risk bottles of wine, etc., over the event. She had gone through the linen gallery, in order to get to the handkerchief counter, which was at the further end. They saw nothing but white goods: cottons, madapolams, muslins, etc.; then came the linen, in enormous piles, ranged in alternate pieces like blocks of stone, stout linen, fine linen, of all sizes, white and unbleached, pure flax, whitened in the sun; then the same thing commenced once more, there were departments for each sort of linen: house linen, table linen, kitchen linen, a continual fall of white goods, sheets, pillow-cases, innumerable styles of napkins, aprons, and dusters. And the bowing continued, they made way for Denise to pass, Baugé had rushed out to

smile on her, as the good fairy of the house. At last, after crossing the counterpane department, a room hung with white banners, she arrived at the handkerchief counter, the ingenious
decoration of which delighted the crowd; there were nothing
but white columns, white pyramids, white castles, a complicated
architecture, solely composed of handkerchiefs, cambric, Irish
linen, China silk, marked, embroidered by hand, trimmed with
lace, hemstitched, and woven with vignettes, an entire city, built
of white bricks, of infinite variety, standing out in a mirage
against an Eastern sky, warmed to a white heat.

"You say another dozen?" asked Denise of her brother.

"Yes, like this one," replied he, showing a handkerchief in his
parcel.

Jean and Pépé had not quitted her side, clinging to her, as they
had done formerly, on arriving in Paris, knocked up by the journey.
This vast shop, in which she was quite at home, seemed to trouble
them, and they sheltered themselves in her shadow, placing themselves under the protection of their second mother by an instinctive awakening of their infancy. People watched them as they
passed, smiling at the two big fellows following in the footsteps of
this grave thin girl; Jean frightened with his beard, Pépé bewildered in his tunic, all three of the same fair complexion, a fairness
which caused the whisper from one end of the counters to the
other: "They are her brothers! They are her brothers!"

But whilst Denise was looking for a saleswoman there was a
meeting. Mouret and Bourdoncle entered the gallery; and as the
former again stopped in front of the young girl, without, however, speaking to her, Madame Desforges and Madame Guibal
passed by. Henriette suppressed the shiver which had invaded
her whole being; she looked at Mouret and then at Denise. They
had also looked at her, and it was a sort of mute catastrophe,
the common end of these great dramas of the heart, a glance
exchanged in the crush of a crowd. Mouret had already gone
off, whilst Denise lost herself in the depths of the department,
accompanied by her brothers, still in search of a disengaged
salesman. But Henriette having recognized Mademoiselle de
Fontenailles, in the auxiliary following Denise, with a yellow

number on her shoulder, and her coarse, cadaverous, servant's-looking face, relieved herself by saying to Madame Guibal, in a trembling voice:

"Just see what he's doing with that unfortunate girl. Isn't it shameful? A marchioness! And he makes her follow like a dog the creatures picked up by him in the street!" She tried to calm herself, adding, with an affected air of indifference: "Let's go and see their display of silks."

The silk department was like a great chamber of love, hung with white by the caprice of some snowy maiden wishing to show off her spotless whiteness. All the milky tones of an adored person were there, from the velvet of the hips, to the fine silk of the thighs and the shining satin of the bosom. Pieces of velvet hung from the columns, silk and satins stood out, on this white creamy ground, in draperies of a metallic and porcelain-like whiteness: and falling in arches were also poult and gros grain silks, light foulards, and surahs, which varied from the heavy white of a Norwegian blonde to the transparent white, warmed by the sun, of an Italian or a Spanish beauty.

Favier was just then engaged in measuring some white silk for "the pretty lady," that elegant blonde, a frequent customer at the counter, and whom the salesmen never referred to except by this name. She had dealt at the shop for years, and yet they knew nothing about her—neither her life, her address, and not even her name. None of them tried to find out, although they all indulged in supposition every time she made her appearance, but simply for something to talk about. She was getting thinner, she was getting stouter, she had slept well, or she must have been out late the previous night—such were the remarks made about her: thus every little fact of her unknown life, outside events, domestic dramas, were in this way reproduced and commented on. That day she seemed very gay. So, on returning from the pay-desk where he had conducted her, Favier remarked to Hutin:

"Perhaps she's going to marry again."

"What! is she a widow?" asked the other.

"I don't know; but you must remember that she was in mourning the last time she came. Unless she's made some money by speculating on the Bourse." A silence ensued. At last he ended by saying: "But that's her business. It wouldn't do to take notice of all the women we see here."

But Hutin was looking very thoughtful, having had, two days ago, a warm discussion with the direction, and feeling himself condemned. After the great sale his dismissal was certain. For a long time he had felt his position giving way; at the last stock-taking they had complained of his being below the amount of business fixed on in advance; and it was also, in fact chiefly, the slow working of the appetites that were swallowing him up in his turn—the whole silent war of the department, amidst the very motion of the machine. Favier's obscure mining could be perceived—a deadened sound as of jaw-bones working under the earth. The latter had already received the promise of the first-hand's place. Hutin, who was aware of all this, instead of attacking his old comrade, looked upon him as a clever fellow—a fellow who had always appeared so cold, so obedient, whom he had made use of to turn out Robineau and Bouthemont! He was full of a feeling of mingled surprise and respect.

"By the way," resumed Favier, "she's going to stay, you know. The governor has just been seen casting sheep's eyes at her. I shall be let in for a bottle of champagne over it."

He referred to Denise. The gossip was going on more than ever, from one counter to the other, across the constantly increasing crowd of customers. The silk sellers were especially excited, for they had been taking heavy bets about it.

"By Jove!" exclaimed Hutin, waking up as if from a dream, "wasn't I a flat not to have slept with her! I should be all right now!"

Then he blushed at this confession on seeing Favier laughing. He pretended to laugh also, and added, to recall his words, that it was this creature that had ruined him with the management. However, a desire for violence seizing him, he finished by getting into a rage with the salesmen disbanded under the assault of the customers. But all at once he resumed his smile, having just perceived Madame Desforges and Madame Guibal slowly crossing the department.

"What can we serve you with today, madame?"

"Nothing, thanks," replied Henriette. "You see I'm merely walking round; I've only come out of curiosity."

When he had stopped her, he lowered his voice. Quite a plan was springing up in his head. And he flattered her, running down the house; he had had enough of it, and preferred going away to assisting at such a scene of disorder. She listened to him, delighted. It was she herself who, thinking to get him away from The Ladies' Paradise, offered to have him engaged by Bouthemont as first-hand in the silk department, when The Four Seasons started again. The matter was settled in whispers, whilst Madame Guibal interested herself in the displays.

"May I offer you one of these bouquets of violets?" resumed Hutin, aloud, pointing to a table where there were four or five bunches of the flowers, which he had procured from the pay-desk for personal presents.

"Ah, no!" exclaimed Henriette, with a backward movement. "I don't wish to take any part in the wedding."

They understood each other, and separated, exchanging glances of intelligence. As Madame Desforges was looking for Madame Guibal, she set up an exclamation of surprise on seeing her with Madame Marty. The latter, followed by her daughter Valentine, had been carried away for the last two hours, right through the place, by one of those fits of spending from which she always emerged tired and confused. She had roamed about the furniture department that a show of white lacquered suites of furniture had changed into a vast young girl's room, the ribbon and neckerchief department forming white vellumy colonnades, the mercery and lace department, with its white fringes which surrounded ingenious trophies patiently composed of cards of buttons and packets of needles, and the hosiery department, in which there was a great crush this year to see an immense piece of decoration, the name "The Ladies' Paradise" in letters three yards high, formed of white socks on a groundwork of red ones. But Madame Marty was especially excited by the new departments; they could not open a new department without she must inaugurate it, she was bound to plunge in and buy something. And she had passed an hour at the millinery counter, installed in a new room on the ground floor, having the cupboards emptied, taking the bonnets off the stands which stood on two tables, trying all of them on herself and her daughter, white hats, white bonnets, and white turbans. Then she had gone down to the boot department, at the further end of a gallery on the ground floor, behind the cravat department, a counter opened that day, and which she had turned topsy turvy, seized with sickly desires in the presence of the white silk slippers trimmed with swansdown, the white satin boots and shoes with their high Louis XV. heels.

"Oh! my dear," she stammered, "you've no idea! They have a wonderful assortment of hoods. I've chosen one for myself and one for my daughter. And the boots, eh? Valentine."

"It's marvellous!" added the young girl, with her womanly boldness. "There are some boots at twenty francs and a half which are delicious!"

A salesman was following them, dragging along the eternal chair, on which was already heaped a mountain of articles.

"How is Monsieur Marty?" asked Madame Desforges.

"Very well, I believe," replied Madame Marty, bewildered by this brusque question, which fell ill-naturedly amidst her fever for spending. "He's still confined, my uncle had to go and see him this morning."

"Oh, look! isn't it lovely?"

The ladies, who had gone on a few steps, found themselves before the flowers and feathers department, installed in the central gallery, between the silk and glove departments. It appeared beneath the bright light of the glass roof as an enormous florescence, a white sheaf, tall and broad as an oak. The base was formed of single flowers, violets, lilies of the valley, hyacinths, daisies, all the delicate hues of the garden. Then came bouquets, white roses, softened by a fleshy tint, great white peonies, slightly shaded with carmine, white chrysanthemums, with narrow petals and starred with yellow. And the flowers still ascended, great mystical lilies, branches of apple blossom, bunches of lilac, a continual blossoming, surmounted, as high as the first storey, by ostrich feathers, white plumes, which were like the airy breath of this collection of white flowers. One whole corner was devoted to the display of trimmings and orange-flower wreaths. There were also metallic flowers, silver thistles and silver ears of corn. Amidst the foliage and the petals, amidst all this muslin, silk, and velvet, where drops of gum shone like dew, flew birds of Paradise for hats, purple Tangaras with black tails, and Septicolores with their changing rainbow-like plumage.

"I'm going to buy a branch of apple-blossom," resumed Madame Marty. "It's delicious, isn't it? And that little bird, do look, Valentine. I must take it!"

Madame Guibal began to feel tired of standing still in the eddy of the crowd, and at last said: "Well, we'll leave you to make your purchases. We're going upstairs."

"No, no, wait for me!" cried the other. "I'm going up too. There's the perfumery department, I must see that."

This department, created the day before, was next door to the reading-room. Madame Desforges, to avoid the crush on the stairs, spoke of going up in the lift, but they had to abandon the idea, there was such a crowd waiting their turn. At last they arrived, passing before the public refreshment bar, where the crowd was becoming so great that an inspector had to restrain the people's appetites by only allowing the gluttonous customers to enter in small groups. And the ladies already began to smell the perfumery department, a penetrating odor which scented the whole gallery. There was quite a struggle over one article, The Paradise soap, a specialty of the house. In the show cases, and on the crystal tablets of the shelves, were ranged pots of pomade and paste, boxes of powder and paint, boxes of oil and toilet vinegar; whilst the fine brushes, combs, scissors, and smelling-bottles occupied a special place. The salesmen had managed to decorate the shelves with white porcelain pots and white glass bottles. But what delighted the customers above all was a silver fountain, a shepherdess seated in the middle of a harvest of flowers, and from which flowed a continual stream of violet water, which fell with a musical plash into the metal basin. An exquisite odor was disseminated around, the ladies dipping their handkerchiefs in the scent as they passed.

"There," said Madame Marty, when she had loaded herself with lotions, dentrifices, and cosmetics. "Now I've done, I'm at your service. Let's go and rejoin Madame de Boves."

But on the landing of the great central staircase they were again stopped by the Japanese department. This counter had grown wonderfully since the day Mouret had amused himself by setting up, in the same place, a little proposition table, covered with a lot of soiled articles, without at all foreseeing its future success. Few departments had had a more modest commencement, and now it overflowed with old bronzes, old ivories, old lacquer work. He did fifteen hundred thousand francs' worth of business a year in this department, ransacking the Far East, where his travellers pillaged the palaces and the temples. Besides, fresh departments were always springing up, they had tried two in December, in order to fill up the empty spaces caused by the dead winter season—a book department and a toy department, which would certainly grow also and sweep away certain shops in the neighborhood. Four years had sufficed for the Japanese department to attract the entire artistic custom of Paris. This time Madame Desforges herself, notwithstanding the rancor which had made her swear not to buy anything, succumbed before some finely carved ivory.

"Send it to my house," said she rapidly, at a neighboring pay-desk. "Ninety francs, is it not?" And, seeing Madame Marty and her daughter plunged in a lot of trashy porcelains, she resumed, as she carried Madame Guibal off: "You will find us in the reading-room, I really must sit down a little while."

In the reading-room they were obliged to remain standing. All the chairs were occupied, round the large table covered with newspapers. Great fat fellows were reading and lolling about without even thinking of giving up their seats to the ladies. A few women were writing, their faces on the paper, as if to conceal their letters under the flowers of their hats. Madame de Boves was not there, and Henriette was getting very impatient when she perceived Vallagnosc, who was also looking for his wife and mother-in-law. He bowed, and said:

"They must be in the lace department—impossible to drag them away. I'll just see." And he was gallant enough to procure them two chairs before going away.

In the lace department the crush was increasing every minute. The great show of white was there triumphing in its most delicate and dearest whiteness. It was an acute temptation, a mad desire, which bewildered all the women. The department had been turned into a white temple, tulles and Maltese lace, falling from above, formed a white sky, one of those cloudy veils which pales the morning sun. Round the columns descended flounces of Malines and Valenciennes, white dancers' skirts, unfolding in a snowy shiver down to the ground. Then on all sides, on every counter, was a stream of white Spanish blonde as light as air, Brussels with its large flowers on a delicate mesh, hand-made point, and Venice point with heavier designs, Alençon point, and Bruges of royal and almost religious richness. It seemed that the god of dress had there set up his white tabernacle.

Madame de Boves, after wandering about for a long time before the counters with her daughter, and feeling a sensual desire to plunge her hands into the goods, had just decided to make Deloche show her some Alençon point. At first he brought out some imitation; but she wished to see some real Alençon, and was not satisfied with the little pieces at three hundred francs the yard, insisting on having deep flounces at a thousand francs a yard, handkerchiefs and fans at seven and eight hundred francs. The counter was soon covered with a fortune. In a corner of the department Jouve, the inspector, who had not lost sight of Madame de Boves, notwithstanding the latter's apparent dawdling, stood there amidst the crowd, with an indifferent air, but still keeping a sharp eye on her.

"Have you any in hand-made point?" she asked. "Show me some, please."

The salesman, whom she had kept there for twenty minutes, dared not resist, she appeared so aristocratic, with her imposing air and princess's voice. However, he hesitated, for the salesmen were cautioned against heaping up these precious fabrics, and he had allowed himself to be robbed of ten yards of Malines the week before. But she troubled him, he yielded, and abandoned the Alençon point for a moment to take the lace asked for from a drawer.

"Oh! look, mamma," said Blanche, who was ransacking a box close by, full of cheap Valenciennes, "we might take some of this for pillow-cases."

Madame de Boves not replying, her daughter on turning round saw her with her hands plunged amidst the lace, about to slip some Alençon up the sleeve of her mantle. She did not appear surprised, and moved forward instinctively to conceal her mother, when Jouve suddenly stood before them. He leant over, and politely murmured in the countess's ear:

"Have the kindness to follow me, madame."

She hesitated for a moment, shocked.

"But what for, sir?"

"Have the kindness to follow me, madame," repeated the inspector, without raising his voice.

Her face was full of anguish, she threw a rapid glance around her. Then she resigned herself all at once, resumed her haughty look, and walked by his side like a queen who deigns to accept the services of an aide-de-camp. Not one of the customers had observed the scene, and Deloche, on returning to the counter, looked at her being walked off, his mouth wide open with astonishment. What! this one as well! this noble-looking lady! Really it was time to have them all searched! And Blanche, who was left free, followed her mother at a distance, lingering amidst the sea of faces, livid, divided between the duty of not deserting her mother and the terror of being detained with her. She saw her enter Bourdoncle's office, but she contented herself with waiting near the door. Bourdoncle, whom Mouret had just got rid of, happened to be there. As a rule, he dealt with these sorts of robberies committed by persons of distinction. Jouve had long been watching this lady, and had informed him of it, so that he was not astonished when the inspector briefly explained the matter to him; in fact, such extraordinary cases passed through his hands that he declared the women capable of anything once the rage for dress had seized them. As he was aware of Mouret's acquaintance with the thief, he treated her with the utmost politeness.

"We excuse these moments of weakness, madame. But pray consider the consequences of such a thing. Suppose someone else had seen you slip this lace—"

But she interrupted him in great indignation. She a thief! Who did he take her for? She was the Countess de Boves, her husband, Inspector-General of the Stud, was received at Court.

"I know, I know, madame," repeated Bourdoncle, quietly. "I have the honor of knowing you. In the first place, will you kindly give up the lace you have on you?"

She again protested, not allowing him to say another word, handsome in her violence, going as far as tears. Anyone else but he would have been shaken and feared some deplorable mistake, for she threatened to go to law to avenge herself for such an insult.

"Take care, sir, my husband will certainly appeal to the Minister."

"Come, you are not more reasonable than the others," declared Bourdoncle, losing patience. "We must search you."

Still she did not yield, but said with her superb assurance, "Very good, search me. But I warn you, you are risking your house."

Jouve went to fetch two saleswomen from the corset department. When he returned, he informed Bourdoncle that the lady's daughter, left at liberty, had not quitted the doorway, and asked if she should also be detained, although he had not seen her take anything. The manager, always correct, decided that she should not be brought in, for the sake of morality, and in order not to force a mother to blush before her daughter. The two men retired into a neighboring room, whilst the saleswomen searched the countess, even taking off her dress to search her bosom and hips. Besides the twelve yards of Alençon point at a thousand francs the yard concealed in her sleeve, they found in her bosom a handkerchief, a fan, and a cravat, making a total of about fourteen thousand francs' worth of lace. She had been stealing like this for the last year, ravaged by a furious, irresistible passion for dress. These fits got worse, growing daily, sweeping away all the reasonings of prudence, and the enjoyment she felt in the indulgence of this passion was all the more violent from the fact that she was risking before the eyes of a crowd her name, her pride, and her husband's high position. Now that the latter allowed her to empty his drawers, she stole although she had her pockets full of money, she stole for the pleasure of stealing, as one loves for the pleasure of loving, goaded on by desire, urged on by the species of kleptomania that her unsatisfied luxurious tastes had developed in her formerly at sight of the enormous and brutal temptation of the big shops.

"It's a trap," cried she, when Bourdoncle and Jouve came in. "This lace has been placed on me, I swear before Heaven."

She was now weeping tears of rage, and fell on a chair, suffocated in her dress. The partner sent away the saleswomen, and resumed, with his quiet air: "We are quite willing, madame, to hush up this painful affair for the sake of your family. But you must first sign a paper thus worded: I have stolen some lace from The Ladies' Paradise, followed by the details of the lace, and the day of the month. Besides, I shall be happy to return you this document whenever you like to bring me a sum of two thousand francs for the poor."

She got up again, and declared in a fresh outburst: "I'll never sign that, I'd rather die."

"You won't die, madame; but I warn you that I shall shortly send for the police."

Then followed a frightful scene. She insulted him, she stammered that it was cowardly for a man to torture a woman in that way. Her Juno-like beauty, her tall majestic body was distorted by vulgar rage. Then she tried to melt them, entreating them in the name of their mothers, and spoke of dragging herself at their feet. And as they remained quite unmoved, hardened by custom, she sat down all at once and began to write with a trembling hand. The pen sputtered, the words: "I have stolen," written madly, went almost through the thin paper, whilst she repeated in a strangled voice: "There, sir, there. I yield to force."

Bourdoncle took the paper, carefully folded it, and put it in a drawer, saying: "You see it's in company, for ladies, after talking of dying rather than signing, generally forget to come and redeem their *billets doux*. However, I hold it at your disposal. You'll be able to judge whether it's worth two thousand francs."

She was buttoning up her dress, and became as arrogant as ever, now that she had paid. "I can go now?" asked she, in a sharp tone.

Bourdoncle was already occupied with other business. On Jouve's report, he decided on Deloche's dismissal, as a stupid fellow, who was always being robbed, never having any authority over the customers. Madame de Boves repeated her question, and as they dismissed her with an affirmative nod, she enveloped both of them in a murderous look. In the flood of insulting words that she kept back, a melodramatic cry escaped from her lips.

"Wretches!" said she, banging the door after her.

Meanwhile Blanche had not gone far away from the office. Her ignorance of what was going on inside, the passing backwards and forwards of Jouve and the two saleswomen frightened her, she had visions of the police, the assize court, and the prison. But all at once she stopped short: Vallagnosc was before her, this husband of a month, with whom she still felt rather awkward; and he questioned her, astonished at her bewildered appearance.

"Where's your mother? Have you lost each other? Come, tell me, you make me feel anxious."

Nothing in the way of a colorable fiction presented itself to her, and in great distress she told him everything in a low voice: "Mamma, mamma—she has been stealing."

"What! stealing?" At last he understood. His wife's bloated face, the pale mask, ravaged by fear, terrified him.

"Some lace, like that, up her sleeve," she continued stammering.

"You saw her, then? You were looking on?" murmured he, chilled to feel her a sort of accomplice.

They had to stop talking, several persons were already turning round. A hesitation full of anguish kept Vallagnosc motionless for a moment. What was to be done? He was about to go into Bourdoncle's office, when he perceived Mouret crossing the gallery. He told his wife to wait for him, and seized his old friend's arm, informing him of the affair, in broken sentences. The latter hastily took him into his office, where he soon put him at rest as to the possible consequences. He assured him that he need not interfere, and explained in what way the affair would be arranged, without appearing at all excited about this robbery, as if he had foreseen it long ago. But Vallagnosc, when he no longer feared an immediate arrest, did not accept the adventure with this admirable coolness. He had thrown himself into an armchair, and now that he could discuss the matter, began to lament his own unfortunate position. Was it possible that he had married into a family of thieves? A stupid marriage that he had drifted into, just to please his father! Surprised at this childish violence, Mouret watched him weeping, thinking of his former pessimist boasting. Had he not heard him announce scores of times the nothingness of life, in which evil alone had any attraction? And by way of a joke he amused himself for a minute or so, by preaching indifference to his friend, in a friendly, bantering tone. But at this Vallagnosc got angry: he was quite unable to recover his compromised philosophy, his middle-class education broke out in virtuously indignant cries against his mother-in-law. As soon as trouble fell on him, at the least appearance of human suffering, at which he had always coldly laughed, the boasted skeptic was beaten and bleeding. It was abominable, they were dragging the honor of his race into the mud, and the world seemed to be coming to an end.

"Come, calm yourself," concluded Mouret, stricken with pity. "I won't tell you that everything happens and nothing happens, because that does not seem to comfort you just now. But I think you ought to go and offer your arm to Madame de Boves, that would be wiser than causing a scandal. The deuce! you who professed such scorn before the universal rascality of the present day!"

"Of course," cried Vallagnosc, innocently, "when it affects other people!"

However, he got up, and followed his old school-fellow's advice. Both were returning to the gallery when Madame de Boves came out of Bourdoncle's office. She accepted her son-in-law's arm with a majestic air, and as Mouret bowed to her with respectful gallantry, he heard her saying: "They've apologized to me. Really, these mistakes are abominable."

Blanche rejoined them, and they were soon lost in the crowd. Then Mouret, alone and pensive, crossed the shop once more. This scene, which had changed his thoughts from the struggle going on within him, now increased his fever, and decided him to make a supreme effort. A vague connection arose in his mind: the robbery by this unfortunate woman, the last folly of the conquered customers, beaten at the feet of the tempter, evoked the proud and avenging image of Denise, whose victorious grip he could feel at his throat. He stopped at the top of the central staircase, and gazed for a long time into the immense nave, where his nation of women were swarming.

Six o'clock was about to strike, the daylight decreasing outside was gradually forsaking the covered galleries, already dark and waning at the further end of the halls, invaded by long shadows. And in this daylight, barely extinct, was commenced the lighting of the electric lamps, the globes of an opaque whiteness studding with bright moons the distant depths of the departments. It was a white brightness of a blinding fixity, extending like the reverberation of a discolored star, killing the twilight. Then, when all were lighted, there was a delighted murmur in the crowd, the great show of white goods assumed a fairy splendor beneath this new illumination. It seemed that this colossal orgy of white was also burning, itself becoming a light. The song of the white seemed to soar upward in the inflamed whiteness of an aurora. A white glimmer gushed from the linen and calico department in the Monsigny Gallery, like the first bright gleam which lights up the eastern sky; whilst along the Michodière Gallery, the mercery and the lace, the fancy-goods and the ribbon departments threw out the reflection of distant hills—the white flash of the mother-of-pearl buttons, the silvered bronzes and the pearls. But the central nave especially was filled with a blaze of white: the puffs of white muslin round the columns, the white dimities and other stuffs draping the staircases, the white lace flying in the air, opened up a dreamy firmament, the dazzling whiteness of a paradise, where was being celebrated the marriage of the unknown queen. The tent of the silk hall was like a giant alcove, with its white curtains, gauzes and tulles, the dazzle of which protected the bride in her white nudity from the gaze of the curious. There was now nothing but this blinding white light in which all the whites blended, a multitude of stars twinkling in the bright clear light.

And Mouret continued to watch his nation of women, amidst this shimmering blaze. Their black shadows stood out vigorously on the pale ground-work. Long eddies divided the crowd; the fever of this day's great sale swept past like a frenzy, rolling along the disordered sea of heads. People were commencing to leave, the pillage of the stuffs had encumbered all the counters, the gold was chinking in the tills; whilst the customers went away, their purses completely empty, and their heads turned by the wealth of luxury amidst which they had been wandering all day. It was he who possessed them thus, keeping them at his mercy by his continued display of novelties, his reduction of prices, and his "returns," his gallantry and his advertisements. He had conquered the mothers themselves, reigning over them with the brutality of a despot, whose caprices were ruining many a household. His creation was a sort of new religion; the churches, gradually deserted by a wavering faith, were replaced by this bazaar, in the minds of the idle women of Paris. Women now came and spent their leisure time in his establishment, the shivering and anxious hours they formerly passed in churches: a necessary consumption of nervous passion, a growing struggle of the god of dress against the husband, the incessantly renewed religion of the body with the divine future of beauty. If he had closed his doors, there would have been a rising in the street, the despairing cry of worshippers deprived of their confessional and altar.

In their still growing luxury, he saw them, notwithstanding the lateness of the hour, obstinately clinging to the enormous iron building, along the suspended staircases and flying bridges. Madame Marty and her daughter, carried away to the highest point, were wandering amongst the furniture. Retained by her young people, Madame Bourdelais could not get away from the fancy goods. Then came another group, Madame de Boves, still on Vallagnosc's arm, and followed by Blanche, stopping in each department, still daring to examine the articles with her superb air. But amidst the crowded sea of customers, this sea of bodies swelling with life, beating with desire, all decorated with bunches of violets, as though for the bridals of some sovereign, Mouret could now distinguish nothing but the bare bust of Madame Desforges, who had stopped in the glove department with Madame Guibal. Notwithstanding her jealous rancor, she was also buying, and he felt himself to be the master once more, having them at his feet, beneath the dazzle of the electric light, like a drove of cattle from whom he had drawn his fortune.

With a mechanical step, Mouret went along the galleries, so absorbed that he abandoned himself to the pushing of the crowd. When he raised his head, he found himself in the new millinery department, the windows of which looked on to the Rue du Dix-Décembre. And there, his forehead against the glass, he made another halt, watching the departure of the crowd. The setting sun was yellowing the roofs of the white houses, the blue sky was growing paler, refreshed by a pure breath; whilst in the twilight, which was already enveloping the streets, the electric lamps of The Ladies' Paradise threw out that fixed glimmer of stars lighted on the horizon at the decline of the day. Towards the Opera-house and the Bourse were the rows of waiting carriages, the harness still retaining the reflections of the bright light, the gleam of a lamp, the glitter of a silvered bit. Every minute the cry of a footman was heard, and a cab drew near, or a brougham issued from the ranks, took up a customer, and went off at a rapid trot. The rows of carriages were now diminishing, six went off at a time, occupying the whole street, from the one side to the other, amidst the banging of doors, snapping of whips, and the hum of the passers-by, who swarmed between the wheels. There was a sort of continual enlargement, a spreading of the customers, carried off to the four corners of the city, emptying the building with the roaring clamor of a sluice. And the roof of The Ladies' Paradise, the big golden letters of the ensigns, the banners fluttering in the sky, still flamed forth with the reflections of the setting sun, so colossal in this oblique light, that they evoked the monster of advertising, the phalansterium whose wings, incessantly multiplied, were swallowing up the whole neighborhood, as far as the distant woods of the suburbs. And the soul of Paris, an enormous, sweet breath, fell asleep in the serenity of the evening, running in long and sweet caresses over the last carriages, spinning through the streets now becoming deserted by the crowd, disappearing into the darkness of the night.

Mouret, gazing about, had just felt something grand in himself; and, in the shiver of triumph with which his flesh trembled, in the face of Paris devoured and woman conquered, he experienced a sudden weakness, a defection of his strong will which overthrew him in his turn, beneath a superior force. It was an unreasonable necessity to be vanquished in his victory, the nonsense of a warrior bending beneath the caprice of a child, on the morrow of his conquests. He who had struggled for months, who even that morning had sworn to stifle his passion, yielded all at once, seized by the vertigo of high places, happy to commit what he looked upon as a folly. His decision, so rapid, had assumed all at once such energy that he saw nothing but her as being useful and necessary in the world.

The evening, after the last dinner, he was waiting in his office, trembling like a young man about to stake his life's happiness, unable to keep still, incessantly going towards the door to listen to the rumors in the shop, where the men were doing the folding, drowned up to the shoulder in a sea of stuffs. At each footstep his heart beat. He felt a violent emotion, he rushed forward, for he had heard in the distance a deep murmur, which had gradually increased.

It was Lhomme slowly approaching with the day's receipts. That day they were so heavy, there was such a quantity of silver and copper, that he had been obliged to enlist the services of two messengers. Behind him came Joseph and one of his colleagues, bending beneath the weight of the bags, enormous bags, thrown on their shoulders like sacks of wheat, whilst he walked on in front with the notes and gold, a note-book swollen with paper, and two bags hung round his neck, the weight of which swayed him to the right, the same side as his broken arm. Slowly, perspiring and puffing, he had come from the other end of the shop, amidst the growing emotion of the salesmen. The employees in the glove and silk departments laughingly offered to relieve him of his burden, the fellows in the drapery and woollen departments were longing to see him make a false step, which would have scattered the gold through the place. Then he had been obliged to mount the stairs, go across a bridge, going still higher, turning about, amidst the longing looks of the employees in the linen, the hosiery, and the mercery departments, who followed him, gazing with ecstasy at this fortune travelling in the air. On the first floor the employees in the ready-made, the perfumery, the lace, and the shawl departments were ranged with devotion, as on the passage of a king. From counter to counter a tumult arose, like the clamor of a nation bowing down before the golden calf.

Mouret opened the door, and Lhomme appeared, followed by the two messengers, who were staggering; and, out of breath, he still had strength to cry out: "One million two hundred and forty-seven francs, nineteen sous!"

At last the million had been attained, the million picked up in a day, and of which Mouret had so long dreamed. But he gave way to an angry gesture, and said impatiently, with the disappointed air of a man disturbed by some troublesome fellow: "A million! very good, put it there." Lhomme knew that he was fond of seeing the heavy receipts on his table before they were taken to the central cashier's office. The million covered the whole table, crushing the papers, almost overturning the ink, running out of the sacks, bursting the leather bags, making a great heap, the heap of the gross receipts, such as it had come from the customers' hands, still warm and living.

Just as the cashier was going away, heart-broken at the governor's indifference, Bourdoncle arrived, gaily exclaiming: "Ah! we've done it this time. We've hooked the million, eh?"

But observing Mouret's febrile pre-occupation, he understood at once and calmed down. His face was beaming with joy. After a short silence he resumed: "You've made up your mind, haven't you? Well, I approve your decision."

Suddenly Mouret planted himself before him, and with his terrible voice he thundered: "I say, my man, you're rather too lively. You think me played out, don't you? And you feel hungry. But be careful, I'm not one to be swallowed up, you know!"

Discountenanced by the sharp attack of this wonderful fellow, who guessed everything, Bourdoncle stammered: "What now? Are you joking? I who have always admired you so!"

"Don't tell lies!" replied Mouret, more violently than ever. "Just listen, we were stupid to entertain the superstition that marriage would ruin us. Is it not the necessary health, the very strength and order of life? Well, my dear fellow, I'm going to marry her, and I'll pitch you all out at the slightest movement. Yes, you'll go and be paid like the rest, Bourdoncle."

And with a gesture he dismissed him. Bourdoncle felt himself condemned, swept away, by this victory gained by woman. He went off. Denise was just going in, and he bowed with a profound respect, his head swimming.

"Ah! you've come at last!" said Mouret gently.

Denise was pale with emotion. She had just experienced another grief, Deloche had informed her of his dismissal, and as she tried to retain him, offering to speak in his favor, he obstinately declined to struggle against his bad luck, he wanted to disappear, what was the use of staying? Why should he interfere with people who were happy? Denise had bade him a sisterly adieu, her eyes full of tears. Did she not herself long to sink into oblivion? Everything was now about to be finished, and she asked nothing more of her exhausted strength than the courage to support this separation. In a few minutes, if she could only be valiant enough to crush her heart, she could go away alone, to weep unseen.

"You wished to see me, sir," she said in her calm voice. "In fact, I intended to come and thank you for all your kindness to me."

On entering, she had perceived the million on the desk, and the display of this money wounded her. Above her, as if watching the scene, was the portrait of Madame Hédouin, in its gilded frame, and with the eternal smile of its painted lips.

"You are still resolved to leave us?" asked Mouret, in a trembling voice.

"Yes, sir. I must."

Then he took her hands, and said, in an explosion of tenderness, after the long period of coldness he had imposed on himself: "And if I married you, Denise, would you still leave?"

But she had drawn her hands away, struggling as if under the influence of a great grief. "Oh! Monsieur Mouret. Pray say no more. Don't cause me such pain again! I cannot! I cannot! Heaven is my witness that I was going away to avoid such a misfortune!"

She continued to defend herself in broken sentences. Had she not already suffered too much from the gossip of the house? Did he wish her to pass in his eyes and her own for a worthless woman? No, no, she would be strong, she would certainly prevent him doing such a thing. He, tortured, listened to her, repeating in a passionate tone: "I wish it. I wish it!"

"No, it's impossible. And my brothers? I have sworn not to marry. I cannot bring you those children, can I?"

"They shall be my brothers, too. Say yes, Denise."

"No, no, leave me. You are torturing me!"

Little by little he gave way, this last obstacle drove him mad. What! She still refused even at this price! In the distance he heard the clamor of his three thousand employees building up his immense fortune. And that stupid million lying there! He suffered from it as a sort of irony, he could have thrown it into the street.

"Go, then!" he cried, in a flood of tears. "Go and join the man you love. That's the reason, isn't it? You warned me, I ought to have known it, and not tormented you any further."

She stood there dazed before the violence of this despair. Her heart was bursting. Then, with the impetuosity of a child, she threw herself on his neck, sobbing also, and stammered: "Oh! Monsieur Mouret, it's you that I love!"

A last murmur was rising from The Ladies' Paradise, the distant acclamation of a crowd. Madame Hédouin's portrait was still smiling, with its painted lips; Mouret had fallen on his desk, on the million that he could no longer see. He did not quit Denise, but clasped her in a desperate embrace, telling her that she could now go, that she could spend a month at Valognes, which would silence everybody, and that he would then go and fetch her himself, and bring her back, all-powerful, and his wedded wife.

THE END

For more by Émile Zola, look for the

The Beast Within

Translated with an Introduction by Roger Whitehouse

Set at the end of the Second Empire, when French society seemed to be hurtling into the future like the new railways and locomotives it was building, *The Beast Within*—also known as *La Bête Humaine*—is at once a tale of murder, passion, and possession and a compassionate study of individuals derailed by the burden of inherited evil. Considered his "most finely worked" novel, Zola expresses the hope that human nature evolves through education but warns that the beast within continues to lurk beneath the veneer of technological progress.

ISBN 978-0-14-044963-1

Thérèse Raquin

Translated by Robin Buss

The numbing tedium of Thérèse Raquin's loveless marriage is suddenly shattered when she embarks on a turbulent affair with her husband's earthy friend Laurent. Their animal passion for each other soon compels the lovers to commit a crime that will haunt them forever. An uninhibited portrayal of adultery, madness, and ghostly revenge, Zola's novel is also a devastating exploration of the darkest aspects of human existence.

ISBN 978-0-14-044944-0

The Drinking Den
Translated with an Introduction by Robin Buss

Considered perhaps the first classical tragedy of working-class people living in the slums of a city, *The Drinking Den* is part of the Rougon-Macquart series, a naturalistic history of two branches of a family traced through several generations. Influenced by contemporary theories of heredity and experimental science, the behavior of the two families is shown to be conditioned by environment and inherited characteristics, chiefly drunkenness and mental instability.

ISBN 978-0-14-044954-9

Germinal
Translated with an Introduction and Notes by Roger Pearson

A clever but uneducated young man with a dangerous temper, Étienne Lantier is forced to take a backbreaking job at Le Voreux mine, where he discovers that his fellow miners are ill, hungry, and in debt. When conditions in the mining community deteriorate even further, Lantier finds himself leading a strike that could mean starvation or salvation for all. The thirteenth novel in Zola's great Rougon-Macquart sequence, *Germinal* expresses outrage at the exploitation of the many by the few, but also shows humanity's capacity for compassion and hope.

ISBN 978-0-14-044742-2

The Debacle
Translated with an Introduction by Leonard Tancock

Zola's only purely historical work, this realistic, detailed, and accurate account of France's defeat in the Franco-Prussian War is a grim testament to the human horrors of war.

ISBN 978-0-14-044280-9

Nana
Translated with an Introduction by George Holden

Born to drunken parents in the slums of Paris, Nana is soon discovered at the Théâtre dés Variétés and becomes the most famous high-class prostitute of her day. Nana's hedonistic appetite for luxury and decadent pleasures knows no bounds—until, eventually, it consumes her. The rich atmosphere and luminous language of this "poem of male desire" transform Nana into an almost mythical figure: a destructive force preying on a corrupt, decaying society. George Holden's lively translation is accompanied by an introduction discussing *Nana* as a key work in Zola's Rougon-Macquart cycle, representing a powerful critique of France's Second Empire.

ISBN 978-0-14-044263-2
